RED ROCK WEDDINGS

RED ROCK WEDDINGS

THREE-IN-ONE COLLECTION

LAURALEE BLISS

Cover Design: Kirk DouPonce, DogEared Design

Published by Barbour Publishing, Inc., P.O. Box 719, Uhrichsville, Ohio 44683, www.barbourbooks.com

Our mission is to publish and distribute inspirational products offering exceptional value and biblical encouragement to the masses.

Member of the
Evangelical Christian
Publishers Association

Printed in the United States of America.

Dear Readers,

Welcome to the unique and wondrous state of Utah and the setting for this series of three contemporary novels. I ventured there with my husband for on-the-spot research and was truly amazed at the variety of scenic beauty I discovered. From arches, to canyons, to rivers and the rugged Wasatch range, Utah has it all, and each book reflects Utah's unique and varied scenic wonders. But I also wanted to use such rocky ruggedness to bring forth the idea of "ruggedness" within each of the characters. The characters struggle with different trials in their lives. As they let go and trust God, the seeming ruggedness of those trials can turn into a thing of beauty as well as knit them with the special person God has brought into their lives.

I hope you enjoy visiting Utah within the pages of this book and journeying with the characters as they discover true beauty and worth within. I look forward to hearing from you.

May God bless you as you journey with Him,
Lauralee Bliss
www.lauraleebliss.com

LOVE'S WINDING PATH

Dedication

For all those with prodigal sons and daughters. . .there is hope!

Chapter 1

When are you planning to help out around here?"

Dan glanced out the corner of his eye at his older brother, Rob, clad in mud-streaked jeans and boasting smears of dirt on each cheekbone. Dan smirked and returned to his magazine on river rafting. What a spectacle Rob was, standing there like Farmer John from the back hills. He ought to be playing a mouth harp and doing the jig to complete the picture.

"I'm taking a break," Dan informed him, flipping a page in the magazine.

"You've been on a break for the last few years around here," Rob grumbled. "When are you gonna snap out of it? Pop knows how much you sit around here doing nothing."

"Aren't you a little old at twenty-seven to be ratting?" Dan snapped, scanning an article on the best places to raft along the Colorado River. He ignored Rob's complaining and returned to important business at hand. Like seeking another career. . .and another life. How he would love to be one of those river guides in the rafts, though he knew nothing of it, save the one trip he took a few years back in West Virginia. Even then he remembered the thrill of the trip in foaming white water, manning his paddle with vigor while trying to keep himself in the boat. And out in Utah, surrounded by raw, red cliffs glistening in the hot sun, the weather was sweltering but different from steamy Virginia with the humidity level at 80 percent. And different, too, from being surrounded by hundreds of acres of peanut plants and a nagging brother.

Dan used to love peanut butter as a kid. He thought it cool that his father grew the very nuts that made his sandwich filling for lunch. Now if he even smelled a hint of peanut butter, he became nauseated. All his life, Dan had worked his pop's peanut fields. He gathered it was his duty as a farmer's kid to help make the land profitable, to do his share of the work. A generational kind of thing. And of course, the peanut was the mark of a fine Virginia crop. Pop proudly sold his peanuts to the processing plants at Wakefield and received nice profits in return. Rob often remarked that Dan wouldn't have his iPod and iPhone if not for their blessed peanuts. To Dan, he couldn't care less that the family icon was the Planters peanut man. All he wanted to do was get as far away from this place as possible. If only he didn't feel obligated to stay and keep the farm going. Pop always said he would rather work with his sons than hire outside help. He liked them by his side, tending to the operations. He was confident of their abilities. But Dan felt he was slowly being smashed into peanut butter with each passing day.

"As usual, you don't listen to a word I'm saying," Rob grumbled. "Pop ought to just tell you to leave."

Sounds good to me. If only he would. But he won't. Instead of answering, Dan hid behind the magazine. Rob stormed off. Dan read another paragraph then pitched the magazine onto the stand and stood to his feet. He liked the work he and Pop did in his early teens, renovating the two-story farmhouse built in the late nineteenth century. Those days were fun. He worked side by side with Pop, creating a home they could be proud of. Putting in wallboard. Making bookshelves. Redecorating his own personal place of refuge. At that time anything was better than working the fields and watching Rob tend to the peanut plants as if they were his pals. In Dan's mind, peanut plants were akin to mosquitoes, sucking the lifeblood out of him.

With a halfhearted gesture, Dan moseyed on out to the yard where Pop was in the middle of showing Rob how to operate the new tractor he'd acquired. Instead of concentrating on the tractor, Dan imagined rafts, hiking equipment, a raging river, and adventure.

"Come on over, son, and let me show you how this works."

Dan shuffled over, staring into the sky, his thoughts higher than the fluffy clouds passing by, while his father explained the vehicle's operation.

"Give it a try, Dan."

"Huh?"

Rob burst out laughing. "I wouldn't unless you want him to wreck it."

"Excuse me, but I know how to operate a tractor," Dan retorted. He brushed past his snickering brother and climbed onto the narrow metal seat. Looking at the controls, he realized at once this machine was not the same as his father's old clunker. He engaged the engine, ignoring his father who tried to shout out the operating instructions above the loud noise. Dan put the gears in high range. The tractor lurched forward, heading at a fast clip toward a field of healthy, green peanut plants. By the time he put his foot on the clutch, the tractor had succeeded in crushing a patch of plants.

Pop shook his head in dismay.

Rob hooted. "What did I tell you? He's not worth anything here."

"Both my sons are worth everything I have and more," Pop said, offering his hand to Dan.

Dan ignored the gesture. He jumped off the tractor to the ground and promptly fell flat on his face in the field, squashing more tender plants. When he came to his feet, his clothes were plastered with dirt, including his new jeans. He strode off in a fury, kicking up a stone as he went, vowing to get out of here as soon as he could.

He flew into the house and headed for the shower. If there was one thing Dan couldn't stand anymore, it was the filth of a peanut field on him. Life itself had become one big pile of dirt, forever encrusted on his hands and clothing. At times it took an hour to scrub the dirt out of every crevice. The red clay of Virginia seemed permanently etched into his flesh.

Dan stayed in the shower for twenty minutes until he heard someone rap on the door. When he finally toweled off and dressed, Pop was waiting for him downstairs.

"Something bothering you, son?" he inquired. "You don't seem like yourself today."

Dan wanted so much to say what was going on in his heart. If only he could. He would let it all out—all the reasons he hated the farm and the idea of being the peanut man's son, and how life seemed to be on a dead-end road. There were places to see and things to do. He didn't want to find himself a permanent fixture in a field, listening to Rob complaining about his work habits and getting all the glory. If only Pop could understand that a man needed to get out and explore the world, to find his place and what he's meant to do.

Instead Dan lied, telling his father he was just fine and scooting off into the kitchen. Mom stood at the counter making pies. She spent most of her time in the kitchen, cooking up a storm to feed her three boys, as she called them. Dan never had a want for great food. Mom cooked up the best steaks, potatoes, cakes, and breads. She worked day and night to feed them well. Never once did he recall thanking her for the meals either—a thought that, for a moment, pricked his conscience. Then again, he worked his fingers to the bone on this farm of his father's. The reward, he supposed, was a good dinner to end a nondescript day.

He snitched some raw piecrust from the pastry cloth where she was rolling out the dough. He then planted a kiss on her cheek for good measure. "Hey, raw dough's not good for you!" she exclaimed with a smile then kissed him back.

"I know, like most stuff it seems." He opened the refrigerator, took out a plastic bowl, and began eating the casserole left from last night. He didn't care that it was ice cold. It was still good, with homemade noodles and chunks of chicken.

"I've been trying to find out what's bothering Dan here," Pop said to Mom. "He won't say a word."

"He's probably hungry. Look at how he's eating."

11

I'm hungry all right, he thought. Hungry for adventure, for a nice woman, for eating out with the boys, maybe even sharing in a few cold beers—though his godly parents would surely balk at the idea of their nice son drinking anything except milk and soda. He never told them how he went out once while they were away and bought a six-pack of beer. He took the six-pack, went up to his room, put on the loudest music he could, and drank all six cans. Having consumed little in the way of liquor in his life, those six cans on an empty stomach immediately made him woozy. He drank half a bottle of mouthwash, hoping to disguise his breath before realizing the mouthwash also contained alcohol. Finally he collapsed on the bed, telling everyone through the closed door that he was sick. His Christian parents never knew about the drinking escapade, or if they did, they said nothing.

And then there was Lenora, whom he met during a two-year stint on the community-college scene. Beautiful Lenora. Dark hair, fair skin. His parents disliked her. They said he shouldn't be dating a non-Christian, that her foul mouth and other points did not a match make. He said he was old enough to decide who he wanted to date. It was the only time he'd seen his father angry over his decision. As it was, time took care of the problem. Lenora captured another guy's heart, and they ended up marrying last year. And the college career ended soon after when he flunked out and ran out of money. Dan assumed his parents' prayers were answered, having him safely back on home turf, alone, unattached, and broke, to continue in the Mallory tradition of peanut keeping.

That was another thing that bothered him. His parents' praying and other religious habits. He went to church like a dutiful son should, but it meant little. His parents prayed constantly for him and his older brother. On occasion he overheard the praying, especially late at night when his parents were in the family room. They would sit together side by side with their hands clasped, offering long intercession for the family. Dan didn't want to admit it, but he felt those prayers calming him when life turned sour. Nor did he want to admit it when his father pointed out his call for salvation back at age thirteen, but how it meant little to him now. No doubt those prayers were acting like Super Glue, trying to keep his feet planted on this peanut farm and under a righteous umbrella. But inside, Dan remained restless, and he didn't know why. He just knew that if he didn't break away soon from all this, he'd turn as nutty as the legumes they grew.

"Now don't eat too much," Mom said with another smile, gently taking the container out of his hands. "I'm making one of your favorite meals tonight. Pot roast."

"Sounds good, Mom. You make the best." He strode out of the house, the screen door banging shut behind him, only to stop short in the yard. Beyond the house lay the peanut fields. Rob was behind the wheel of the new tractor that pulled a cart, expertly driving it back and forth, hauling supplies dropped off by a delivery truck into the barn for storage. Dan ground his teeth. Rob was perfect at everything about farming. Dan would be perfect in his job, too, if he found a job to his liking. He took out the magazine he had rolled up and stuck in his back pocket after his shower. A wilderness adventure was more his style. Like rafting the wild Colorado River. Feasting on the great meals the rafting outfits cooked for dinner. Wearing all the newfangled sports clothes and sandals instead of jeans that smelled like cow dung and boots stained with the red clay of Virginia. Seeing the wild beauty of places like Arches National Park, unlike the fields of nothing around here. Oh how he wanted a new life. He swatted at a mosquito looking to take a bite out of his flesh. He wanted it bad.

"So what's going on, son?" a voice inquired.

Dan whirled to find his father behind him, peering at the magazine he held. He rolled it up quickly. "Nothing."

"Mind if I take a look?"

Dan reluctantly handed him the magazine. Now he would hear the proverbial lecture, how he should be thinking about the family and not chasing after some dream. Instead his father looked it over until he came to the back of the magazine where Dan had circled several ads for work as an adventure guide.

"Is this what you want to do?"

Dan blinked at the question he posed. He decided to answer just as succinctly. "Yes."

"Why? I didn't know you liked it so much. You only went rafting that one time, if I recall."

"I don't know. It was a blast the time I went. It's something completely different and in a different state. Something totally new."

Pop squinted at the fields and then looked at the barn where Rob was unloading supplies. "You really don't want to be a farmer, do you?"

Dan looked at his father. He thought for sure he would hear stories about how the peanut farm had been in the family for generations and that it was his duty to keep it going. "No. I can't stand it, Pop. I've tried to be happy, but this is not what I want to do. It's not for me. Rob is better at the farm stuff anyway. You don't need the both of us working here. He does everything."

"But I do need you, son. I need both my sons to make this place work. If you left, I would have to hire another helper."

"No, you wouldn't. Rob does it all. Look at what a great season you had last year while I was taking classes. He's a one-man show, all by himself."

"But look at us now, working side by side, making the farm happen with the people you love. It's knowing that together we can roll up our sleeves, work hard, and watch a harvest blessed by God. We can enjoy the fruit that comes with it. You have to admit there's been good fruit from working here in the past."

Dan couldn't argue with that. He had a nice smartphone, and last year, a new tablet waiting for him at Christmas. But there was more to life than those things. There remained the constant nagging in his heart to go places. Here on the farm, he felt like life was passing him by. All the guys out West were having fun, and he was stuck shoveling manure and waiting for peanuts to form beneath the ground.

"So you have your heart set on being a river guide?"

"Maybe. I need to get my feet wet first. See what the possibilities are out there. Try my hand at something different."

He handed back the magazine. "Well, I can't force you to stay here. If you want to leave, it's your decision." He began to walk away.

"Hey, Pop? If I decide to leave, I'll need some money to settle down with. You said that we were earning money as we worked here. I'm sure I've earned something these past fifteen years."

"You mean the money that's in the trust fund I set up for each of you boys?"

Dan nodded without reservation. "I need money. Can't move and get a place to rent without money."

Pop sighed long and hard. "I'll take your share out of the bank if that's what you want. I hope you've prayed about this and you're certain this is what God wants you to do. You realize that once you use up the money, that's it. There won't be anything left."

Nothing to it, Dan thought gleefully. *With the kind of money these guys must be making in the adventure business, I'll be able to return the favor and then some.* Excitement surged through him at the possibility. "Sure, I understand. But I don't plan to waste it, Pop. I'll be making money, too, so it won't matter."

Pop looked at him, his mouth open to say something, then nodded. The conversation had ended, and Dan had won. He smiled to himself. This had gone better than he ever could have hoped or dreamed. He figured Pop would fight him all the way, but he'd acquiesced as if it were nothing at all. Surely this must mean it was the right thing to do.

Dan waved the magazine flier like a banner for the world to see. "Moab, Utah, here I come!"

Chapter 2

hat's on your mind?

        Jolene. . .is tired of red rocks, heat waves, muddy water, and irate customers.

Jolene, or Jo, as she liked to be called, hit the ENTER button on the keyboard and watched the statement appear on the "wall." She sat back in her seat, staring at her avatar—her cheerful face parked inside a raft, of course. What other picture would she have on her Facebook page? And what other link would she have posted except one for Red Canyon Adventures of Moab, owned by her cousin, Todd.

Now she reread the words she'd posted. How cynical they seemed. Thankfully Todd rarely accessed his Facebook page, or he would wonder why she wrote such a thing. And he'd make some remark, too, about how a posting like that could hurt his business. Jo never shared her feelings with her cousin these days. She'd come out here from the East to help but found herself being scorched instead, just like the fiery red rocks under the intense Utah sun. If he knew her thoughts, he would decide she was suffering another round of PMS—of which on those days he told her to take the day off. If only he knew everything. But guys don't usually notice things like that. Instead they loved food, electronic gadgets, a girl, a good time.

"I'd like to book a one-day trip, please."

Jo continued to stare at her phone until she heard a loud "Ahem." She looked up to see a rather plump man with sunglasses attached to a colorful band encircling his throat. Beside him stood his equally rotund wife. They looked like typical vacationers to Moab. Probably came here in their RV from who knows where, parked it in one of the expensive RV parks north of town, and now wanted to experience all that the area had to offer.

"How can I help you?"

"We want to book a one-day rafting trip for two."

Jo tried not to snap her gum like some teen bored by the routine and the customer. She looked at the company computer screen. "Let's see. We have room on a raft of ten leaving at 8:30 a.m. tomorrow."

"We want to arrange our own private rafting trip. Just the two of us."

Jo looked at him. "We usually like to place you with other passengers.

And it adds to the trip, sharing it with others." She already had that icky feeling that this was not going to be a pleasant encounter. Another irate customer who wanted his way would further substantiate her posting on her Facebook wall.

The man went on to explain how he'd promised Tootsie—she guessed that was the woman's name—her own boat ride down the Colorado.

"I'll ask Todd what he can do for you. He's the manager." She picked up the cell phone and turned away, not wishing to look anymore at the man's irritated face. She put forth the question.

Todd answered.

"Okay, thanks." She turned back to the guy. "Todd will take you on a private excursion, but it will cost extra."

He didn't seem to care but plunked down a debit card. It didn't surprise her that Todd had agreed. He always had dollar signs for pupils in his eyes these days. How Jo wished she could convince him there were more important things in life than making money. Like having God in the picture. But these days, everyone was looking for money and making it the only way they knew how.

The man bustled over with his and her bottles of suntan lotion, energy bars, and drinks. Jo rang up the purchases, thinking about the time when she first tried to share about God with Todd. "Please don't get into that religious stuff, Jolene. I've been doing just fine without God for twenty-six years."

Jo wondered how she ever existed without God now that she knew Him. Scratch that. Even a single moment. She'd found out the hard way she couldn't. . .which made her think of something different to write on the wall of her Facebook page. When the couple left, she returned to the Internet and deleted the last post. She entered her favorite verse from Philippians. *I can do all this through Him who gives me strength.* She smiled at those faith-filled words that infused her spirit with strength. If there was one thing she needed right now, it was a zap of faith. And maybe a new lease on life.

"Wow, it's great to be finally here. This place is amazing."

Another bright and cheery customer. Though she shouldn't complain. Business was tough enough with the fierce competition between the numerous rafting companies here in Moab. She looked up and this time allowed her gum to snap at the college-aged guy who wandered in, no doubt seeking the wildest rafting experience they had to offer. Jo already had the sales pitch on her lips, ready to recommend the two-day excursion into Cataract Canyon with Class IV and V rapids. Her fingers curled around the brochure.

He strode up to the counter with confidence oozing out of every pore. He wore expensive shades that could use a fancy band to hold them in place. Jo looked over to see the eyeglass bands sadly lacking on the display rack, including her favorite color—purple. She made a mental note to remind Todd to reorder a few more. "I've got just the trip for you. Cataract Canyon." She launched into her sales pitch.

The man whipped off his shades and gently pressed a finger against her lips. The contact made her leap to her feet. How dare he touch her like that! And how dare she find it exciting for a brief moment. She stepped back and shook her head as if to ward off the thought.

"Sorry. I didn't mean anything. I just wanted to quiet you for a second so I can explain why I'm here. I'm looking for a job, not a trip."

"We already did our hiring back in the winter. Sorry." She didn't bother to add that Todd was thinking of cutting back on employees, as profits had been slipping with the wavering economy.

"Well, I see there's tons of rafting companies around here. Any you know of that might be hiring river guides?"

"You know the rivers around here?"

He thought for a moment. "I'm a fast learner."

She laughed. How typical—boast first for an attention-grabber then admit later that he knows nothing about what he wants to do. "There's a lot to learn about running a raft down the Colorado. You can't just walk off the street and expect to paddle a boat safely with paying customers on board. And you need to be licensed by the state before you can conduct a trip. Do you have any experience?"

"Well, I went on a rafting trip in West Virginia, on the Gauley River. Ever hear of it? Some of the wildest rapids you've ever seen."

"What class were they?"

His forehead furrowed. "Oh, the best class. Top of the class, if you know what I mean. First-rate white water." He winked.

Jo wondered if he was joking around with her or he really didn't know the first thing about rafting. "Well, you can check with Todd to see if he could use an extra hand. He might need someone to help with cooking on the family trips. Driving the bus. Or organizing gear. But honestly, we're rather tight right now on our budget. Like everyone else these days, we're cutting back."

"I'd rather paddle a boat than fix a meal."

"I know, but you have to start somewhere. Most of the trips we do include either a picnic lunch or full meals for the overnight trips. So you need to know it all. We serve some of the best food, too, I might add." She wanted to boast about her involvement in that aspect, helping Todd discover that serving customers satisfying meals brought them back, or in the least, served as a way to spread a good word about their company. "Did you know our meals were rated one of the top of the companies here in Moab? I used to help with the cooking, but now I mostly man the reservation desk."

He leaned over the counter, his rugged face with a five o'clock shadow and breath scented with peppermint a bit too close for comfort. "And I'll bet you're the best cook around. That's why you won the awards."

"I can charbroil a steak quite well, thanks. And I make fabulous brownies." She felt her cheeks warm as his hazel-colored eyes leveled on her and then began tracing her facial features.

"Sounds great. How about having me over for dinner so I can taste some of your cooking?"

She snapped her fingers. "Wouldn't you know it, I'm booked solid." She thought about her social calendar, which included the Internet and gathering with church friends Wednesday nights. Besides, the guy was getting a little too friendly for comfort. "Well, if you're willing to do some tasks like cooking, equipment handling, stuff like that, Todd might be interested."

"I suppose that's better than nothing. I have plenty of money to start up here anyway. Which reminds me, can you suggest a place to rent? Any place will do, just until I get settled and have time to look for a house."

"You can check the classifieds in the local paper for apartments and rooms for rent."

"Okay, thanks." He paused. "Do you know when Todd might be back?"

"Not sure. He had to make a run this afternoon. Should be back by six."

"Six, huh? Guess I have time then to get acquainted with the town. Maybe you can take a lunch break and show me around. It's getting to be that hour, and I'm hungry."

Jo looked at the clock and the hands moving toward the noon hour. A break would be nice, even if it was with an overly eager guy who had no idea what he was doing or where he was going in life. "Okay. I can get Christine to cover."

"Super. Know any good places to eat?"

"I like the Moab Diner. It has great Mexican food."

"Mexican food at a diner? This I've got to see."

Jo felt like a mom ready to escort her eager son. She'd never seen such excitement in someone who couldn't wait to see what Moab had to offer. If only she could tell him how dull this life would soon become. But she supposed someone eager to run the river would find it all exciting. Maybe if she had stuck it out with the camping and cooking part of the deal and not demoted herself to a desk job, life would be more interesting. Though that was her fault. Todd needed someone capable to man the desk. And she agreed to do it. Besides, *godliness with contentment is great gain.* Wow, did she need to work on the contentment part of life. Like this guy, who seemed content just to be here in Moab. And here she was, contemplating how to get away from Moab.

They arrived at the Moab Diner with its red plastic booths and granite-colored tables, a hangout for many of the rafting guys. She and the guy quickly nabbed a seat. To her dismay, she spotted their competitor Chris Rhodes and some friends at another table. She wondered why he wasn't out on the river today. She hoped he didn't notice her. That's all she needed to top her day.

"So what's good here?" he asked. "I suppose the tacos."

Jo kept her eye trained on Chris. So far so good. With the empty plates before them, she hoped they were about ready to leave. She still recalled the painful episode that erupted between Chris and Todd over a huge group looking to hire a rafting company for a special weekend excursion. Todd did everything he could to land the contract, even spreading a rumor about Chris and his company, which Todd thought was legit and used it to his advantage. When Chris got wind of it, nasty words flew and nearly fists as well.

"You look like something's on your mind," the guy interrupted. "Hey, do you realize we haven't even introduced ourselves? I'm Dan Mallory."

Jo turned her attention to him. "Jolene Davidson. But I like to go by Jo."

"Jolene. Nice southern name, like from Tennessee. Or Georgia."

"Well, if it isn't the Red Canyon Adventures co-conspirator," came a voice.

Chris had spotted her. *Super.* Jo tried to focus her gaze on the menu, which turned blurry.

"I'm still amazed your cousin can sleep nights after the stunt he pulled last month," Chris went on.

"I had nothing to do with it," she said quickly.

"Sure, sure." Chris then looked at Dan. "And who's this? Another one you managed to con into an adventure? Or into the company?"

"I'm Dan, fresh from the East," Dan said, offering his hand. "I'm looking for a job here in a rafting company."

"Well, if you want my advice, don't work for Red Canyon Adventures. Their only adventure seems to be spreading lies and running everyone else out of business."

"It wasn't an out-and-out lie. You were rumored to have a salmonella problem," Jo said in a low voice.

Chris stared with daggers in his eyes.

"There's nothing wrong with making a profit as long as it's honest work," Dan added.

An eyebrow raised on Chris's face. "There's a big difference when that profit comes from unethical means. I'm sure Jolene can fill you in. And for your information, we were cleared of that salmonella thing."

"Hey, are you by chance looking for workers?" Dan interrupted.

"Nope, we're not. Sorry." He then returned to Jo. "Tell Todd I don't forget things easily, Jolene. And he ought to be making apologies real quick, 'cause time's running out." He gave one last steely-eyed look before whirling about and leaving.

"Wow, I had no idea you companies were out to spill each other's blood," Dan said, his eyes wide. "What's he talking about?"

"My cousin likes to make money, and he got the group Chris wanted. Todd will do whatever's necessary to make things work to his advantage, even if he has to tell a tall tale. I mean, there was a rumor that Chris's company had an outbreak of salmonella poisoning, but like Chris said, it was never proven. Because of it, Todd got Chris's groups."

"Not a good idea to spread a rumor unless it's true," Dan said slowly as if thinking on his own words. "I mean, I'll admit I sometimes fibbed or took shortcuts, but I always ended up getting burned by it. It never seems to work out in the end."

"I wish Todd would learn that lesson." She suddenly considered the idea of Dan joining their company. Maybe it would be good for her cousin to have a guy who had some moral backing to him. One who might be able to point out questionable activities before it was too late and they all suffered as a result. Like giving people trips they didn't want or taking away groups from other companies by telling everyone their food was bad or spreading other rumors. Todd might listen to a guy over her, not that he hadn't listened to her past objections. But if Todd got a guy's take on things, it might work out for the better. "Hey Dan, if I got Todd to interview you, would you consider working for our company? I mean, you weren't spooked by what Chris said, were you?"

"Are you kidding? 'Course not. I'll take what I can get. That's why I'm here. I mean, I'd rather not end up the official company cook. I would really like to help guide a boat or something."

"Well, you need training, you know. But I'll see what he can do for you."

The waitress ventured up to take their orders. Dan took the initiative, ordering the specialty—the Navajo taco. Jo wasn't sure she could handle the food right now with the painful twinge in her stomach, made more intense by all this commotion. But God had divinely arranged for this meeting, maybe to bring back to the rafting company some semblance of virtue that had been lacking. She decided on a Mexican stir-fry then returned her attention to Dan. "So what kind of shortcuts have you taken in the past?" she wondered aloud.

Dan looked at her in surprise. "Why are you asking me that?"

"It's good to know a person's background. Call it a background check, so to speak. And to make sure you're not bringing any surprises into the company."

"Look, I came here with a clean slate. No police record or anything, I promise. Even got that one speeding ticket cleared up before I left the state. The only employer I worked for was my pop, and I know he would vouch for me. Maybe. I mean, sometimes you take shortcuts on the home front, like Pop tells you to do something, and suddenly you get a call on the cell phone and forget to complete the project. That sort of thing."

"So you worked for your father?"

"Yeah, we raise peanuts for a living, if you can believe it. How's that for a nutty profession?" He laughed so long and loud, Jo had to wonder if something else lay hidden behind the laughter. She'd known many people who hid some untold pain behind a joke or laugh. "Now you see why I wanted to come here."

"Well, this isn't all that glamorous either. If you like broiling days and river water sloshing all over you and customers who aren't always friendly. . ."

"Are you kidding? Sounds great. Anything is better than watching peanut plants grow. Believe me."

To Jo, the idea of working with plants, waiting for the fruit of the earth to come forth, even if it was sight unseen in the ground, seemed like a nice change compared to red rocks, hot sun, and trying to work through the idiosyncrasies of people in the rafting business. Maybe they should switch jobs. "How about I go work on your dad's peanut farm and you can work for Todd," she suggested with a laugh. "It will be our own reality show. I'd love to watch plants grow. And I like honey-roasted peanuts. After a while, all these rocks can get to you. Makes you feel like you're living on Mars or something."

Dan laughed, too, this time in a friendly manner that sent warmth radiating through her. "Pop would sure love to meet you—and Mom, too, but then I wouldn't get to know everything about you." At that moment their meals arrived, the scent of cumin and cilantro rising into the air. "And I'll need lessons in cooking, if that's where I end up. You can show me how to do a steak up right and make me a first-class Iron Chef like Bobby Flay."

Jo bent her head to pray and set the future in God's hands. "And help us know, dear God, if you wish Dan to be a part of our rafting company. In Jesus' name, amen." When she looked up, Dan sat there, hazel eyes wide open, fork in hand, ready to take a bite. *Okay, so this guy is different.* He certainly had enthusiasm. Maybe he can help put the business on the right footing. Fresh blood in the company, so to speak. New life. And she prayed, maybe new hope, too. The business sure needed it. She could use some of it as well.

Chapter 3

So far Dan could not have been more pleased with how things were working out. It had been smooth sailing from the moment he arrived in Moab and then fell into company with the very attractive co-proprietor of Red Canyon Adventures. Jo got him a job as soon as she introduced him to her cousin Todd. Not that he cared much when she mentioned he would cook. But if the cooking part got his foot in the door, or rather, in a raft, he would take it from there and become the captain of his own ship in no time. With training, that is.

Dan lingered before the mirror on his first official day in the rafting business, gelling his hair, checking out the new tight-fitting polyester shirt, board shorts, river sandals, and of course, shades. He looked the part, even if he didn't have the slightest idea what he was doing. But in this game, looks and confidence mattered. It worked well in sealing this deal when he put the charm on Jo and snagged a job. How he wanted to call home and gloat over the fact with mighty bro and Pops.

He did call once, letting the family know he'd arrived safely in Moab. Pop said little. He received a text message from Rob who told him how Mom was in his bedroom looking over some of his belongings that he'd left behind. Dan thought about that for a few moments before deleting the message. He loved Mom and missed her fine cooking. The more he thought about the family back home, the worse he felt, so he chose not to think about it. Mom would pray anyway, and that would make her feel better. And when she learned how happy he was here, how many bucks he was making, and how life was sweet for him in Moab, she would be okay with his decision. Maybe he could even invite her and Pop to come out, and he'd take them on a rafting trip. He'd cook Pop a steak the way he liked it. They would know without a doubt this is where he was meant to be.

But all the niceties still didn't make things feel right. Somewhere deep inside, he had a nagging doubt. He didn't know what to make of it either. Like a black cloud trying to dull the sunshine, of which there was no lack in this place. In fact, the other items he bought besides the clothes were a bottle of heavy-duty waterproof sunscreen and a hat. But once he thought of the action to come today—his first trip on the river to see all that there was to see—the doubt fled. Maybe it was just nerves.

He took up his iPod and made tracks. No way did he want to be late on his first day. Hopping inside his newly purchased used Jeep—he wished he could afford a new one but didn't want to use up all his money—he peeled off down the road, gunning the engine for effect. Ah, life was good.

Suddenly he saw the flashing strobe lights of a police car in his rearview mirror. "Oh, man," he mumbled, looking at the speedometer, wondering how fast he'd been going. He pulled over to the shoulder.

The officer sauntered up as if he were used to pulling over beach guys in their red Jeeps. "I need to see your license and registration, please."

"I have a Virginia license. The registration hasn't arrived yet. I just got here and recently bought this Jeep."

"Hmm. Not a great way to be introduced to Moab's speed limit of thirty. Especially doing fifty."

Dan blew out a sigh. "Any chance you can let me off with a warning? I'm on my way to my job. It's my first day. And I guess I need to get used to the speed limit around here. And this new Jeep. Too many new things."

The officer looked as if he'd heard all these arguments before. He said nothing but walked back to his vehicle to perform a security check. Dan tapped his fingers on the steering wheel and looked at his watch, realizing he was about to be late for his first day on the job. And he was about to see his insurance skyrocket with another ticket. This was not good. Life was bad. He should've skipped the gel routine this morning and given himself extra time.

After a few minutes the officer returned. "I'll let you off with a warning. But the speed limit in town is thirty."

"Thank you so much, Officer. And if you ever want a rafting trip, Red Canyon Adventures has the best! And I'll make sure they give you a discount."

The officer cocked an eyebrow, shook his head, and returned to his car. "Thank you, God," Dan said loudly and took off, this time making sure the speedometer did not inch anywhere near the thirty-mile-per-hour mark. He should be thanking God for a lot of things these days. After all, he had a nice apartment, his fine red Jeep to cruise around in, a rafting job, a friend in Jo. He smiled when he thought of her. She was a neat girl who loved life, even if she seemed a little worn out by it. Maybe he could lift her mood. He would infuse enthusiasm into her dull and dreary life. If only she knew what a dull life really was. . .like driving a tractor in a peanut field. She would thank her lucky stars she lived here in Moab.

He made it to the center with a minute to spare. There he found the boss, Todd, giving directions to the other employees. Paying customers, outfitted in everything from short shorts to one in a pair of jean shorts that hung to his kneecaps, stood ready to embark on their journey down the Colorado. Dan ventured forward and greeted everyone. "Hi, I'm Dan Mallory."

"Nothing like getting here at the last minute," Todd noted.

"Sorry. I'm not used to the speed limit."

"Sylvester pull you over?"

Dan laughed loudly, thinking of Sylvester the "puddy tat," according to Tweety. "Don't know, but whoever it was let me off with a warning. You have a real friendly and forgiving town here."

Todd nodded. "Okay, we're gonna pile into the bus and head over to the loading area. Next time, Dan, I need you here an hour earlier to help load up the boats and other gear."

"Yeah, you can't be showing up anytime you want," another guy added.

Dan detected the sarcasm in the voice and wondered if he might be in trouble. "Sorry, I didn't know that. I'll be early next time."

Todd looked at his clipboard. "Your job today is lunch since you don't have training for anything else. I assume you know how to make sandwiches."

"Like PB and J?" Dan again laughed, only to find Todd and the other guy staring at him in displeasure. "Sorry, that was lame. You see, I used to work on a peanut farm back home."

"Boy, you are from the back hills of the East," the other guy murmured.

Todd went on to explain Dan's job for the day, taking care of the lunch preparations. Just then, Dan noticed Jo walk out, carrying a large cooler. He and Todd went to help her load it onto the bus.

"You need to get here earlier," she told him. "Travis was having a meltdown that you hadn't shown up, and he was stuck with all the work of loading the gear."

Dan nodded. "So that's his name. Better than saying, 'Hey you.' Yeah, I already got bawled out about it. Sorry." He hoped for a smile but instead saw a grim expression on her face. He couldn't see her eyes behind the sunglasses that shielded them. "So what's on the lunch menu?"

"Sandwiches, fruit, cookies, lemonade. The usual." She paused. "Oops, that's right, you don't know the usual."

"And here I thought we'd be cooking steaks."

"That's on overnight trips. But hang around long enough, and you'll get to do that, too."

"Honestly, what I really want to do is be a river guide. Wonder when Todd will let me do that."

"Oh, he might introduce you to it today, just for kicks. You have to train anyway on the river for a solid three weeks. Then pass a test."

"So I might do something today? Wow, I thought I'd have to be at this game forever before I'd get a chance to man the helm."

"This is not a difficult section of the river. He'll probably have Travis give you some pointers on the calmest section. It's a perfect place to learn the ropes."

Dan hoped that they would also be entering calmer waters where he might be able to learn more about Jo. "You're coming today, right?"

"Nope. Someone's got to hold down the cash register and book the trips."

"I guess so." He thought about asking if she wanted to grab a burger afterward, but he heard Todd's impatient voice inquiring if the food was ready. Jo and Dan hurried over to load the back end of the bus with the fixings for lunches, along with the dry bags. "Make sure you put the food like the chips, cookies, and rolls into the dry bags before you load them onto the rafts," Jo instructed, holding up the stiff waterproof bags used on the rafts.

"Wish me luck," Dan said, eyeing her lips when he said it. *Get a hold of yourself, Dan the man. It's too soon to be begging a good-luck kiss. You just met her three days ago. Give it time.* But her lips looked tantalizing all the same. He wished he had her along to help him. He nearly suggested to Todd that an attractive sandwich maker by his side might be a nice addition to his first day on the job. He dismissed it when Todd and Travis climbed on board the bus. He followed suit.

"Have a good time," Jo said with a smile.

It was a pleasant send-off, not as nice as a kiss would be, but nice all the same. He let her sweet words soak into his withered being that was now getting even more withered from the intense heat. "How hot does it get here?" he asked Travis when they settled into their seats.

Travis didn't answer for a long moment. He then said, "Hot."

What was this guy's problem? He must still be mad that Dan arrived late and he was stuck with the work. "Okay, hot as in what?"

"Gets to a hundred plus. Even in the shade."

"Wow. We get some days like that in Virginia. But it was always so humid, too."

"You don't get that here. It's dry heat. Low humidity levels." Travis then pulled out a racing car magazine. Dan frowned in contempt. Travis would have to be reading a NASCAR rag. His brother Rob ate and breathed NASCAR. Rob sometimes went to the speedway in Richmond or the one in North Carolina somewhere to catch the action. He loved the stuff.

Dan pushed the irritation aside to glance behind him at the assorted customers eager to taste a river adventure. They came in all sizes and with various backgrounds. One of the women didn't look too pleased about the whole deal, judging by the way she sat tense in her seat, wrinkles creasing her young face. She had frosted hair and big hoop earrings. Her boyfriend had his meaty arm hooked around her as if trying to soothe her nerves.

"It's gonna be a blast, sweetie. You'll love it."

"If I fall out, I'm suing," she told him flatly.

"If you fall out, I get to rescue you. And it will be great."

She wiggled out of his grasp and folded her arms in a huff. "If I fall out I'll sue, and I'll drop you, too."

Dan had to smirk. There were parts of this job he hadn't anticipated, like the clientele. He never was much of a people observer, but this was already proving to be quite entertaining.

The bus hissed and groaned for the hour ride through a pristine area of genuine Utah wilderness, with tall cliffs and rock formations bordering the river. Finally it came to a stop at the drop-off area. Several other rafting outfitters were already at work, readying their prospective clients and boats. Dan noticed the guy, Chris, from the restaurant the other day. Thankfully the guy didn't say anything but was busy with his own outfit. After the conflict in the restaurant, Dan didn't care to see more blood spilled here. But so far everything looked peaceful.

Dan helped Travis and the other employees unload the boats while Todd gathered the group together for a quick safety lesson. Each was equipped with a life preserver or what Todd called a PFD or personal flotation device. Dan wondered what the guy wearing the jean shorts would do when his clothing became waterlogged. At least it was plenty warm today; they might actually dry. Already the perspiration was rolling down Dan's face. He wanted to ask about drinking water, but Travis was barking at him for not having the dry bags of food ready.

"It would be nice if someone filled me in on what to do," Dan said.

"Jolene said you knew everything about rafting trips. I didn't think we'd have to go back to grade school."

Oh man. Me and my bloated ego. Dan remembered how he'd tried to sell himself to Jo with all that talk of rafting in West Virginia, when he'd only been on one trip. He was eating his own words. "Well, every rafting company does things differently, so I want to make sure I don't mess things up."

Travis seemed to accept this explanation and began to explain their routine for the trip. Dan felt better about it all when Todd signaled to them. Dan buckled on his PFD and climbed in with Todd and half the company, which included the nervous woman with the large earrings and her manhandling boyfriend. Travis skippered the other boat with the remaining passengers and the food.

Pure excitement pulsated through Dan as they each picked up paddles, ready to attack the river. The passengers all talked excitedly as they took off down the Colorado. An azure sky reflected in the bounding waters. The rocky formations of cliffs and spirals, painted dark orange and red, fascinated him. Dan began to learn the names of the formations. Fisher Towers. Castle Valley. Even one that looked like a church with rock people standing before it. They stopped at one point on the river to play a game with the paddles and take a nature walk. Dan had never felt such a thrill in all his life. To witness all this before his very eyes after months of reading about it in magazines seemed too good to be true. Rob would be jealous if he could see him now. *The whole family would be jealous*, Dan thought. This was life at its best, and he was being paid for it. Nothing could be better.

The boats drifted easily over a few rapids in the river to the delight of the passengers. Everyone seemed to be enjoying it except earring girl who complained to her boyfriend that the up and down motion of the boat was making her sick. "Just have fun," he told her. "This is great!"

"I don't think this is fun at all. I just know I'm gonna fall out of this thing."

Dan shook his head, wishing that she, like the others, could put a smile on her face, relax, and enjoy the splendid Utah scenery. He certainly was and couldn't wait to help man the boat later on.

❧

Dan had just finished arranging the meats and cheeses in semicircles on plates, complete with snippets of parsley for decoration, when Todd ventured up. "Hey, that looks awesome, Dan. You look like a regular chef, arranging everything."

"Thanks to Mom. She liked to put on these lunches at church and always made sure everything looked good." For a moment he became lost in thought, thinking of Mom at those church functions and how she wanted everything to be perfect. Dan knew she only wanted to bless others and make them feel special. Could some of her be rubbing off on him, even out here in Utah?

When the lunch was ready, the guests gathered to make sandwiches. Dan looked on, pleased with himself as everyone commented on the fine spread. "Yo! Having fun yet?" he asked earring girl as she helped herself to the pasta salad.

She looked at him in surprise. "I guess. Bobby here tells me this afternoon we're going to another beach area for some swimming and sunbathing. Know anything about it?"

"Well, uh. . ." Dan looked over at Todd. "I'm sure we are. I'm rather new here, so I'm just learning about this trip myself. But so far, it's been great."

"Yeah," she said before moving on to the plates filled with cookies. When everyone had been served, Todd, Travis, and Dan fixed themselves sandwiches and found a place to eat. Travis immediately complained about his raft and how the people refused to listen to instructions when it came to paddling.

"I've got a decent group," Todd remarked. "How about I switch with you, Travis, and you man my boat. You can show Dan some of the technique. This stretch of the river is perfect for learning some basics."

"I thought Dan was hired to cook."

Dan opened his mouth to object, only to find Todd coming to the rescue. "I could use a substitute guide, so the quicker we teach him, the quicker we can put him on a boat if we need to."

Dan tried to eat, but the expectation within him was growing by the moment. Here Jo had given him tales of doom and gloom stuck in a chef's apron and hat. Now, Todd was talking about him skippering his own boat. Was God doing things for him or what? Was God happy that he'd taken his inheritance and abandoned the family to go do his own thing? *Where did that thought come from?*

"Something up?" Todd asked him.

"No, no, just glad to be learning about rafting. That's why I came here."

"Well, I like your enthusiasm. And if the attention you gave to the lunch is anything like you will give to rafting, you're gonna do just fine."

Dan ate the rest of his sandwich with gusto, all the while thanking dear old Mom and her church luncheons for helping him out. He owed her a *Life Is Good* T-shirt. He'd seen that saying on shirts inside the store. But honestly, he owed her a whole lot more than he was willing to give.

❧

"Don't worry about it."

But Dan did worry about it, big-time. He sat on the bus, trying to avoid earring girl and her boyfriend who were likely staring at his back with daggers in their eyes. Okay, so his first time at the helm of the raft wasn't the best. He was told this was an easy stretch of river. How did he know there was a rock hidden under the water? Like he had X-ray vision or something. Who put it there anyway?

"I can't believe you didn't see it," Travis yelled at him. "You have to look at the water and the way it's flowing to see the obstacles and alert the passengers. You could clearly see how the current was making a vee around the rock."

When the raft sideswiped the rock, the motion sent everyone lurching. And suddenly earring girl was in the frothy river. She screamed, frantically waving her hands as if she were about to be swallowed up, even though the water was only waist deep. To make matters worse, her boyfriend sat in the boat and laughed. Travis held out a paddle to assist her back into the raft. Then to cap it off, she moaned how she'd sacrificed one of her precious earrings to the deep.

"Dan, are you hearing me?" Todd said.

"Yeah, sure."

"These things happen. It's not the first time, nor will it be the last. Passengers fall out. It's part of the river. That's why they wear a PFD and are taught what to do if they fall overboard."

Dan glanced at the rear of the bus to see earring girl and her red face. "She looks pretty mad. But she didn't help matters. I mean, she was leaning over the side of the boat already when it hit. Something about losing an earring."

"Don't worry about it, okay?"

Dan was happy that Todd seemed to be rooting for him. He felt certain after such apparent ineptness he'd be shown his way to the company exit. Especially after the big deal Travis made over it.

When they arrived back in Moab, Dan felt as if he had just completed an all-day marathon. His legs ached, and his arms even more so. His face felt as if it were on fire, and he had a pounding headache to boot. Inside the store he grabbed a cold bottle of water out of a refrigerated case and began gulping it down.

"Yo! You'll have to tell me what you took," said a sweet voice from across the way.

He looked over to find Jo tidying up the shirt rack.

"I have to know what you took out of the case so I can mark it down as employee compensation," she explained.

"I'll pay for it," Dan said.

"You don't have to. Just let me know. I mean, you can't walk out with merchandise, but you can take a drink and an energy bar now and then."

"Thanks." He had to admit Jo was a pleasing sight after this mixed-up day that had seen him go from exultation to exasperation.

She went to the cash register to begin signing out for the day. "You look bad. Got a nasty sunburn, too. You need to wear more sunscreen. That's some of our primary instruction to the customers. Wear sunscreen and drink plenty of water."

"I feel bad. As for the sunscreen, I remembered everything else but forgot to put that on today." He leaned across the counter, feeling very weary indeed.

She gave him a sympathetic look. "Better grab a tube of aloe vera there. You can pay me for that. And would you be interested in stopping for ice cream after work?"

Dan immediately straightened. "Thanks. That'd be awesome."

"Just have to finish up. Be right back."

Dan waited with as much patience as he could muster, downing the rest of his drink. He took the tube of aloe vera and left the money on the counter, then applied the gooey blue gel to his burned face.

When Jo returned, she was carrying her purse, which was shaped like a small backpack. "Todd's gonna inventory out. He said you did fine today. The lunch was awesome." She took the money for the aloe vera and put it in the cash register.

"Thanks." Dan followed her into the hot sunshine of Moab that made his face and eyes hurt. "I guess if you can call running the raft into a rock fine."

"Oh, rafts hit obstacles all the time. They bounce."

"Yeah, but it bounced a little too much and earring girl got tossed out. She wasn't happy."

Jo laughed with a sound that warmed his sunburned soul. Oh, how he would love to curl his arm around her and soak up some of her sweetness. But he kept his arm to himself.

They entered the ice cream shop where Jo ordered them both extra large twist cones. "We'll have to eat in here. Outside they'll melt into a puddle in about five minutes." She led the way to two seats in the corner.

"Someone should do a test to see how long it takes for an extra-large twist cone to melt in one-hundred-degree weather."

Jo laughed, licking away at the ice cream. Dan watched in spite of himself until he felt stickiness on his fingers and saw his ice cream already melting. He began taking big bites.

"Slow down, or you'll end up with a brain freeze."

"That would be all right. My head is hot enough as it is. At least my headache is better." He paused. "I just wish I hadn't rammed that boat into a rock. Everything was going so good. Todd really liked how I'd set up the lunch. And he's all interested in me becoming a substitute guide soon."

"Really? Then you did have a good day, even with the bump on the rock."

"If Travis would only be cool about things. I think he has it in for me as the newbie in all this."

Jo shrugged. "We were all new once. But don't let it get to you, Dan. You'll fit in just fine, and pretty soon you'll be guiding a trip with the best of them."

Dan was liking Jo more and more—and after only three days filled with lunch, ice cream, conversation, and laughter. He wanted so much to call her his girlfriend. Once again, he had to tell himself to slow it down. But maybe she was thinking the same thing, that she wanted him for her boyfriend. She didn't let on that she did. He would like to ask her and make it official. But he couldn't have everything he wanted in less than a week. An awesome job and a girlfriend to boot. Could he?

"You look like something's on your mind."

"I. . .uh, I'm happy to have a friend. When you're new in town, a friend is awesome."

"It's important. Friends make things better. And so can ice cream when you've had a tough day. I get a cone whenever I've had a tough day." She paused as if lost in her own thoughts.

"Has today been a tough day?"

"No, it's been pretty good, actually."

Dan was liking this more and more. He'd give it a few more days, tops. Jo was sure to be in his relationship status on Facebook. He hoped.

Chapter 4

Jo couldn't help but feel compassion for Dan, even if he was brash at times and thought a bit too much of himself. Seeing him with his face burned that first day and looking as if he had run a marathon—it must be that motherly feeling creeping up in her. Though Jo could hardly think of motherly things at her age. Twenty-three years wasn't exactly a teenybopper, but neither was she old enough to think like a mother. She was just the age to enjoy life as a single person, though at times it proved challenging. At least Dan's arrival added some zip. He kept her on her toes when she needed to explain simple protocol. The other evening he'd stopped by the store asking for advice, claiming he needed to know all the ins and outs of this place if he was going to fit in. And other things, too—like handling irate customers such as earring girl, as he called her. Jo had to admit she admired his tenacity.

Jo entered the gear room that evening to sort out the PFDs left behind from the day's trips. Besides motherhood, there was another thing she wasn't looking forward to. Cleaning up after everyone. If the husband wasn't going to at least pitch in on a few of these assorted duties, life would be a struggle. But, then again, if he arrived home with a vase of red tulips—she missed seeing tulips blooming in Moab—and a box of those new candy-coated mint-chocolate candies, she would be in heaven, and all the mediocre jobs in the world would not sway her happy mood.

A few swear words echoing into the storeroom now sent her whirling. Travis was delivering a fresh set of wet gear, which he dumped on the floor. He swore again until his gaze rested on Jo.

"Do you mind?" she said. "We're trying to run a family business."

"We're in the storeroom, for crying out loud! And that guy Todd hired doesn't know what he's doing."

Uh-oh. Travis was complaining about Dan again. Poor Dan, who only wanted to do what's right. "What did Dan do this time?"

"We had him on dinner duty last night, and he burned the steaks. You know how much beef costs? Then another guy wanted his rare. Dan looked like he was going to be sick and refused to cook it that way. I had to do it. The guy's crazy. He doesn't belong with this outfit."

"He just needs some more training. We all had to go through training,

Travis. Even you. I'll go next time on the overnighter and teach him the ropes. He really wants to learn."

"Yeah, the first time he's out, he nearly wrecks the boat by hitting a rock and throws that girl overboard."

"Travis, aren't you being a little melodramatic? The rafts can take it. I'm sure you've hit plenty of rocks."

"He belongs back on his old man's peanut farm." Travis uttered a few more choice words when he thought she wasn't listening.

Jo sighed and picked up the PFDs to sort them out by sizes. There had to be a way to smooth things over and make Dan accepted among the employees. It wasn't good for company morale to have employees not working together as a team. The customers were sure to notice it, and this business was highly competitive. If other rafting companies knew what was afoot, they would gladly pounce on it. She could already see their competitor, Chris, making the most out of it. *If you want your steak burned, your life in peril, and people at odds with each other, then take a trip with Red Canyon Adventures. But if you want succulent meals and a smooth, friendly trip to see the wonders of nature, then come raft with us.*

Jo wondered what the strategy should be. Talk to the guys about it? Talk to Dan and give him more lessons? She already knew she needed to go on the next overnighter to offer him lessons on camp etiquette. But she knew, too, her reputation was on the line. After all, she was the one who asked Todd to hire the guy. She needed to save herself embarrassment and settle everyone's nerves—a tall order Jo was uncertain she could fill.

Jo finished the work in the storeroom and headed back to the main building. Todd stood at the cash register finishing some paperwork. She lingered at the doorway, observing his movements to see if he was as irritated as Travis. He stood composed, his tanned face smooth, his eyes focused on his work. Todd was usually quite levelheaded. While Travis acted out his frustration, Todd did it undercover. It would not surprise her, for instance, if he'd already fired Dan yet stood there without displaying a hint of emotion.

"So how was your overnighter?" she finally asked him.

"It went great. The customers had a good time."

Hmm. She expected to hear about the steaks burning and Dan keeling over in the sand. "Travis said Dan is having a hard time settling into the routine."

Todd glanced up. "Huh? Not from what I'm seeing. I mean, he didn't cook right the first time, but I remember Travis scorching pancakes on his first cooking duty. Dan did a good job setting up the tents. And the kids love him."

These comments made Jo glow inside. Perhaps she'd not blown it after all in suggesting that Todd hire him. "So you think he's gonna work out with the company?"

Todd shrugged. "Not sure. We're still in the training phase. But he's eager to please and wants this job bad, so that's good. He's not like a certain know-it-all who thinks he has everything figured out when he doesn't." Todd opened the register to take out the day's cash and put it in the safe. "I just wish he'd keep his mouth shut about the way I do things. He's not the head of this place, even if he feels he's earned it."

Uh-oh. Todd and Travis were having issues? They had other employees in the company—Sheryl, Christine, Larry, Chip, Evan—but no one worked more closely together than Todd and Travis. She thought of them like brothers in a way. They often hung out evenings at the tavern, not that she agreed with their habit of having a beer, but they talked business and discussed ways of doing things. Jo wondered if one day Todd might make Travis his business associate. Now to hear they may be butting heads—this was not a good sign.

He went on. "Just the other day he was talking to me about something that Chris was offering at his place. Frankly, I don't care to know what Chris or any of the other competition is doing. I'll run my business the way I want."

Todd was venting, which was probably a good thing. Oftentimes he didn't.

He suddenly backpedaled. "Sorry, I've said too much."

"You need to get it out. Remember what your mom used to say. 'Todd will explode one day if he doesn't get all those things out of him. He just sits there and stews.' "

"Yeah, but it's not good for my employees to hear me talking about them behind their backs. It makes for bad blood. And the customers are going to sense it if we're not a team. So forget I said anything."

Jo could only admire Todd for putting his customers first. And his business, too. No matter what it took. And she was there to make sure it ran smoothly, and he was on an even keel with everything. She owed that to their mothers who were as close as sisters could be. They were all close as kids growing up in New York where her parents still lived. Holidays were shared with the entire clan. The cousins hung out and played games or talked until 1:00 a.m. It was only natural that Jo would choose to come out West a few years ago to help Todd with the business when he put out the call. What probably wasn't natural was the true reason she responded to his need for help. Jo had come here to Moab to get away. . . .

She shook her head, not wishing to delve into that memory right now. First thing's first. Make sure her owner-cousin and fellow employees were happy, and the business remained afloat. "Todd, you know I'm here to help. If there's anything I can do to make things better, let me know."

"Just be sure you help out where Dan is concerned. I'm having you go along on the next overnighter, too, and teach him how to cook."

"You know, he's really looking forward to skippering his own boat. But I know to be a skipper, you gotta first mop the deck."

Todd gave her a smirk. "And you know he needs to be trained for a solid three weeks. I have no problem with Dan manning a boat after instruction and passing the state test. It will take time, but I think he has what it takes."

Dan would love hearing that. And for some reason, Jo felt eager to give him the good news. Leaving work that night to return to her apartment, she wondered where he lived. Not that she dared go to his apartment, but he talked of renting a nice place and had already bought himself a Jeep. He had the money to settle down. A far cry from when she first came here and had to resort to sleeping on Todd's sofa until she could afford a place of her own. Her vehicle right now was her own two feet or begging off Todd for the use of his car. But there were advantages to living in a town. Her feet did fine, taking her places. Everything was convenient.

Just then she heard a horn toot. A red Jeep pulled up beside her. Dan looked over with a smile parked on his face. "Hey there. Need a lift?"

"Actually, I prefer walking, thanks."

"Okay." She watched in amusement as he attempted to parallel park in a nearby space. After three tries he finally got the Jeep into the space, though cockeyed, and pocketed the keys. "So where are we walking to?"

"Well, I'm walking home."

"Great. I always wanted to know where you live."

Jo didn't say that she wanted to know where he lived, too, but the thought of him discovering her place of residence left her uncomfortable. "Look Dan, I'm not into that kind of thing."

"You mean you're not the kind of girl who invites guys into her apartment. Of course I know that. I mean, Mom lectured me about it long ago. The 'I won't invite myself unless I'm asked' kind of thing. But I can walk there, can't I?"

"I guess so." As they walked, he yammered away about rafting and his first day cooking, leaving out the details about burning the steak. Obviously no one thought it a big deal but Travis. Yet she was curious about his take on what happened. "Travis said you had a problem with the steaks."

"Oh, he got all uptight because I burned one, and I didn't care to cook a raw one for a customer. Travis had to do it himself. I guess because he guides trips, it's beneath him now to cook. Though I thought everyone was supposed to help out."

"I'm not sure why Travis is acting like this and giving you a hard time."

Dan shrugged. "It's no big deal. So long as the boss isn't upset, that's what counts. I mean, I get along fine with everyone else. Guess Travis gets upset easily over things. Not sure why. Maybe he's wired that way, with a short fuse."

Dan seemed to know a lot about people. The mere thought intrigued her. "Yeah, sometimes people don't react well to difficulties. Though I never thought anything bothered Travis until you came on the scene."

"Maybe we're like oil and water. I mean, Pop once had a fellow farmer he couldn't get along with no matter what he did. The guy insisted that there was only one way to raise peanuts. Pop had other ways of doing things. They even got into a shouting match once about peanuts. I mean, what good does it do? It's probably the same with this guy. He has his way of doing things, and I guess I'm messing up his plan. But he doesn't realize that it makes no sense to get uptight. Life's too short."

"It's good it doesn't bother you."

"Well, not so fast. It does if I let it. Besides, I have you to give me my pills of encouragement each day. Better than a bottle of vitamins." He gave her a huge smile, his face reflecting the setting sun. "I mean, you've been a blessing. Oops."

"What?"

"Now I sound like my mother. She's always saying how this person and that person is a blessing."

"There's nothing wrong with that. It's why God made us, to love Him and to help each other. Love your neighbor as yourself."

For the first time, Dan lapsed into thoughtful stillness. Now another question surfaced in her mind—Dan's faith. Jo's relationship with God meant everything to her. She wondered if it was the same with him. "Your mom must be a strong Christian woman," she said.

"To the T or capital C, I guess. Follows every rule and regulation there is. Hey, you want to stop for a drink? I'm thirsty. Seems I never can get enough to drink out here. It's so dry."

"Yes, it is dry."

She followed him into a café where they sat down and ordered sodas. He consumed his in a few minutes then promptly let out a loud belch. "Oh man, sorry about that."

"That's what happens when you swallow soda quickly." She sipped hers slowly through the straw, even as Dan ordered another one. "So what are you going to do on your day off?"

"Well, I'm hoping you might have the same day off so you can take me on a tour of Moab. I still don't know the half about this town, though I see the Colorado flows nearby on its way south. I kind of wonder why the rafts don't go all the way to town."

"It's too shallow for the boats to make it this far. But Moab is a great little town with its own character. I'll see if Todd can give me the day off; then we can look around." She hesitated. "But I'm not sure. . ."

His smile grew even broader as if she were making his evening complete. She cautioned herself not to become too involved. There were interesting things about Dan, but she should take it slow. She dared not trust her heart to him or lead him on, for that matter. *A simple walk around town would be all right*, she thought, *as was having a cola*. It didn't send up a smoke signal for a relationship. They were just being friends.

When Dan downed his third cola, he flew to his feet. "Wow, I feel like I can race around the block. With all that caffeine and sugar, I'll be up all night. Then I'll be tired for work tomorrow, and that's not cool." They went outside to find the sun had dipped below the rocky landscape beyond, igniting the area a fiery red. Dan paused to appreciate the scenery. "You never see anything like this in Virginia. It's like something out of an inferno. I can't get over how red the rocks are or the interesting formations. To think that eons of wind and rain did it all."

"You need to visit Arches some day. The national park near here. It has over a hundred natural arch formations inside the park."

They walked along the sidewalk until Jo paused before a kiosk displaying area information. "See?" She pointed to a picture of the famous Delicate Arch, glorified by the sunset.

"I remember seeing that in a magazine back home. That's fantastic."

"Yes, it really is pretty. There's a nice hike to it where you can view it up close." She paused, realizing she was again trying to plan their activities together. She needed to put the brakes on this before she found things careening out of control down the road of life.

"We have a national park in Virginia called Shenandoah. It has a road running the length of the mountains to different overlooks."

"I've been there many times."

He turned to stare at her. "You have? I didn't know that."

Jo paused, realizing her slip. "Well, we traveled a lot," she managed to say.

"We never did. Pop refused to leave his peanuts. He never trusted anyone else to look after them. But now I don't have to worry about it, because I'm doing the exploring on my own. Seeing all there is to see in life. Everything I've been missing out on. I'm having a great time, too."

Jo listened to the tone of his voice, almost as if he were challenging his father's rule, though the man was a thousand miles away. What happened in Virginia to send Dan here? She would love to explore it more, but again she didn't want to open her heart further. As it was, she'd probably said too much already.

"Well, this is where we part ways. My place is over there."

He stood still, his hands in his pockets. Thankfully he kept them there and made no move to take her hand or anything else. They stood on the sidewalk in the fading sunset, looking into each other's eyes. This was getting more uncomfortable by the second. Jo looked to a small gift shop across the street. "Guess I'll see you in the morning, bright and early."

"Yep. I'm with an early morning group. Same river trip. I think Todd will let me do the boat again, and this time, no rocks."

"You'll do fine." She saw him take his hands out of his pockets. He took a step forward. *Uh-oh. He's on the move.* She gave a brief smile, turned, and walked away. He didn't follow. She hastened for her apartment, and when she arrived, closed the door behind her and breathed a sigh of relief. *What are you doing, Jo? Why are you letting this guy into your life? Taking you out for a soda? Talking to him? And then of all things, you offer to spend your day off with him!*

She sighed and accessed Facebook. She typed onto her wall—*I refuse to open up my heart until the timing is right.* She then saw a friend request from Dan Mallory. She went to his page to see his smiling face. The background scenery of the photo appeared like the kind found back East. There were no red rocks or bright sun, just lots of green. She missed the greenery of the eastern forests and farmlands. Lush trees and tall grasses. An abundance of flowers in springtime, like the colorful mixture of dogwood, redbud, and azaleas. She hit the key to accept his request. It shouldn't change the status of their relationship if they were simply friends on a computer.

She looked around at various pages until suddenly the chat box popped up. Dan had logged on.

AHA. THOUGHT YOU MIGHT BE ONLINE. THANKS FOR ACCEPTING MY FRIEND REQUEST.

Jo pondered how to answer. WELL, ONE FRIEND'S AS GOOD AS ANOTHER, she typed.

YES, BUT WE HAVE A UNIQUE FRIENDSHIP. WE ARE FRIENDS OF THAT GREAT RIVER KNOWN AS THE COLORADO. AND THOSE FRIENDS MUST STAY TOGETHER AND SEE WHERE IT LEADS THEM OR DROWN.

Jo considered that one. ARE YOU DROWNING?

NO WAY. I'M ALIVE AND I'M AFLOAT, THANKS TO YOU.

Jo felt warmth rush into her cheeks and decided she'd better end this session quickly. WELL, I'M PRETTY TIRED. ANOTHER BIG DAY TOMORROW.

OKAY, NIGHT NOW. SWEET DREAMS.

Even at home she couldn't seem to get away from the man. Closing the laptop, she realized she needed to cool this off somehow. Give him the proverbial cold shoulder. Claim she was too busy for get-togethers. Though she was the one who agreed to a tour of Moab on a mutual day off. She sighed. *God, I know You brought Dan here for a reason. I'm not sure what to make of it all. But until I know his heart and where he stands with You, Lord, I pray that somehow You keep us separated. Please don't let me lose my heart over this or be tempted. Provide me a way out. I want my heart to belong to You and You alone until the time is right for a man to enter my life. In Jesus' name.*

She felt better after the prayer but still wondered in the days ahead how she would relate to Dan. She would still be seeing him day after day. There was that camping trip together coming up. A day off sometime in the future to explore Moab. Maybe even a hiking trip to Delicate Arch. None of this lined up with the prayer she'd just offered. Well, God would have to change the plans. Or change Dan's interest. Or do something wild and crazy. Or maybe she needed to do the changing. Take charge of her life and her destiny. Let Dan know that being pals on a social network was fine, but that was all. At least for now.

Chapter 5

ooyah! Dan, you're the man. He was feeling good today, and not just because the sun was shining as it always did. Or the blue skies loomed above without a hint of clouds. Or there was another round of hot, dry weather as was typical. He was just glad to be here, doing what he could only dream of doing a few months ago. Sure, there had been a few hiccups along the way and the steely-eyed look of Travis whenever something minutely went wrong. But Todd liked what he did. Everyone else was friendly. And plans for a relationship with Jo were coming along nicely, with online chats and the one afternoon when they toured the sites of Moab. Sometimes Dan wished their relationship would take off on a swift jog or even a fast run. But Jo was not that kind of girl. He could read between the lines. She had principles. For instance, she never wore anything out of line. Her clothing was conservative—mainly hiking apparel. She wore little makeup and tiny hoop earrings. She was perfectly tanned, nicely proportioned, and had fabulous legs. She was also careful with online social network places. They'd chatted a few times about nothing personal but everything friendly.

Dan knew, though, that something must be happening between them, because everyone else seemed to sense it. He realized it the day he stumbled into the office to find Travis there with a friend of his. Usually the boss didn't approve of outside friends moseying around the place, but Travis ignored the policy and brought his friend in anyway to help himself to the doughnuts and coffee. It was then that Dan overheard Travis complaining about him, intermixed with whispers about Jo.

"Yeah, you can tell Dan and Jo are already starting something. And of course, whenever something good is coming Jo's way, Todd wants to make sure it works out. Guess he thinks Jo deserves a guy in her life after coming here to help him."

That didn't sound too bad to Dan, until Travis began pointing out Dan's faults. And how Jo had to come on the next overnight trip to babysit him. "Isn't that just cozy."

Though Dan did like the idea of Jo being by his side, he didn't appreciate Travis gossiping to his friend and patronizing him. So Dan strode into the office with what he hoped was a cheesy "gotcha" smile on his face and asked

40

what they were talking about. Travis stood his ground, but the friend looked away. Dan continued to make small talk while pouring some freshly brewed coffee and then walked out whistling a jingle.

Now Dan was looking forward to the overnight trip planned for this weekend. They had a decent group reserved—three families each complete with mom, pop, and kids. The best part of all was that Jo would help him smooth out the kinks in the cooking arena, though Dan knew perfectly well how to cook. The burned steak had been a fluke. Could've happened to anyone. But if it opened the door for Jo and him to interact, he'd take it.

Just then he heard a greeting and whirled to find Jo entering the building. She looked great to him even if she wore hiking shorts, a T-shirt, and had her hair pulled back by an elastic band. "C'mon Dan, we've got shopping to do."

One day we're gonna go shopping for that diamond. . . . He halted. Where did *that* come from? He'd only known her a few weeks. Marriage was a huge step. He could see it a year from now, arriving back at the farm with Jo in tow and the looks of astonishment on Pop and Mom's faces when he announced, "Hey folks, meet the wife!"

"Dan, are you listening to me?"

"Sure, I like to shop, depending on what it is. What are we shopping for?"

"We need to get the rest of the food for the trip. Normally Todd does it, but he asked us to go so he could check on a raft that we need for this trip. Somehow it isn't inflating properly."

"Is that bad to be one short?"

"It is when you're fully booked like we are this weekend. So I hope we can get it fixed, or we're gonna have to rent one somewhere."

She slung her backpack purse over her shoulders. It certainly wasn't like the huge bag his mom carried. He liked it. "Nice bag."

Jo looked at him in surprise and wrinkled her face. "What? You mean my purse?"

"Yeah, it's not huge. Just right for an outdoorsy girl like you."

"What do you know about a woman's purse?"

"Nothing, except the one I see my mom lugging around. She has one you could fit car parts into."

Jo laughed. "I like this one 'cause it's more like a day pack than a purse. Sometimes people frown on carrying a day pack into stores."

"When I went to DC for a trip a few years back, you couldn't carry anything bigger than a camera case into public buildings." His voice faded. Another memory surfaced, of a family trip to Washington DC to celebrate Pop's birthday. It was one of the few times they managed to lure Pop away from the peanut field for a family outing. He wanted to see the Air and Space

Museum. They had a great time exploring the Apollo spacecraft, the airplanes, and the cases of moon rocks. And of course, watching the IMAX film. For a moment he was transported to that time, and the laughter of his family in his ears was real.

"Dan? Hello? Are you alive?"

Jo's concern brought him back to reality. "Just thinking." He didn't elaborate on his thoughts. If he did, she was sure to ask questions about family stuff, maybe even tell him he needed to go back home and straighten things out. That he shouldn't have up and left his family like he did with no one to take his place. "But I have a life, too," he argued. "And I plan to live it."

"Dan, you'd better tell me what this is all about."

"Sorry. I was thinking aloud. It has nothing to do with you, I promise." He smiled, and she smiled back. All was forgiven and hopefully forgotten.

They walked down the road to the grocery store where Jo suggested they each grab carts. His cart was soon filled with fresh vegetables and meats, hers with snacks, soft drinks, and desserts. "This looks like enough to feed the first battalion," he commented.

"Everyone always gets hungry when they're out on these trips. They'll eat you clean. But that's okay. They're paying for it."

Dan nearly flipped over the amount Jo forked over at the cash register. Several hundred bucks gone. But it would certainly make for happy campers when the adults saw the steaks, and the kids the Kool-Aid and cookies.

Jo wheeled the cart loaded down with bags until she suddenly stopped. "I don't believe how dumb I am."

"What? You're not dumb."

She threw up her hands. "How are we going to get this stuff back to the shop? I forgot to borrow Todd's SUV."

Dan should have thought of that, too, though he had been slightly distracted. But now he could be the hero and rescue a damsel loaded down with two dozen shopping bags. "No problem. I'll go get my Jeep. It's not that many blocks away."

"Thanks. And can you hurry? We have pricey perishables. I'll go back inside and keep this stuff in air-conditioning."

"Be right back."

Dan wasted no time jogging down the street toward the rafting center. He dodged in and around shoppers cruising the town, young couples holding hands, and older citizens gawking at the postcards and trinkets in souvenir shops that said Moab in a dozen different ways. All signs of a thriving tourist town and a place he was glad to be a part of. He arrived and climbed into his Jeep, returning to the store where Jo stood waiting by some soda machines.

"I'm sorry about this."

"What are you sorry for?" He hauled bag after bag, loading each into the back end of the Jeep until it was full.

"Sorry that I'm not thinking. I hope I can get my act together before the trip. I'm supposed to be the trainer, and you're the trainee."

"I think it's good if people can help each other out of situations. Can't get much better training than that. Two are better than one anyway."

Jo turned quiet. He started the engine, hoping he didn't scare her with the hint of some diamond solitaire in the future with the "two are better than one" comment. It just seemed the right thing to say.

"I know you're right," Jo finally answered. He perked up at her agreement. Maybe he wasn't so off track with the relationship angle after all.

Having placed the meat and veggies into the large refrigerator unit and packing the rest into dry bags, he and Jo began sorting out camping gear. They packed tents, cots, and sleeping bags for everyone, along with other gear like lanterns, tableware, and cooking supplies. "There's a lot to think about with this kind of trip," he mused.

"Normally we have a checklist, but I know the routine by heart. Still, I should show it to you." She left and soon returned with a clipboard holding multiple pages. "See what I mean?"

"This is good for someone like me who's always disorganized." He scanned it carefully. "Looks like we've covered all the basics."

Jo laughed. "You'd better read the list and make sure we haven't forgotten anything. I don't think Mr. and Mrs. Harris would like it if we have the tent but no cots for them to sleep on."

"But sleeping on nice, soft sand isn't so bad."

"No, it's not." She paused. He saw a red flush enter her cheeks that could not be from the wind and sun. Again he wondered if he'd said the wrong thing, but he was just making a camping comment. He liked cowboy camping in the great outdoors on the soft ground. He and Rob used to do stuff like that when they were young. Wander into the woods, pick out a nice spot, and bed down for the night. He went ahead and told her about it to ease her discomfort.

"Oh sure, I totally agree with you. I don't know, I guess I feel weird talking about that kind of stuff with you."

Now it was Dan's turn to feel a flush creep into his face. "I don't understand."

"Never mind." She took off in the direction of the office. He dearly wanted to follow, to press the issue and find out what was going on underneath that gorgeous mound of thick brown hair caught up in a hair band. Maybe this meant she did have feelings for him. Maybe she thought about him. Admired his physique and his winning personality. At least he was tanning up nicely after the initial sunburn, along with sporting a lean build, nifty sunglasses, and of course, the fantastic red Jeep. If all that couldn't land him a girl, what would?

His heart began to pound in anticipation. He had no worries. They were going together on a camping trip to help the customers but also to work as a team. And when the customers drifted off to sleep, there was the moonlight creating that shimmering effect on the river and Jo sitting beside him, taking it all in. What a perfect opportunity for a kiss and a cuddle. *Take it easy, Dan the man. One step at a time.*

❦

The rafting part of the trip went well, with the kids and their parents loving every minute. They screamed and cheered and laughed all the way down the rapids. They were modest rapids according to Todd, good enough for little guys and girls who found small bounces in the boat a great thrill. For his part, Dan was mesmerized by Jo who sat in the other boat. The wind tousled her hair, and the loosened strands floated in the breeze. Her face broke out in smiles. One time she raised her hand as if she were waving at him. He waved back, and she turned away to focus on her paddle. It didn't matter. She was still amazing to look at. He couldn't wait for the camping part of the trip when they would work together.

The spot Todd chose for camping was an area utilized by other rafting companies—a large stretch of sandy beach surrounded by red rocks and cliffs, and flanked by the gentle flow of the river. Here the kids could play around with their parents—building sand castles or wading in the river while he and the crew readied the camp. Dan wanted Jo to help him erect the tents, but she was setting up the camp kitchen. He didn't worry. They would be working together soon enough.

"You're the first guy I've ever hired that knew about tents right off, Dan," Todd commented. "You're a natural at this."

"Virginia is for campers. Lots of places to camp with the mountains and all."

Todd laughed. "Must be why Jo knew about it, too, having lived there for a while. Guess with the mountains, there's plenty of recreation."

Dan was suddenly caught up in the first part of Todd's statement. *Jo is also from Virginia?* Where? Why didn't she mention it? What was her reason for coming here?

He turned and saw Jo waving at him, and this time she meant it. "C'mon, Dan. I need you to help make the salad."

He walked over. "Did you say make the salad? But I'd rather cook the steaks. Isn't salad making the woman's job?"

She cast him an evil eye. "Don't start with me now. Here's the tomatoes. Go ahead and cut them up."

Dan tried to hide his displeasure as Jo worked on getting the other parts of the meal ready. "Todd says you're from Virginia."

She gave him a look he couldn't decipher while she held bags of dinner rolls in each hand. "So what?"

"Well, I am, too. You knew that, didn't you?"

She shrugged.

"C'mon. Isn't that interesting that we're both from the same state? Where did you live? Why did you come out here? Don't you find it a lot different than Virginia?"

"A man of a thousand questions. Yes, I did live in Virginia for a time, near Leesburg. And of course, Utah is different from Virginia."

She answered the questions but left out all the juicy details that women usually loved to provide. In the meantime, he just missed chopping off the tip of his finger. "So you're not going to elaborate."

"There isn't much else to say. I came out here to help Todd. And because things weren't working out too great with my brother in Virginia."

Ah. . .some description at last. He watched Jo set out the steaks on a board and season them. Again he wished she were here at the cutting board dicing tomatoes and he were manning the grill. He felt like a housewife.

"You really have an ego problem," she suddenly remarked.

His chopping abruptly halted. "Me?"

"Yes. I can see it in your face. Don't worry. You're gonna cook the steaks like a barbecue maestro. I understand these guy things, being around my brother and Todd."

He chuckled. "Jo, you can read me like a book. Do you also know that. . ." He paused. It almost came rattling out of him. *Do you also know that I think you're something else? More than something else? That I would like to date you and maybe kiss you and see where the future leads us. . . .*

"C'mon, let's get the steaks on the grill."

He reluctantly abandoned his attraction for Jo, which shouldn't be rearing its head right now, anyway, since the moon hadn't yet risen. He went over to the grill. Charcoal smoke smarted his eyes but made his mouth water at the same time. He stood by the steaks, turning them every so often. As they cooked, the guests wandered by, taking in the deep aroma of the food while enjoying the summer evening. Dan heard a variety of remarks, everything from how yummy the steaks looked to "I hope you didn't forget that I asked for tofu burgers." Jo had those tucked away in the cooler.

"You're doing a great job, Dan," Jo observed. She stood fairly close to him now, and though her eyes were focused on the steaks, his gaze was focused on the top of her head. He could see the long part down the middle of her hair, the way she often wore it. He wondered what her hair smelled like—probably a combination of the great outdoors and charcoal.

When the meal was cooked and the guests served, it was time for the staff to eat. Jo cooked the rest of the steaks and tofu burgers for them. Dan was all set to help himself to the remaining steak when Travis came along and snatched up the last hunk. "Sorry," he said with a grin.

Dan shrugged and looked at the three tofu burgers staring back at him. He could have a tofu burger. Combining it with lettuce and onions, drowned in ketchup, it would be just fine and healthier, too. *You ain't gonna win either, Travis.* He sat companionably with everyone else, watching Jo from where she sat opposite him, indulging in her nice piece of steak and salad that he'd fixed. They talked about the trip thus far, the pancake breakfast the next morning, and who would be leading the night stalk with the kids after dark.

"I nominate Dan to do the night stalk," Travis announced.

"Dan cooked tonight," declared Jo. "Why don't you do it, Travis?"

"I don't mind," Dan said. "I like doing the night stalk. As a kid, we did one with our flashlights in a campground with a ranger, near the Blue Ridge Parkway. Someone saw a bear. That was the quickest stalking we ever did."

Everyone laughed long and loud, including Jo. Everyone, that is, but Travis. Dan laughed, too, in spite of himself. He was quickly nominated night stalk captain of the evening.

When they began cleaning up, Jo sauntered up to him, her face beaming. "Dan, you are nothing short of the man tonight."

"I am?" He tried to hide his pleasure behind a straight face, but it was tough. A small smile managed to seep out.

"Sure. I mean having a good attitude about things, even if you didn't like making the salad. And volunteering to do the night stalk. You're pretty amazing."

Thank You, God. I'm in heaven. And he meant it. Not that he talked much to God these days, but maybe he ought to. God was blessing him big-time, and Jo was getting more and more intriguing. Especially when she announced that she wanted to tag along on the night stalk with the kiddos. *We're a team, God; we're a team.*

And a team they were, leading the kids along the riverbank by flashlight where they found creatures that came out at night—different kinds of bugs and lizards, and they even heard the howl of a coyote on a distant cliff. As they headed back for the yellow glow reflecting in the propane lanterns that lit up the campsite, Jo walked beside him, her flashlight shining this way and that.

"Well, this has been a great day, Dan."

"It sure has." And it was only just the beginning. The night was still young.

"You know, when I came here from Virginia, I wondered if I'd ever have days like this. I mean, I came here not only to help Todd but hoping for a change in my life. And then I found out life is pretty much the same wherever you go."

"No way."

"Huh?"

"It's been great for me so far. This is where I needed to be. Do you think I had this much fun raising peanuts? No way."

"But stuff still follows you. The discontent that brought you here. It doesn't matter how far you travel either. You may not see it right now. It took me awhile to see that life was not any different than back home. There were still troubles and trials and my own problems to work out. I'm just glad I know God. He's helped me so much in many areas."

Dan began kicking up sand as he walked. "You sound like Mom and Pop."

"What do you mean?"

"They talk like God is some kind of buddy in the sky waiting to offer a lift on His go-cart. I'm not sure how anyone can see God like that."

"I'd hardly call God a buddy, but He is a friend in times of need. And above all, He is Lord of my life."

Dan nearly tripped over a stick. He caught himself in time and then stopped, even as the kids raced over to be reunited with their parents and share in the marshmallow roast now in full progress. God was Lord of her life? No longer just a friend but also some great King on a fancy throne, giving out dos and don'ts? How could He be both? What did this really mean?

When they heard Todd asking them to hand out the makings for s'mores, Jo left him to pitch in with the work. Dan could only stand and watch her place a child's well-charred marshmallow between chunks of chocolate and graham crackers. She handed it back to the wide-eyed, eager kid.

God is Lord of Jo's life? *And* God is a friend? He realized then he didn't know God at all. Maybe in name only, but that's it. And maybe he didn't know Jo that well either. If a pin could burst a balloon, it just did with several simple yet profound words. *He is Lord of my life.*

Chapter 6

What Jo said that evening at the campsite stuck like one of those burrs, not in Dan's sock but in his brain. Though he tried hard not to think about it, the message continued to remain in his thoughts. She was just like his folks when it came to things of God. If there was one thing he wanted to do, it was to escape all the religiosity. He certainly didn't want Jo to know this, however, as it was obvious God meant a great deal to her. That was okay by him, so long as he didn't have to believe it, too. Or maybe he could give the semblance of being part of the religious gang. Like saying the proverbial "Well, praise God!" when something good happened, or bowing his head in dutiful prayer when it came to thanking the Lord for his food. All the things he'd grown up with back at the farm.

At times though, Dan felt like he owed God a great deal more than just platitudes. God did see fit to give him a fantastic job here in Moab. Dan had a great apartment with a huge bedroom. The main living room held the fifty-five-inch plasma TV and a gaming system. He had his red Jeep to cruise around town. Nice Oakley shades to wear. Everything a man could want, save a girlfriend clinging to his arm, which he hoped to remedy soon.

Jo did like the way the camping trip turned out, so Dan felt he was making strides in the area of a relationship. He knew when she was surfing the Internet and managed to snag her for a few impromptu chats. They saw each other quite a bit on the business front, even though the rafting trips kept him busy most days. They hadn't gone out to eat in a while, but Dan knew he also couldn't appear overly eager by asking for dates and risk sending her in the opposite direction. He had to take this all step-by-step. Except for the God part. The-Lord-of-her-life part. That he had a hard time reconciling.

Dan arrived home after a day on the river, overheated as usual and looking for a drink to quench his thirst. Despite the copious amounts of suntan lotion, he still felt like a chicken cooking in the hot Utah sun. The sun was relentless in this place, shining day in and day out. He had seen one afternoon thunderstorm since his arrival. No wonder the ground was baked to hard clay. The red rocks kept the heat, too, reflecting the intensity of it at night, long after the sun went down. But it was still a neat place, even if it felt like an oven. And he never stopped marveling at the rock formations they passed by each day on the rafting trips. He knew them all by heart and liked pointing out things like the Gummy Bear formation to the thrill of the kids. He was at ease explaining to the guests the various geological features and even the version of how old the formations were—made a zillion years ago from the big bang or something like that, though it went against everything Pop taught him about Creation. He also liked the water antics they played on the raft—the tug-o'-war games, sneaking up on other rafts for water fights, and taking a dive backward out of the raft to the delight of the passengers.

Dan now relaxed on the sofa of his apartment, sipping a cold drink, feeling a bit drowsy. The air-conditioning felt good. He was ready to drift off to happy land when his cell phone played a rock-and-roll tune.

"Hey-lo," he answered, his eyes still closed.

"Hi, Dan."

A sweet feminine voice filled his ear. Instantly he was awake, as was every nerve in his body. "Hi, Jo. Wassup?"

"Not much. I just closed down the store and. . ."

"Great, you wanna get a bite to eat?" He cringed, realizing how swiftly the invitation came streaming out of him.

"No, not that. The reason I'm calling is that Travis says you lost some gear today."

"Huh?" His hand squeezed the tiny phone he held. "What's he talking about? I checked in all the gear from my boat."

"The numbers aren't adding up. We're short on PFDs and two sets of paddles."

"Well, see if it's from his boat." He tried not to let the words come out in a snarl.

"Dan, I don't know whose boat they're from. I'm just telling you what he told me."

"Yeah." He was ready to let it all out—what he truly thought of Travis. "I'll be right there." He stood to his feet, his muscles stiff from being in near-sleep mode. He felt a strange twitch in his neck, probably from the day's paddling. Todd told him that soon he might be ready to tackle some of the more adventurous parts of the river. Dan wasn't sure he'd ever be ready for a place like Cataract Canyon. But maybe if it got him away from Travis, he would take Todd up on it.

He put on his baseball cap and grabbed his car keys, wallet, and drink bottle. Well, maybe all things were working out for good. If he went over there and straightened this out, then maybe Jo would feel better about going out to eat with him. He wouldn't appear to be playing the guy chasing after the girl scenario. He could make it one of those buddy-type meetings to discuss work, maybe even ask her about the Cataract Canyon rafting trips as a cover. That sounded like a good plan.

The Jeep was steaming hot to the touch, thanks to the one-hundred-degree heat that had not dissipated despite it being 7:00 p.m. It didn't take him long to drive over and head directly to the building where the equipment was stored. Jo stood there along with Todd, trying to sort it all out. "I turned in all my stuff," he announced to Todd.

"Well, we're off on the count. You checked in each of the PFDs?"

"Yes, along with the paddles."

Todd scratched his head. "It's not adding up. And I don't like being short. We have a sold-out excursion tomorrow. I have to find the missing gear."

"We must have more life jackets lying around," Jo said. "The paddles could be in a different area."

"I don't like this when I have a mega-group coming the next day. They're a business group, too. I wanted everything ready to go. This stinks."

Dan was unsure what to say or do. He did recall at the river earlier that day, when they had stopped for a break, that Travis appeared tense. And some of the people on his raft were not wearing life jackets.

"Dan, is something up?" Jo asked.

He blinked, wondering how she would know. Did his face have neon words filtering across it? Could she read what was in his mind? She couldn't possibly know his ulterior motive—that his coming here and showing interest was actually a cover-up for a planned dinner date later tonight. "Uh. . .only that a couple of Travis's passengers didn't have PFDs on when we left the beach area. I noticed it when we were already on the river, but I thought the guests had taken them off for some reason."

Todd stared. "What? But that's against company policy. Are you sure?"

"Yeah, but I know he'll deny it. He's been after me ever since I started this job."

"I wonder why Travis would do that," Jo said. "It doesn't sound like him."

"No, but I'm about to get to the bottom of this," Todd said.

Todd strode away while Dan watched in apprehension. If Todd opened his mouth that he'd blabbed about Travis, it could land him in hot water. "Hey Jo, I don't want him telling Travis that I said anything." He swiped his hands together in agitation.

"He won't."

Dan wasn't so sure. He thought again about Jo's words. *God is the Lord of my life.* If He is Lord, then He is in control. And He could handle people like Travis and his jealousy, keeping dear old Dan out of boiling water and from getting beat up by the bullies of Moab. Right?

"Dan, it will be okay." Again came Jo's soothing voice, so much like nice cold ice cream easing his dry throat.

He swallowed to find his throat raw like sandpaper. He badly needed a cold drink. He headed over to the back door that led to the store and helped himself to a drink out of the case. He then checked it off on the employee list posted by the cash register. Jo followed him and now stood in the doorway. The fading red hues of sun framed her like a fiery halo effect. She looked stunning to him. And mysterious. And ready to pronounce once more—*God is the Lord of my life*. And he, Dan, might have to bow down right there.

"You really are bothered by this."

He finished the drink in several long swallows. "Travis and I have never gotten along. Maybe he thinks I'm here to take over the roost. All I wanted was a fun job on the river. But he doesn't like how I handle the customers. What I do with the kids. How I cook. How I pack the gear in the boats. And he says I don't give correct safety instructions. Like what is there to give? Stay in the boat and love your guide stuff, mostly."

"Well, he certainly can't talk about safety if he's allowing passengers to ride without wearing the proper safety equipment. If Todd finds out its true, he'll can him."

Dan stared. "You mean he'll fire Travis?"

"It's a violation, and if one of those passengers fell overboard and drowned, do you know what would happen to us? A lawsuit, maybe even charges of negligence."

Dan never thought about that. He then remembered the first time he manned a craft and the girl with the earrings who fell overboard while trying to retrieve her shiny jewelry from the Colorado. It never dawned on him the other aspects of this job, like safety and people getting hurt and lawsuits. He was glad then he didn't hold the reins of control over this operation. He was only a measly employee thankful for a job.

Todd finally arrived back, his face redder than it had been when he left. "Travis insists his people were all wearing their PFDs. He says it was you that didn't have them on your people, Dan."

Dan stood there, feeling as if one of those orange water coolers filled with ice were dumped on him. He felt a chill. There were actual goose bumps breaking out on his tanned forearms. He could barely choke out the words, "But that's not true." He looked to Jo for help. "I did everything by the book, boss. I will swear on. . ." He hesitated until he saw Jo's brown eyes soften. ". . .on a stack of Bibles. I mean, the Lord knows it and everything. I wouldn't do something like that. I know the rules, and I care about people's safety."

Todd's hands flew in the air. "So who am I supposed to believe? It's your word against his. And frankly, Dan, you're the new kid on the block. If I had to go on my gut reaction, I'd say it's the new one on board who may have overlooked a safety measure."

Oh, no. Would he be walking the streets of Moab with a Give Me a Job, Please! sign dangling from his neck? He thought fast and furiously. The group he handled today was all one family. The parents and four kiddos. And he recalled the mom and dad saying they were staying at a certain RV park outside of town. "I'll do what I need to do to clear my name then," Dan said stoutly. "I know where the family is staying that I helped guide today. I'll go right now and ask them if they all had on life jackets and if they will swear by it."

Jo stared at him, as did Todd. "Todd, don't you see? If Dan is willing to go find the family to clear his name, then it's obvious who the guilty party is. And I don't know why Travis won't admit it."

"And I'm willing to prove it," Dan declared. "Anything so I won't get canned."

Todd's eyebrow rose. "Nobody's talking about canning you, Dan. You're a great worker." He began to pace. "I'll talk to Travis again and try to find out what happened. But if you want to get a statement from the family, go for it. It will give me proof with Travis, too, and make things a whole lot easier."

Dan was more than happy to oblige. Anything to clear up this matter once and for all. He immediately headed for his Jeep and jumped in. Only then did he see Jo standing nearby, watching him. "You can come along if you want. Probably should, as I have no idea where this RV park is located."

"How will you find the family?" she asked, entering the passenger seat. "I mean, there's a ton of campers this time of year. It will take a miracle."

"Well, you believe in them, don't you? I'm sure you do. Quoting God and all."

"Of course I do. Every day is a miracle. Don't you think so?"

"I hope there's one for me today. So start praying for a miracle, my dear."

And that's just what she did. She prayed as if God were actually sitting in the backseat of Dan's red Jeep, listening, nodding His great head, or whatever kind of head God possessed, ready to act on his behalf. Dan was at a loss for words when she finished and sat back with a slight smile on her face. She looked as if she enjoyed the one-way conversation. Or maybe it was two-way—though Dan admitted he was hard of hearing these days.

Heading north out of town, they arrived at the Red Rocks RV Park mentioned by the father of the family. At least Dan had the name of the family from the roster. He went to the campground office and checked in with the owner. A grizzly man looked at him over the tops of his reading glasses and shook his head. "Look, I don't know who you are from Adam. I'm not going to tell you where those people are camped."

Dan always wondered why older people compared a person to Adam. He tried to stay calm, but the agitation within was clearly building. His job was on the line. His integrity. And the need to nail Travis and prove him a liar.

"Sir, this is an important safety issue we're dealing with in our rafting company," Jo intervened. "We're hoping to find out about some missing life jackets and paddles. And we need to know if the family accidentally kept them in their possession or if they know where they might be."

"Guess you don't do good inventory at your company then," he said with a huff.

The door creaked open just then and two girls walked into the store. "Hey, look, it's Raft Man!"

Dan whirled. The kids on the trip had christened him by that name. Sure enough, he recognized the two girls that had been on the raft that day. "Hey there!" he managed to say.

"Hey, Raft Man. We had a great time today. We're just here to buy ice cream."

Dan saw the startled look on the manager's face that matched the disbelief in his heart. "Hey, I was wondering if your dad is around. I gotta ask him something about the trip today."

The girls grabbed his hand. "C'mon, our campsite isn't too far away."

Dan looked over at Jo with a grin. She came alongside as the girls chatted away about the trip.

"Did you find the life jacket okay to wear?" Jo asked.

"No, but Raft Man made us wear them. Though I'm a good swimmer. See, here's our camper. Dad cooked hot dogs for dinner."

Dan went over, introduced himself, and promptly told the man what had happened. In no time the man had written on a piece of paper confirming that his family wore life jackets the entire trip and had turned them in, along with their paddles. "I wouldn't even think of letting my kids go without," he said. "Or my wife and me, for that matter. Why, is there a problem?"

"Just a personal matter we need to clear up about equipment check-in," Jo said with a smile. "But we appreciate you taking the time to help us."

"Well, have a hot dog. I've got plenty left. The kids had a great time out there today. Glad we chose your company. There's so many. We just happened to stumble on it while walking in town."

Dan munched down his hot dog while thanking the man between bites. When he and Jo headed back for the Jeep, his thoughts swirled from the entire scene.

"There," Jo pronounced with a smile.

"There what?"

"You got your miracle. Now do you believe?"

"Yeah, it was definitely a miracle. I mean here we were, asking that manager about the family. He's looking at us and saying there's no way he's gonna tell us anything. Then presto, in walk the two girls from the trip. Pretty amazing stuff."

"There," she pronounced again. "Now do you see why God is Lord of my life? I mean, who else could have orchestrated things so perfectly? You could not have planned it better if you tried. God knew where we were going. He knew the girls would want to buy ice cream. He knew we would meet them and you would get the information you needed to save your job. Dan, God cares about you."

Another proverbial statement often spoken to him in his younger days. But coming from Jo and on the heels of what they had just witnessed at the campground, there was truth behind it. God cared. Why He did. . .Dan didn't know. He never gave God a reason to care. He'd left Him behind for Utah, along with everything else. The thought suddenly made him uncomfortable.

At least he did end up with a date night of sorts with Jo, even if it was eating a hot dog together and seeing a miracle take place at an RV park. His job was spared, his reputation intact. And he had Jo to thank, in part, for it. But one thing was for certain. He had to get Jo completely on his side. Not just the friendly side of things or the religious side of things either, but the serious side. The relationship side. And he thought he knew just how to do it.

Chapter 7

Jo loved her days off. She could sleep in and read the Bible or a good novel while lounging in bed. Turn on the laptop and tweet or look at Facebook. Make cinnamon swirl coffee and lounge around in sleepwear until noon. Glance out the window to see the air rippling from the heat and watch people sweating as they went about their daily duties. Sit back and whisper thanks for sweet air-conditioning. Doze in the recliner. Check the clock and see if there's time to munch before polishing off a bag of reduced-fat Oreos.

Jo had elected to indulge in the lounging part so far today, a mug of java in her hands, when the doorbell sounded. She tensed. That could only mean one thing, and as far as she knew, he was working today. *Thank goodness*, she told herself. As much as she liked hanging around with Dan, he was starting to dampen her spiritual nerves. He had a capability of wheedling his way into her life while trying not to look like it. She probably shouldn't be reading into their innocent activities of late, but she had a distinct impression that he was attracted to her. And that wasn't a good thing at this stage of the game.

Jo glanced through the security hole to see the deliveryman with his magic clipboard. She cracked open the door in curiosity to see a large box resting at the man's feet. "I didn't order anything."

"Jolene Davidson?"

"Yes, but. . ."

"Sign here." He thrust the electronic board at her.

Who sent me this huge box? she wondered as she signed her name. She then saw the logo of an outdoor shop on it. Okay, someone had stolen her ID and was now sending her weird stuff via her credit card. She considered refusing it, but the deliveryman had disappeared, leaving her with the box.

Might as well see what it is, she mused. She carefully zipped open the box with a small paring knife. Inside a plastic bag rested a brand-new backpack. "What?" She rummaged inside the box for the shipping information. The form clearly had her name on it, along with the purchaser's name. Daniel J. Mallory.

"Dan, this isn't going to change things one bit," she mumbled, even as her curiosity got the better of her. She lifted out the backpack to find a newfangled lightweight model with plenty of outside pockets, a padded hip belt, and a place for a hydration system. It certainly was nice—and expensive, too. "I can't accept this, God," she said aloud. Oh, how a part of her wanted to. She always wanted a nice backpack, especially with the camping trips on the river. A place to store her stuff. And then opportunities for backpacking into the wilds of Arches or even Canyonlands. But not from a man she really should be avoiding. If anything, this ought to be raising the red warning flag that the hurricane winds were starting to blow, and she'd better take cover fast.

With reluctance, Jo placed the backpack in its plastic bag and back into the box. She didn't relish the idea of having to pay shipping to send it back, but she couldn't keep it either. *But maybe if I did keep it, use it for a good purpose, tell Dan that it means nothing, but if he wants to spend his money so foolishly. . .*

Quit it, Jo. You can't accept this. It amounts to accepting a relationship. And you're not the dating type. You're the wait-on-God type.

So much for a day off to lounge around and relax. Now her nerves were standing on edge. The package, combined with two cups of coffee, multiplied it. Her stomach began to churn. She made herself a piece of toast spread thick with strawberry jam and sat watching the people on the street. Neighbors were doing their daily routine. A few dog walkers were out and about, inter-mixed with tourists holding digital cameras. On a distant horizon loomed the fiery splendor that made up the national park nestled beside Moab. Maybe she should take advantage of the day and spend some time in Arches National Park. Pack up an early dinner and go for an evening hike to watch the sun set behind the park's most famous natural feature, Delicate Arch. Get back in tune with God's purposes for her life rather than tuning in to Dan's actions, like sending her the backpack. She needed God's tuning, certainly. His voice speaking to her spirit and directing her path.

Some of this is my fault, also, she admitted. *I was too friendly with Dan in the beginning.* He seemed so eager to please. Todd did like him a great deal. Despite the friction with Travis, Dan was working out with the company. He liked kids, too, which was a bonus. He loved a good outdoor adventure— another plus. But he would have nothing to do with God—a huge minus that erased all the plusses. She refused to shirk, either, when it came to telling Dan about her Christian beliefs. She wanted to wear it like an ad on her shirt in the hopes that something might rub off on him.

But now she looked at the big box. So much for conviction. The only thing he was being convicted of was the idea that they were a couple. Phooey on that.

Her cell phone played *Amazing Grace*. It was Dan calling in. She ignored it. Then it signaled an incoming text message. She couldn't resist checking it. DID YOU GET THE SURPRISE?

Jo stared at the words. *Yeah, some surprise. Why didn't you just send a big note with it and the words, You're Hot. Will you be mine?* She chewed on her lower lip and finally texted him back.

SENDING IT BACK, she keyed in.

WRONG SIZE?

No.

DON'T LIKE IT?

NO, NOT RIGHT.

Her phone signaled again with an incoming text message, but this time she turned the phone off. No doubt he would be knocking on her door next, wondering why she'd refused his thoughtful gesture. He'd be looking to make things right, for the pack and for them, which might not be for a while with the rafting trips scheduled for today. By the time Dan got off work at 6:00 p.m., she would be long gone to Arches National Park for an evening hike with God.

Jo packed up her day pack for the journey. In it went snacks, a water bottle, a hat, and sunglasses as the sun would still be quite bright in the height of summer. On a whim, she turned her phone back on to check the messages. Two more text messages came up, both from Dan, along with a voice mail from Todd. The text messages were:

WHAT'S NOT RIGHT?

WHAT'S WRONG?

And from Todd. "Hey, can you call me when you get this? I need to ask you a question." Good, as she also needed to ask him if she could borrow his car for the trip to Arches.

Todd was manning the desk when she called, wanting to check her numbers on an order sheet for the store. "So, how's your day off been?" he asked.

"Okay." She nearly spilled the beans about the backpack but decided to make it a nonissue. She planned to stop off at the post office anyway to mail it back. "I haven't been to Delicate Arch in a while, so I thought I'd take a hike there tonight. Can I borrow your car?"

"Sure. Man, I wish I could go with you, but there's too much to do here. I should lead a group into the Fiery Furnace again. You can make some good money with a hiking group."

Jo recalled how he liked to conduct hikes within Arches, and one being the famous but tricky labyrinth of trails within sandstone formations called the Fiery Furnace. "Don't you remember that one kid who got lost, and you had to call the rangers in to help find him?"

"You would remind me of that. Guess I'd better stick to rafting then. Anyway, have fun, don't get lost, and don't wreck my car."

"I don't plan to do either of the first two. But I hope your insurance is good." She ended the call before he could issue a retort. Like she planned to smash his car into an arch or something. Wouldn't that make an interesting stunt—sending a car careening right through the South Window Arch. Jo sighed, put on her day pack, then lugged the large box toward the front door. This box was going to be a hassle, she had to admit. She'd have to come back home to pick up the box and fight traffic to take it to the post office before it closed. She decided to leave it for now. Maybe Dan would stop by and return it for her if she asked. Anything could happen.

When she stepped outside, heat like a blast furnace, typical of a summer day in Utah, greeted her. It amazed her how wonderful air-conditioning felt when encountering these weather extremes. As usual, the town teemed with tourists. She waved to a few of the permanent residents who seemed like victims lost in this onslaught of tourism. But the residents also knew that tourism was their livelihood and never complained. Neither did she. Visitors brought in money, and money paid the bills.

Jo arrived at the shop to pick up Todd's car and saw Todd and Dan at the desk talking. Both of them looked up, but it was Dan's grin and large hazel eyes that she tried to ignore.

"Here you go," Todd said, surrendering his spare set of keys. "I filled up the tank today, too."

"Nice. Thanks so much."

"So where are you off to?" Dan asked.

"She's going to hike to Delicate Arch," Todd said.

Jo tried to give Todd the evil eye, but he was looking in the opposite direction. *Great. Now Dan knows my plans.*

"Delicate Arch, huh?"

Todd continued. "It's fantastic at sunset. You should go see it, Dan. Why don't you take him along, Jolene? I'd feel better, anyway, if you didn't hike alone."

"I can take care of myself. I don't need an escort. I've done the trail plenty of times."

Todd gave her a strange look, accompanied by the look of expectation on Dan's face. She hesitated. "All right, c'mon," she said to Dan. "Better take water with you. Even though we're walking in the evening, it can still be in the nineties."

Dan obliged, grabbing some water and giving Todd a thumbs-up signal as if he'd just scored major points. Jo wasn't impressed by any of it. Nor did she want Dan tagging along. This was to be her hike, after all. Her hike with God. Once again, Dan had wheedled his way into her life.

"I'd be glad to drive," he now said.

"That's okay. I know where to go. Easier than trying to navigate you through it all."

They said nothing until they entered the car. "Did you get my text messages? I left like a dozen," Dan said as she started the car.

"Look, if you're going to get into that, then please stay here. As it is, I wanted to do this hike alone."

Dan looked as if he'd been slapped. "Sorry I'm bothering you." He fumbled for the door handle.

"Wait. Don't worry about it, okay? I know we did talk about seeing Delicate Arch when you first got here. And it is nice at sunset. I just don't want to go into the text messaging thing. Or anything else, if that's okay. Can we call a truce?"

"Sure." Dan instantly relaxed, and the confident smile returned to his tanned face. His skin had begun to accept the extremes of Utah sun. At least he didn't look like the lobster of days past. He even looked like he'd lost a little weight. His upper arms were showing muscle. Jo wondered why she was examining him up close and personal like that. He then cast a small smile as if glad for her observing eye.

"So, what's wrong with the backpack?"

"I thought we weren't going to get into that." She blew out a sigh. "Okay, look. There's nothing wrong with it. I just don't think you should be buying me expensive presents."

"It's no big deal. It's just a way to say thank you for getting me the job with your cousin's company. For helping me learn all the ropes about cooking so I didn't look like a fool. For being there during our miracle day at the RV park. That kind of thing."

"It's still an expensive gift to be giving someone just for doing the right thing."

Dan sat back, his fingers tapping on the door. "Jo, I had nowhere to go when I got here. You were the first friend I ran into. It's fine to give a friend a gift. At least, I thought it was. Maybe in Moab it's not."

Jo bit her lip, wondering if she had read too much into this whole deal. Dan obviously had money to burn and had tried to bless her. All she wanted to do was ship the gift back the moment she saw who it was from. Now she was glad that she hadn't dragged the box to the post office but had left it in the living room. Still, she had to wonder if something else lay hidden behind the high price tag and tough Cordura fabric. "Okay. I just think you spent too much."

"I have the money. In fact, I'm thinking of taking a new leap and buying a house." He withdrew a crumpled real estate brochure from his pocket. "The price has gone down, and it looks good. Has everything I want. And I've got enough money to put a decent down payment on it."

Jo glanced out the corner of her eye to see a picture of a humble, one-level ranch home. She recognized the area. "You have that kind of money on you?"

"Yeah. I left Virginia with my inheritance, so to speak. I mean, if you're going to start over somewhere else, might as well have enough money to do it with."

Jo turned onto the road leading into Arches National Park. "Do you want to stop at the visitor center?"

"Naw. You've seen one, you've seen them all."

Jo drove on, up the steep park road and into the bowels of red sandstone and tall rock formations. They bypassed Courthouse Rocks, boasting huge, house-sized boulders; passed Balanced Rock; and approached the turnoff for the Windows section, a series of arch formations. On a whim, Jo drove around the loop to observe Dan's reaction.

"Wow, this is amazing. I've never seen anything like it. I mean, to think that it took a million years of wind and water to carve these out." He began taking pictures on his cell phone. "Have to send these babies to Rob. Boy, will he be jealous!"

"It only takes God's finger to form an arch, you know. He doesn't need a million years to accomplish it."

He glanced over at her. "So you're one of those who doesn't believe the earth is a million years old?"

"I learned back in school how land can be altered in a moment's time. Like Mount St. Helens back in 1980, where two new lakes and a river valley were formed. It doesn't take God a zillion years to create something fantastic. It's just man's idea of what happened, to lessen the idea that there is a God."

"I don't know," Dan began dubiously as Jo drove back to the main park road. "Well, however the arches were made, they're still awesome."

Jo continued the drive as Dan stared out the window at the scenery until they arrived at the trailhead for Delicate Arch. She had to admit, she was enjoying his enthusiasm, as if everything was new and interesting to him. Maybe it was the Lord's doing that she'd changed her mind and allowed him to tag along. It made the time fun.

Once on the trail, Dan immediately began comparing the hikes he'd done in Virginia to the slippery sandstone beneath their feet and the red rocks and soil all around. It was like being on another planet, as he said. Jo listened to his chatter, thinking how nice it was to have a friend who enjoyed hiking as much as she. But could she count on Dan to keep this friendship status? Or was he looking to take advantage of the moment? If only she could be certain.

After negotiating the rock face, they found that the trail leveled off for a time before following a narrow ledge. In the distance, Jo could see the visitors gathered to take in the evening sunset. The thrill of expectation rose up within her.

"So how long does it take. . ." He never finished his statement. Instead his mouth dropped open. "Wow. Would you look at that? It's fantastic!"

Jo found a place on a nearby rock to watch the sun's fading rays make its final impression on the natural wonder of Delicate Arch. "It's best to come here this time of evening. You can see the arch so much clearer and even watch it change colors with the setting sun. See it turning from gold to orange and pretty soon, red."

Dan sat beside her on the rock, taking it all in. "I wish I had a better camera," he confessed. "Not sure how it's gonna come out on my cell phone. But better this than nothing, I suppose."

Jo sat quietly as the colors muted with the setting sun. What a wondrous spectacle made by God for His people to enjoy. It amazed her still every time she came here. And satisfied her with the knowledge that He was still at work in her life, creating something beautiful, even if it took time. The One who began the work in her life would complete it in the day of Christ Jesus.

All at once, Jo felt unexpected warmth settle around her. She tugged her gaze away from the beauty of Delicate Arch to find that Dan had slowly curled his arm around her. He tipped his head to one side as he looked at her. His eyes reflected the reddening skies above and the rocks below. He searched her face. He was going to kiss her, and to Jo's dismay, she was going to let him. At the last moment she turned away and stood to her feet, angry that she'd nearly slipped. "I need to head back before it gets too dark to see the trail." She grabbed her day pack, her feet moving swiftly as Dan hurried to keep up.

"Jo, I didn't mean anything. Sorry."

"You meant every bit of it, Dan. Life is like some game to you. I'm just one of your many playing pieces."

"No, you're not. Believe me, you're not. I wouldn't do anything to hurt you."

Jo stopped and whirled. "Well, you have hurt me. You said you wanted a friendship, but now I see what you're really after."

He paused also. "I do want a friendship. But, c'mon. We were enjoying a super sunset and a great view of the arch. It felt like the beach. What's a guy and a girl supposed to do on the beach at sunset?"

"Enjoy God's scenery without being taken advantage of," she retorted. "That's all I wanted to do, and you ruined it. Now I'm sorry I asked you along."

She hurried on, knowing she could hardly outwalk him with his long legs and healthy male stamina. But she could definitely outwit him in other areas. Especially this game of the heart where he thought he was the master.

"Look, I'm sorry for what I did," he said again when they arrived back at the car. "You aren't going to drive off and leave me in the parking lot now, are you? It's a long hitch back to Moab."

"No, of course not. But you'd better take back that backpack of yours. It's not right."

He heaved a sigh. "Jo. . . ," he began.

"You can't just buy a relationship, Dan. And you aren't going to buy me. Or do anything else your devious mind is trying to think of right now. I like my life the way it is. I'm not looking for a relationship. So please, leave me alone."

They said nothing more the rest of the trip back to Moab. When Jo dropped the car off at the rafting center, they still had not spoken. Jo didn't care. It was better this way. She hurried to her place, nearly tripping over the box still sitting in the middle of the living room. Her phone signaled. It was a text message from Dan.

I'M SORRY.

I am, too, she thought. *Sometimes I just wish we'd never met. But sometimes I'm glad we did. . . .*

Chapter 8

Okay, so things were not as cool as Dan once thought. Not that anything was cool in this place. He asked Todd when the weather began to change, and he said not until late fall. Dan liked the fall season with the rich autumn colors and plenty of apples to pick at the nearby orchard. Then he reminded himself he wasn't in a color-changing, apple-picking place. Far from it. He was in Moab, Utah, the land of red rocks, canyons, and arches. The land where a feisty woman lived and now would have nothing to do with him.

Since the episode at Delicate Arch, he and Jo only spoke when necessary and mostly about business. A few days ago, he noticed on his credit card statement that the backpack had been returned. She said little to him about it or anything else. Yet Dan often thought about that evening jaunt they had taken to watch the sunset over Delicate Arch. He couldn't help himself, watching Jo perched on the rock, gazing at the spectacle before her with strands of her hair dancing around her shoulders. It was a ripe moment that had unfortunately turned a bit rotten. Maybe if he'd concentrated more on the friendship angle and not rushed things. Now she thought of herself as only a playing piece in his game of life, which she wasn't. She was so much more.

His thoughts turned to the rafting business. Things had changed drastically in the last few weeks, and it wasn't only in his relationship with Jo. Everything had changed since Todd decided to let Travis go after the life jacket incident. Now that they were short one man, Dan found himself up to his neck in work. He had long since passed the river guide test and now was a fully licensed guide, among his other titles. He often arrived early in the morning to do the count that Travis once did. He did the river trips with gusto. Then he went home late at night after performing the same equipment check. He wondered why Todd didn't ask others on the workforce to do it, until it dawned on him that Todd trusted him. He'd developed a good enough reputation that Todd was giving him more and more responsibility. But with it, Dan felt himself beginning to drag under the weight of it. He yearned for free time to explore more of Moab and the surrounding area. Not that he wasn't outside enough. He'd done the river so many times, he knew it like the back of his hand. He'd even gone on a multiday excursion to Cataract Canyon, led by Todd. What a wild time that was, with Class IV and V rapids that dashed the rafts about like toy boats, to the delight of the college-aged gang that bought the trip. But Dan decided he preferred camping with families after witnessing the guy and girl entanglements on the college trip, complete with couples walking along the river and kissing behind the sagebrush. Without Jo, there was no sense thinking about kissing or anything else long term. He wouldn't put her in that kind of position even if he wanted. But why worry about it? She wouldn't have anything to do with him, period.

"Hey Dan, can I see you for a moment?" Todd called into the shop. Since it was now the middle of August, the number of trips was already beginning to wane as families returned home to get their kiddos into school. The river was running low, too, which affected the trips they conducted. Dan wondered how he would spend the winter without the usual work to keep him occupied. Maybe he would need to pick up a part-time job. Especially since he was seriously planning to buy that ranch home and had already begun the paperwork for the loan.

"Hey, Todd," Dan said, occupying a chair inside Todd's office. The place was typical of a single working guy, complete with awards for sporting competitions on the walls; a desk lined with empty sports drink bottles and crumpled potato chip bags; and samples of gear, such as sandals, water shorts, sunscreen, and even paddles propped up against the wall.

"The reason I asked you in here is to talk about your employment with Red Canyon Adventures."

Dan straightened. *Uh-oh.* Could Todd be giving him his pink slip? But why? He hadn't done anything wrong that he knew of. . .unless Jo spilled the beans about the Arches trip. Maybe Todd was angry he'd taken advantage of his innocent cousin—wooing her with a backpack and then trying to kiss her while watching the colors of Delicate Arch change in the setting sun.

"You know I had to fire Travis. So I was wondering if you might consider taking his place in the company. He was like my VP, if you think of it that way."

"I thought Jo was."

"Jo? You mean Jolene? Family name thing, I guess. She just joined the company to help me out. She's not looking for a managerial position. Travis had been here from the get-go and helped with arranging the trips and everything. Now that he's gone, I could use another guy for feedback on those kinds of things. Of course, I know you're still getting used to how the business is run, but I can tell you're a quick learner and you like what you do."

"Thanks." Dan had to wonder why Todd didn't ask any of the other employees who had been here far longer than he. There must be something about him Todd liked, and that made him feel confident. "So what do I need to do?"

"I'll give you the details. Clue you in on the business part of the company. Let you in on decision making. But you're also still in learning mode, so this doesn't mean you get to run things. At least not yet." He added a grin.

"I wouldn't want to." But he did like the idea that someone thought him capable and trustworthy. Back home on Pop's peanut farm, Rob ran everything. Including Dan's life, it seemed. But Dan didn't feel the least bit intimidated by Todd. He found in him a certain camaraderie and a willingness to work together to make things happen. Not so back on the peanut farm. There it was a competition for his father's affection. Or maybe that was Dan's perception. Rob always seemed to win out in those instances. At dinner time, Pop praised Rob for one thing or another. Now, at last, Dan was making a name for himself. He was being promoted, even over others who had been there a lot longer. He planned to pin his new title on his chest for everyone to see.

"Don't tell me you're already zoning out on me, Dan," Todd said, staring at him. "It's not even 3:00 p.m."

"No, no, just thinking of home. How I never got a fair shake there, but here you trust me. Wish everyone thought as you do."

"I wish we could trust others. I mean, I trusted Travis, and he flat-out lied to my face. But I don't think you'd do that, Dan. You care about this business. I know you love the river, and the kids call you Raft Man. And that day with the missing PFDs, just to see your determination to make sure you came clean, well, that spoke volumes right there."

Dan must file that episode away for future reference. But honestly, he did want to clear his name and make himself look good. What did he have if he didn't? A bad name is not what he came here for. But was trying to secure a good reputation good enough reason to abandon home and head for the red rocks? He grimaced at the thought.

Todd began going over some of the company records. Dan didn't know a whole lot about the business side of things, as Pop always took care of the paperwork. He did do some computer work for Pop, like the billing. Todd showed him the database of customers. He asked if he and Jo could do a mailing soon to prepare for next year. "We have to make sure we're up and running for the next season, even as this year is winding down."

"Yeah, it's hard to believe I've been here nearly three months. I guess that means this place is gonna change."

"Like how?"

"Well, for one, it won't feel like I'm stepping into the neighborhood pizza oven every time I leave my apartment."

"Moab does cool down," Todd said with a laugh. "We can get some snow, too. Of course, if you head four hours northwest of here, there's plenty of snow starting in a month or so near Salt Lake. The best skiing, too, at Park City. The Olympics were held there, you know."

Dan had done no skiing in his life and wasn't sure he wanted to learn.

"Jo loves to ski. She's first-rate."

Booyah. That sealed it. He'd learn to ski no matter what it took. And whatever else Jo liked to do. Though right now, he wasn't even sure they could get through the company mailer together without a major blowup. She was still angry over the Delicate Arch episode. Or he assumed she was angry as he hadn't heard much of anything from her except company business. There were no more tacos or nice drives or even runs to the store for food, which she did herself for the campouts. She was putting him on her ignore list. And the final slap was when she removed him from her friends list on Facebook.

Suddenly she appeared in the office doorway. "Hey Todd, I wanted to know. . ." She paused when her gaze leveled on Dan. Or rather she leveled a set of blue daggers in eyes the shape of crescents. Yep, she was still mad.

"C'mon in, Jolene. I was just telling Dan here about his new job. Since Travis is no longer with us, I have him taking up some of the company responsibility. And I need you two to work on the mailer soon."

One cheek muscle twitched in her otherwise smooth face. "Okay, fine. But I need to know if you plan to go out this afternoon as there's a family here who wants a rafting trip."

"I'll take them," Dan said happily.

"Can you go with him, Jolene? I still need to figure out some things here with the files."

"Yeah, sure." Jo marched out.

Dan followed, peeking into the store to see Mom, Dad, and several young boys pleading with the parents to buy them each new kids' sunglasses. "Looks like fun," he commented.

"Just remember, we're here to do a job," she told him. "We're taking the family rafting, and that's it. You take advantage of this situation, and I'll make sure Todd knows all about it."

"Understood, ma'am." He even saluted for effect.

Jo rolled her eyes and strode off to gather the PFDs and other equipment. Dan met the family in the rear of the store and told them briefly where they would be going and some safety pointers.

"Are we going out in the boat soon?" asked one of the boys.

"Real soon. And here's my assistant." He acknowledged Jo. "We're going to take you over in the van to the drop-off point to begin the trip. And you're in luck. You'll have your own private guides, the two of us."

"So you and your wife are taking us?" asked the mother.

Dan looked out the corner of his eye to see Jo's face blanch. "We're just co-workers, ma'am," Dan said swiftly.

"Oh, I'm sorry. I thought maybe you were a husband and wife team. You seem to work well together."

Thank you, God! You're making my day big-time. This couldn't have begun any better, even if the look on Jo's face told him otherwise. It wasn't as if he'd paid the mom money to say that. He shrugged in Jo's direction as if to communicate, Hey, don't blame me; I didn't set them up.

She turned away.

&❦

The rafting venture went smoothly. Dan liked seeing the way Jo tackled the trip. She had good strength and know-how of the river. When they arrived back at the shop, he decided one compliment shouldn't throw her off too badly. "You were good out there today. Did you see the nice tip the family gave us?"

She pushed back strands of hair from her face. "Yeah. Thanks."

"Maybe we should spend it on a nice, thick steak. And onion rings. What do you say?"

She shook her head. "No thanks."

Dan hesitated. Suddenly he felt the urge to say something, anything to calm the tension between them. "Look, I'm really sorry about what happened on the hike the other night. I should've never done what I did. I mean, I broke your trust. It wasn't what you bargained for."

"No, it wasn't. I just wanted to have a good time with God, and you had to move on in. And the problem is, I nearly gave in. I don't like that."

Dan tried to hide his utter delight at this revelation. *She almost gave in? She wanted to kiss me, too? She has feelings for me? Yeah!*

"Dan, you need to know there's more to life than you. There's a much bigger picture here. Other people have feelings, and they're trying to do what's right in life."

"I know that."

"Do you? I know you say we're friends, and you're just helping. But then you move in like the doors are wide open. Even if I was tempted to give in, I won't do it. I'm not that kind of person. You may have come from the open arena of dating with any girl that pops along. But I would rather wait on God to bring the right man into my life."

God does that kind of thing? Since when? Dan never equated the God of the stained-glass window to a God who cared about a person's relationship status. Jo made God sound so. . .personal. "Don't tell me you've never been in a relationship."

Jo hesitated. "Yes, I have. And maybe that's why I've decided not to go shopping around the neighborhood. It hurts too much. I'd rather wait on God and see where He leads me. He's never let me down. He knows what's best for me."

Dan thought about it. How often did he think that God had let him down? Except now when God seemed to be smiling everywhere Dan turned. All but this one small problem standing before him. "I still don't see the problem in spending our nice tip on a steak or taking a walk or watching a sunset on a trail."

"But you saw firsthand what happens when you even try to do the most innocent of things. Like taking a hike to see Delicate Arch, and you take the opportunity to make your move."

"Look, it's a guy thing. I didn't mean anything by it, and I sure didn't mean for it to upset you. If it makes you feel any better, I promise it won't happen again." He watched Jo remove her hair band and allow her hair to flow free. He sighed. Maybe he wasn't being totally honest. If he saw Jo by another sunset and with her hair blowing in the breeze like that, he probably would try to kiss her again. But right now he was willing to say anything to stem the flow of anger until things changed. And he believed they would in time. Todd was making him one of the head honchos. He and Jo would be working more and more together. It would naturally flow that they would get to know each other, and with that would follow a closer relationship. He just had to learn to put the brake on and not do a free fall that would scare her away. "If I promise to be on good behavior and be a friend, can you accept a friendship?"

Jo hesitated. "Look, I don't want to seem tyrannical or something. I just want to guard my heart. And you should guard yours, too, Dan. Unless you don't care about it. Obviously you aren't a one-woman kind of guy."

That comment stung. No, he couldn't say that Jo was his first interest. She was about the sixth, maybe, counting the girls he knew back in high school. And then his two-year stint on the community college scene with Lenora before financial necessity brought him back to the peanut field. But none of those girls had the kind of principles Jo did. Or her stubbornness when it came to her religion. Like thinking God was a matchmaker, of all things! That really threw him for a loop.

"But I will spend a little of the tip on ice cream," she suddenly announced.

Dan spun about and stared. "You will? Great! I mean, okay."

She laughed. "Besides, we have business to discuss. With Travis gone, there are some things I probably should go over with you since you're basically taking his place."

"Todd has been doing that."

"Well, other things. What to expect in your new role, working with Todd. It takes a lot to keep things going, Dan. And it has to be taken seriously."

He nodded. *Get serious, Dan.* He needed to do it on the job front as well as in this relationship. No more games. No more kid stuff. Time to act like a man. Whatever that meant.

❧

"Well, we made it through," Dan said with a smile, sitting back to allow the banana split to slowly digest.

"Made it through what?"

"A nice dessert without blowups, confusion, or misinterpretations. Just straight talking." He watched her scrape the last bit of chocolate syrup from the sundae cup. He averted his gaze while she licked the spoon to watch other customers coming in and out. Suddenly he straightened in his chair and stared. His ice cream turned to a cold rock in his stomach.

"What's the matter?"

"Travis and Chris just walked in the door. Wouldn't you know it? I swear they must have homing beacons attached to their baseball caps. Like those little lights I've seen." He looked around to see if the store had a rear exit. No such luck. And no luck either in the nonrecognition department as Chris strode over, hands in his pockets, a grin parked on his face.

"Hey, I just wanted to thank you two."

"For what?" Dan said before feeling Jo's foot nudge his shinbone.

"For giving me Travis. He's excellent."

"Well, you'd better watch it. He also takes shortcuts and tells tall tales." Again he felt Jo poke him and shake her head.

"Oh yeah, and let's get on the topic of telling outright tales, shall we? Like the salmonella lie? I'm sure you don't want me to go there, Jolene, do you?"

"Look, we were just leaving, Chris. Glad Travis is working out in your company. He didn't with us, and that's fine." She took up her backpack purse and stood to her feet.

Dan had no intention of leaving, not when he saw Travis already beginning his manipulation tactics on Chris through fancy storytelling. Until he felt the pressure of Jo's hand on his arm, urging him to leave. He looked over at Travis to see a smile on his face that grated his nerves.

Outside the shop, he whirled to face her. "Why did you drag me out of there like I'm some kid?"

"Because if we didn't leave, you were looking to start a brawl. All that's needed is a few accusations to fly, and then it begins. Chris was baiting us both. You just have to stop taking the bait."

"I don't care. You can see Travis has been filling Chris's head with lies about the company. Doesn't that bother you?"

"So what if he has? It won't go anywhere."

Dan couldn't believe her calmness in the midst of this battle. He wanted to fight. His manly muscles were crying out for it. But somehow he allowed the soothing balm of Jo to calm the tide. With reluctance, he walked away.

"Now do you feel better?"

"No, because that guy is still sitting there, lying through his teeth."

"Dan, the only person he's hurting is himself."

"How did this whole salmonella thing with Chris come about anyway? He mentioned it again. I remember you telling me about it when I first got here."

She let out a sigh. "We heard complaints from several people that they had become sick soon after a rafting trip using Chris's company. Of course, whenever you hear of a stomach bug mixed with food, you think salmonella. Well, Todd questioned the possibility. The rumor leaked out. Chris lost business, and state health inspectors even showed up. He was cleared of the allegation, but the damage had been done."

Dan sighed. "I don't know, but I'm worried. Chris isn't going to forget what happened. And with Travis there, adding in his bad feelings about Todd, I smell trouble."

"Then you need to pray about it, Dan. It's all you can do."

Pray about it? What a strange concept. Maybe he should. But he really didn't know the One he ought to be praying to. Not like Mom and Pop did. Or Jo even. Just the mere thought made him feel uncomfortable. No, he'd put the praying aside and let Jo take over that part. Instead, he'd spend the rest of the evening thinking about the company and how to keep Chris and Travis from showing up on the company's front doorstep when they least expected it.

Chapter 9

The activity at the rafting center slowly began to die down after Labor Day. As vacationers went back to work and students to school, there was less and less demand for trips during the week. Weekends still proved busy, but Jo could take a day or two off midweek to do the things she wanted. And those days didn't amount to much. The laptop became her friend. She sometimes gathered with friends she knew from church. She thought about taking up some kind of craft and even bought a card-making kit, thinking it might be nice this year to give out handmade cards for Christmas.

Jo turned on the laptop to see what was happening. Once again, Dan asked for a friend request on the social network. Ever since she'd taken him off her friends list after the escapade at Arches, he inquired if he could come back. And each time she hit the IGNORE feature. Until today, when she felt in a more jovial mood and accepted. After she hit the button to access his profile page, she noticed the new picture of him making some strange face while sitting in the raft. She wondered then about his background. She still knew so little about him. Why he really left Virginia to come here. What his plans were in life. If he would ever consider putting God in the equation.

The chat box popped up. I STRUCK OIL, Dan wrote.

WHAT DO YOU MEAN YOU STRUCK OIL?

I MEAN I'VE BEEN TRYING TO GET YOUR ATTENTION NOW FOR WEEKS. DID YOU KNOW I'VE CLOSED ON MY HOUSE? AND I'M HAVING AN OPEN HOUSE THIS FRIDAY NIGHT. LIKE TO HAVE YOU COME IF YOU CAN.

Jo thought about it. Like her social calendar was booked these days. I'LL HAVE TO SEE. YOU CAN'T HAVE TOO MANY PEOPLE COMING TO IT. YOU DON'T KNOW THAT MANY IN MOAB.

TRUE. JUST EMPLOYEES FROM THE COMPANY. MAYBE I SHOULD INVITE OUR ARCHENEMIES.

Jo could imagine the confrontation if Chris and Travis showed up. Thankfully, after the ice-cream encounter several weeks ago, things had been quiet. No more chain rattling.

YOU KNOW BETTER THAN THAT, she typed.

I KNOW. I HAVE YOU TO STRAIGHTEN ME OUT.

Jo thought on that one. She remembered that tonight was their young

adult fellowship at the church. Well, why not? Hey, since you like parties so much, come on over to the gathering at my church tonight.
We're going to play board games.

What time?

8:00.

I'm there.

That was easy, Jo thought, reminding her of the commercial with the
same slogan. She grimaced and closed the laptop, wondering what she had
just gotten herself into. Had she opened herself up to more trouble? She
thought not. This was a good group to join. Dan needed to see how Christian
guys and girls interacted with each other. He could use basic lessons on what
it means to have a real relationship with the Lord. Not engaging in romantic
encounters at every bend in the road, but serving each other and waiting on
God for Him to open the doors. She smiled, thinking of it more like a trap to
capture Dan's soul than anything. *Hope you're ready, dear ol' Dan*, she thought
smugly.

Jo arrived early that evening to clue the group leaders in on the coming
intrusion by Dan Mallory. They were a married couple named Brian and
Trish. "He's a transplanted Virginian who isn't sure what he's supposed to do
in life," she told them. "And he's Todd's assistant in the company."

"We look forward to meeting him," Brian said with a smile.

The meeting soon came to order. Brian led the group in prayer and asked
for testimonies and prayer requests. Jo glanced at her watch. No sign of Dan.
Jo tapped her foot, feeling her agitation rising. How she wanted him here to
listen to the testimonies and find out what was happening in other people's
lives.

A half hour later, just as Brian was bringing out the games, Dan showed
up. Jo tried not to let her irritation get the better of her, but she did wonder if
he'd planned all along to avoid the first part of the meeting. She went ahead
and introduced Dan to Brian.

"So are you settled here in Moab?" Brian asked.

"Sure am. Just got myself a nice place, too. Wheels. A job. Life's been real
good. It's been a blessing for sure."

Jo tried not to bristle as Dan smoothly threw out a few colloquial
Christian expressions. He went on to tell Brian about God's blessing over his
life ever since he arrived here and how he'd wanted to meet other people. "So
this is a real answer to prayer."

I wonder when's the last time you really prayed, Dan? She looked to Brian
to see if he could read through it all. Brian only smiled and invited him to
play a game. Dan looked to Jo and asked what she would be doing. When

she mentioned entering the Monopoly challenge, Dan agreed to play also. But now she wasn't in the mood to do anything. Especially having Dan sitting right next to her at the table, flashing a smile now and then, and using Christian lingo with everyone around him.

God, can't people see who he is?

And then a still, small voice responded. *"Who is he?"*

The question startled her. *He's just pretending, to get what he wants.*

"Like someone else I know."

Jo sat stunned, even as Dan gave her the dice and told her it was her turn. She looked at the board game and rolled the dice, all the while wondering if she, too, had been playing the game of Christianity. Throwing dice and moving her piece to get ahead. As it was, she didn't leave Virginia on the right footing. She left because of personal things she'd never revealed to anyone but Brian and Trish, and of course, Todd. She thought she'd made the right decision when she did it, but was she running instead of confronting the past? Pretending to play the game without reconciliation?

"You aren't into this anymore, are you?" Dan asked.

"No, not really." She looked around and found another woman, Meg, to take her place at the table. She walked off, catching Dan's thoughtful gaze as he continued to play the game. Life was too confusing. She'd been rebuked at her own game of life, it seemed.

"What's up, Jo?" Trish asked, coming up to her. "Is it Dan?"

"Dan isn't a Christian, Trish, but he's pretending like he is."

"The only one who really knows his heart is God, right?"

"Yes, but. . . I don't know. He's looking to be more than just friends with me. I've tried to hold him off, but there are nice things about him."

"You did the right thing by bringing him here. Sometimes when we get away from a church family and strike out on our own, temptations happen we don't expect. Getting him involved with other Christian guys is a good way to go. Hopefully he can come to church on Sunday."

"That may be difficult right now as many of the rafting trips are still going strong on weekends. But when the fall season ends, he should be able to come."

"That would be even better. But you do what you need to guard your heart, Jo. Give it over to God. Let Him continue to work through you. And feel free to have Brian intervene with Dan whenever you need him to. He's glad to help."

"Thanks." With Dan still immersed in the game, Jo decided this was a good time to disappear. Hopefully Dan would make new friends and set his sights on other things rather than her. And she could finish her own soul-searching and seek to discover what she needed to resolve in her life.

ॐ

Jo was happy with the way things were going. There had been a distinct change in Dan ever since she introduced him to her young adult group. To her surprise, he was faithful to come every Wednesday night, even though he often ran late, avoiding much of the prayer and testimony time. Yet she was encouraged to find him interacting with other brothers in the Lord and making friends.

The rafting season had ended and life turned quiet. She and Dan spent workdays doing inventory, mailing out brochures for upcoming business, and checking out new stock for the store. The cooler temperatures brought out long-sleeved shirts and jeans from the closet. When a faint dusting of snow painted the red rocks, Dan was out there with his cell phone camera, taking shots of it. He continued to remain courteous with her. Things were definitely looking better.

"So are you coming?" Todd asked her one day as she was counting out sunglasses on the counter.

"Of course. Why would I miss your New Year's Eve party?"

"Just wondering. You seem so quiet these past few months. Are you upset?"

"About what?"

"That I made Dan my assistant in the company instead of you. I know you've been here longer and all. In fact, you've essentially become part of the company in many ways."

"Believe me, I don't want the aggravation of being a VP."

Todd whistled a sigh. "Okay, good. I just thought maybe you were mad at me or something." He paused. "By the way, do you ever hear from Ross?"

Jo froze when he mentioned her older brother. "No, actually I haven't. Why would you bring that up?"

He shrugged. "I don't know. With the holidays and all, you start thinking about family."

"I'm sorry your mom isn't here anymore." She saw a pall come over his face, as he recalled how his mother died in a car crash a few years back and how his dad had nothing to do with him. *Why were there all these family difficulties in life?* she wondered, thinking of her own falling out, not only with Ross but with her parents, too.

"I think about her around Christmas. But hey, we're family now. Cousins, anyway. I'll let you get back to your counting."

Jo watched him move off to the office. He was being melancholic again, like her, thinking of family and all that they had lost. If only they could gain something back. But she had no plans yet to get in touch with her brother Ross or her parents. Ross had made life a challenge in so many ways, being the proverbial older brother by telling her what to do and where to go. Saying it was his responsibility to take care of her, especially with their vast differences in ages. Fifteen years to be exact. She didn't want to let on to anyone, especially Dan, of her troubled years as a teen. Having to leave home and move in with Ross when her parents couldn't deal with her. Ross was the only one who opened his door to her. And what did she do? Left him, too. Dan didn't realize she wasn't a Goody Two-Shoes. She'd had tough breaks in life. But all that was better kept locked away for now.

Jo heaved a sigh and stared at the pile of sunglasses. Now she would have to recount them with all these distractions. Why did these things have to come to the surface now? She'd received acceptance and counseling when she first came here. She'd found forgiveness for what she had done in the past and moved on with life. But now the past was coming back to haunt her. Maybe because she was being nitpicky and judgmental of Dan.

"What's up?" She heard a cheery voice call out.

Dan arrived with a grin parked on his face, looking as if he'd conquered the world.

"Sunglasses." She modeled one for him. "Rather, counting them."

"Wow, that is too sweet. So, are you going to Todd's party?"

"Of course. I'm his cousin. I do the serving."

"You gonna wear a little waitress outfit?"

Jo's face heated, and she looked away.

"Sorry. That was a tactless comment." He stepped back, the cheerfulness evaporating from his face. "Moab looks like a great place to celebrate Christmas though."

Jo moved sunglasses from one pile to another. "Dan, do you ever think about your family?"

"My family? Of course. Why?"

"Just wondering, with it being Christmas and all."

"Actually, I've been trying to figure out what to give them this year. I thought about giving them free tickets to a rafting trip next year. Rob would love it. I mean, I've got the money to fly them out. I just don't see my mom heading down the Colorado in a raft." He leaned over with his elbows resting on the counter. "How about yours?"

"Well, Todd is having the party, so we exchange gifts then."

"No, I mean your family. Mom, Pop, brothers, sisters."

"They. . .they're in New York. Except for my oldest brother."

"I went to New York City once. Saw all the famous places. Went up the

Empire State Building. Saw the Statue of Liberty. And of course, the footprints of the Twin Towers. That was a sobering moment."

"Uh. . .sorry, I really need to get back to counting these."

"Oh, sure." He looked at her thoughtfully before moving on toward Todd's office. Jo didn't want to relive the rest of the story, that she'd not seen her family since she was fifteen, that she'd been cared for by her brother for several rough years until fleeing to Moab. That she'd put her family through worse fiery furnaces than anything Arches National Park could dish out on the Fiery Furnace trail. That she likely still nursed some unresolved guilt for gumming up her life and theirs. For thinking they had raised a model daughter, only to find her caught up in drugs and a crude boyfriend. *God, why is all this coming out now? It's been safely buried away for so long. Are You trying to do something by resurrecting this? But why now, and why with Dan around?* Maybe because she wanted to appear the solid Christian to him. That he wouldn't know the down and dirty parts, that she wasn't all she was cracked up to be, at least before she came to know the Lord.

For now, Jo settled herself into the Christmas festivities. Todd closed down the shop for two weeks. Jo got out her ski equipment and took off for a day on the slopes near Salt Lake to be by herself and think. When she turned her cell phone on, there were at least a dozen messages from Dan asking where she went. She grimaced, feeling no inclination to give him daily updates on her life, especially when she was trying to sort things out.

Jo brushed out her hair and put on a shiny top and black jeans for the New Year's Eve party. Todd always threw a nice bash at his place, with great food and plenty of soda—though he did have beer for the drinking crowd. She planned to be in the kitchen helping wherever she could. And staying out of Dan's sight, even though he'd been on good behavior these many weeks.

Jo arrived at Todd's. The place twinkled with strings of multicolored lights lingering from the Christmas holiday. With the warm evening, many gathered out on the front porch, sipping whatever was in their glasses and talking. Jo slipped by, giving swift greetings, and entered the kitchen. Dan stood at the counter, making an hors d'oeuvre tray. "What are you doing in here?"

"Todd asked me to help out. He likes my flair for arranging food. What do you think?"

Jo liked the way he had arranged the crackers and cheese to spell out the New Year. "Very creative."

"Thanks." He stood there for a moment, gazing at her, looking as if he liked what he saw.

Jo felt her face grow warm. She hurried out to find Todd and see if anything else needed to be done.

"Don't worry about it," he told her. "Just have fun. Dan's my cook tonight."

Super. She tried not to read into it and grabbed a soda instead. There were several hours left to wade through before the stroke of midnight. She wondered how she would pass the time. She wandered outside to find the moon had risen, bathing the landscape in a drapery of white. It looked peaceful, as if God would bring His peace on the upcoming year. How she needed to embrace the way of peace, especially with what He'd been doing in her heart these past few weeks. She sipped her soda, thinking of the Christmas card she'd received from Ross. It was simple and friendly, asking how she was and telling her they were thinking of her. Even Dad and Mom had sent one, as well as a gift card to some store that she would have to drive to Salt Lake to shop in. At least they were thinking of her.

Just then she felt someone touch her arm. Dan came up, holding a small plate of food. "Got you some of these before everyone else dives in. Sausage balls, cheese, and crackers."

"Thanks, but I'm not hungry."

He put the plate down. "Jo, you've seemed lost now for a while. What's going on?"

"I don't know. Just thinking." Her gaze encompassed the velvety rocks once more. "I'm glad I'm here in Moab."

"Me, too. I mean, I think of Pop and Mom. You know, this is the first holiday I've spent away from them?"

"Was it hard?"

"Not as bad as I thought. I talked to them on Christmas Day. I think Mom was crying on the phone, but I couldn't tell. Rob said he liked the idea of going rafting sometime. Pop was pretty quiet, except to ask how I was getting along. Told me he was praying for me. That kind of thing."

"That's good. It's good that your family cares about you."

"Jo, I care about you, too." His fingers began to sweep her forearm. "I think about you all the time."

"Dan. . ."

"It's almost the New Year. I would really like to make a resolution."

"So would I."

His hazel eyes reflected the moon. "You would?"

"Uh-huh. Never to be alone with you at sunset or in the moonlight. It's not a good idea."

"Jo, c'mon. Stop playing."

"Playing?"

"Look, I've played along now for a while. I went to your church group and all. But let's be honest. You know you've got feelings for me. You said so yourself not that long ago. It's getting kind of boring waiting for you to come around. Let's just make a resolution this year to spend more time together."

Jo felt the anger rising up within her. "Hey Dan, I've got an even better suggestion."

"Yeah?" He drew closer, the look on his face betraying his desire to kiss her. His arms began to curl around her.

"I'm into a totally new game for the New Year."

"Sounds good. Just let me know the rules." He began to nuzzle her neck.

"Okay. It's called Hands Off. I mean it." She pushed him away and hurried off. She walked fast, away from the merrymaking all around Moab, and headed straight for her apartment. *Oh God, how I hate the mess I'm in. With love. With life. I pray this will be a year of new beginnings. That somehow my life will count for something. Things can be made new again. But, please, leave Dan out of my life right now.*

Chapter 10

L ove is supposed to be thicker than water. He'd heard it from an oldies song somewhere. He wanted it like the flour and water paste he used back in grade school to glue projects together. But nothing could paste this relationship back together, as much as he wanted. Love was too runny right now, running right out of his life. It did not bind them together. In fact, it was nonexistent, though Dan could say with his heart that he was falling head over heels in love with Jo. But since the last few episodes, she'd once more resorted to ignoring him. She'd hardly spoken to him except to pass on something from Todd. There were no more ice-cream socials or other gatherings. At least she did show up at the game night Wednesday nights at her church, but she made certain she didn't play the same game as he. For a time he stopped going to the event in a protest of sorts, but after a while, he missed the camaraderie. He liked hanging out with this bunch. They were interesting and godly. He hoped that if he continued to hang out with Jo and her friends, she would warm up to him.

But as usual, he let his feelings get in the way of his plans, and now he was back to square one. Or rather he seemed to be flirting with the negative region. At least he was secure in other areas of life. He enjoyed having his own house. Work was okay though quiet. He spent his free time exploring Moab to see all that there was to see. Like walking the river walk. Cruising the outdoor shops. And yes, enduring other run-ins with Travis and Chris when he inadvertently stumbled upon their rafting center. He should have remembered the name of the place when he entered it, but it had slipped his mind until he saw them.

"What are you doing here, Dan?" Travis immediately called out. "Scoping out our place for Todd?"

"It was purely accidental. I was just seeing what Moab had to offer. I didn't know this was Chris's place."

"Sure. Nice try."

Dan tried to exit, but it seemed Travis was more interested in conversation. He asked how the company was doing. If Todd had received any bad news lately—though Dan couldn't begin to figure out what *that* meant. So Dan decided to change the subject slightly and loosen up the talk. "The only grim news I've got to report is the girl angle. Jo doesn't seem interested in me no matter what I do. Guess I don't have it or something. Any thoughts on the subject, guys?"

His question brought the reaction he'd hoped. The talk turned from his place of employment to girls. Chris began to relate about his past and present girlfriends. Travis said Jo didn't look at anyone or anything. "But she's got quite a past, so what do you expect?"

This comment piqued Dan's interest. "What do you mean by that? I mean, we all have sordid pasts in one form or another."

"Oh, why she left New York and then Virginia and all. I mean, she originally left home when she was fifteen. Or rather her parents kicked her out from what I hear."

Dan tried not to look interested, but on the inside he was riveted. He pretended to study a rack of water shorts, hoping and praying that Travis would continue to run his mouth. And he did for a time, talking about how she moved in with her older brother in Virginia, but even he couldn't deal with her. "She's got an attitude, and now she walks around holier-than-thou when she's messed up. Can't figure out how getting religious all of a sudden makes you perfect."

Dan was intrigued. Why was Jo kicked out at age fifteen? It never dawned on him that she would have any troubles in life. She seemed so. . .well, perfect and pretty. And holy, as Travis said, like trying to stay holy in her relationships. The more he thought about it, the more curious he became.

Back home, Dan turned on his computer tablet to check Facebook. Once again Jo had dumped him as a friend on the social network after the New Year's incident. Round Two. He wished there were some way to look into her heart and see what was happening. It would be nice to know she also struggled with things. They would be so good for each other, helping each other through the tough parts of life. Wasn't Pastor Brian just saying the other day that lessons learned from troubling times can help someone else?

Now he had an overwhelming desire to help Jo with her past. She'd helped him when he first got here, and now he wanted to do something in return. At least be there for her. Though he knew what would happen if he tried to intervene. She would push him away with the "Hands Off" game again. *Jo, I wish you could understand that I care about you. Okay, so I like you, too. I like being with you. I would very much like to kiss you, even though it's probably not a good thing right now. But I care. I'm not just out for your body or something, even if you are good-looking. I care about you personally. And if you're in trouble, I want to help.*

Wow, what a unique concept. He wasn't thinking about himself for a change. He was finally getting the eyes off Dan Mallory and onto someone else. Considering someone else's feelings instead of harping on his own.

Dan checked his hair and appearance today. He wanted to look his best but not appear as if he were trying to play up the moment. He chose a long-sleeved polo shirt and cargo pants. And for kicks he added a Bible, one Mom gave him when he turned sixteen. How she dearly wanted him to read it. Dan never opened it. Now it would make a good prop for this meeting. Maybe he could go on the guise of needing some kind of biblical lesson. He tried to think of something Pastor Brian said that he could use to pose a question. That would appear innocent enough. And then he could find out more about her in the process and especially her past. Patience was the key to turning love into glue. And when they did come together, he would let nothing tear them apart.

He arrived at Jo's apartment to see a light shining in the window. *Good, she's home.* He came to the door and heard singing. He wasn't familiar with the tune, something about God and the need to go deeper or something. He paused for a few minutes to listen. She had a nice voice. He looked at the Bible he held, thinking he ought to do his own deep searching sometime.

He knocked. The singing continued. He knocked harder. It suddenly stopped and there came the patter of footsteps.

"No way, Dan." He heard the muffled response behind the door.

Great, she can see through the security hole. "Jo, this will only take a minute. I've got a question about what Pastor Brian said Wednesday night."

"Look, I know that game. Pretend to have a question when your real motive is to find a way inside. Forget it."

Man, she does know everything. She must have lived on the other side of the tracks. "Okay, look, I'm concerned about you."

She didn't respond.

"Travis said you'd been through things when you were younger, how your parents made you leave and all. I—I just wanted to let you know if you ever want to talk about it. . ."

The door suddenly burst open. He jumped back and nearly dropped the Bible.

"What in the world is Travis doing blabbing about my personal life to you?"

Dan sensed the water getting quite hot. "We were just talking about relationships and all. He said you'd been in some tough situations when you were a teen."

"Todd!" she shouted, stomping her foot. "He must have said something to Travis. For crying out loud, it's *my* personal life. So Todd told Travis, and Travis told you. What's next, the *National Enquirer*? And no, I'm not some Hollywood star's ex-lover or an alien from outer space. And yes, I did have a tough time as a teen. Who doesn't?"

"I know." He saw then she was staring at the Bible he carried. The next thing he knew, he was standing inside her apartment for the first time. It was a nice place, too. Lots of feminine touches. Magenta curtains. Framed prints of puppies. A clock hanging on the wall with numerals in the shape of rosebuds. Totally girlish but sweet. How could this woman have any problems? She was sweet, kind, tenderhearted, fabulous looking. . .

Jo flopped down on the sofa. "I just don't understand why people have to go telling everyone their life's history. And of course, now you know mine."

"Well, not really. Only that you've had a tough time. I mean, being a teen these days is not easy. Lots of peer pressure."

"Tell me about it. That's all I've had. Pressure coming from every direction. And James was a total idiot."

James? Dan tried not to look interested, but he was very interested, especially if there was another guy in the picture.

"I should've never gotten involved with that guy." She paused. "Maybe you need to understand why I don't care to date or hang out with guys. You see, a guy ruined my life. Or rather, I let him ruin my life. He got me involved with drugs. My family kicked me out. They said they couldn't deal with it, that I needed to go live with my brother Ross who had a better handle on things, being older. Then Ross kicked me out, too. Well, that's not true. I kicked myself out. I came here to find a new life. Then I got involved in the church here. Brian and some of the others helped me. I got saved. And now I have a new outlook on life."

Dan tried to absorb all this, but he must have had a stunned expression on his face, because Jo wriggled her nose.

"So I'm not the queen of the castle as you thought, huh? I've got faults."

"Well, who doesn't?"

"I don't know. You seem to think you have your act together."

"I do, don't I?" He laughed shortly. "No one's perfect. But sometimes it's good to start over again. I couldn't stand where I was either. Moab seems to be the place where people find help. I mean, you've helped me so much. And I'm sorry I keep trying to take advantage of it."

She sat massaging a sofa pillow with her fingertips, a move that distracted him. He inhaled a sharp breath and looked away, back to the rosebud clock. Boy, would Mom love a clock like that.

"Yeah, you sure have," she finally said. "And I'm still not convinced you aren't trying to do the same thing now. So with that"—she stood to her feet and went to the door—"I hope you don't mind me asking you to leave now."

"Okay, sure. I just wanted you to know that you can always talk to me."

She said nothing more. He left, wondering if anything had been accomplished this night. One thing was certain. He really didn't know the true Jolene at all.

෨෪

Dan felt better about the situation with Jo, but not about work. Something was definitely eating Todd. He'd not been right for several weeks now. He'd lost his friendliness, his zing for things, and the way he used to invite Dan into his office to talk about stuff. And then there was supposed to be all the planning for the upcoming season, which Todd had done little of since the winter mailer. All of this concerned Dan. Especially when he got a call from Todd that he didn't need to come to work for a few days. Sometimes things were slow, and he wasn't needed. But days off in the spring when stuff should be moving left him wondering what was afoot. He called Jo to ask what was happening, but she offered little in the way of information. He thought about the last few outings on the river but could think of nothing he'd done wrong. Maybe he was just being paranoid.

He decided to be of good cheer anyway, despite his reservations, and walked into the shop whistling. He didn't bother to notice the CLOSED sign on the front door. Jo should be at the cash register, ready for the day, but she was strangely absent. In fact, the place didn't feel or look right. He walked to the back of the shop and looked in Todd's office. He saw Evan, one of the other employees, walk past him with his head down.

"Hey Evan, what's up, man?"

Evan ignored him. A strange feeling came over Dan. He peeked into the office again to see Todd running his hand through his hair. Todd looked up and flinched when he saw Dan. "Well, you'd better get in here."

Dan looked at his watch as he slipped into a chair. "I know I'm a little late. Where's Jo?"

"Dan, we've got a major problem." He smacked some papers on his desk. "We've been served with a lawsuit."

"What?"

"Yeah, by one of the customers that went on a trip early last season. I don't know if you recall, but you were learning to help guide on that trip. It's from the girl who fell in the river."

"You mean earring girl?" Dan thought back to the conversation she had with her boyfriend on the bus. *And if I fall in, I'm suing.* She wasn't kidding.

"I have insurance, but as you know with the economy and everything, it's been getting tough. And this girl's got a top-notch lawyer who's trying his best to find loopholes in the agreements each of the customers sign. It seems she's a state representative's daughter."

This was going from bad to worse.

"You should have treated her with kid gloves," Todd added.

"How was I to know that? I mean, it was my first day on the job. Travis was in charge of the boat."

Todd again ran his fingers through his hair. "Well, whatever. But this is going to kill me once word gets out. And it already has."

"Just fight it."

"Easier said than done. You know how much this will cost me in business and money? Especially with her kind of lawyer. She's claiming she got some kind of neck injury from the fall. Had to wear a neck brace. Even though customers are supposed to take responsibility for what happens according to the disclaimer they sign, they're claiming that because an unlicensed guide was at the helm, the paper she signed is null and void."

Dan flew to his feet and began to pace. *I don't believe this!* "She's making all this up. She wasn't hurt."

"Even if she is, I don't see how we can win in the long run. She'll play the innocent girl, and she'll get sympathy. And then witnesses saw you at the helm when the boat hit a rock and she fell out."

Dan whirled. "Todd. . .I. . ."

"Look, Dan, there isn't anything else to say. But this is your notice. I'm going to have to let you go. I can't have you here with this going on. Even if Travis was there with you, he's already gone."

Dan attempted a sick chuckle of disbelief, but inside he felt like he was dying. "You've got to be kidding."

"No, I'm deadly serious. I don't know how I'm gonna keep going as it is. Especially when word of this gets out."

This was a nightmare come true. "Todd, I don't know what to say."

"There's nothing you can say. It was my fault for putting you out there on your first day. It was a dumb thing to do. Even dumber having Travis in charge. Maybe I'm being burned for things I've done in the past. Looks like God is getting back at me."

Dan wished he could address this, but right now he felt like God was out to get him, too. Now he understood why Evan left the building with his chin on his chest. Dan was about to have his head on the floor. "Todd, I wish you would let me stay on."

"Wish I could, too. I'll keep in touch."

Dan took his final paycheck and left. He stared at the floor, tracing the patterns of linoleum just as Evan had done. *I don't believe this. I–I've just been fired.* He looked at his paycheck. Only a week's worth. He had his mortgage coming up. His car payment. And he hadn't saved a dime like Pop always taught him to. He'd spent it all. *Okay, don't panic. There has to be other places hiring guides for the upcoming summer. You can get a job.*

Dan tried to calm himself, but all he felt was despair. And questions. And anger toward earring girl and her fancy-pants father. And everything else.

Now he did what he thought he'd never do. He went directly to the competitor's place. Inside was hopping with eager customers shopping and looking to book tours. Travis looked very happy. "Is Chris around?" Dan asked.

"He's real busy. What's the matter with you?"

"I just got fired. So I'm in a lousy mood."

"Now you know what it feels like, huh? C'mon back." Dan's spirits rose as he followed Travis into a back office. It was a much classier place than Todd's, he had to admit. Professional. Even had an espresso machine parked on the counter. Through the window he saw air-conditioned transports. Shiny boats. Dan knew he would love working here. Maybe.

When Travis told Chris that Dan had lost his job, Chris invited Dan to have a seat.

Dan filled him in on all the gory details and then some.

Chris sat there, drumming his fingers on the desk. "Well, as you can imagine, I can't have someone inept handling my boats."

Dan stared. "I wasn't inept. Your employee, Travis, was the one training me. It was my first day on a boat. He can tell you."

Chris shook his head. "Sorry, can't help you."

"So it's okay to keep an inept guide on your force who can't train worth beans?"

Chris's face darkened. "Travis is an excellent employee. If you don't mind, you can leave my office. There's the door."

Oh man, Dan, what did you do? He took off as fast as he could. Now he walked the streets like a robot. Everyone had smiles on their faces and a lift to their step. The sun was hot. The rocks were flaming red. The sky was blue. And he felt like junk inside. He entered another rafting place and introduced himself. They shook their heads when he asked about employment. So did a third. Dan then spotted a saloon open for business, despite it being 10:00 a.m. Well, why not? He had nothing better to do today.

He ambled in, took a seat right at the bar, and ordered a beer. How could this have happened? Not long ago, everything was going perfectly. And a month ago, Jo had invited him into her apartment of all things! Now this. He downed his beer in several gulps and ordered another.

"Better watch it, guy," said the bartender. "Little early for this."

"I don't care. I just got fired."

He shook his head. "Sorry to hear that."

"You wouldn't be hiring, would you? I'd even bus tables."

"No one is now, I'm afraid. Sorry."

What am I going to do? He intended to bury it all in his beer, but the liquid made him feel worse. It did not deaden the pain but created a lump in his throat. He nearly asked for a third beer when he heard the door open and close. And then he saw her. Jo. Why would Jo be at a saloon of all places on the globe? These places were off-limits to Christian people. It was beneath them. Saloons were only good for lowlifes like himself.

Instead Jo walked over and sat down beside him. If he were not losing his senses now in the beer, mixed with his problems, he would have considered this another miracle of God. But it also made him feel strange, too, knowing Jo's Christianity and her seeing him nurse his troubles over a beer.

"I'll have a root beer," she told the bartender.

"How'd you know I was here?"

"I followed you. Took me a bit to get the nerve to walk in here. This isn't my usual hangout."

"You shouldn't be in here at all," he said shortly.

"Neither should you. Look, I knew this was coming. Todd told me about it a few days ago. He likes you a lot, Dan. More than you know. But until this blows over, we felt it best to get you out of the picture."

"So will you go out of business?"

"I hope not. I pray not. But we're already feeling it. Word is out there and our trips are already down. People are canceling trips. Which is why we had to let Evan go, too. We'd hired him just before you."

Despite his own troubles, Dan realized that Jo had troubles of her own.

"I'm sorry this happened," she added.

"I am, too. I gave it all I had. I tried to do the best I could."

"Todd knows that."

"But it wasn't enough to see this through. I mean, to let me go just like that." He snapped his fingers. "I went to see Chris, thinking maybe I could find work at his place. Of course, now he knows what happened."

"Oh, Dan!" she groaned. "Why did you do that? Now it's going to make things worse."

"Because I need the work to pay my bills, Jo!" His voice was louder than he intended, but he didn't care. He wasn't going to be blamed for going to Chris. Or anything else. "I need work. I got bills coming. Man, what a time to lose a job."

"I thought you had savings."

"I used to, but. . ." He refused to tell her how he'd spent it all, everything his father had given him when he left Virginia. Gone to personal things like going out. The Jeep. The house and everything inside it. "I've got bills due.

I've got to find something quick."

"C'mon, let's go see if we can find some leads." She downed her root beer and tugged on his hand.

Dan didn't budge. For some reason, Jo's willingness to help rubbed him the wrong way, and he didn't know why. "Look, you don't have to pity me. I can take care of myself. I'll be fine."

"Dan, I'm just trying to help."

"Thanks, but I'll be fine on my own." He managed a lopsided grin before standing and leaving the saloon. He didn't need advice or anyone's help at this stage. He'd made it once in Moab; he'd make it again. But the wall of doubt was rising quicker than his confidence.

Chapter 11

Life on the fast track had suddenly come to a screeching halt, and Dan felt numb by it. For the first time, he watched other rafting companies load up their vehicles with equipment and personnel, but he was not among the ones helping. Or guiding trips. Or setting up camp and leading night stalks with the kids. Despite his best effort, scouring out at least a dozen outfitters, no one wanted to hire him. Word had gotten around about the lawsuit, and somehow they believed he was at fault.

"Can't take the risk," said one owner, his shades hanging from the strap at his neck. He was wearing fancy board shorts and a sleeveless shirt.

"I'm not a risk. Look, you can try me free for a week. If you like what I do, we can make it permanent. I've got a license and everything."

The guy shook his head. "It's all over that you were involved in the act that led to the lawsuit at Red Canyon Adventures. There's no way I can take a chance like that with my company."

Dan couldn't believe it. Now he was branded a work hazard all because he was learning the ropes that first day under Travis's tutelage. Travis had a job and he didn't. How he wanted to trash the guy's name from here to Salt Lake City. The more he thought about it, the angrier he became. The guy who was to blame got off scot-free and even had a good job to boot. Dan was innocent, and yet he was the one with the brand on his neck.

He took the Jeep that day and scouted out the hidden places in and around Moab. But even the interesting rock formations and town hangouts failed to comfort him. No longer did he lead enthusiastic groups down the Colorado, hearing their exclamations along with the thrill of the moment as the rafts bobbed over the rapids. Instead he listened to the anxiety of his heart thumping madly in his chest and the endless questions circulating in his brain, wondering how this could have happened.

To make matters worse, he still felt guilty over the way he'd treated Jo at the saloon. For having had such an interest in her in the past, to cast her away like he did went beyond his comprehension. He should've accepted her advice with open arms. She might've had some ideas about employment. She'd been here much longer than him anyway. And he threw her away like a hunk of scrap. Many times he wanted to call her cell or even knock on the door of her apartment. But instead he sat brooding in his house, looking at his tablet, wondering how much longer he would have these comforts before he must sell things to make ends meet.

Dan sighed. He'd had such wild expectations for a future in Utah from the glossy pictures and attention-grabbing ads. A new home away from the old. Now he considered it all. The old homestead was never like this. Oh, he'd had his brotherly spats with Rob, which amounted more to jealousy than anything. He'd had his times of boredom working the family farm. He poked fun at Mom and Pop who did everything by the Holy Book, so to speak. Here in Moab, he wanted to make a name for himself. To show everyone, the world, himself, God, that he could make it and make it big. Now what did he have to show for it? Zip, zero, zilch.

A knock on the door drew him out of his contemplation. Surely it couldn't be the employment office with news of a job for him. Maybe Todd was coming to relent and offer him his old job back. He'd even cook if that's what it came down to. Dan opened the door to reveal Jo. Normally an encounter like this should have knocked him off his feet and allowed love to take over. But he looked at her as if she had a sign around her neck saying, *You deserve it. If only you'd kept your big paws off me.*

"Hi, Dan."

"Hey." He made no move to invite her in. Instead he moved to the two deck chairs on the porch and plopped down in one. She followed suit.

"We missed you at game night. All the guys were asking where you were, especially at the Monopoly table. I told them that Todd had to let you go."

Great. Now all of Moab knows. Mr. Big Shot is now The Biggest Loser. And it wasn't because of a weight-loss competition on reality TV—he was a loser in life. "Thanks a bunch."

"Dan, c'mon. You can't do this alone. There are people who care about you. By the way, Brian said to give you this. He saw it on a bulletin board in town." She handed the paper to him.

Dan took it halfheartedly and stared at it. It described an employment opportunity in the sanitation department. "You're kidding, right? Isn't this the same thing as a garbage collector?"

"Dan, it's a job. Moab is pretty short on them these days. You need to take whatever is out there. It's only temporary, just to make ends meet until something else opens up. Or this thing with Todd blows over and business picks up, which we hope it does soon."

Dan perked up at this. Maybe there was a light at the end of this dark tunnel. "You mean Todd might hire me back?"

"I don't know. We're having the case reviewed to see where it stands and where we stand as a company. We probably won't know anything for a while. And I'm sure you're gonna need money soon."

"But there has to be something better than a garbage worker. Hauling trash cans. . . You've got to be kidding."

"You can try and ask around, Dan, but all I've seen is part-time work. And part-time is not going to pay the bills, I'm sure."

Her gaze drifted to his fine ranch house, which among other things had a mortgage attached to it. He couldn't argue with her. If there was one thing Dan couldn't do, that was default on his loans and have more bad stuff attached to his name, such as a bad credit rating. Besides, this was sure to be temporary. Todd might hire him back at a moment's notice. Or something else would open up. Maybe if he was patient enough, one of Jo's famous miracles from God would pop up. Like the miracle at the RV park when they ran into those girls from the very family he needed to find.

He took out his cell phone and dialed the number on the paper while Jo sat there expectantly. He spoke to the guy in charge. "It's not a job most people will do," the man said, "but it's good pay." Dan noted the details of the job in his brain. He hung up and pocketed the phone.

"Well?"

"They need workers. It looks promising."

Jo jumped to her feet as if he had just been given the word of the day with sunbeams attached. "I just knew it! I know this is God."

He stared. "This is my answer from God, to demote me from river guide to trash hauler?"

"No, that He provided you with work. It's His provision, Dan, and His blessing, too. If only you don't get too close-minded to see it."

He felt the defenses rising quickly, like metal barricades. "Let's not go down that road, please. I'm not in the mood for a religious lecture."

"It's not a religious lecture. There is more to life than you or me or anything. You need to see the big picture. Other things are at work here. All this may not be just for you."

"Really. Who else is gonna benefit?"

"There's eternal things. Trials come up in life for a reason. They test us and shape us into the person God wants us to be. And it's not only us who are affected, but others, too."

Dan again felt his irritation on the rise. Jo was trying to be helpful, but her words were more akin to rubbing red desert rock in raw wounds. "Look, I've got some stuff to do. The guy wants to interview me as soon as possible. Guess he needs people to do his dirty work for him." His face scrunched up at the words. "Sorry, bad pun."

"Okay, see you later." She didn't seem put out, but he was definitely putting her out. Or rather putting out her godly ideas that were grating on him, reminding him of his lack of interest in religious things. He thought of dear Mom, picturing her on her knees in his old room, praying for her wayward son. Maybe even praying that something like this would happen in his life. That he would rise to the pinnacle of his career and then hit bottom in a Dumpster along with the rest of the garbage. He wondered how he could ever come out smelling like a rose after all this.

The next afternoon Dan arrived home, newly instated in the trash collecting business as garbage man number five. There could be worse things in life, he reasoned, like no employment at all. He should be grateful for small things, however small they seemed to be. But he found no comfort. He'd come here to make a living by leading rafting trips. Now he would make his mark on Moab by dealing in their trash.

He turned on his computer tablet to find a friend request from Jo. He accepted it. And lo and behold, the chat box popped up.

So how did the interview go? she typed in.

Got the job.

Wow, that's great.

What's so great about collecting trash? Please enlighten me.

I've heard you can tell a lot about people by their trash.

So I'm going to study food wrappers to see what they eat or the magazines they're dumping out. Better than interviewing them to get the inside scoop, I suppose.

I was trying to be funny. I guess I wasn't.

Dan thought about that. No, I guess I didn't think this would happen to me. I had such great expectations about everything.

Sometimes things happen when you don't expect it.

Tell me about it.

The chat box remained empty. He nearly closed it down when another message popped up.

So how about some ice cream when I get off work? You know the old saying, life's short, eat dessert first.

Ice cream. What a novel idea. Dan sighed, wishing he didn't feel so sour. Sure, why not? he typed.

Okay. Meet you at the shop around 6:00.

He closed down communications. Jo really was a special person. And he was realizing more and more how much he didn't deserve her. Oh sure, he once thought himself the perfect male, ready to capture a woman's heart. But Jo was too good for him. Too innocent. He should do the right thing and allow her to find the right man for her life. He certainly wasn't the one.

For the first time, Dan climbed in his Jeep feeling humbled. He wasn't all giddy, flexing his biceps, his head held high, looking down on others who were worming their way through life. He thought of Rob then. How he looked with contempt on his brother's life. But Rob had stuck it out on the family farm. He was there helping out while Dan wanted to escape it all for some dumb dream. Dan knew he should have waited to see if this path to Utah was the right one rather than going headlong into something that may have been wrong from the beginning. He got a feeling that he should talk to Brian sometime about this stuff. Maybe let him sift through these thoughts and come up with a solution. But right now Dan punched a number on his cell.

"Hey, Rob? Hey, it's Dan." He sensed the surprise over the phone. "Oh, me? Doing okay, I guess. Just wondering how things were going on the farm." He listened as Rob told him of some minor things happening—machinery that needed fixing and then Pop sick for a time with something like the flu. "Well, glad he's better." Pause. "No, I hadn't seen the weather. I sure hope you get some rain soon. Man, six weeks is a long time without any." Pause. "Yeah, it's dry here, too. Never rains, but that's normal." Rob then talked at length about the girl he'd been seeing, one Dan barely remembered. Dan saw that he'd arrived at his destination—the ice cream shop. "Hey, I'll have to catch you later. Good talking to you."

Jo walked up to the Jeep.

"Guess what? I just called my brother." He hoped for a pat on the back, a verbal "Good for you" or something. Instead she said nothing. He shrugged and followed her into the shop.

"My treat," Jo added.

"Thanks. That makes me feel like a man." She gave him a look, and he responded with a smile. "I'm not being very funny. Really, I appreciate everything you're doing, Jo. I'm sorry my attitude is so bad. I'm just trying to work things out."

"Yeah," she said absently as if lost in thought. He wondered what spawned the sudden disquiet on her part as they both ordered sundaes. He thought she would be jumping up and down over his family contacts. He stepped back to mentally analyze it. Likely Jo was going through things, too. She must have burdens in her heart. The lawsuit thing wasn't just about him. Her cousin's company was affected. *Get your eyes on someone else for a change, Dan. And that doesn't mean looking at the body. The heart would do fine right about now.*

They wandered over with their sundaes to a corner table, the same table where they ate once before. Maybe they should carve their initials in the tabletop or something. "So how are you doing?" Dan asked. "All we've done is talk about me."

"Oh, I'm fine. But I was glad to hear that the job worked out. Which trash are you picking up, residential or commercial?"

"Residential. I'm one of those happy guys that roll out trash cans to the garbage truck or something to that effect. The manager wasn't too specific on official duties, which is fine with me. But hey, since I didn't do so well guiding a raft, maybe I can learn to drive a truck!" He laughed in spite of himself. "Might as well make the most of every opportunity. Just think. Here I am in the red rocks, the arches, and the glory of the Colorado River, and what am I doing? Basking in the garbage of Moab. Yo, baby."

Jo remained silent, and again Dan chastised himself for being full of it as usual. He simmered down enough to ask, "So are you still doing any trips?"

"We try. Our business is down 50 percent. We get people wandering into the store, too, which helps."

"Boy, I miss that place. And grabbing my daily drink and energy bar. But most of all, I miss the family trips. Taking the kids on night stalks. Remember that one you and I did together? And you taught me how to grill the perfect steak."

"It was a nice trip. You were excellent at making the salad."

"All I really want to do is those raft trips. But right now I'll even make salads and do equipment detail. Why I got demoted to garbage detail, I'm not sure. Something has to work out, huh? I mean, like you said, there's got to be a reason for this."

"That's a good way to look at it, Dan." She scraped out the last bit of ice cream coated with fudge from the bowl.

"You're really quiet today. I hope I'm not lording over you with my mouth."

"No, just thinking. When you said how you called your brother today, it got me thinking about my brother. I haven't talked to him in ages."

Dan tried not show it, but inside everything suddenly stopped. He recalled then what she'd shared about her past and her older brother who took her in when her parents kicked her out of the house. He decided to go gently. "I thought it would be hard. But I just picked up the cell and called. Rob was real cool about it. Talked nonstop about his girlfriend. I didn't say anything about you, of course, because I know you're not into that. I mean, the girlfriend issue and all. We're just friends."

"Thanks, I appreciate that. I never know where things stand with you. One day we can be having a good friendship; the next, you're making another move."

"You don't have to worry about that. The only move I'll be making is to the garbage truck. I've learned my lesson, I think. Or whatever. I'm not exactly sure what the lesson is in all this. To look before I leap into the Colorado River, maybe? Anyway, I was glad I talked to Rob. Maybe you should try calling your brother. Just to say hi. Can't hurt, and it might help."

He saw something flash in her coffee-colored eyes; a certain glint to them. Then they softened as if she were considering his suggestion. Could it be he'd finally had something to offer that might help Jo? Maybe he wasn't such a bad guy after all. Maybe there were some redeeming factors about him.

"I don't know. We haven't talked in so long. I don't even think he'll recognize my voice."

"Sure he will. You're related, for better or for worse. Well, that's a marriage thing. But you know what I mean. Honestly, I couldn't stand Rob. I thought what he was doing in life amounted to nothing. But he really likes what he does, even if it's harvesting peanuts. And it helps Pop out."

"Well, I didn't leave because I was jealous of my brother. It was for other reasons."

Dan felt the wave of happiness in him come to a screeching halt. Something rose up in him, something he hadn't planned on. "What makes you think I was jealous of Rob? I hated what he did is all."

"Of course you were jealous. I know the sibling rivalry stuff. One parent giving more attention to the other sibling, making you feel inferior, like you can't do anything right. That they will never be happy with what you're doing. You can never please them enough, so you try and please yourself to make up for it."

Dan's knees bobbed back and forth under the table. He felt a sudden chill as if something major had happened. Had he been jealous about his father's feelings for Rob and his attention in the family? Maybe he was trying to hunt down approval to make up for what he thought he lacked on Pop's part. All he knew was that another whammy had just been hurled his way, and he wasn't sure how to handle it. "Okay, fine. But what about you? What do you have to deal with concerning your family?"

"I have plenty to deal with, Dan, but I don't want to get into it. I have others who are helping me in those areas, thanks." She stood to her feet. "Well, I'd better go on home."

"I'll drive you."

"That's okay. I like to walk. See you around."

Dan stared after her, watching her petite form and curvy legs walk to the door of the shop. Her ponytail swished as she opened it and hurried out. He wondered what thoughts lurked beneath that ponytail. Deep thoughts that she couldn't yet share with him. If only he didn't find himself in his own personal storm, he might have been able to offer some wisdom. But he had to get his act together first. Find out what was holding him back from being available for Jo and from having her trust him with her personal struggles. He thought he knew. . .but at that moment, the God issue still scared him. *I'm not ready to make that step. Yet. . .*

Chapter 12

The first week on the job seemed to last forever. Instead of the feel of the river and pleasant water cooling him off, Dan sweated buckets while his flesh fried in the hot sun. Not to mention what garbage did in the heat. His nose would never be the same after smelling things souring and decaying. Dragging another huge garbage can toward the back of the truck, Dan decided nothing could be worse than this. He wanted to quit after day two, but when he found his bank account down to nothing, he knew he had no choice. His concern mounted over how he would make ends meet. As it was, he wondered how he would get the money to make the payments until the first paycheck rolled in. The money from Todd paid a few bills, but now he had nothing.

Dan sighed, taking a break to guzzle water out of a cooler tucked in the cab of the truck. The driver, Charles, who'd been at this stuff for years, he said, pointed to the road.

"Get going, Dan. We're already behind schedule."

"C'mon, I need a break," Dan groaned.

"You told me you needed this job. So you'd better keep hauling cans, or you'll be out of a job real quick."

Dan bit back a retort and walked down the road to roll over the next container. He stopped when he saw two people on the front porch. A man and a woman, both wearing swimsuits, sat in lounge chairs opposite each other. They then turned and looked at him. He thought he heard one of them laugh but couldn't tell. He averted his gaze and rolled the can along the street toward the open end of the truck where the odor nearly knocked his dirty sandals off his feet.

"Hey, Dan!" a voice called out.

He whirled, wondering if he'd actually heard his name or if the garbage was calling to him. The guy bounded down the driveway, dressed in board shorts and wearing shades. Dan thought about his expensive shades and decided he ought to put them on craigslist to help pay the electric bill.

"What are you doing, man?" Travis stood before him, wearing a grin.

"I'm having fun," Dan said sourly. "Looks like you're having fun, too. The real kind."

"It's my day off." He looked at Dan, the garbage can, and then the truck. "You're kidding. You're working with the sanitation department now?"

"Why not? It's a living. Besides, I hear you can learn all kinds of things about people from their trash." He opened the lid to the can. "Anything I should know about you in here? I suppose it's all legal, too."

The smile disappeared from his face for only a moment before a grin returned. "Wow, I really thought Todd would hire you back. He liked what you did for the company. Kind of got to me a couple of times, but hey, having him fire me actually saved me. Got my job with Chris, and now I'm secure."

He didn't say it, but Dan could finish Travis's thought pattern. *You got yourself let go when no one was hiring. Better you than me.* "Well, things tend to work out in the end," Dan added in a burst of faith.

Travis swiped his sandal across the ground, stirring up red dust. "Too bad it happened. Guess if Todd had kept his nose out of other people's business, he wouldn't be in the mess he's in. He got what was coming to him."

"Hey Dan, get back to work!" Charles called from the driver's window. "You're putting us way behind schedule!"

"You'd better get back to your garbage detail, Dan. Don't want to keep the cans waiting."

The snicker grated on him more than a cheese grater rubbing against his skin. He felt anger burn in him as well as questions. Like what Travis said about Todd. He knew the company Travis worked for had problems with Todd, especially over the salmonella incident. He had to wonder if there was some correlation between that and the current lawsuit.

"You'd better quit with the socializing, kid," Charles said, scratching his head beneath his hat. "That's the problem with hiring you young kids. You don't know what hard work means."

"I've known plenty of hard work in my life," Dan retorted. "I worked my old man's peanut field for years, since I was seven years old."

"Then why are you here and not back there helping him out? That kind of thing usually stays in the family."

"I—I've got a brother who seems to know it all." His voice faded away as he went to roll over another can. Why was he here anyway? That was a good question. Why had he sacrificed the good life with the family—everything he needed, like shelter, food, clothes, peace—for this place? Sure it had been the lure of the river. The glory of rafting. The feel of being a big shot behind the paddle. But what did it bring him now? And especially this mess of the lawsuit and maybe even a rival company out to bury Todd in the red Utah dust.

When they finally finished the route for the day, Dan decided to give Jo a call and tell her what he'd learned from Travis. Or what he thought he might have learned. The cell rang, but she didn't answer. He left her a message on voice mail. He wished he had time to go over to the store, but he hadn't set foot there since the day he was let go. Too many painful memories and probably leftover anger with Todd as well, though now it seemed to have lessened. In fact, he felt sorry for the guy who had enemies out to get him. Dan sure didn't want to be in that kind of predicament, though he didn't relish his current predicament either.

Right now he had other things to worry about, like his finances. He decided to be bold and ask his boss for an advance on his pay. He had bills nearly overdue, like his cell phone and the electric bill. He had to get his hands on some money, and another week without income wouldn't cut it.

Dan ventured inside the building, stood before the wooden door for a few moments to gather his courage, then knocked.

"What do you want?" the boss called out. "I'm on the phone."

Oh, man. "It's Dan Mallory. I. . .uh, I need to talk to you about something, Mr. O'Donnell."

He heard the man talking loud and fast, discussing dinner plans and the drink he wanted after work. The phone slammed. "All right, come in."

The door creaked open to reveal the man lighting up a cigarette. The office was cluttered with all kinds of things Dan couldn't begin to sort out in his beleaguered mind. Most of it probably deserved to be part of the trash they hauled. "Sir, I have a question. I'm, well, I'm running short on cash right now, having switched jobs and all. I was wondering if I could get an advance on my paycheck."

"I pay on the fifteenth of the month," the man stated, blowing out a puff of smoke.

Dan tried not to sneeze as the smoke tickled his nose, and his throat turned raw. "I know it's unusual, but I've got some bills due right now and—"

"Gotta budget, kid. That's what I keep telling my eighteen-year-old who goes and spends his cash like it's water. Gotta save. And you get paid on the fifteenth. That's that."

He felt a chill descend on him despite the stuffiness inside the office. "Sir, I—"

"Look, go have a bake sale. Wash cars. But that's how I run things here. I don't give handouts. You get paid when you work and on my schedule." The man's glare showed Dan the conversation had ended.

Dan meekly closed the door. In his mind he saw the bills lining the counter at home, all with ominous due dates on them, outlined in red. He was going to be late paying them, and even three weeks late on some. What was he going to do?

He thought then of people he could ask for a loan. Maybe someone at church, but he couldn't bring himself to do that. He could never ask Pop either. As it was, he'd taken his inheritance and spent it all. Jo didn't have any, especially with the way business had dropped off in recent weeks. She was surely hurting financially, too.

He strode outside and looked around until his gaze rested on his Jeep. There was only one thing he could do—take Mr. O'Donnell's advice. He needed money, and he needed it now. Selling other things in classifieds would take time. He got in and drove to a used car lot. From the dust the Jeep had been purchased, and now it would return to the red dust of a used car lot in Moab.

An hour later, he had lost another two thousand dollars with the trade-in, but at least he had the cash to pay the bills. But none of this really helped. He was sinking into the mud, or rather, the dust, as it was too dry around here for anything else. He was being swallowed up by things he couldn't control. As he walked along, he began to cough. He smelled garbage. He saw a few garbage cans still sitting by the curb, and he shuddered. What had he become? What had his decisions led him to? They were supposed to lead him to Shangri-la, but instead, they led him to the bowels of life and the stench to match.

As he walked along staring at the red ground, he thought of green fields. The smell of the rich earth. The pleasant breeze. The joy of a harvest. He was back in Virginia at Pop's peanut fields. Pop was coming home that day after seeing the first harvest. He was there to divvy up the money with Dan and Rob after going to the bank. And Mom had ordered an extra large pizza to celebrate. His favorite, too. A meatza with everything on it.

Now Dan reluctantly passed Zack's and their pizza, along with the Moab Diner. There was no money for pizza or a taco supreme but enough for boxes of mac and cheese, which he bought at the store the other day. His legs ached as he walked, and he realized he'd been on his feet all day. Charles complained he should have work boots and not the fancy river sandals. And it was a long walk from his place of work to home. A very long walk. Several miles at least, or it felt like it.

Now he realized what Jo went through. She had no vehicle and walked everywhere. She lived a life of humble means. He paused to check his cell, which had remained silent all day. She'd still not returned his call, which was strange. She'd vanished like everyone else, no longer interested in keeping company with a garbage collector. And he couldn't blame her.

He continued to ponder it all when he noticed a figure in the distance. He stopped short, recognizing the familiar brown shorts, the hair caught up in a ponytail, and a purse in the shape of a small backpack. It was Jo, and she was laughing at something, or rather, with someone. And it wasn't the fact of her smiling face but who she was smiling at. Some guy he'd never seen before. Tall. Suntanned. Clad in shorts and a polo shirt. The guy said something. She laughed again and waved her hand. They began walking. Dan knew he had no business following them, but he did anyway. They soon headed into Jo and Dan's private haven, of all places in Moab. The ice cream shop.

Dan stopped dead in his tracks. Peering into the window, he saw them order his and Jo's favorite treat, two sundaes. He licked his dry lips, wishing he were feeling the cold creaminess running down his throat. But soon the feeling became replaced by anger. Frustration. Bitterness. Pain. And the feeling of a very dry mouth. Jo had found someone with the right look, driving the right car, who had all the right stuff and a wallet loaded with cash. Now that Dan was in the garbage business, she had linked arms with someone else.

He whirled and continued the long walk back home. But even the word *home* didn't feel right. This place was not home anymore. He'd tried to make Moab a home. He'd given it his all, his soul even, to make this place his. But Jo had warned him long ago that he was only bringing his problems with him. That no matter how far he strayed from Virginia, all the things he thought he left behind still remained. His dissatisfaction with life. His search for true meaning. What he was supposed to do. How he was supposed to live.

Dan finally arrived home an hour later, his feet aching, dirty, and blistered, vowing to find himself a clunker somewhere if there was any money left from paying the bills. He had several boxes of mac and cheese in the otherwise bare cupboard and made himself a large potful. He then went to check in on the social network and saw a friend request from Rob, along with a note.

Hey, bro. Glad we talked. I'm thinking of scrounging together some money and coming out to see what you do there in Moab with the rafting and all. Let me know when would be a good week. Maybe you can get me a good deal on a rafting trip.

Dan stared. Rob wanted to come out here and see what he did? He could see it now. The snickering Travis offered today would pale by comparison. He'd hear Rob's laughter and "I told you so" and "You never had it so good in Virginia," and other assorted sayings to make him feel lower than the landfill site. He accepted Rob's friend request but did not answer him right away. Instead he sat back to think about a response. If he didn't answer, Rob might book a flight immediately. Whether he said something now or later, Rob would eventually find out he was a simple trash collector. If only there was some way he could find another job in a rafting company somewhere. He straightened. Maybe Jo and Todd would let him take a raft for one day. He could pretend to be a part of the company. Show off his stuff to Rob and then send him on his way.

Instead he slumped down in the chair. Like that was the solution, pretending everything was fine and dandy when it wasn't. Living a lie, which is what he'd been doing for eighteen months. He took up the tablet and composed a message.

> *Hey, Rob. Sorry, but now's not a good time for a visit. Things haven't worked out right with the rafting company, and I was let go. So I won't be able to take you up on a rafting trip right now.*

He conveniently left out the part about the lawsuit and his new job. Rob didn't need to know the particulars. He read it over and hit the ENTER key. At least he was able to confess that he was no longer working for Red Canyon Adventures.

Rob was online, for a message came back within a few minutes.

> *Sorry to hear about your situation. It's been tough here, too, and with the drought, Pop is looking at a major loss. I'm already looking for another job.*

With these words, Dan sensed a change in his attitude. The feelings of anger and jealousy and the sibling rivalry that always reared its ugly head when they came together began to fade. Now he was seeing a brother. Someone who cared. Someone who wanted to share in life's difficulties. And he felt something else, too. Shame on his part that he wasn't there to help Mom and Pop in their time of need. That while they were hurting, he was having his own pity party in the red clay. He'd not even spoken to them since Christmas, he thought. He couldn't remember the last time. It was amazing to see how things that once tore at him now opened his heart. Like his family.

Dan leaned back against the chair, thinking about him and Rob in a tent in the backyard, tossing peanut shells at each other. He was adrift then in memory, to water floats down the James River, a lesson with Pop behind the wheel of the tractor and the car, a Mother's Day brunch he and Rob fixed for Mom. . .

A knock came on the door. Dan jumped and looked at the time. He'd been dozing for a half hour, his head on the table. He came groggily to his feet, swaying. It was already 7:00 p.m.

A knock came again.

He stumbled forward, wiping his face, and opened the door. Jo stood there with the aroma of Chinese food wafting in the air. "Hi, Dan."

He stared from the top of her head to the leather sandals on her feet. "What are you doing here?"

She stepped back. "Well, hi to you, too. What kind of a greeting is that?"

"Sorry about that." He stepped aside.

She walked in and went to the kitchen table where the bills were spread out. "Paying your bills?"

"Yeah," he said, plunking down into a chair. He put away the computer tablet.

"Don't worry. It will get better. How's the job?"

"Nice and smelly." He inhaled the Chinese food as she opened the little white cartons to reveal shrimp lo mein, moo goo gai pan, rice, and egg rolls. "I don't have a lot of money. . . ," he began.

"My treat. I wasn't in the mood to eat alone."

"I didn't think you were alone," he added a bit stiffly, flying to his feet to retrieve some plates and forks. At once the vision of her with the guy at the ice cream store took over.

"What's that supposed to mean?"

Dan shrugged. "I saw you at our hangout—the ice cream shop today."

Jo stared, puzzled, until her eyes widened. "Oh, you mean you saw Neil and me?"

"Sure, you and Neil. Is he the new guy Todd hired?"

"What? Of course not. He's Brian's brother."

Great. Brian had a holier-than-thou brother. And now the holy brother had his holy hooks in Jo. So much for that. Easy come—well, it wasn't easy by any means—easy go.

"I was showing him around town. And he was hot, so we went for ice cream." Her head tipped to one side. "Dan? Do you have a problem?"

I have multiple problems. I want you to be my girlfriend, but I can't begin to keep you with the kind of life I'm leading right now. And now a holy brother comes to town, probably with lots of cash to treat you right, standing on a good, solid foundation, leaving me out and him in. Dan looked at the Chinese food that was slowly starting to cool, but nothing came out of his mouth.

"Neil is a lawyer, Dan," she explained to his unspoken inquiry. "He's going to help Todd look over our situation. He actually flew in to be with Brian, and it so happened he had some spare time to help out our company." She paused then added, "Before he flies back home to his family in Texas."

"His family lives in Texas?" Dan repeated in a high-pitched voice.

"His wife and two daughters. Yes, he's married, so you can relax." And suddenly she was grinning as if enjoying this little game.

If Dan wasn't so famished and Jo wasn't who she was, he would have taken her in his arms right then and planted a big fat kiss on her juicy red lips. Instead he ate his egg roll before commenting. "So you think it's funny to lead me on like that?"

"It was kind of neat watching you squirm. I'll have to admit, I've never had a guy do that."

"Sure you have. That James guy."

"Are you kidding? He didn't care about me. He had his drug habit. It's kind of nice, actually, to have a guy jealous. Makes me feel wanted." She ended it with a giggle before tasting her moo goo gai pan.

He would have enjoyed this time more if not for the present circumstances of poverty and trash collecting and everything else grotesque. And feeling as if he could never match up to Jo's expectations. Yet she did come by with a great Chinese dinner, which he now took over to the microwave to reheat. He then volunteered to heat up hers as well. When they sat down, something passed between them. What was it about sharing meals that brought about a certain bonding?

He shared then about his meeting with Travis earlier and his suspicions.

"I'm not going to worry about it. Trying to make a connection between the two scenarios of Todd and Chris will only make things worse. I'm just glad Neil's here. It shows God is on our side. We can be victorious through Him." She cast him a look when he stayed silent. "Yes?"

"I'm just thinking how much I feel like a loser right now. Cool is out and poor is in. Maybe you'd do better to hang out with the lawyer types. I know this Neil guy is married, but you know what I mean. I'm sure there's plenty to choose from, or at least from the rafting guys in Moab."

"Dan, c'mon. You're in some tough times right now, sure. Lots of people are in your situation. That doesn't make you any less of a quality human being, despite other flawed areas."

"Aha, I knew we would get into it. What flawed areas in particular are you referring to?"

"Well, like your Christian walk. Before you can do anything else in life, you really need to see where you stand with God and what He is in your life. If you want to talk to Brian about it, I'm sure he would be glad to help."

Dan paused to consider her words. He admitted he did murmur a prayer or two these days. He had no choice, with his ever-shrinking wallet and ever-increasing bills. But then there were the feelings of anger over Travis. The disgust at his present job. Wondering if God was saying from the great throne room of heaven, "You deserve it all, Dan, you poor man. Leaving your family in the peanut field to come here to seek your fortune. And for what? Look at what's left."

"I can see you're thinking about it," Jo added.

"I'm trying to sort things out, yeah. But religion is something I need to do on my own schedule. No one else's, you know what I mean?"

"The only religion you need is what lies between the covers of a Bible. In there is everything for salvation and the true meaning of life. Our purpose for existing."

Jo's words stayed with Dan long after she said good night. He had a Bible somewhere, the one he used as a prop the night he went to Jo's apartment, seeking answers. But now he really needed those answers. Maybe it would do him good to look at the Bible and see what it had to say. Something different might come out of an exercise like that.

Chapter 13

Jo always believed there was more to life than what meets the eye. God did not make mistakes. Despite everything that had happened with Dan, the job, Todd, her life, God knew it all. He knew what would happen, which people would be involved, and the outcome. And right now, Jo's thoughts and prayers were centered on a particular outcome. She wanted to see good come of all that was happening, even if Dan couldn't see the good right now. And sometimes she struck gold with seeing it, too. Now was the time for faith to take over and trust for a godly outcome.

Not a day would go by when Jo wasn't thinking about Dan or praying for him. At first she found him rather obnoxious. A bit full of himself and his own desires in life. But these days she was seeing him in a new light. He'd been handed a raw deal, finding himself saddled with a job he disliked and barely able to make ends meet. But good could come of something like that. The situation could move him to do some soul-searching where the things of God were concerned and place him at a point where God could reach him.

Jo thought about it as she sat before the silent cash register. With their rafting business slowed to a crawl because of the lawsuit, just a few visitors came by to look at the leftover merchandise. Only a few employees remained, with barely enough to cover the rafting trips they did conduct. When they didn't have the personnel to do extra trips, Jo asked the visitors for their information so they could be alerted when the trips became available. She hoped they would soon be able to hire employees back, especially Dan.

At that moment a family of four came strolling in with smiles on their faces. The kids immediately headed for the aquatic toys while Dad and Mom came up to speak with Jo. "We were here last year for the family rafting trip, and we just had to do it again with your guide named Dan. It was a marvelous time, and the kids loved it."

Jo sighed. Another family requesting Dan's presence. "I'm sorry, but he no longer works here."

Mom and Dad stared at each other in surprise. "Oh no," Mom groaned. "The kids asked for him."

"This is the only trip the kids wanted to do," the dad explained. "They just loved Dan. He took them on that night hike or something by the river. They said that was their favorite part. He's a natural at it."

Jo smiled and offered them another trip with a different guide, which they reluctantly accepted. The kids then came over with their selections—aquatic glasses and bubbles. Jo liked seeing the cash register open with business, but even more than that, she liked what the mom and dad had to say about Dan. With every word they spoke, Jo sensed something welling up in her heart. *Dan would make a great dad*, she mused before straightening in her seat. He would make a great dad? *That means he has to be a husband.* Jo shook her head, just as Todd walked in.

"What's the matter?" he asked.

"Another family came in here wanting a trip with Dan. They said he was the best." She squinted as she looked at Todd. "Isn't there any chance we can hire him back? He's miserable as a garbage collector."

"Not until things have cleared up. I can't take the chance."

"I'm not asking, I'm pleading. People love him. The kids think he's the greatest. He's a hard worker, Todd."

"I know he's a hard worker."

"And he had nothing to do with the lawsuit."

"I know that, too. I'm just trying to figure out what to do. We're running into trouble financially as it is. I'm not sure how we can keep our head above water."

"Todd, if you advertise this as a family-oriented rafting company, with overnight trips and night stalks to complement it, you're going to generate more business."

"I can't just do that. I do need some high-level trips like Cataract Canyon for the college crowd."

"But I think we should gear this company toward the family. Like those water parks and other places that are family friendly. We could get some playground equipment, too."

"Oh, Jolene, honestly." He rolled his eyes, but a smile remained on his face.

"I'm just thinking out loud. But one thing you really need to consider is Dan. It's a waste having him deal in Moab's trash. He's got talent that our company can use."

"Yeah, and he knows it, too."

"But he's going through a lot right now. A complete spiritual makeover is in full progress, I'd say."

Todd's eyebrow rose. "I'm sure you've had a hand in that department."

"I've shared about God, if that's what you mean. Same as I'd do with you, if you wouldn't give me the I-can't-listen-to-that-kind-of-thing routine."

"Believe me, Jolene, I've done my share of thinking these past few weeks. It was an answer to prayer when your youth pastor's brother came by, willing to help me with the lawsuit." He paused. "From what Neil is saying, he believes he can get the case dropped due to insufficient evidence. He plans on contacting the lawyer of the insurance company to see if the details can be worked out to our benefit."

"Wow, that's great!" She stood and gave him a hug.

"Guess you have it in good with that church of yours and the Man upstairs."

Jo sighed and shook her head. "Man upstairs, ha. He's also downstairs and all around. And He cares, Todd."

Todd took off before she could say any more. Hope was rekindled with Todd's announcement about the lawsuit. Hope was also growing to a roaring blaze where Dan was concerned. Especially on the heels of the family visit to the shop, with the mom and dad praising his ability. She ought to go see him and tell him. Give him something positive to gnaw on. Hope deferred makes the heart sick. But in this case, hope could bring health and healing to a man's troubled heart. And Jo couldn't wait to give the remedy.

❧

Jo drove up to Dan's house in Todd's car. The place appeared quiet to her, even melancholic in a way. The windows were dark. Not a flower could be seen anywhere, though guys rarely had flowers anyway. A cloud of depression seemed to hang over the place. How she wished she'd stopped and bought a basket of flowers to hang on his porch. Flowers to Jo symbolized hope. She didn't see many flowers in Moab except for those that came out in spring, struggling to find life in Utah's red soil. But the markets still carried baskets of flowers that people often displayed in front of their homes.

Jo backed out of the driveway with an idea in mind. She hastened for the nearest market and wasted no time buying a basket. Driving back, she saw a figure marching down the sidewalk, head held high. She pushed down the button of the window, receiving a blast of hot air. "Hi, Dan. Want a lift?"

"Hey. Guess I'm getting used to this walking routine, even though I need to get myself a car. Know any cheap ones?"

"C'mon, hop in. I have something for your home, so I'm headed that way."

"I hope it's a check." He laughed shortly and entered the passenger seat. "So what do you have?"

"You'll see. How was work?"

"The usual. Can't you smell it?"

She shook her head. "Maybe. I smell outdoors stuff and a guy whose deodorant is wearing off. But I've worked around Todd now for a long time. You get used to guy smells in the great outdoors." Jo smiled, hearing

Dan laugh a bit as he settled in the seat, adjusting the vents so that the air-conditioning blew on his face.

"This feels so good. I've decided that I may never go back to walking. You can pick me up and drive me home every day if you want."

"I'm not sure how Todd will react to his vehicle becoming the Moab taxicab."

"I was kidding. But it's easy to get spoiled. Probably why I'm in the mess I'm in. I was too spoiled. I've been thinking it over. God had to knock me over somehow. And it might as well be with a garbage truck. I've heard how people make idols out of their personal stuff and how God ends up taking it all away."

"Well, sometimes He does. But sometimes it's just the natural course of things. The point is, He can still work through them." She arrived at his home and opened the side door to retrieve the planter. Dan stood beside her, staring at it.

"You're kidding, right? You're turning my masculine bachelor pad into a *Gone with the Wind* plantation home?"

"I don't know, but the house looked kind of sad to me. Flowers mean there's life. You have to admit that plants can really speak things."

"I used to make fun of Pop's peanut plants. The only thing they spoke to me was a dull and dreary life. But I'm thinking more and more that I would like to see them again. The folks, that is."

"You should go back for a visit."

His face colored. He scraped his sandal along the ground. "I don't think I could do that."

"Why not?"

"I don't know. I acted like the Clyde part of Bonnie and Clyde when I took the money and ran. I lost all of Pop's inheritance. I don't think it would be a warm reception."

Jo took the planter and, to her delight, found a hook ready and available on the front porch. She watered the pot from the outside spigot, hooked it up, then stepped back for a view. "There. Perfect. One big happy home."

"Made by the happy homemaker, which I most definitely am not. I'd invite you in, Jo, but the house is hotter than that place no one wants to go to, and I have nothing in the fridge."

"Why is it hot in your house?" She then thought about it and nodded. "You really are living the life of a vagabond."

"I'm barely keeping the house. I've already missed a mortgage payment. I have to make the next or I'm going to be experiencing camping in a whole new way."

"Okay, then. Let's go somewhere. What about Arches?"

Dan stepped back. "Arches? I'm surprised."

"I love that place. Why not?"

"I don't know. Maybe because I burned you there. Took advantage of a situation that I shouldn't have."

"I'm not in the habit of keeping count of it all. You said you were sorry, didn't you?"

"Yeah, but. . ."

From the look on his face, she didn't think he was that sorry for what happened on their hike to Delicate Arch. And she had to admit, at this point, she wasn't sorry either. "Arches would be good," she decided. "We'll stop at the market for fried chicken and drinks. My treat."

"You're gonna spoil me if you keep this up. The only time I don't eat mac and cheese is when you stop by with food."

What else does a wife do? . . . Oops. There it was again! The husband and wife angle. How could she be thinking that?

The errands for food didn't take long. Dan kept the bag of chicken on his lap, inhaling the aroma as if it were the best thing on earth to him. Jo encouraged him to go ahead and eat a piece if he wanted, but Dan shook his head, vowing to show restraint until they arrived at their destination. Within the hour they were at the Windows section of Arches and spread their picnic near the North and South Window formations.

"They look like a pair of humungous eyes staring at us," Dan commented, munching down his chicken and biscuits as though he had not tasted food in a long time.

"They are windows made by God. Look through them, and what do you see?"

Dan paused, and to Jo's surprise, stood to his feet. She sat there, watching him head up the trail toward the open archway that overlooked the rugged Utah landscape. He returned and sat down on the bench beside Jo. "The view looks cool, that's for sure. It's better up there. Back in Moab, all I see are my problems. Here I can see things in a whole new way. The problems don't seem as big anymore."

"That's why I like it here. If we see those rocks up close and personal, they're just rocks. But from a distance, they form a pretty setting. Just like we're seeing things we've done under our own microscope. But from afar, God sees our mistakes as something He can redeem for His glory."

Dan smirked. "I'm not sure how He can take a life like mine and make it into something cool like an arch."

"He already is. You said how you're seeing God in a different light. And maybe if you go home to Virginia and patch things up. . ."

He picked up a small rock and tossed it. "Maybe. I don't know. I've lived my life the way I wanted. Or thought I wanted. But the idea that now I should ask God's opinion seems kind of strange. What if He calls down from heaven, ignites that bush over there on fire, and says, 'Get thee out of this land of Utah and back to where you belong'?"

"Well, He might. But I think He really wants to know if you're ready to listen and willing to trust Him with your life. I mean, Dan, you've been trusting in your own way of doing things for a lot of years. Not to speak against the mistakes, because I've made a ton myself. But do you think you've done a good job with your life?"

"As a boss of my own identity, hardly."

"Then why not let the true Boss of heaven and earth give your life a try? You certainly don't have anything to lose, and maybe a whole lot to gain."

He tossed another rock. "It would sure make Pop and Mom proud."

"Don't worry about that. Think of what it will do for you, personally." She pointed at the huge round arches of solid stone before them. "Look through God's eyes and not yours. And you're going to find a whole new view on life, guaranteed."

Dan got quiet then, which was unusual for him. The stillness persisted as the sun began to disappear below the horizon. Jo packed up the dinner. She had to return Todd's car before it got too late. As she headed back for the car, she felt a hand on her arm, drawing her to a stop. "Hey, Jo?"

"Yeah, Dan?"

"Don't worry, I won't take advantage of the sunset again. But I do want to tell you that you're something else. I mean, I always knew people cared about me. Like Mom and Pop. I never really appreciated them until now, when I see everything you've done for me these past few weeks. Thanks."

"Sure, Dan." She smiled, spawning a similar smile on his face. They began drifting back to the car. Her arm still tingled under the touch of his hand. She thought that a kiss beneath the setting sun would be nice. When they were both ready for it, that is. And it might be coming sooner than she expected if they could work out the snags of life that remained. But at least she found in Dan a listening ear, more so than ever before. Even if the sun was setting right now, a new dawn may be rising.

№

"Well, Jo, thanks again for everything," he said, exiting Todd's car at his house. "They talk of heroes rescuing damsels in distress, but it's interesting and humbling to have the damsel rescue the hero."

"Dan, believe me, you're doing your fair share of rescuing, too. See you soon."

Jo thought on her comment as she drove back to Todd's place. All this talk of reconciliation made her reconsider her own life. Her brother, Ross, for example. Everything he'd done for her, which she threw away when he challenged her to make things right. And then her parents in New York, with whom she'd had no real relationship for many years. Yes, Dan might need to make amends with his family, but so did she.

Chapter 14

If only Dan could believe in Jo's statement. That he was somehow rescuing her with his situation. How he could possibly be doing such a thing, he had no idea. But the thought continued to pester him as he went about his work after a promising weekend filled with interesting conversation and deep thoughts.

Something must have changed up there in Arches, because today he felt more energized. Charles wasn't grumpy either, and in fact, praised Dan for his quick work. "You taking pep pills or something?" the older man finally asked when Dan came jogging up with a can.

"No. Just want to do what I'm supposed to and give it all I have."

The man's eyebrows formed a perfect arch. "Been a long time since I've heard a young person say those things. I hear them say all kinds of stuff and never mean a word of it. But you seem to mean it today."

"I had a good day yesterday."

"Aha. Bet there was a girl in it, huh?"

Dan paused. "Well, yeah, I was with a friend of mine. We went to Arches and hung out. Got to talking and all. Did you know there are arches up there that look like huge eyes staring at you?"

Charles chuckled. "I haven't been there since I was a young man."

"You need to go back. It's great. I'd take you, but I had to sell my Jeep to pay the bills."

Charles stared at him. When Dan entered the cab after finishing with the cans on the street, instead of roaring off to the next neighborhood, Charles sat back and stared at him. "You know what, Dan? You're gonna be all right. And you're gonna go far."

For the first time in a long time, Dan sat dumbfounded. It was hot in the cab, and the sweat was rolling off his forehead, nearly blinding his vision. But he didn't move a muscle. Maybe because he couldn't believe what the man had just said.

"I see you don't believe me. You know why I say it? Because I've been there. I was young like you, you know. A dumb hotshot. Came here seeking my future. And ended up in the garbage business. Which is fine. I don't mind it. I meet interesting people. It pays the bills. But I think, too, about what I

112

could've become and what I had lost. And I don't want you ending up like me. You have a lot going for you. You told me you left your father's farm to come here, right?"

Dan had a difficult time answering; his mouth was so dry. "Yeah."

"You need to start by going back and making things right. No matter what happened or what others have done, it's the right thing to do. Begin where you left off and go from there."

Dan looked off into the distance at the row of garbage cans waiting in expectation for them on the next street. "I don't know if I can. I wasted a lot of things. Money. Life. Choices. And I kind of ran out on the folks."

"It's not too late. When you think it's too late is when the hope is gone, and then you've got nothing to fall back on. But that isn't so in your case. You're young. Don't end up like me, stuck behind this wheel. Don't even end up on a boat either, going nowhere fast. Find out what you're supposed to do in life. But no matter what, don't leave your loved ones out of it. They need you, and you need them."

Dan snickered. "I never thought I was getting anywhere working in a peanut field. But maybe I was only looking at it from one point of view."

"Did you have money? A place to live? Good food? People who loved you?"

"Yeah, everything." He stared out the window to see the heat reflecting off the pavement.

Charles put the truck in gear. It groaned and hissed to the next street. Dan opened the door. When he did, he felt like he was ready to open a new door to life, one he never thought he would open again. Taking hold of another garbage can, he thought about his big getaway plans. He'd gotten away, sure. And learned a heap. Maybe to ready himself for a bigger plan. Something he couldn't have done elsewhere. But what the plan could be, he wasn't entirely sure.

"Just remember what I said," Charles said when he returned. "And know you've got God watching over you. He cares big-time. He's just waitin' for you to make your move and stop saying no to everything and everyone around you."

At the end of the day, Charles and he were buddies. Or rather mentor and mentoree. Charles gave him a smile and a firm pat on the back. Dan soaked it in as he walked home, whistling. He didn't have all the answers, but he was looking at peace for the first time in his life. And Jo had been right about making God the big part of it all. Not in words, a church building, even Mom and her apple pie. But making God personal. Real. Before he handled anything else in life. *I need that*, he thought as he walked along. *I don't want the stained-glass window God. Or the leather book with pages written about God. But the real honest-to-goodness Person. God, make Yourself real to me. The real deal. Let me say yes.*

"Hey, Dan!"

Dan whirled to see a smiling face peering at him from a car window. It was Brian, the minister from Jo's church. "Need a lift?"

Dan thought of declining, but instead pounced on it and occupied the passenger seat. The air-conditioning felt good. Brian gave him another smile and asked about work.

"It's a living."

He laughed. "Yeah, we need to be happy for any kind of work these days. I'm hearing more and more how people are being laid off. Have to keep a thankful heart, even if the job may be different than we planned." He pulled into a convenience store. "Gotta make a quick stop. I'll leave the engine running."

Dan drummed on the dashboard, letting the cold air blow on his face. It felt refreshing on his hot and dried-out flesh. When Brian returned, he carried two huge slushies and handed one to Dan. "These are great when it's hot out."

Dan stared. "Well, I don't have—"

"Hey, it's on me."

Dan took it slowly, unsure of what to think or say, until the words of his prayer came back to him. *God, make Yourself real to me.* Was God doing just that by presenting him with Brian's friendship and a slushie?

Brian headed onto Main Street, talking about the game night and hoping Dan would come back soon. "We miss you. Monopoly hasn't been the same."

Dan smirked. "Yeah, it was a good time. But I think now I kind of need to start showing up earlier. For the testimonies and all." He looked at his slushie cup, thinking about the testimony in the cold cup he held in his hands. Of God's love and care.

"Hearing testimonies is a good thing. They stir up our faith, especially if it's been cold for a while. Faith can get buried by all kinds of things. But when you stir it up and make it come alive, you realize then that God is love, too. And He becomes real to us."

"Wow, that's just what I've been asking for. That God would be real to me."

"Then let's agree on that together."

Brian prayed a prayer that reached deep into Dan's soul, stirring his faith to life. After it was over, Brian asked if he'd heard about the rafting company and the lawsuit.

"I haven't heard anything yet."

"Might want to head over there sometime soon. I think you'll be surprised."

Dan looked at him, but Brian said nothing more. When Brian pulled into the driveway, Dan invited him in, but he said he had to pick up his kids from soccer practice. "Keep your chin up, Dan. With God in the picture, it can only get better."

It's already getting better, he thought, looking at his empty slushie cup. *Much better than before.* A thirst-quenching, life-giving slushie given to him by a guy who cared. From a guy who had made God commander in chief of his life, but a guy who also showed him how real God could be.

Just then his cell phone played a tune. He could barely make out Jo as her words rushed forth. Something about the rafting company, the lawsuit, and a job. He couldn't quite comprehend it all. Finally, she said she was coming right over and bringing a pizza.

Slushies. Pizza. Charles patting him on the back. He was overwhelmed, so much so that a tear sprang into his eye.

He went into the house to straighten up the few sticks of furniture that remained. The wall was bare—he'd sold the plasma TV. He'd sold his tablet, too. But the bills had finally been paid, and he'd managed to keep the house. He was living a humble life with all the clutter out of the way. Maybe once he had his act together, he could handle some of the stuff again. But without it, he was seeing and hearing so much better.

A knock came about a half hour later. Jo stood there, her face beaming like the sunrise, holding a huge pizza box. "Dan, we are celebrating!"

Behind her stood Todd along with several other employees from the rafting company. "What's going on?" he asked incredulously. It wasn't his birthday. That had come and gone without anyone knowing about it. They all marched in and occupied the few chairs he had as well as the floor. They tore into the pizza—a meatza loaded with everything.

"We got our place back!" Todd said with his mouth full of pizza.

"What Todd means is, the lawsuit's been dropped," Jo added. "Neil helped out. The case is closed."

"I want you back, Dan," Todd added. "I've got big plans to turn the company into a family-friendly business. With you and Jo at the helm, it's gonna be great!"

Dan sat there with a piece of half-eaten pizza on his plate. It had all come crashing down so suddenly, he didn't know what to say or think. When he stayed silent, everyone stopped eating and stared at him.

"Something wrong?" Todd asked. His eyes narrowed in concern. "Look, I'm sorry I had to let you go, Dan. I hope you'll forgive me for doing it. I didn't have a choice. . . ."

He continued to sit in silence until his gaze focused on the bare wall where the TV once hung. The empty place where the sofa stood. He could have it all back. He could have his old life, complete with his board shorts and shades. His Jeep, which he sorely missed. The kids loving him as he manned the helm of a raft. And Jo by his side.

"I'll have to think about it, Todd."

In an instant the joy of the celebration evaporated. Within a half hour, the group began to break up. Dan felt no remorse for what he'd said. But he couldn't say yes. Not now. When Todd left, Jo still sat cross-legged on the floor, looking up at him in curiosity.

"So what's going on, Dan? I can't believe you're not jumping all over this."

"God."

Jo sucked in her breath.

"I wasn't swearing. God is doing something in me, Jo, something big. I know I should be throwing another huge party with this announcement of getting back to the river and all. But like you said, I used the river as an escape. A problem solver. If I went back to the river, I'd still be floating in the same old raft of trouble." He paused. "I—I need to make a visit home."

Jo sat still, with a face he couldn't begin to read in a million years. He thought she would be happy for him. But instead, he watched a pool of tears collect in her soft brown eyes and roll down her cheeks.

"Jo, please. It's not like I don't want to be with you and help your cousin. . ."

"Oh, Dan, it's not that. It's just. . .I've been praying, too. Asking God what to do about my life. The mistakes I've made in the past. And if I should go back. I think you just gave me the answer."

"But you shouldn't be doing what I'm doing."

"Yeah, I should. We're more alike than you think. Just because I talk the God-talk doesn't mean I always walk the God-walk. I needed someone to take me by the spiritual hand and lead me. I knew in my heart I had to confront my brother Ross. To tell him I'm sorry and thank him for everything he's done. And make amends with my parents, too, and ask for their forgiveness."

"I need to do that." He paused. "Okay, so when do we buy our plane tickets? Bet if I ask Rob, he'll let me have the cash for it. He's got another job besides the farm and is making decent money now."

Jo stood to her feet and drew forward. His arms curled around her. Suddenly they were kissing, not in pent-up passion or for any other reason, but in thankfulness for the decision they had made.

116

Chapter 15

He could not believe his nerves. He, Dan the man, was now Dan the soul of humility. He was doing what he thought impossible in days gone by. He was going home to reconcile what was and see where God might be leading him next. He wished then that Jo had come with him, but she had her own time of reconciliation to perform. They parted ways at the airport where he caught a flight to Richmond and she to Dulles near DC. But before that, they shared a kiss and vowed to pray for each other. How Dan needed that prayer now. His hands tensed around the steering wheel of the rental car he'd picked up at the Richmond airport. He'd not let his folks know he was coming back home. Rob knew, of course. He'd loaned Dan the money to make the trip. He hoped it wouldn't be too much of a shocker on his folks, but this needed to be done.

Soon the familiar green fields he'd seen all his life began to materialize before him. It looked as if the ground had received a good soaking of rain. He hoped Pop would have a good harvest. He wanted the man to receive God's blessings in his life. And he realized then how much he'd been blessed by his father's hard work. He never lacked for anything. And yet he had taken all of the hard-earned money and spent it on frivolous things. Sure, some of the money was his. He'd worked for it. But really, they'd all worked for it by way of managing the farm they called their own.

A tear or two teased his eyes, wondering what would happen. His hands trembled as he turned onto the road leading to the Mallory farm. In the field ahead, Rob was driving the tractor—the one Dan crushed the peanut plants with in the days leading up to his exodus from this place. He brought the car to a stop and sat watching his brother. The tractor rolled along with Rob oblivious of his arrival. He waited until Rob turned the tractor around and drove it back in his direction. The engine hissed and groaned. It then came to a stop. He saw a figure stand up. And then Rob jumped down.

"Dan! Wow, it's so good to see you, bro." Rob gave Dan the strongest hug he'd ever received.

"Do Mom and Pop know I'm coming home?" Dan asked.

"No. I kept it a surprise for them. Come on back to the house. They will be so glad to see you." Rob turned serious. "But I need to tell you something,

Dan. Pop isn't well. His heart's been acting up. We just found out yesterday he may need surgery. I knew you were on your way here, so I waited to tell you in person."

Dan stopped walking. "His heart's not right?" he managed to croak out.

"Yeah. He had some tests done and the results came back. They say there's a blockage or something in a few arteries. He has to go for more tests."

"Maybe I shouldn't see him now. I don't want to cause him any more stress."

"I think you're just the right medicine for him. He's missed you a lot."

Dan wished that were true, but he couldn't help thinking what a disappointment he'd been to his parents, leaving them as he did, wasting his inheritance, not being there to help when they needed him most. With the work Rob could not do in his absence, Pop was obliged to handle it. For all he knew, Dan was to blame for his father's heart condition. His trepidation at the reunion was now magnified. He slowed his feet to a snail's pace as Rob went ahead of him to announce his presence.

Mom came running out, clad in her frilled apron, her arms extended. "Oh, my boy! My precious boy. And I don't care how old you are; you're still my boy. I'm so glad you're home."

"Hey Mom," was all he managed to croak out. His beloved, praying mom who never gave up hope, no matter where life carried him. He used to make fun of her godliness. Now he relished it. She smelled good, too, like moms usually do, of fine cooking and flowers and a hominess he couldn't begin to describe.

She took up his hand. "Come on into the house. Your father will be so glad to see you."

"I'm not so sure. I don't. . .I don't want his heart acting up because of me."

"It will be all right. Go on in and see him. He's in the den. And we're having your favorite dinner, too."

Dan couldn't help the tear that trickled down his cheek. *God, I don't deserve any of this*, he thought. He stopped short at the doorway to the den where Pop sat in his easy chair, reading the newspaper.

"Hi, Pop," he managed to say.

The paper fell into his lap. "Dan." He stood to his feet. "Son, you're back."

"It's okay. Don't hurt yourself."

"I'm fine. Especially now. Come on in. Sit here. Tell me how you are."

Dan did so, slowly. "I wish I could say that everything is fine, Pop. I did find a job but also did some dumb things. Thought I was a hotshot, really. Made some stupid decisions. I—I spent all the money you gave me. And when I needed it most, it was all gone. But then there was the whole beginning. Leaving you all like I did. And I know I'm responsible in large part for your heart problems." The tears came fast and furious. "I've caused you all kinds of pain and stress and—"

"Son, you're home, and you're safe. That's the only thing that matters." He paused. "You look like skin and bones, son."

"Yeah, it got tough in Moab. I lost my job. Barely made ends meet. Then I got a job hauling garbage. But it was good for me, Pop. Real good."

Pop nodded. "Things like that can be, son. They really can. God works everything together for good."

Later that evening, after a lavish dinner of pot roast with all the trimmings, Dan shared with the family about his life in Moab. Everyone listened quietly. No one offered any rebuke. No "I told you so." Or anything else. They just sat there with thoughtful faces. After it all, Rob suggested they catch the new sci-fi movie out sometime. Mom said she needed to make a run to the grocery store for more food now that her boy was home.

"I met someone special, too, in Moab," Dan went on. "Her name is Jolene. Jo for short. She's a strong Christian woman, Mom and Pop. You'd love her. She talked a lot of sense into me. I owe her so much."

"Well, when do we get to meet her?" Mom asked. "But she's in Utah, isn't she?"

"Actually she went home, too. She's up north near Leesburg. Like me, she had some things to work out with family here in Virginia."

"All things work together for good," Mom said with a smile. "Even with all our plans, God is still in control of it all."

How glad Dan was for the reminder after all he'd been through. But now his thoughts were on Jo. He missed her a great deal and wondered how things were going for her.

A few days later, he heard from Jo. His heart beat rapidly, the love surging through him as she shared her excitement over her time at home. How she'd made amends with her brother and even gotten to speak with her parents for the first time in years. She said her mother cried. She then talked about Dan to her family, along with their adventures in Moab.

"I talked about you, too," Dan said with a laugh. "And my parents want to meet you bad."

"I'll be on the bus to Richmond tomorrow, if you want."

"Booyah!" he shouted, louder than he intended. Mom ducked in the doorway, asking if everything was all right. "Jo's coming to meet you," he told her.

Mom smiled and nodded.

☙

Jo's coming! Dan's heart sang. He couldn't wait to see her—her streaming hair, bright eyes, and magnificent smile. And to remember all they had been through together. He didn't know what would have become of his life if Jo hadn't been there. If he hadn't worked for her cousin's company. And if he hadn't personally met the God who made Arches National Park, the God of rivers and red rocks, the sun, and yes, of people like Brian and others who cared. All of it made him rejoice.

When Jo arrived on the bus, she was like a vision sent from heaven. He swept her up in his arms and gave her a kiss, which she returned. He held her hand the entire time he drove back from the bus station, telling her about the reunion with his family and God's grace over it. "After it was over, all I could think about was you." He stopped at the fields on the road to the house. "This is where I come from, Jo. These are the famous peanut fields."

"Oh, it's so lush and green. No red rocks and dust. Just green everywhere. It's beautiful."

Peanut fields are beautiful? What a wild concept to him. But it showed him how different everything was now, with the right attitude in place. He parked the car. "Come see what we grow, up close and personal."

She obliged, walking the fields with him as he explained how the peanuts were grown and harvested. "So, do you think you'll live here now?" she wondered.

"I need to stay, at least for the time being. Pop's heart's not good. They need the help. Maybe when he's better. I'm hoping Brian can find me someone to sublet the house in Moab. Maybe someone from church."

Jo sucked in her breath. "You need to do what God is calling you to do."

"But Jo, I don't want you to go back to Utah and leave me here. Please, if there's any way you could stay, too?"

"Dan, even if I lived with my brother, we'd be hours away."

"Better than a thousand miles."

She shook her head. "I don't think I can."

"Then let's get married. You can be here with me."

Jo released his hand and stepped back. "What? Dan, you can't be serious."

"I have no choice but to be serious when I'm standing in a peanut field. I love you, Jo. You're the best thing that's ever happened to me. I feel alive when I'm with you. I want you to be with me, forever."

"Oh Dan." She thought for a moment. "I love you, too. It's been hard for us, I know. Lots of bumps in the road. But it's amazing to see what God has done and what He's continuing to do." She looked out over the fields. "And the way He's restoring things and making everything alive and new. But let's not rush something this important. Let's keep getting to know each other and see what God has in store for us." She thought for a moment. "I can tell Todd

I need to stay here for now—he knows I came out here and had things to do. He can find others to help at the company. Maybe there's a place I can stay nearby, at least temporarily. And we'll take it from there."

Dan squeezed her hand, thankful to have God in his heart and Jo by his side. "Let's go meet the family." His gaze lifted to heaven. *Thank You, Lord. I was lost and now am found. Delivered, from stuff, from life. But most of all. . .from myself.*

HEART OF MINE

Dedication

To JoAnne, Margie, and Rachel for making my very rough draft of an idea a real book. Thanks so much for all you do.

Chapter 1

So many questions and so little in the way of answers. Marissa Jones tried not to let it grate on her, but the constant day in, day out pondering was wearing her down. She shifted her cell phone to the other ear while throwing more books into a box. "Mom, remember, the caterer told me the deposit was forfeited. Don't worry, I handled it months ago." Pause. "Yes, I did read the fine print when I signed the contract." She wanted to add, *And how was I to know that Eric would die? Why are we talking about this? There are so many other things that we need to discuss. Like my move back home.* She bit her lip, refusing to say what she thought—Mom was being difficult once again.

"Why are you so short with me?" Mom went on. "I know it's been hard, but we need to make sure everything is set."

Marissa believed she had good reason to be on the sour side of things. After all, she'd lost her fiancé several months ago. Life had been turned on its head. Now she was about to move back to her hometown of Cedar City, Utah. Leave Nebraska and its memories. "I'm sorry. Look, I know you're only trying to help me tie up loose ends."

"Well, it's good you're coming back here. You were never the same when you left. Really, ever since you left for college and then moved so far away. You changed so much."

Yes, I've changed. In ways I never thought I would. Who wouldn't, when your fiancé dies unexpectedly a month before the wedding?

But she had to wonder, too, if Mom held some hidden thankfulness that things turned out the way they did. After all, Mom had been lonely since she and Dad divorced. She never wanted her and her sister Phyllis to move away. "Who will I go shopping with?" she'd mourned. "Who will I eat with?" But in time, it seemed Mom had overcome much in her life. And maybe they could do a little reconnecting now that it was just the two of them, without a husband or fiancé.

"Marissa, are you still there? Oh, how I hate these cell phones. I never know if someone has a decent connection or not. Betty uses one all the time, and then suddenly she's gone. I'll be talking away and find out she hadn't heard a thing I'd said."

"Yes, Mom, I'm still here. Hey, I'm sorry, but I have some more packing to do before the movers get here. I'll give you a call before I leave."

"Well, all right. You sure you're still coming? You won't change your mind or anything?"

Marissa thought she detected worry in her mom's voice. "Yes, I'll be there. Trust me. I've packed up everything."

When the call ended, she thought to herself, *I'll never be more thankful to leave here. I see Eric everywhere.* She forced away the tears that tried to well up. *Sometimes I think I hear his voice. Smell his cologne. I hear the cell phone ring and think it's him. And of course, all his friends and family are here. It's time to move on. And Cedar City is the place I believe God wants me to be.*

Marissa consoled herself these last few weeks by preparing for the move. Six months had passed since Eric's death, yet the memories were still so raw. It was difficult enough having to drive by the church where she was supposed to get married or the fancy hotel they had booked for the reception. She'd sold her wedding gown on craigslist. She had yet to take off her engagement ring. She stared at it even now—an exquisite one-carat diamond set in solid gold. Eric never went cheap when it came to what she wanted. From jewelry to bouquets of flowers on their engagement anniversaries to an iPhone one day as a surprise gift. At least she could look at the engagement ring without tears welling up in her eyes. Maybe it was a sign her heart was on the mend; that she was ready for this move. No longer did she feel paralyzed by her circumstances. The door was open, and she intended to walk through with her head held high and her emotions held in check.

Marissa continued to load up a box. Many things had already been packed into boxes, ready for her and Eric to begin their life together, when the terrible news came. He'd been in a car wreck out on the interstate and was killed instantly at the scene. She recalled how everything went into slow motion in those terrible days that followed. The parade of sympathy in the form of calls, casseroles, and cards. The funeral where Marissa sat without family, while all of Eric's family and friends were there, consoling each other. The lonely times that followed. It was then she realized how important family was in tough times. And friends, too. Like the friends she'd left behind from the church youth group in Cedar City. Denise and Joy. Last she'd heard they were still around, though Joy had recently gotten married. And of course, Mom had all her friends.

Cedar City was a good place to be, as it was nothing like Omaha. The town was small, filled with touristy-type places like the historic downtown and array of shops. Unlike Omaha's river bluffs, Cedar City was surrounded by the natural beauty of red rock canyons, hoodoos, rivers, and even a mountain that provided skiing in the winter. But she wasn't returning for all that.

She was going back to discover new things. A new purpose. Perhaps new love. And Utah held plenty of interesting memories. High school, prom, an old boyfriend, ski trips, even college where she met Eric for the first time. Utah had memories but not the painful feelings like here in Omaha. It was a place to start fresh.

The cell phone played a tune once more. Mom again. Marissa groaned. "I'm never going to get this packing done. . . ."

"Oh Marissa, I have the most wonderful news! I just got off the phone with Betty Newberry. You must remember her, I'm sure. Well, she and I are in the craft club together. And guess who's also moving back to Cedar City? Just in time for your arrival!"

"Who's that, Mom?" She tried positioning the phone on her shoulder so she could wrap glasses in tufts of newspaper.

"Wayne. Betty's son. Remember him from high school?"

Wayne Newberry. She hadn't heard that name in a long time. Memories rose to the surface, of a tall guy with thick, wavy hair who was voted most successful in the high-school yearbook. They'd dated a few times. And he was her prom date. "What about Wayne?"

"He's coming back to Cedar City to set up his practice. He's a successful psychologist according to Betty. He helps people with their problems, like Dr. Phil. Isn't that wonderful? He'll be making plenty of money, too, I'm sure. Maybe even become famous and have his own talk show. There are so many doctor-type shows out there now. Everyone wants solutions to their problems."

Marissa could already see where this was headed. The mothers getting together, whispering about their children while making greeting cards or whatever craft project was on the docket. Mom confiding in Mrs. Newberry about her brokenhearted daughter in need of a quick love fix and the psychologist son who appeared to fit the bill. A dinner date was sure to follow the moment she stepped out of the car. "I don't think I'm ready for that right now, Mom. I mean, I haven't even gotten there yet."

"Ready for what? I just wanted to tell you there are others coming back to Cedar City the same time you are. You're not alone."

But Marissa was feeling very much alone at that moment. . .so alone that she wondered what could fill the void. Even if she was going back to what she knew first, with hometown streets and familiar names, old friends and her mom, nothing could claim to be the remedy. Though Mom was trying her best to stick a bandage on the wound.

"Well, thanks for the news." *I guess.*

"And the lemon bars will be waiting for you when you get here."

Marissa smiled. Mom remembered her craving for homemade lemon bars when she was a little girl. Oh, how she loved the mixture of sour and sweet the bars delivered in every bite. Maybe there was a lesson to be learned—that the sour things in life, tempered with the sweetness of God, could make things yummy in the end. And the thought of freshly baked lemon bars might be a good enough reason to return to Cedar City. "Thanks so much, Mom. That means a lot."

ᴥ

Before leaving Omaha for good, Marissa decided on a visit to the cemetery one last time. She walked across the grass, past the marble blocks of stone in various shapes and sizes, until she came to Eric's grave. A smattering of grass seedlings had begun to turn the carpet of brown dirt into one of living green. "I'm leaving, Eric," she whispered. "I'm heading back to Cedar City. I know you'd want me to do this. . .to be happy and go on with my life." She twisted the engagement ring that stayed on her finger even during the months following his death. "Thanks for all the great times we had. For the way you loved me for who I am. But it's time for me to go. I can't keep looking at the past, and I know you'd understand that."

She tugged on the ring, allowing it to slip off her finger and into a zippered pocket inside her purse. This was it. She was saying good-bye to a part of her life forever. She would not look back but forward, with God's grace and mercy. It's all she could do.

Marissa turned to walk back to the car but stopped short. Another car, a huge white sedan, had pulled into the cemetery. She recognized it and the shape of the figure with a short, stylish hairdo and chic glasses sitting behind the wheel. Eric's mother. She inhaled a swift breath, thinking about the ring in her purse, wondering if she should slip it back on her finger for the woman's sake. Instead she hid her left hand behind her back as the woman got out of the car and headed toward her. Marissa always thought if they had been closer in age, Eric's mom might have become one of her good friends. She seemed so youthful in many ways. Vibrant and carefree. Different from her own mom. Only this woman had lost her beloved son. And now she appeared to have aged rapidly in the last few months.

"I thought you might be here, Marissa. I know you're about ready to leave town. I just wanted to give you a hug farewell."

"Thank you so much." She didn't quite know what else to say. Eric had always been the talker, bridging the gap between her and her pending mother-in-law. Mrs. Donaldson seemed to like her well enough. She frequently had both her and Eric over to the house for dinner. She was there the day Marissa tried on different wedding gowns. She helped Marissa pick out the place for the reception. She had ideas on a caterer, flowers, even a photographer. Eric said his mother was looking forward to having Marissa as her daughter-in-law.

"You're going to be just fine," his mother added, patting her arm. "You're a strong and beautiful young woman with so much ahead of you." She sighed, and Marissa saw the tears glimmering in the woman's eyes.

"I hope you don't think I'm abandoning Eric or the family by moving away," Marissa began.

Mrs. Donaldson stepped back as though surprised by the comment. Her gaze drifted across the cemetery. "Of course you're not. Eric's gone. He would want you to go on with your life. He always wanted you to be happy, you know. I only wish. . ." She paused, looking past Marissa in the direction of her son's grave. She shook her head. "Too many thoughts. So many memories, good and bad. It's hard. I only wish. . ."

"Only God can carry our losses, Mrs. Donaldson."

"Yes, you're right. He's strong enough to carry every burden." She seemed lost as she continued to stare at the grave site. She then looked back and managed a smile. "Now you take care of yourself. Where are you moving to again?"

"Cedar City, Utah. Remember, it's the place where I was born and where I grew up. I'm moving in with my mom temporarily." Marissa opened her purse and took out a small notepad and pen. "Here's my mom's address. I'll be staying there until I get a place of my own. And you have my cell number and e-mail address."

Eric's mother nodded, taking the slip of paper. "I should go back to Utah one of these days. It's been so long." She wiped a tear from her face. "Please keep in touch. Let us know how you are. I will always think of you as a daughter, you know."

Marissa and the woman embraced. She felt the dampness of the woman's tears across her cheek, the final living reminder of Eric. Marissa kissed her cheek and tasted the salty remains of the teardrops. "Good-bye and thank you for everything."

Marissa returned to her car, thinking of the ring in her purse. She opened the zippered pouch to see it there, safe. Mrs. Donaldson's car rolled along the narrow road of the cemetery, tires crunching gravel, and then headed into the street. She wondered if the woman had noticed the ring missing from her finger. Not that it should matter. It was over. Would the memories fade with time as she embraced a new future?

Returning to the apartment, she gazed about the three bare rooms with boxes ready for the movers. Resting on the sofa was a scrapbook she had not yet packed away. Mom had put it together as a surprise gift one year. In it were memories of Cedar City and her childhood. There were photos of the downtown area. The walking trail into Cedar Canyon. A camping trip in Dixie National Forest with the youth group. And Bryce Canyon, where she went with the youth group on a retreat and where God spoke to her through the strange-looking rock formations called hoodoos. God was ready to set her feet on solid ground, or rather rock, as rocks were famous in Utah.

She made a mental reminder to return to Bryce one day for a visit. Maybe book a room at the lodge and wait for God to speak to her again. Ask Him what to do with her future now that the door had been shut to her hopes and dreams. Especially with Mom looking to arrange another relationship with the arrival of Wayne Newberry to town.

Marissa sank down on the sofa to look at the album once more. There were pictures of family at holiday time, including her dad before her parents' divorce when she was thirteen. Her older sister, Phyllis, who lived out in California. The family dachshund, Sunny, who died not long after Marissa moved to Omaha. She decided then she should think about getting another dachshund. They were such funny dogs, a veritable wiener doggie for sure. A puppy to train would certainly fill her days.

She turned the pages. There was a picture of her in the black evening gown she wore for the senior prom, standing beside her date, Wayne Newberry. Tall, dark-haired, a winning smile, a fine catch. She couldn't imagine him single. *Maybe he's divorced.* She shook her head, refusing to be mixed up in a situation like that, with some ex-wife in the picture.

She examined a few more pages. Pictures of college. Ski trips. And then a few of Eric with the blue eyes she adored. She traced the defining features of his square jaw and the lips she tasted many times, though it seemed like ages ago.

What should she do with such memories of Eric? Try to keep a semblance of them alive? Or take the pictures out of the album and surrender them, perhaps to Eric's family? They might like them, after all. For her, at times it was too painful still to even look at them.

But she couldn't let them go. Not yet. Eric was her life for a long time, ever since college. Even with the move, he would not simply vanish from her thoughts. Not with the memories of an engagement and sharing kisses on pleasant evenings, along with plans for a future and a family.

Marissa leaned back against the sofa. Eric was such a good kisser, too. He picked the most romantic places to sit and talk or share dinner over candlelight. He always remembered their engagement anniversary each month with a bunch of roses. She had so many glass vases, twelve of them to be exact, that she'd finally given them to Goodwill. He was a nice man, too nice to have his life shortened like that. But now he was enjoying heaven. He loved God, like she did. He was ready to enter eternity, even if God had called him to heaven sooner than anyone expected.

Marissa closed the scrapbook. She was ready now to close the book on this life in Omaha and open a new book and a new page. *God, I give this all to You. My move back to Cedar City. My life, my future. The future I once thought I had has changed so much. It wasn't the future You wanted me to have, I guess. So I ask You to please open the right doors for me and show me what to do with my life. In Jesus' name.*

She knew at that moment she was placing her destiny in God's capable hands.

ु

Marissa watched the movers carry out her boxes and furniture. This was really happening. Life was changing. Good-bye to the old. Hello to the new. Thankfully Mom had a friend who could keep her furniture until a future apartment became a reality. And Mom had made room in a large closet for the rest of Marissa's belongings.

The cell phone rang. "So are you really coming?"

"Of course I am, Mom. Why would you think I'm not?"

"I don't know. Maybe it was a bad dream I had last night. I woke up thinking you were married and staying in Nebraska for good. And worried that you might be blown away by one of those awful tornadoes. We don't get storms like that here. At least I never heard of one. We just have to watch out for forest fires. Thankfully I haven't heard of any yet this season."

Marissa wanted to tell Mom that she wished the dream had come true. She didn't want to move, after all. She loved Eric and wanted them married. But that was no longer the plan.

"Are you there, Marissa? Hello?"

"Yes, Mom, I'm still here, but I have to go. The movers are loading the van right now. I should be there in a few days. It takes time to get there. It's a long way."

"You were too far away, living in that place. Now at least one of my girls is coming home. Your sister won't, of course. She's staying in California. Oh, by the way, I'm having a party to welcome you."

Oh, no. Marissa sighed. A get-together filled with well-meaning guests was not something she wanted to endure right now. Peace and quiet seemed better remedies. Time to readjust and settle down. "You don't have to do that, Mom. In fact—"

"Don't worry, it's nothing big. Just some family friends and others you might know. You're going to be very surprised."

Marissa wondered if she would see friends from the youth group. Or the old high school days. Until she thought of Wayne. Mom would no doubt invite him if he was in town.

Marissa thanked her and hung up, just in time to instruct the movers to be careful with a chair that had a loose arm. She was glad at least for the "welcome home" sensation that flowed through the conversation. It sounded as if Mom couldn't wait. Marissa only hoped she could find a smile to plaster on her face. She wished she didn't have to pretend. There was still some heart mending to be done. If only it hadn't come to this. *But it has. And I will make the best of it, Lord, with Your help.*

Chapter 2

Y ou're looking just great, Marissa."

He stood there wearing a smile, dressed in a sports jacket over a polo shirt, leaning against the frame of the door inside Mom's home. Wayne Newberry. He still had the wavy, dark brown hair she remembered from high school, but he now sported a mustache. He fit the bill of a successful doctor as if he were ready to embark on his own syndicated show. He had all the right everything, it seemed.

"Thank you." She managed to slip by him and to the refreshment table. As usual, Mom had outdone herself. It came from her work at the grocery store deli, where she got bargains on everything. There were ribs, tacos, cold salads, a relish tray, and, of course, a huge glass plate filled with her mom's famous lemon bars.

"I'm sure it must be difficult coming back here."

Marissa turned to see he'd followed her. For an instant, she scanned his left hand and saw no wedding band. She shook her head, hoping he hadn't seen her looking. Mom had already told her he was single. Not that she should think about such things. She'd only just arrived. She had boxes to unpack, a job to secure, people to reconnect with, her life to rearrange. And maybe a dachshund puppy to complete the picture, if she could talk Mom into the idea.

"Well, this is still home to me," she now said to Wayne and bit into a carrot. "And everyone has been really great. Did you know I got to see Denise for a little bit? You remember her from high school. She said Joy was here, too, but Joy's been sick. Come to find out, she's expecting."

She couldn't tell if Wayne was listening as he picked up a plate and selected some food from the buffet while she talked. Marissa looked around to see many of the guests giving her looks ranging from the curious to smiles to faces laced with sympathy. She knew they were probably considering her circumstances. What happened in Nebraska with her fiancé. Her move back here. And probably thanking God they were not in her shoes.

"How about going out for coffee sometime and catching up?" Wayne now asked.

She barely heard his invitation amid the thoughts cluttering her brain. "Huh?"

"Go out for coffee sometime?"

"Oh sure, that would be fine." She gave a small smile and then felt a tug on her arm. It was another of Mom's friends from her craft club, a Mrs. Carson.

"You look so thin and pale, Marissa. It's a good thing you came back to Cedar City. We'll have you looking healthy in no time."

"It's very nice to be back, Mrs. Carson," she said politely.

"Oh, come now, I know how it is. I lost Stanley a few years back. Remember that, Rosie?" She yelled at Mom above the noise of the guests.

"What was that?" Mom yelled back and then came over. The two had an open conversation over Mrs. Carson's husband, who'd passed away, and how long it took for her to recover. She then told Marissa how she cried every night and couldn't cook but resorted to eating those horrid frozen dinners and bags of store-bought cookies.

Marissa fanned herself with a napkin and wished she could escape from all the chatter to the back deck for a bit of air.

"And I felt the same way when Ralph left me," Mom said, giving Marissa a look. "I was so lonely." A broad smile filled her face. "But no more!"

Marissa managed a smile. With everyone now engaged in conversation or occupied with the food, she slowly made her way to the back door that led to the deck. Opening it, she stepped out into the warm summer evening. The sun's fading rays had just begun to set fire to the red rocks and earth of the Utah landscape. She breathed in the strange air. How different this was from the hustle and bustle of Omaha.

She and Eric had taken a road trip to the western part of Nebraska once to see rock formations reminiscent of what existed here in Utah. That day she'd felt a longing for her native state. They stopped to tour the national monument called Scotts Bluff and the landmark of Chimney Rock that pioneers ventured past on their way westward along the Oregon Trail. It was all so interesting to her. Eric and she had a good time together, though he said he was glad to be back in Omaha. He liked trips on occasion, especially if it was to the ski slopes. But he preferred the closeness of people and neighborhoods with houses one after another, as if he found security in numbers and social networking.

Marissa walked onto the deck and down the steps to the backyard, where the grass was wilting from the intense heat. Mom must have forgotten to put the sprinkler on the last few days, which was the only way grass could survive the harsh Utah summers. She thought back to when she was little, playing in the backyard with Phyllis. Pretending to be a queen in a court. Playing with Barbie dolls. And then her teen years, of trips to canyons and ski trips in the rugged mountains. Of walks around town, sipping sodas and laughing. Now she was back to begin life anew. Or find out what her life should be now that it had taken a radical detour into the unknown.

After a while, a few guests began drifting out into the backyard to share a few sentiments with her. Others joined in, and the party moved outdoors. Mom threw on a switch, and an array of party lights in glowing colors, strung along the back railing, enlivened the atmosphere. Marissa sighed. Now was not the time for thoughtful contemplation. It was back to mingling and trying not to be a party pooper at her own party.

When the guests finally left, Marissa collapsed into the chair and flung away her flip-flops, glad to be off her aching feet. She was still buzzing from all the conversation and too many lemon bars. Mom pronounced the party a success and occupied the chair opposite Marissa, holding a steaming cup of coffee warmed in the microwave.

"Won't that keep you awake?" Marissa asked.

"It's decaf. You want some?"

Marissa shook her head and looked down to see food that had been dropped on the carpet.

"Did you have a good time? I saw you and Wayne talking."

"We chatted a little. He asked me out for coffee."

"Oh, how nice. I hope you said yes."

"We'll go eventually. I need to settle in, look for a job and a dog, things like that."

Mom's eyebrows rose. "A dog! Heavens, Marissa, why do you want a dog?"

"Because I miss Sunny. I feel like she should be here. I was looking over pictures from that scrapbook you gave me. She was such a sweet dog."

"She was a nuisance. And dumb as they come."

"Mom!"

"I don't see how you'll have time for that. There are so many things to do here." She paused. "But I know you didn't come back here to have me tell you what to do. You're grown up, after all."

"Uh, yeah. Twenty-five, to be exact." Marissa added silently, *Too old to have my mom directing my life, but too young to be nearly a widow.* She couldn't exactly call herself a widow, as she and Eric hadn't exchanged wedding vows. But at times they had acted as if they were married. For instance, a week before he died, Eric had put her name on his bank account and even gave her money. Why, she didn't know. He'd told her it was for a rainy day, to use when she needed it. That was like a husband in her mind, trusting her with his worldly possessions.

"Oh, I wanted to tell you. I have a friend who would be glad to hire you for her gift shop. This is the time of year when it gets busy, with visitors coming to Cedar City on their way to canyon country."

Work at a gift shop. Now wouldn't that be just the thing to reintroduce herself to the climate of Cedar City reeking with tourism. She nearly laughed but diverted her attention back to the crumbs sprinkled on the carpet. She stood and went to fetch the vacuum.

"I don't think I've had anyone clean my house in years," Mom mused, staring after her. "Thank you."

Marissa realized it had been a long time since she'd been back here. She had visited while on college breaks. But since her move to Omaha after college, she'd only been back twice. "It's been a while, but now I'm here. Let's tackle the dishes and get them out of the way."

"I'm too tired." Mom leaned back against the chair and closed her eyes.

Marissa headed for the kitchen, where she spent the next hour washing dishes and cleaning up the refreshment table. She thought then of Wayne, piling his plate with food. And then his offer for coffee. Maybe she should try this new route and see where it led. "Hey Mom, do you have Wayne's phone number?"

"Hmm. Whose number?"

"Wayne Newberry's?"

"His mother's number is on the refrigerator door. I should remember it, but I can't even think right now. I'm so tired."

She didn't want to call his mother but dialed it anyway. After speaking to Mrs. Newberry, who gushed over how well Marissa looked and how happy Mom was to have her back, she obtained the number. "I just know Wayne will be tickled pink to hear from you," Mrs. Newberry added.

Wayne's deep voice answered when she called. "Marissa, this is a surprise. You okay?"

"Hey, I was wondering if that coffee invitation is still valid."

"Of course it is. I just asked you tonight. Want to make it tomorrow morning? Eight a.m.?"

"Okay. After tonight, I'm going to need a good latté to get me going."

He laughed. "There's a good coffee place in town called The Grind. Mom was telling me about it. I think it's new since we both moved away."

"Great! See you there." Marissa hung up the phone. Wayne Newberry. Old high school flame. Well, why not? Might as well see if any of the flame was still burning.

&♥

Marissa arrived for her morning brew to find Wayne at a table with the newspaper spread out. He stood to his feet the instant she walked in and smiled.

"What will you have?"

"Oh, you don't need to buy me coffee."

"Of course. That's why I suggested it. A latté, right?"

"An iced hazelnut latté and an apple cinnamon muffin would be great. Thanks." She took a seat opposite him to see the newspaper opened to the classifieds, and in particular, real estate. Wayne must be thinking of buying a house. Which reminded her that she should be looking for a place. She took up the paper and began scanning ads for apartments when he came back with her latté and large muffin on a plate. "Thank you. So are you looking to buy a home?"

"I'm thinking about it. Looks like there are some good deals."

"I need to find myself an apartment sometime in the future, once I get a good job lined up." She sipped the latté, strong but cold on her throat. "So what have you been doing since high school?"

He closed the paper and folded it in half. "I took off for college like most everyone else and lived away for a few years. I decided to come back here and set up my psychology practice. I deal with teen and college issues. Runaways, drug addiction, that kind of thing. Being a college town, there's plenty of that to go around. Not to make light of a problem. Too much pressure on kids these days. But it seemed like a good idea."

"It sounds like a good thing to do." She took another sip, sensing the latté would have her flying down the street with its potency. "I have to find a job. Mom says she can get me something to start in one of those downtown gift shops. Can you believe that's why I went to college. . .to work at a gift shop?" She grinned. "But it's better than nothing, I guess."

Wayne's face crinkled as he laughed. "My mother says we still get plenty of tourists on their way to Cedar Breaks and Bryce. It's that time of year. First the tourists, then the college kids."

"I saw the RVs passing through when I arrived. The town pretty much looks the same. Still has the historic district, the nice parks—though the walkways are looking better."

"Not that much has changed from what I've seen, and I've only been here a week myself." He finished his coffee, then stood to get a refill. Marissa took time to admire his tall, athletic build and broad shoulders. The wavy, dark hair and dark eyes. And large hands. Wayne had a lot going for him. She wondered why things didn't work out in the marriage department. She would love to ask but knew it was highly personal.

He returned to his seat opposite her. "I was very sorry to hear about your fiancé. How are you doing?"

"Well, what can one do after something so unexpected? But I'm doing better. I've had time to work through it. Everyone here's been great since I got back. I mean, the party Mom threw was nice. I think I made the right choice in leaving Omaha."

"Of course you did. This is home, and people care about you. When a crisis hits, most find comfort and security in the things they know and love."

"When I saw the red rocks and canyons and little trees, I thought, yes, this is where I grew up. This is where my friends and family are. It isn't where I went to college, of course. . ."

"You took off for Salt Lake or something, didn't you?"

"I went to Utah State, and that's where I met Eric. He was in one of my classes, but we found out we both loved skiing. We spent a year on the ski team together. He taught me quite a bit. He was a year ahead of me and graduated, then moved back to his home state. But we stayed in contact through texting and the Internet. And phone calls, of course. He'd come to ski sometimes. Then he got a good job in Omaha, where his family lived, and asked if I'd be willing to move out there after graduation so we could be closer. I thought I was doing the right thing by moving there. Even if Mom wasn't happy with my decision to live out of state." Her voice trailed off as she sensed the doubt creeping in.

Why did she let such thoughts rise up? Like the idea she'd made a mistake by agreeing to marry Eric, which is why he died. It was foolish to even consider it. But she wondered, too, as Wayne sat looking at her, if he thought this was a perfect orchestration of events to bring them together after years of separation. "I wonder sometimes if I made the wrong decision. Marrying and living so far away."

"I know it's hard figuring out why things happen the way they do. I get people psychoanalyzing themselves all the time about their personal choices. Sometimes we have to make choices and see how they work out. And sometimes decisions lead to unhappy and even tragic results, and for no reason at all." He leaned closer, his coffee-colored eyes burrowing into her. "But you are *not* to think you did anything wrong here, Marissa. You followed your heart. And I'm sure you and Eric had a great time, even if it was brief."

"Yes. I'm glad for the time we had. He was a great guy." She sipped her latté. "Sorry I'm bringing all this up. I'm sure it's not what you wanted to hear."

He smiled. "I have no agendas. I just want to catch up with a friend from the old days and find out what's happening in her life."

"Well, now you know the nitty-gritty. And why aren't you married? A guy like you with a potentially successful and profitable career. Lots of women to choose from, I'm sure."

He lowered his gaze to stare at his coffee cup, and she wondered if she'd unintentionally hit a nerve. "It didn't work out for me."

"Oh, I'm sorry. Divorce?"

"No. I suppose it's good it ended when it did, or it might have turned out that way. We were all set to head down the aisle. Had wedding plans prepped and everything. Then Leslie got cold feet. She wasn't like you."

Marissa sucked in her breath, wondering what he meant.

"A levelheaded person," he finished. "Knowing what you wanted in life and going for it, even if it didn't always work out. Leslie had some nice traits, but she and I, we just didn't mix. Locked horns a lot. Argued. She had some problems left over from childhood."

"I guess it's good you didn't go through with anything, then."

"Marissa, I could never see you and me arguing. We seemed to hit it off real well in high school. I kind of wish now that we hadn't gone our separate ways when we graduated. Maybe things would have turned out differently."

"I don't know. Like you just said, Wayne, it makes no sense trying to dissect what we each did. But right now, I'm asking God what to do about my life. I hope you will give me the chance to do that. I. . .I'm not ready for anything right now."

His face reddened slightly. "Of course. I'm sorry if it sounded like I was hinting at something. I'm just glad to see you back and doing well, all things considered. But you always were a strong woman." His face softened as if appreciating that characteristic, among other things.

Marissa was glad the conversation had gone well up until this point. She decided now might be a good time to part ways. She thanked him for the coffee and left the shop, thinking about the conversation and the look in his eyes that conveyed a longing to embrace the past. Wayne and she had had good times together. But it was a long time ago, and they were different people. *God, it's too soon for dating or anything else. I don't even know what I'm doing right now. I need time. Please let others know I need to sort things out. Where to go and what to do.*

Marissa entered her car and drove the streets of Cedar City. Familiar sights began to come back to her. The storefronts of Main Street. Then the entrance to the canyon walk, where she parked on a side street and decided to go for a wander. Many times as a high-school student, she had walked the gravel pathways with friends, laughing over a guy they liked or the next activity in the youth group. They talked about the festivals that hit the town or gawked at strange tourists carrying their cameras. She should call up Denise and Joy and have them rendezvous here for a reunion and catch up. Just like she had with Wayne. But everyone was busy with their lives.

Marissa walked the path, or rather took a stroll through a multitude of memories. She gazed at the rocky canyon and landscape dotted with sagebrush, allowing the pungent aroma to fill her. She was so absorbed by it all, she didn't notice the man walking opposite along the path until she nearly collided with something yellow and furry at her feet.

"Oh, please excuse me." She jumped back. "I nearly stepped on your dog's paw."

"No harm done. Likely Goldie would have leapt out of the way. Sit," he commanded the large golden retriever. The dog promptly obeyed.

Marissa smiled and petted the dog's furry head, thinking on her promise to buy herself a dachshund puppy when she had the chance. She stared down at the dog sitting so obediently, waiting on the next command from her master, when the man swiped off his sunglasses. She looked up, and suddenly the air left her. She felt cold all over.

It can't be!

The man's cheerful face evaporated. "Are you okay? Did Goldie do something? She's usually real gentle. I've never known her to scare even a flea, though she doesn't have any. I use the monthly spot treatment." He laughed.

Even the laugh! Her breath quickened. It had to be some kind of dream. Or a vision of her own making. Maybe even a hallucination. All she knew was. . .her beloved Eric was standing right before her very eyes!

"Are you all right?" he asked in concern. "Are you sick?"

"I. . .I. . ." She began to back away. "I. . .you look so familiar."

He laughed. "Wish I could say you did, too, but I'd be telling a tall tale." He chuckled again.

Oh, dear God, have You brought Eric back to life? Is this real? Did something strange happen? A miracle maybe? Or had he come back and now he had amnesia or something? "Is your name Eric?" she suddenly blurted out.

"What? No. I'm Anson." He held out his hand. She made a feeble attempt to grasp it before her hand fell away. "Have we met?"

"I–I'm sorry." She spun about and hurried away. When she turned back to look, the man was walking in the opposite direction. He then turned, too. Their gazes met. *Dear God, what am I going to do? It's like he's come back. Eric's alive! But. . . he's dead. We buried him.*

Didn't we?

Chapter 3

Anson could not get the woman's stricken face out of his mind. He gripped Goldie's leash. It was like she'd seen a ghost. She'd asked if his name was Eric. He must look like someone she knew. Someone close to her heart. That was obvious. He walked the trail leading farther into the canyon then turned. She remained where she was, still staring at him. Compassion stirred inside him. How he wanted to help. He should go back and reassure her that he was not who she thought he was. He broke into a brisk walk, hoping she wouldn't leave. Her feet shifted. Her hand swept her face. But she stayed where she was.

"Hi. I'm not sure, but you seem upset about something," Anson said gently as soon as he got within speaking distance. "Want to talk about it?"

"I—I just can't believe how much you look like. . ." She paused. "Have you. . .have you ever lived in Nebraska?"

"No. Never been there, actually. I spend too much time traveling this state for my job."

"Did you ever go skiing in Park City?"

"Of course, though I'm not very good at it. Am I being interrogated or something?" He meant it in a friendly way, but she took a step back as if his words had been a swipe.

Her face colored. If it were not for all the questions, he might have enjoyed studying her features more. She was certainly lovely to look at, with her long, dark brown hair and eyes to match. If only he could wipe away that strange look on her face that spooked him even now.

"I guess I'm losing my mind. You see, I lost my fiancé a few months ago."

Goldie took that moment to lie down on the ground and take a rest. The woman seemed to breathe easier as if things were more relaxed. Silently he thanked his dog. "I'm very sorry to hear that."

"I mean, he died just a few weeks short of our wedding. In a car accident. I used to live here in Cedar City, back in my childhood. I decided to return after it all happened, to start over again. And now I can't believe I'm seeing things. Thinking you look like him or something."

"It happens. Don't worry about it. But rest assured—Cedar City is my home and not anywhere else. Except I did grow up in St. George. But I do get

141

around to other places."

She straightened. "Like where?"

"I work for the National Park Service, so I travel to other parks in the region. But I come back here on my days off to take care of Goldie. She has to stay behind when I travel, and I hate leaving her here."

"I hope to get a dog," she blurted out. "I had a dachshund growing up. I simply love them."

"A wiener dog!" he exclaimed with a smile.

She gave a shaky smile in return. "They do look like little wieners. But I love dogs. Eric and I would have gotten one once we settled, I think. I never did ask him about that. He had a saltwater tank filled with exotic fish. Some were the size of my hand. He even had a few living coral and those strange-looking anemones." Her voice drifted off, lost in thought, until she centered her attention once more on him as if studying his face. "Have you ever been in an accident?"

"Look, you don't really think I'm your dead fiancé come back to life," he hedged.

"No, of course not. It's silly. I—I thought I was over him is all. Guess I'm not if I'm seeing things."

"It takes time to get over something this tragic. You can't do it overnight. Or even in a few weeks, I know. I lost both my parents within a year of each other. My mom to cancer, my dad to diabetes and probably a broken heart. Dad never got over Mom's passing." His face colored when he realized maybe he shouldn't have used that comparison. Not that he wanted anything to happen to this pretty woman before him, like losing herself in a thick fog of grief.

"He's been gone over six months. I thought that was plenty of time. I even took off the engagement ring he gave me. But now maybe I'm going over the edge instead. Especially after this." She began sidestepping away. "I'm really sorry to have bothered you."

"It's no bother, really." Anson watched her walk away, trying her hardest not to look back at him again. Inwardly he sensed she wanted him to be her dead fiancé resurrected from the dead. And that fact saddened him. He remembered Dad mourning for Mom. Clutching her picture to his chest, weeping. Saying he didn't want to live anymore, that he wanted to be in heaven with her. At this, his feet began to shift. He wanted to dash back to that woman and tell her to live. Not to throw her life away. Or imagine him as the one she'd lost. She was young. She had so much of life ahead of her. And love, too. Things bright and sunny, not dark and dreary. *God, help this woman in her grief.*

When he arrived home, he immediately called his friend Carl to tell him about the events of the day. Carl would be glad for the encounter, as strange as it had turned out. He'd been on Anson to start looking into the dating scene. Anson had decided to irritate his friend and take his own sweet time. Until now.

"Interesting," Carl remarked when Anson told him of the abrupt meeting on the canyon walk.

"Is that all you can say? Interesting?"

"Well, it's an interesting way to meet. Not that I would want to look like someone's dead fiancé. Too bad. I've been saying a prayer for you, Anson. For a miracle. Not exactly the way I thought it would happen, though."

He frowned, even if his friend couldn't see his reaction. "Thanks a lot."

"The problem is you're never around town long enough to make things happen with a woman. Especially with the kind of work schedule you keep. Don't you leave for Cedar Breaks tomorrow?"

"Actually, I have a few days off. They switched my schedule around."

"So that means I don't have to take care of Goldie for a few more days. Yahoo!"

"Yeah, and I'm sure she'll miss you." He looked down at the golden retriever nestled at his feet, her furry head resting atop his tennis shoe like it was a pillow, dog drool staining the nylon.

"Everyone has their doubles walking around out there. I guess you were hers."

"Yeah. She asked all the questions, too. It was really strange. I wonder if she might need some help. A little grief counseling or something."

Carl chuckled. "She should have said you looked like a crown prince from Saudi Arabia. That would net you all kinds of attention."

"Yeah, a modern-day *Prince and the Pauper* come to life. But she was pretty insistent. In fact, she asked me if I'd ever been to Nebraska. If I'd ever been in an accident. Things like that."

"Sad. You're right, it sounds like she could use some help."

"Yeah. Made me think of Dad when Mom died. I kind of wish now. . ." He hesitated. A lump formed in his throat, and he was unsure why.

"Don't go that route, Anson. You didn't do anything wrong."

Maybe God was putting his finger on something. That he still blamed himself for not seeing the warning signs in Dad. Of his depression. Not caring for himself, like the diabetes that eventually stole the man's life. The way Dad slipped away so fast. Anson should have watched over him better.

"Anson? Did you hang up? Hello out there."

"No. Just thinking."

"Bad thing to do sometimes."

"Yeah. It's not good to dwell on this anyway. It brings up things that should be gone. I need to read the Bible. I don't like what this is doing." He didn't want to elaborate on what still bothered him. Carl wouldn't understand it anyway. The only one who could was Lucy, his sister.

"Don't let it get to you. Think of the opportunities, instead. Like the attention of this lady." Carl went on, talking about the woman Anson had seen on the canyon walk. "Maybe it gives her comfort to know her fiancé will be resurrected one day. I mean, I once had someone who thought I was a dead ringer for a guy that played in a rock band. Now there's an interesting double to be. A Christian rock star who won a Dove award."

Goldie began pawing at Anson's leg, summoning him to dinner. "Look, I gotta go, Carl. Thanks for everything."

"Not sure I did anything, but you're welcome. And about the encounter? Don't worry about it. Just a knee-jerk reaction on her part. I'm sure you'll meet again, and it will go much better. Then you can ask her out."

Anson smirked and said good-bye. Rousing the dog from her comfortable position on the carpet, he went and poured kibble into a bowl for Goldie. He thought then of the woman and how she wanted a dog. Goldie had been a find at the city kennel. Dogs brought comfort when life dealt a bad deck. A dog would be just the ticket for her. Maybe he ought to offer to accompany her to the town kennel and look for a wiener dog. Or look for a dog on craigslist.

Goldie crunched down the dog food in less than two minutes, lifted her furry head, and looked at him with dark eyes.

"That's all you get, Goldie, or you'll get sick. You know it."

The dog cocked her head at him.

"Yeah, forget putting on the charm. So who do you think I look like? Perhaps a guy that a girl might one day want to meet?" He snickered. "Forget it. You don't have to answer that. I'd rather not know anyway." He stood before the mirror in the hall to see sandy-colored hair and a dark shade of blue to his eyes. Fairly tall, despite the fact that Mom said he was a preemie with health problems. He'd overcome whatever ailed him, even the asthma as a child. Mom would be proud of what he'd become and where life had led him, especially his faith in Christ. If only she hadn't died so early from cancer. Then Dad from uncontrolled diabetes. Anson swallowed the knot in his throat when he thought of it. Dad refusing to monitor his sugar. Anson asking him to go see the doctor when he began exhibiting strange symptoms. The man clinging to a picture of Mom with his gnarled fingers, wishing her back in the land of the living. Lucy finding him unconscious on the ground a week later. He died at the hospital. Yes, Anson had sympathy for the young woman he'd met today. The death of a loved one was difficult, especially one who was, or is to be, your life partner. Unfortunately, Anson wasn't sure he would ever see her again to offer his condolences. And maybe more.

⁊❧

Anson decided on another venture the following morning into Cedar Canyon. After yesterday's rather abrupt encounter, he and Goldie didn't get the kind of walk in God's good earth that they both needed and deserved. Usually they would do at least three miles, enjoying the scenery. Today was a new day, bright and sunny, as days usually were this time of year in Cedar City. All sun and little else.

He opened the car door for Goldie to jump out of the backseat. He hooked on her leash. "C'mon, girl. We're going to try that walk again." He yawned, wishing he'd gotten more sleep instead of thinking too much. Like about the young woman and her distraught face yesterday. Dad and Mom. And other things. Such as wondering when he might find that special someone in his life. He inhaled a deep breath, enjoying the scents of sagebrush in the warm sun and the serenity of the river flowing lazily by.

And then he saw her, standing in the same place as if she'd never moved. He checked his watch, realizing he'd been here the same time yesterday.

She stepped forward tentatively. "Hi."

"Well, hi. I didn't think I'd see you again so soon."

"Look, I had to come back to"—she paused, staring, and then focused her gaze on the ground—"to apologize for what happened yesterday. You. . . well, you do look a little like my fiancé, but you're not, of course. In fact, I can't believe I quizzed you like I did." She shook her head. "I guess I'm having problems."

He moved forward in a gesture of understanding then stopped as she moved back. "You don't have problems. You're in mourning."

"Huh? I shouldn't be after six months."

"My dad mourned for a year after my mom died. He never really got over it. There isn't a timetable on things like that."

She pushed back strands of her hair. "Okay. Well, again, I'm really sorry." She managed a small smile and backpedaled.

He wanted to offer to go on a walk, to ask more about what happened. But she looked as if she'd rather make her escape, despite his interest in getting to know her. Her long, dark hair whipped about in the breeze. She had a perfect figure. When he was a bit of a distance away, he finally turned to see that she'd vanished. He sighed and looked down at Goldie, who paced back and forth as if reminding him of their three-mile jaunt. Time to let this go. He should center his thoughts on his upcoming work this week anyway in visitor relations—his area of expertise within the Park Service.

He frowned. So much for interacting with visitors and making them feel comfortable in their surroundings. Looks like he hadn't done too well in that area with the young woman. When problems arose with visitors or other situations that needed attention, he hoped for a calm and confident manner that would soothe a frazzled soul. Not so today.

He jogged the rest of the way back to the car, allowing his mind to go blank. He drove home, reaching it in a mere five minutes, just as his cell phone played a tune. It was his sister, Lucy. Must be God's timing, what with these memories of Dad and Mom, plus the encounter with the distraught woman. Lucy would know what to say and do. As he escorted Goldie into the house, he gave Lucy an abbreviated version of the encounter on the canyon walk.

He expected to hear her usual female inquiries and explanations, as only Lucy could do. "So she really said you looked like her fiancé?"

"Dead ringer, I guess. Oops, that didn't come out right. Sorry. I feel badly for her."

"Ever had anyone tell you that before, Anson?"

"Tell me what?"

"That you look like someone?"

"Not that I remember. But she just lost her fiancé, so it makes sense. I can understand the reaction. I mean, remember Dad?"

"Yeah, I guess so." There was silence. Finally she said, "Hey, are you busy tonight? Got time to come over to my house for dinner? We haven't seen each other in a while. The boys would love to see you again. They miss you."

Something wasn't right in her voice, but he couldn't put his finger on it. "Luce, is everything okay? I don't know if I can take another troubled woman. Totally kidding," he said hurriedly. "I'm there for you, you know that."

She chuckled in bursts. "Of course. Sweet of you. But I'm fine. So. . .can you come?"

"Am I known to turn down a home-cooked meal?"

"Good. Look, I need to run."

He heard nothing more, but the unspoken words were loud. Especially the silence after he mentioned Dad and Mom. He prayed something wasn't wrong. Then he thought how cancer can run in the family. He shook his head, running fingers through his hair. *Don't go that route, Anson. Don't read into anything, okay? Think about the great meat loaf she makes. You get to play with your nephews. Just go and be together as a family.*

God, she's the only family I have. Please don't let there be anything wrong.

❧

"Anson!" the boys screamed when he entered, bearing gifts. He never came to Lucy's house in St. George without gifts in hand, and his nephews knew it. He watched them take the bags and open them to reveal the latest Lego kits. "Cool, Anson! Thanks so much." He'd asked them long ago to call him by his first name. Uncle Anson just didn't make the cut for a worthy title. And the kids obliged.

Lucy stood in the kitchen doorway, a small smile on her face as she wiped her hands on a towel. "I'm making your favorite, little brother."

"Meat loaf and potatoes au gratin. I was hoping you would."

"You demand the best," she said with a smirk.

He came to her and bestowed a hug. Her body stiffened under the embrace, but he forced himself not to read into it. "Will Frank be here, or is he working late?"

"He'll be here. Meal's just about ready." She turned and headed into the kitchen to check on dinner. He followed, watching her. Something wasn't right. She couldn't look him in the eye. She stood hunched over and not because she was fixing the meal. A heavy burden lay on her shoulders.

God, what could it be? He decided to go gently. She would tell him eventually. "So is work going okay?"

"Oh, work is fine. Thanks." She shook her head as if to dismiss something else that had popped into her mind. How he wanted to know what lurked beneath her fine, raven black hair. They had always been open with each other. Especially after losing both Dad and Mom. They talked often. He about work and Lucy about family. Sometimes she confided in him about her and Frank, who could be a difficult man.

Just then the front door burst open to admit the burly man, who worked in postal delivery. Immediately the boys showed their father the kits Anson had given them.

"Nice."

Frank politely shook Anson's hand. They didn't share much in common, but Anson was pretty sure Frank loved Lucy. Though right now, Anson couldn't be sure about anything.

Dinner was a quiet affair for the adults while the boys chattered away about school ending in a week and what they planned to do this summer. Frank asked about Anson's job and if he expected a good tourist season this year.

"Shouldn't be any different," he said, stirring cream into his coffee. "But I hope it will be another quiet summer." He looked over at Lucy, who had not spoken a word the entire meal. *Maybe she and Frank are having issues.*

Lucy jumped to her feet and began clearing the dishes from the table. "Let me do that, Luce," Anson told her. "You made a super dinner."

She managed a smile. "Glad you liked it."

"And I hope we're going to get a chance to talk."

She looked over at the clock and then her husband. "I don't know. It's getting kind of late, Anson, and you've got work, I know." Her eyes darted back and forth.

"I always have time for you."

She shrugged. "Yes, but. . .well."

"Can I at least talk to you? About relationships? Get a woman's perspective to help this lowly bachelor see things better?"

Her eyes grew large. "Oh, of course!" For once he saw her perk up, as if he'd offered some life-changing announcement. He had none, of course, only that he wanted to know what was going on with her. But sitting there, he didn't know the words to say. She asked Frank to take the boys upstairs to play before leading the way to the sofa.

"I've been praying you'll find someone to settle down with, Anson. I mean, time is passing on. You're what, twenty-six?"

"Twenty-seven. Remember, you made me a big birthday cake with two and seven candles on it back in March. Had a great party. You even invited some of my ranger pals." He laughed, then grew quiet. "We're it as far as family goes, though. It's just you and me."

She grew quiet then. "I never thought we wouldn't have our parents. They will never see their grandkids grow up. I miss them a lot."

"I do, too. I guess the visit with the woman at the park made me think of them. Losing the ones you love. Dad never got over it." He paused. "Sometimes I want to blame myself, Luce, which I know isn't right. If I'd been more forceful with Dad when he wasn't feeling good. Got him to the doctor in time. . ."

"Anson, don't you dare blame yourself. Dad was a stubborn man. But he was more stubborn in handling his grief. Even if he wasn't accepting of your advice in the end, you brought a lot of joy to his life. To both of them. They never had any more kids, you know. Maybe Mom was having issues even then. I never did ask her. And then she died of ovarian cancer."

"Yeah." He hesitated. "Are you okay?"

Lucy straightened. "What do you mean?"

"Not sure, but you look like something's up. Trying to read a female mind, forget it. But you did seem rather distant tonight. I never knew you to go through an entire meal without talking."

She looked away for a moment. "Just trying to sort things out. Looking for the right time for things."

"There is a time and a season for everything under the sun. Are you and Frank doing okay?"

148

"What? Yes, of course. Oh Anson, please don't try and figure everything out." She rested her hand on his arm. "I'm sorry if I look like I'm leading you on. We're fine here, really. I just wanted to see you again. We're all that's left in this family, like. . .like you said. Everyone else is gone. Though Dad's brother, Uncle Roy, might be alive somewhere. I'm not sure."

All this talk of family was good. A blessing. Something to cherish. He vowed to see her more often. To try and be there for her, despite what lay hidden. "Don't forget the Jamboree coming up soon."

"You know I wouldn't miss it. But you'd better be heading back. It's getting late."

He stood. "Take care, Luce."

"I'll tell the kids good-bye for you." She walked with him to the door, standing by his side like the older sister she'd always been. And a good sister, too. He didn't want to lose her. He spun around. "Luce, you don't have cancer or something, do you?"

Her eyes widened until they looked as if they might pop. "Anson! Whatever made you think that?"

"Just be sure you get yourself checked out. Cancer runs in the family. And I'll be sure to get checked, too."

She opened her mouth as if to say something, then nodded and answered with a simple, "Okay."

When the door closed behind him, the uneasiness still stirred within him. As much as he loved his sister, for the first time in his life, Lucy was like a stranger. And he didn't know why.

Chapter 4

I feel so silly and stupid," Marissa said, stirring the ice cubes floating in her iced latté. "I can't believe I walked up to a perfect stranger and asked if he was Eric. I must have been completely out of my mind." She took a long drink, hoping to find some solace in the man who was a doctor as well as a friend from long ago. Right now she needed both.

Maybe she ought to occupy the sofa in the corner of the coffee shop and confess all her woes of late, like the scene in a psychiatrist's office. The troubles seem to be piling up one on top of the other as each day played out.

"Maybe it's better it happened," Wayne said. "Now you're dealing with it. It's out in the open, so to speak."

She leaned over the table. "But I was so convinced for a moment it was him. He. . .he looked just like him. The same color hair. The blue eyes. The same build, well, actually this guy was taller."

"I hear that all the time. Everyone has a double walking around somewhere. Look at how many have sworn they've seen Elvis walking around. And now it's Michael Jackson. And other people. Like the people never died, which is unrealistic and unhealthy."

"Well, I don't care to make this the latest scoop in the *National Enquirer*, I'll tell you. I feel so dumb about it."

"It's going to be okay." Wayne smiled and gently took hold of her hand. "You'll be fine. Just let it go."

She craved his reassurance more than she realized. She'd been so uncertain since that meeting at Cedar Canyon. She didn't know which way to turn or what to think. She was glad Wayne told her that seeing doubles was commonplace, but it still proved discomforting. Maybe because the feelings were still raw. As Anson pointed out, she hadn't truly recovered from Eric's death. She was still a basket case running around Cedar City, looking to find him alive in the people she met. Maybe it would take years and not months to get over this.

She glanced at her left hand, which Wayne still held in his, the hand that once displayed the brilliant diamond Eric had given her over a fancy dinner one night. She'd thought she'd said good-bye to it all that day in Omaha. She'd convinced herself it was time to move on. She believed she'd made the right decision by moving back here to Cedar City and starting over. Then why was she being plagued by another emotional storm?

Marissa shook her head and tried to forget it. She prayed with all her might she wouldn't see Anson again, as kind as he had been. She didn't think she could handle the emotional strain. She must bury it along with all the other unhappy memories.

"You need to do something for fun," Wayne suggested. "Take your mind off things. You know the Shakespearean festival is starting up. And I just happen to have two tickets." He released her hand and took the tickets out of his wallet, flashing them before her eyes. "I would love to have you accompany me."

"So they're still doing that every summer, huh?"

"Of course. It's Cedar City's trademark. Everyone's been talking about it. The hotels are starting to fill up. And of course, *Romeo and Juliet* is extremely popular. In fact, I think many of the shows are already sold out."

Marissa smiled, thinking how nice it would be to enjoy a play and allow the moment to carry her away from the complexities of life. "I'd love to go."

His face brightened. "Great! Looking forward to it."

She was, too, as she sipped her cold latté. "Did you know that I did some acting in Omaha? We joined this little theater group. Eric said I had a knack for it. Of course when it came time for me to say my lines, I goofed them up. The other guy I acted opposite from was a professional, so he helped me. But Eric loved it." Her voice faded away to a whisper, realizing what she was doing. Allowing it all to drift to the surface. "There I go again."

"What?"

"Talking about Eric and everything. Sorry."

"Why are you apologizing? Of course you're going to talk about him, and probably for a long time. Memories serve as a way of accepting what's happened. Especially in the area of grief and loss."

"I thought I was having more problems by continuing to mention him like I do." *And running around Cedar City, looking for his double in strangers*, she chastised herself.

"Marissa, you can't pretend he never existed. That would be unhealthy. He was a big part of your life. Almost your other half. I'm sure you knew each other very well."

Marissa nodded before taking another long drink of her latté. Yes, she knew him. Everyone said they made the perfect couple. When she met him in college, they just clicked. She wanted to borrow his notes for chemistry one day after class. He was happy to oblige and came by with the pizza, too. From that moment on they were a couple. The relationship led them to his parents' hometown of Omaha where they both landed jobs and apartments after college. Wedding plans began in earnest until everything came crashing down that one awful afternoon.

Her thoughts flashed back to the guy she saw at Cedar Canyon and his similarity to Eric. Then she stared at Wayne. He was nice looking and not a bit like Eric. A dimple formed in the corner of his mouth when he displayed his wry grin. And he had dark hair and eyes. She told herself to stop dwelling on the past, Eric's double, or anyone else and concentrate on what the future may hold.

Now she watched Wayne take out his smartphone and show her the house he wanted to buy. As if it might yield some kind of exclamation from her. She hoped he wasn't expecting her to say something like, *I'd love to live in it, too!*

"It's very nice. But are you sure you want to live way up there in the hills? What will you do when it snows?"

"That's why I've got four-wheel drive. It seems like the perfect place to get away from it all. You can come see it with me later on this afternoon if you want. A woman's perspective on things would be nice to have."

"Well, maybe. I have to go job hunting."

Wayne looked at his phone. "And I have an appointment in the next half hour, so I need to run. Call me if you want to see the house." He stared for a minute, looking as if he wanted to kiss her good-bye. She flushed at the thought. Instead he pocketed his phone and headed for the door.

❧

I remember you saying how much a dog would help you right now. Maybe this would work. He practiced the lines in his head while staring for several moments at the screen, which displayed the pet listing on craigslist. Anson glanced over at the corner table, still using part of a newspaper to conceal his features while the woman he saw on the canyon walk pawed through her purse. He hoped to bless her by this announcement and maybe make things easier with regards to her loss. She took out a tube of lipstick. He thought of the man she had shared coffee with. He knew him. Or knew of him. Wayne Newberry. He and the woman had shared some deep conversation, though Anson couldn't hear the words. Occasionally her long finger would sweep a tear away from the corner of her eye. She then exclaimed over something Wayne showed her on his cell phone. He hoped it wasn't a dog as he looked at his own phone. He really should make his move now that Wayne had up and left. He imagined Carl cheering him on, telling him to go for it.

Anson stood and moved to the table. The woman sat back with a start, nearly dropping her lipstick.

"Oh wow. I'm sorry, but every time. . . ," she began, then looked at her purse.

"I didn't mean to startle you. I was glad to see you here. There's something I found online that might interest you." She drew in a deep breath while smoothing back her hair. He gave her his phone. "See? There's someone right here in town who's selling dachshund puppies."

"You're kidding." She read the description out loud—eight-week-old puppies ready for homes. "The price is a bit steep, but for puppies, and miniature dachshunds at that. . .I have to see them." She searched for a pen to scribble down the information on a paper napkin.

"Actually, I already e-mailed them about the specifics." He took back the phone. "Here it is. 'We have two males and a female. I would like $150 cash each. They've had their first shots.' The owner is located on College Street if you want to stop by."

Marissa shot out of her chair. "I'm there." She then sat back down with a sheepish grin. "I suppose I'd better get some doggie stuff first. I don't have a thing. Food, collar, leash. A crate." She then slapped her forehead. "Mom. What will she think of all this?"

"Your mom?"

"I been living with her since coming back to Cedar City. She wasn't too keen on the idea of me getting a dog." She took out her phone. "I'll have to find out if the tide has changed." She placed the call while Anson forced himself to sit still and not fidget. "Guess she's at work at the deli. Wow, even though it will be a lot, this is something I need right now. We had a dachshund when I was growing up. A dachshund is the family trademark."

She sighed, looking so thoughtful and pretty just then, with her long, wavy hair. He was glad he'd been able to discover this. Maybe the tide was turning between them, too.

Anson cleared his throat, shoving any leftover nervousness he felt aside. "You know, we've met a few times, but you never did tell me your name."

"What? Oh, I'm sorry. It's Marissa. Marissa Jones. And you're Anson, right?"

"Right. Does your mom work at the grocery store here in town? I think I've met her a few times. They make a killer chicken that my pal Carl and I enjoy eating while watching the baseball game."

"Yes, Rosie Jones. I guess if you live here long enough, you get to know everyone. But I never met you until now, even though I grew up here."

"I grew up in St. George," he reminded her. "I didn't move here until after high school."

"That's right." She hesitated. "You know, I don't think I ever told Eric where my mom worked. I never talked much about my family. Maybe because I knew Mom wasn't thrilled about our engagement. I'm not sure."

Anson wondered about that and the apparent disagreements she'd had with her mother over things. He'd had a good relationship with his mom and was thankful for it until the cancer took her away. Maybe it was good Marissa was talking to a psychologist like Wayne Newberry. She could get the professional help needed to overcome these bumps in life. Like he wished he'd done for his dad after Mom died.

"Well, I'd better go find a job to pay for my dog," Marissa said. "And get some stuff for her, too."

"I take it you'll go for a girl."

"Of course. Girls have more fun." She blushed redder, looking even prettier than the finest rose. "Sorry, I didn't mean for it to come out that way. I meant that we girls have to stick together."

"If you say so."

"Anyway, thanks Eri. . . Boy, I almost called you Eric, too. This is crazy." She shook her head, managed an embarrassing grin, and headed out.

The aura of her presence still lingered, as did the pleasing aroma of her flowery perfume. Anson returned to his cup of now cold coffee, downing it before looking once more at the ad and picture of the puppies. Perfect. If only there wasn't the stigma of this Eric person hanging over everything. The mere fact sent a slight chill racing through him, despite the hot day. And sadness for her, that she still mourned so deeply. He checked the time on his cell phone, realizing he'd likewise better make tracks. He still needed to buy some chow for Goldie before he left town. Carl would be keeping her for four days while he roamed the Utah parks on business. And he'd better make sure he had enough food, as Carl had it in for him the last time the chow ran out, as did the dog biscuits.

Anson returned to his car and headed for the nearest big chain store and the pet department. Once inside the store, he stopped short. Standing in the aisle, perusing dog leashes and collars, was Marissa. He wanted to say something but instead ducked behind bags of dog food jutting from their places on the metal shelving in the other aisle.

"Can I help you?" a clerk asked her.

"Yes. I'm getting a miniature dachshund. I'm not sure what size collar I should get."

He watched as the clerk pointed out a selection of the smallest collars in stock. She held up several, checking the clasp and design before settling on a pink one. *Guess she's settled on a girl,* he thought. He admired Marissa's long fingers and her hair, which draped like a waterfall of molasses over her shoulders. Hardly any women he knew of wore their hair long. She then moved off to select a dog dish. Finally she tried to pull out a bag of puppy food, only to have several bags fall in an avalanche around her.

Anson immediately came over to her aisle. "You didn't hurt yourself, did you?"

"No. I guess they didn't stack the bags right." When she turned to face him, she gasped and stepped back. "Oh, it's you!"

"I know it looks strange, but I'm honestly not following you. I'd forgotten to get a bag of food for Goldie before I head out of town."

"I didn't think you were a stalker." Marissa smiled. "But guess what? I just talked to Mom, and she's agreed to have a go with the puppy. Reluctantly, with feet dragging, I think. But she's willing." She pushed back hair that had fallen forward. Suddenly she came out with a nervous chuckle. "Thank you so much for finding the dog. I still can't believe what I said to you out on the canyon walk. Talk about a major embarrassment. I mean, you really don't look anything like who I thought you were. I must have just been emotional and all, moving here. Too much to handle all at once."

"Well, a new puppy will surely keep you occupied. You won't be bored." She giggled at this, and excitement filled him. "Let me carry the bag of dog food to the checkout. I'll tell them to hold it for you until you've finished shopping."

"Okay, thanks." She smiled once more—a dazzling smile filled with perfect white teeth. She looked like a glamour girl in one of those commercials. She must be a model, he decided, but she didn't have that kind of outward personality. Still, she was warming up nicely to him. No longer did she stare at the ground or the sky above but looked him straight in the eye as if she were used to seeing him. Things were definitely starting to look up.

He strode up to the cashier and presented the dog food. In an afterthought, he went ahead and purchased it.

A few minutes later, Marissa hurried up, out of breath, to unload the other doggie goodies on the counter. "Oh, and the puppy food is mine, too. I still need to pay for it."

"It's been paid for already," the clerk said.

She stepped back. "What?"

"Welcome to Cedar City," Anson said quickly, managing a small smile before taking up his own bag of dog food and heading out the door.

He stopped to peek in the corner of the shop window and saw her standing at the checkout. She fumbled in her purse for her debit card, appearing quite flustered. She glanced around as if expecting him to still be there. He inhaled a sharp breath, wondering what she was thinking. How he wished he could read her thoughts. Did she like what he did? And consequently, did she now like him? When she saw her load the bags into the cart in preparation to leave, he moved quickly to his car. He must let it go for now. There was work to accomplish this week. But when he returned, he hoped their paths would cross again.

❧

Marissa decided she'd had enough interesting encounters for one day and headed for home, leaving the puppy for tomorrow's adventure. She could barely breathe let alone think after what happened at the store. She thought of the dog food in the trunk, purchased by Eric's double, then shook her head. She mustn't think of Anson that way. True he did have a few similarities to Eric. But he was his own man, as Eric had been. And now she wished she'd said something different in the store. To stop with the apologies and move on as if nothing had happened. Even small talk about the weather would have been better.

She barged into the house and dumped the dog items in the foyer.

Mom hurried out of the kitchen. "What are you doing with all that?"

"Remember, Mom? I'm getting a dog. I don't have it yet, but. . ."

"Oh. I hoped you were joking when you mentioned it."

"What?" *Oh please, Mom. Don't do this to me.*

"I don't know if I want a dog here, Marissa, now that I've been thinking about it. While you were away at college and Phyllis was doing her thing, I had to take care of your dog. And she was so sick. It was awful. Especially when I had to have her put down."

"Mom, I know you did so much for Sunny. And I never thanked you for it. But really, it won't be like that. This is just for a few weeks until I can get an apartment."

Mom looked at her but said nothing.

"I don't want to sound desperate, but I really need this in my life right now, especially after everything that's happened." Marissa didn't spill the rest. . .that life was spinning out of control, despite her best efforts. Having the puppy—caring for it, training it, walking it—would give her something to shower love and attention upon. Something to rid her mind of Eric, Eric's double wandering around town, and Wayne's fingers caressing hers along with that look of interest in his eyes.

Mom stared at her for a moment, shook her head, and returned to the kitchen. Marissa looked at the dog food, thinking about Anson's kind gesture. She so wanted a dog back in Omaha but never broached the subject with Eric. He loved his tropical fish. Did Anson like tropical fish, too? *Oh, honestly, Marissa. Stop with the comparisons.*

"Marissa, I don't see why you need a dog now with everything else going on. You're just getting settled." Mom had reentered the foyer to look once

156

more at the dog bowl, leash, and food.

"That's all I want to do is settle in, Mom. But it's hard. People here have been great. I've liked getting together with Wayne. I haven't been able to connect with others like I wanted, such as Denise and Joy from high school. Joy's been having morning sickness, and Denise is busy with her work. Maybe if I can reconnect with the church, though they have a new pastor. . ." Her voice faded away.

Suddenly Mom had an arm around her, giving a gentle squeeze. Marissa soaked in the comfort that eased the misgivings. She wanted to blurt out all the things going on inside but held back. "I know it must be hard," Mom said. "Give yourself time. And I brought home the ingredients to make you lemon bars. They always seem to cheer you up."

Marissa heaved a sigh. "Mom. . .what about the dog?"

"Look, I'm just glad to have you home. If you need the dog so much, okay. But he's your responsibility." Mom released her hold and said nothing more.

Marissa silently thanked God for this small miracle, one of many she needed in her life. She was doing things she never thought she would do a few months ago. Like returning to Cedar City when she thought she would be married and living a blissful existence in Omaha. She prayed that peace and purpose would reign in her heart again, even if both seemed absent right now.

Chapter 5

So who is she, Anson? Let's have all the juicy details. Please!"

Anson was busy scribbling notes, barely hearing the words of the young female ranger manning the information counter inside the visitor center at Cedar Breaks National Monument. "Who or what are you talking about?" he wondered absently. He was on duty as usual, ready to hear all the complaints and situations involving visitors—like trespassing, damaging park property and protected sanctuaries, people sick or injured or unhappy with the park in general. And he would smooth it over with conventional wisdom and sneak in some godly attributes as well. Like turning the other cheek to an irate visitor. Give good for evil. Deal in justice and the law. Say a kind and encouraging word—things that would soothe a distressed soul. And he'd already done that with a woman who said the park had injured her ankle. He'd smoothed it over with a sympathetic phone call and avoided legal action.

But now his fellow rangers were hammering him today, and he didn't know why. Did his face give away a telltale sign to the two women that something was going on? Like lines of tension running across his forehead or a certain look in his eye or maybe the pen trembling in his fingers. He thought he appeared rather composed, even if his insides were slowly twisting into knots.

"C'mon, I can see it. I actually heard you whistling as you work. Didn't you, Mira?" Sandy elbowed her naturalist friend.

"Yep, Anson was whistling all right. Some oldies song like 'Love Me Tender.'"

He peered up at the two young women who eyed him in anticipation while leaning forward, poised to hear any titillating gossip. "You two sure are nosy."

"C'mon, Anson." Sandy cupped her face with her hands, blinking her lashes rapidly. "We want to hear every detail."

He dismissed their interest to collect his notes, which took up the end of the information desk. A visitor bumped into him then and inquired about hiking trails in the park. Sandy let go of her curiosity to answer the visitor's question, while Anson took the opportunity to write a few more choppy sentences about his phone call earlier to the injured visitor. Thankfully the call had gone well, with the husband apologizing for making a scene and confessing they'd both been on the wrong side of the railing when the log fell on his wife's foot. If only all things could be this easy. He sighed in relief, thankful the situation had been resolved. Yet other situations loomed, ones he had little skill or knowledge in solving.

The visitor moved to the front door, and once more Sandy's attention was focused on him. "Mira and I had been taking bets when you'll find someone to date. So how about it? Who's right and who's wrong?"

"Ladies, you have entirely too much time on your hands. Maybe I should find some work for you to do." He chuckled while stowing away the papers.

"You're a great guy, Anson," said Sandy. "If I wasn't already going out with someone, you'd be on my short list." She laughed. "You should at least have a few prospects."

"Thanks for the interest, but it will happen when it's supposed to happen." Like everything else in life, he decided. But right now things were happening that he wondered if they were of God or not. Like the encounter with Marissa Jones that ended up hitting his heart and soul in an unexpected way. He had to admit, after the various encounters, from the canyon walk to the pet store, he had a distinct desire to know more about her. Like where she lived, for example. Maybe it was close by since she frequented the canyon walk. If she did live in the neighborhood, that would surely mean more encounters. And maybe friendly conversation would occur now that she was over the initial shock of their first meeting. They'd gotten the kinks out, so to speak. Hopefully she would deal with her grief and move on. They could enjoy walks with their dogs once she had her little Fido trained. Talk about their interests. Maybe it would lead to lunch, like a sandwich and coffee. Or dessert. Lucy loved desserts. Women liked chocolate, too, right? Marissa liked that shop, The Grind. And he would like to be the guy on the other side of the table rather than the psychologist, Wayne Newberry, who seemed a bit too friendly during their last encounter, in Anson's opinion.

"See, he's turning red, Mira," Sandy noted. "Anson, you're driving us crazy with all this secrecy!"

"Okay. Here's a little story for you."

The two women leaned over the counter, eager to hear every detail.

"I ran into a woman on the canyon walk in Cedar City who thought I was her dead fiancé come back to life." He expected laughter or looks of wonder. Maybe even sympathy.

Sandy's smiling face disintegrated into a look of bewilderment. "Are you joking or something?"

"Did you see something on a crime drama?" Mira asked.

"That's what happened. In fact she even asked me if I was him, if I lived in the same state as this fiancé and everything."

"You're kidding. You've got some crazy girl chasing after you?" Now both women looked at him with wide eyes.

"No, nothing like that. She's very nice. She's just been through a lot. Her fiancé died a while back, and she moved to Cedar City to be with family and friends. Of course, after a few more meetings, she decided I didn't quite look like him after all."

Sandy shook her head. "Maybe you are her dead fiancé come back to life, Anson. I saw that once on TV. Can't remember where. But the guy had amnesia and didn't know who he was."

He saw them both looking him over, wondering if he'd been smacked on the head. "I assure you I don't have amnesia. I still remember who you both are. Kind of." He grinned.

"Do you like her?" Mira asked.

Anson thought on that. "Yes, as a matter of fact, I do."

The women shrugged. "Well, I'd say you'd better go easy, then. Treat her with some of that mercy heart you give the visitors, Anson. You can't go wrong."

Anson thought it a good idea as he moved toward the door of the visitor center. Still he was embarrassed he'd spilled the beans about the whole "double" scenario. He should have respected Marissa's privacy. But the rangers were hungry for details, and he'd given them plenty to chew on.

He slipped outside and behind the visitor center to a clearing that overlooked the famous vista of Cedar Breaks—a huge bowl-like configuration with rocky formations colored like a mixture of table salt and cayenne pepper. In the distance other visitors gathered along the walkway to take in the beauty. The only thing that spoiled the scene were the dead spruce lining the canyon rim. The lifeless trees, damaged by beetles, stood out in sharp contrast to the colorful canyon. How like life. Beauty that could be easily marred by memories of those who had passed on, or other tragedies and loneliness. He would like to see Marissa stay beautiful. To not let what happened in the past ruin her like the scene before him. He should do as Mira and Sandy suggested—sprinkle mercy and kindness as the necessary ingredients for life and peace.

He returned to his SUV and tried setting his mind on his work. His next stop was the forest service center at Dixie National Forest. But his thoughts continued to drift. He should have another talk with Carl. Watch some sports and eat chicken. Then talk about women. Carl had a girlfriend. Maybe he should get Carl's take on how to approach a woman who'd been engaged. How does he get her to see him with new eyes and not with eyes that only see her late fiancé?

Anson thought over the game plan. He had it in the bag as far as Carl was concerned. Good food and sports go together. And so, too, would a talk about women. When he pulled into the grocery store, another thought occurred to him. Marissa's mother worked in the deli. It would be good to find out a little more about her through the mother. He knew Rosie by face. She was a model of perfection when it came to handling the deli, running it better than any drill sergeant could train the troops. Other than that he didn't know much else about her.

He strode into the busy supermarket and headed for the deli area. He didn't see the older lady. Instead some young woman who snapped her gum stood behind the counter. "Is Mrs. Jones working?"

"She left early."

Great. Anson sighed. So much for that. "Okay, thanks." Now the aroma of fried chicken tugged at him. He set to work assembling the meal—a box of chicken and potato salad to go along with it. He then meandered over to the bakery for an apple pie. Carl would never say no to this. And neither could he as his stomach churned with the thought of food.

Suddenly he spied an older woman wearing a store apron, ready to exit the store. He left the food sitting in a basket on the counter and ran out to intercept her. "Mrs. Jones!"

She whirled in surprise. "My goodness. Did I leave something in the store?"

"No. I'm sorry. I'm Anson McGruder. I often stop at the deli counter."

"Well, you're one of a hundred each week, I'm afraid."

"I was. . .I was wondering about Marissa."

The woman's eyebrows rose. "Are you a friend of Marissa's from high school?"

"Uh. . .well, we've met. . . ," he began. "On the canyon walk."

"Isn't it wonderful how she's come back to town? I'm so thrilled to have her back."

"I imagine you are. Any mother would be."

"I just hope I won't be in competition with her dog. She got herself a dog, you see."

"Really." So she did finally get the dog he'd suggested. The fact warmed him. He now had a connection with Marissa. "Well, I know it must have been tough on Marissa, losing her fiancé. I mean, when I first saw her on the canyon walk, she thought I was him."

At this the woman's eyebrows rose even higher. "Oh my goodness. I had no idea she was taking it so hard. I guess I should have figured it. Probably a good thing she and Wayne are seeing each other. Do you know Wayne Newberry?"

He nodded but was struck by the words. *Wayne and Marissa are seeing each other?* He sputtered, "You mean he sees her as a client?"

"Oh, no. I just talked to Wayne's mother. Something is happening between them. They're going on a date to see *Romeo and Juliet*. He's quite a successful psychologist. And he's in the middle of buying a house, which means he plans to stay in the area. I think they're perfect for each other."

All the anticipation within Anson suddenly vanished. He shifted his feet. "That's nice," he said weakly, knowing full well he didn't mean it.

"Yes, well I'll have to tell her I ran into another one of her friends. She's looking to reconnect with old friends here in town, but they all seem so busy."

"Tell her I'll be walking my dog on the canyon walk tomorrow morning at eight. We can. . .we can talk about old times." Like times in the last few days, he mused. And maybe tell each other good-bye, too, now that Wayne Newberry had arrived on the scene and whisked her away. Anson wished he could probe more—how serious Marissa and Wayne were, and if that house meant she and Wayne were planning to marry in the future. If that were so, what about all that supposed grief she exhibited? Maybe it wasn't as bad as he thought. She must have overcome the melancholy quickly if she and Wayne were on some fast track to the altar. He stood there wondering if he had just wasted the last few days on some whim. *You should have never thought of her in any other way than a stranger you met on the canyon walk. Let it go and stop being selfish. Be glad she's finding a reason to go on.* But he wanted to be that reason.

Anson trudged back inside the store to find his basket of food long gone—disposed of by another gum-snapping clerk, no doubt. He went around picking out his dinner once again, hoping Carl was free tonight. He really needed to talk things over with him. Tell him the big news of the day—that love had once more eluded him, swept away by a psychologist's mind and heart.

⁂

Over a plate of fried chicken accompanied by potato salad later that evening, Anson dropped the bomb. "Hey Carl, I just thought I'd let you know that, once again, love has sent me heading into another Dumpster."

His friend never missed a beat when it came to food, but Carl surely missed the seriousness of Anson's news as he ate. "Well, I'm sure we all feel that way from time to time. Like we've been in the garbage heap of life." He dished up another huge helping of potato salad.

"I mean it."

Carl shoveled down a forkful of salad followed by a swig of cold soda. "Okay, so what's the deal? Where are you going with this? Because I've never known you to take a dive in the trash before." He chuckled and tipped back his chair.

Anson unfolded the details of the last few days and how Marissa appeared to have been seduced by a psychologist who sympathized with her woes. Carl said nothing, but in the middle of the story, his chair hit the floor with a thud. "Well, sorry to hear that, bud. I must say I'm really surprised how this woman has gotten to you. First time I've not seen you head over heels for your work in the Park Service."

"I know when we first met, she was shaken up. Thinking I was her fiancé come back to life or something. Then I thought I was starting to bridge a connection. Finding her the puppy. Buying the dog food. Now this guy comes out of nowhere and takes her away."

"You don't really know what kind of relationship Marissa and this psychologist have. It's hearsay from some overly eager and protective mother who wants things prearranged. Go do a few things with Marissa and see what happens. Like the walks you do in the canyon. Or take her on a road trip to one of your parks." He grabbed a dinner roll and reached for the butter. "We can even do a double date if you think that would help."

He thought silently on it, trying to imagine Marissa on a dinner date, her long hair reflecting in the candlelight along with her inquisitive eyes. Reminiscing over him finding the puppy for her on craigslist. He must still have a connection to her somehow, even with Wayne in the picture. There had to be something to grab hold of, no matter how small it was. "I'll try the walk first and see where things stand. If I can at least determine Marissa's intentions, I can take it from there."

Carl chewed, swallowed, then reached for his drink again. "Do what you want. Just keep your feelings and hers in check. If it goes south, get out fast. Don't wreck your lives over something that may not work out. But I wouldn't worry. You're good at interpersonal relationship skills, Anson. It's why they made you one of the chiefs in the visitor relations department. You're the genuine smooth talker in the area of visitor problems. So use your best skills to your advantage."

"I never thought I'd be solving my own problems."

"Anyway, speaking of your work in visitor relations, when do I get Goldie next?"

As if on cue, the huge golden retriever lumbered over and stretched out beneath the table at their feet. "Seven fifteen Wednesday morning. I head for Zion as soon as I drop her off."

"Okay. You hear that, Goldilocks? It's you and me again. And you'd better be good."

163

"Goldilocks? Look, Goldie is as good as gold. Hence the name."

"Sure, sure." Carl wiped his mouth once more on his napkin, then wadded it into a ball and pitched it unsuccessfully toward a nearby wastebasket. He stood to his near six-foot frame. "Well, thanks for dinner. Keep in touch, okay? I'd sure like to know how this turns out."

"Thanks."

Anson saw his friend to the door then moseyed on over to the living room and sank into a chair. Goldie followed suit and lay down at his feet. Just then a thought occurred to him. He stood and accidentally stepped on Goldie's paw. She let out a yelp. "Oops, sorry girl."

He went to his office and turned on his laptop. Once on the Internet, he typed Marissa's full name in the search engine. Several entries popped up, including a listing in a graduating class from Utah State. He perked up at this, recalling that she'd said something about skiing and clicked on the college ski teams. There he found Marissa Jones with her long hair flowing out of a knit ski cap. She wore a bright smile framed by flaming cheeks, holding a pair of skis upright beside her. She appeared quite attractive in the photo, like a model for a skiing magazine. He then looked over the faces of her teammates. No Eric was listed. Still, he was curious about the man who had nearly married her. What kind of man was he that had captured her heart?

Anson continued looking via the search engine. A news article popped up with Marissa's name in it. The article described the accident that killed Eric Donaldson. Anson bent to ruffle Goldie's fur as he read the difficult story and then the obituary that followed.

> Eric Donaldson, 26, of Omaha, Nebraska, died December 3rd as a result of a traffic accident. He was born February 28th in Park City, Utah, to Henrietta Clay (now Mrs. Eugene Donaldson) of Omaha, Nebraska. He graduated from Westside High School in Omaha and Utah State in Park City, Utah, where he majored in computer science.
>
> Eric was a skilled skier and an active member of the Covenant Church in Omaha. He enjoyed being with family and friends and lived life to the fullest.
>
> He is survived by his parents, Henrietta and Eugene Donaldson; a brother, Mark; his maternal grandparents; aunts; uncles; cousins; and his beloved fiancée, Marissa Jones; who will miss him dearly. He was preceded in death by his paternal grandparents.
>
> A Celebration of Life and Reception will be held Friday, 4 p.m.–7 p.m. at the Covenant Church. Private interment.

He wished there was more about Marissa besides the few photos from college and the simple yet profound statement in the obituary. "Well, Goldie ol' girl, maybe I should take my own advice and let this go. I've got things to do anyway. And it doesn't make much sense worrying about it."

Just then the cell phone played a tune, disturbing his thoughts. Lucy.

"Hi, Anson. I was wondering. . .well, how you're doing and all."

"Doing good. You caught me reading an obituary, actually."

"What! Who died?"

"You remember me telling you about that woman on the canyon walk who thought I looked like her dead fiancé. Well, I was reading about the guy. And I can say that this fiancé and I have nothing in common, which is good news."

"I. . .I don't understand. Why are you doing a comparison? For what purpose?"

How could he confess that he was being nosy, that he liked Marissa and was hoping to find out what kind of guy she liked before someone else, namely Wayne the psychologist, stole her forever under the guise of some mental diagnosis? "I don't know. I just wanted to learn more about the man Marissa nearly married. Aren't you happy that I'm looking into the relationship department?"

"I don't know. Not like this."

He looked at his phone in puzzlement. He thought for sure Lucy would be happy he was attracted to Marissa. But maybe not. "She seems very interesting."

"She sounds like she has problems. Be careful. Anyway, I wanted to let you know that we're coming up for the Jamboree in a week. Will we see you, I hope? The kids are counting on it."

"Of course. Tell my nephews I'm taking them on the midway. And to see the old cars. Maybe I'll throw in popcorn and cotton candy for good measure."

"They will love it, I'm sure." She paused. "By the way, what did the obituary say?"

"Not much. The guy was originally from Park City. I know he and Marissa met in college. He was big skier. Computer guy. Stuff like that."

"Okay. Anyway, I'll see you in a week."

When the call ended he still stared at his phone, wondering what could be plaguing Lucy. Why was she so against Marissa? Was God trying to say something, but he wasn't interested in listening? Was he setting himself up for a big fall if he proceeded outside of God's will? *God, I know You will work this out if it's meant to be.*

Chapter 6

The next morning Anson was treated to a pleasant sunrise, and he prayed, perhaps a new dawn in his life. He took Goldie out early to make certain she had a good walk before delivering her to Carl's. The sky was a perfect blue, as was normal for summer days in Utah. It felt quite warm but not humid. He had to admit, he was glad this was the day the Lord had made. That he would be making tracks for Zion. Visitor problems surely awaited him, but he could also enjoy the splendid scenery, like venturing into The Narrows—a popular walk within a canyon by way of the river.

He took out his phone and checked the calendar. Next weekend was the annual Jamboree, and he made a notation to contact Pastor Ray about helping at the church booth. Maybe he could take Pastor Ray aside then and discuss the issue of relationships. It might be good to have a man of God's take on these things and to keep him accountable in all areas of his life.

Anson began jogging along the walkway with Goldie when he saw a woman approaching in the opposite direction. The dog she handled was so small it could have fit in the palm of his hand. He skidded to a stop. "Now that is one tiny pup."

She stopped also, and suddenly he realized it was Marissa. Maybe the dawn was indeed rising, as he'd hoped. At first she appeared startled to see him, then relaxed. "Well hi, Anson. You're out early this morning. Meet my new boy, Sammy. The one you found for me *and* bought the food for. Which I haven't been able to thank you for until now."

"My pleasure. So it's Sammy, is it? I thought you might be getting a girl instead. You mentioned it when we talked about it at the coffee shop. What happened to the pink collar you bought?"

Her face pinked up, like the collar. "Oh that. I exchanged it for another. The lady just had male puppies left by the time I got there. Which is fine. Sammy, meet your uncle Anson. He's the one who found you. I owe him big-time, on several fronts."

Anson found the comment endearing. He liked it that he and Marissa were already speaking in terms of a relationship, even if that relationship was a simple one through their pets. "And Sammy, this is Goldie."

"Careful. Goldie's just a tad bit bigger than Sammy. More like Goliath

166

meeting David." She laughed. He liked the sound, bubbly and bright like the sunny morning. She appeared more comfortable this time than in previous encounters. Maybe finding a dog and buying a bag of kibble did wonders with the dog owner, and a very attractive dog owner at that. "Don't worry. Goldie likes dogs, large or small." Goldie took the opportunity to nuzzle the pup. "See? Maternal instinct. Bet if you give them time, Goldie will have that pup under her wing. Or paw." He looked at his cell. "But unfortunately I have to run, so I can't see how the friendship materializes."

"Late for work?"

"I have to be in Zion by noon. And inevitably I'll end up behind an RV going twenty miles an hour on the highway."

"What do you do there? Are you a ranger?"

"Not quite. I'm in the visitor relations department. I make sure everyone visiting the parks is happy and fairly healthy. Always something to be done. I'm responsible for several of the parks here. Cedar Breaks and Bryce, mainly. Sometimes I help in the national forest also. Zion, too, if they're looking for a second opinion, like today."

He saw her straighten. "Did you say you work at Bryce? I love that place."

"Maybe we could go there sometime." He knew he'd hit the bull's-eye when he saw her face light up as if a sunbeam fell directly on it. She stood still, pondering it all and, he hoped, him also in the equation. "Anyway, I'd better get going." Though inwardly he wished he had another hour. Or two. Or three.

"Okay."

Hope surged within him and set to rest, at least temporarily, any doubts raised earlier. Then she flashed him a smile, and nothing but her face appeared. He would have asked her right there about a future dinner date, except she'd moved off down the path. At least he had made inroads with the mention of Bryce Canyon. *There's always tomorrow. Or at least the day when I return from work.*

❧

Marissa took stock of the last few meetings she'd had with Anson. *Let's see now. He likes dogs. He likes Bryce Canyon; or rather he has connections to the canyon. He is adventuresome. He does look somewhat like Eric.* But the more she observed Anson, except for his hair and eyes, the more different he appeared. His build, for instance. He was taller, maybe, and thinner. Then of course there were personality differences. Likes and dislikes. She halted. What were Anson's likes and dislikes? She didn't know. Nor did she really know anything about him, save a bit about his job description and his dog. Not like Eric, whom she knew inside and out. Maybe it was time to discover someone new.

And Anson was proving to be new and different. Especially with his love for the canine companions, which spurred her interest. Like the encounter this morning. She stopped again, even as Sammy tugged on his tiny leash and whimpered. "What if he lives near here, Sammy?" She hurried then to the parking lot but found him nowhere in sight. Hopefully they would see each other more on the canyon walk. Talk more. And find out things about each other.

Sammy whined again. Marissa scooped the tired pup into her arms and cuddled him. "I'll get you home, Sammy. Though it would've been nice to know where he lives, I must admit. Then we'd likely see each other more." She trudged back down the road to her mother's house where Mom stood watering the flowers. The harsh Utah sun baked everything in sight. Green lawns were only had by those who watered faithfully, and Mom was one who cared about having a green lawn and flowers. She liked color, and so did Marissa.

"Don't let that dog go doo-doo on my nice lawn," Mom warned.

"He did his business on our walk. I'm training him as quickly as I can so he isn't any trouble. And he's doing pretty good."

Mom said nothing more. At least she appeared accepting of the new addition, even if reservations remained. Marissa hoped it would go better in the days to come. Heading inside to give Sammy some water and then tuck him in his crate, she again thought about the encounter today. One particular tidbit about Anson intrigued her—that he occasionally worked at Bryce Canyon, of all the lovely places on earth. She was already making plans to go there soon, perhaps in the fall when the crowds were smaller and she could spend time in God's creation.

Bryce meant a great deal to her. It was the place where she encountered a personal God interested in her. Or rather He'd always had His eye on her, but she'd chosen to see Him for who He was. Not just in the fascinating hoodoo formations or in the other park features. But discovering that He loved her and cared about her. As the youth pastor said on the retreat long ago, God had shown the supreme act of love by sending His Son to die for her. It made a profound impact on Marissa's life, driving her to who she would become. Yes, Bryce Canyon was one of those places she thought of often and the place she wanted to revisit for a time of personal reflection.

But first things first. She took out the newspaper to circle some ads for a few job openings available in town. Most were temp jobs in gift shops, which Mom pressed her to check out. She needed to do something. Her savings wouldn't last forever, and she was beholden to her mother now that she had Sammy. Work, followed by an apartment, would help make her independent and settled.

"Oh Marissa, did I tell you that Wayne called?" Mom announced. "Something about dinner and a play tonight."

Dinner and a play? She didn't recall the invitation at first until she thought back to the coffee they had that one day and his interest in seeing a Shakespearean play during the annual summer festival. *Wayne! Uh oh.*

"Sounds like you two are getting along nicely," Mom added, venturing into the living room.

"Wayne's a nice guy, I guess. Though sometimes I feel like he's psycho-analyzing everything I say."

Mom laughed. "At least you're getting it done for free. Betty was telling me that he's settling here very well. He plans to have his office up and running in the fall when the college students return. Good thing, too."

"Why do you say that?"

"Kids have lots of stress at college. You did, didn't you?"

Marissa didn't want to confess to Mom that college meant freedom in many ways. There was the intensity of studies, yes, but there were good times, too, like being part of the ski team. She had a great time taking to the slopes where she'd nurtured a relationship with Eric after they met in class. She recalled the times at the ski lodge on a break from the slopes, warming her cold toes before the fake gas fireplace, talking with him about everything. She wondered then if Anson liked to ski. *Stop thinking about him like that*, she chastised herself. Maybe she should be asking Wayne if he liked to ski instead. Did she only have this strange fascination for Anson simply because he looked a little like Eric? Or maybe the idea that he'd opened the door for her to get Sammy and bought the dog food stirred things to life. But then again, Wayne had bought her coffee and a muffin not once but twice.

The phone shrilled. "Get that, will you, Marissa?" Mom called.

She swept it up to hear Wayne's voice on the other end. "Did you get my message about the play? I tried your cell but just got voicemail."

"Is it really tonight?"

"I thought I told you what day it was back at The Grind, but maybe I didn't. Yes, the tickets are for tonight. Is that a problem?"

"I guess not." She looked at Sammy standing before the kennel door, staring longingly as if he couldn't wait for her to take him out of there and cuddle him. "Hey Wayne, do you like dogs?"

"Dogs? Sure, I like dogs. I don't own one myself, but I like them. We always had cats. Pets are very beneficial to their owners. Helps alleviate stress."

"You'll have to come by and see my new puppy. His name is Sammy."

"Sammy?"

"I named him after the seal. You know the children's book, *Sammy the*

169

Seal? I mean, he doesn't look like a seal at all, but it was my favorite book when I was learning to read." She wondered if he would now psychoanalyze this.

"People find comfort in clinging to things from their childhood. It gives them a sense of security."

Is that bad? she wondered. She couldn't tell from his voice. Did he think she was searching for comfort? Or was she simply being a child at heart?

"Marissa, are you still there?"

"Yes, I'm here. So what time is this thing?"

"Our 'thing' starts at eight. I thought we could grab a bite to eat beforehand. I could pick you up at six."

Marissa was on his first sentence—the "thing" part. Did they have some "thing" going? Did agreeing to see the play set "things" in motion?

"Marissa? You don't seem like yourself today. Did you run into that man again or something?"

How would he know that? Was he spying on them? Or was it the psychologist in him at work once again? "Well yeah, but. . ."

"I could tell by your preoccupation. Listen, if you want my advice, which is pretty sound if I do say so myself, you need to stay away from him. It's creating negative feelings in you that are affecting both you and those around you. The further you keep away, the better it will be in coping with your loss."

"That may be a little hard considering Anson lives on a nearby street and walks his dog every day. Anyway, I thought it would be good running into him. Helps me deal with those bad feelings face-to-face instead of pretending they don't exist."

There was silence on the other end for a moment or two. "Actually it will keep reminding you of the feelings instead of moving past them. Anyway, what about your life now? For instance, you said you wanted to find an apartment. I can help you look tomorrow, if you want."

"I need a job first."

"I've been thinking about that. You could work for me. Do you know any secretarial skills? I need a receptionist."

Now wouldn't that be cozy. The mere image of them working side-by-side made her heart jump and her palms sweat. "Yes, I do know some secretarial skills, but Mom circled some ideas in the paper that I might take a look at first."

Again there was silence. Marissa sensed that things were not heading off on the right foot with Wayne, especially if they were supposed to be going out on a date later tonight. Finally he said okay and that he would see her at six. She sighed. So far this was already turning into a mixed-up day, and it was only nine o'clock in the morning. Not a great way to start.

Marissa opened the kennel and picked up Sammy. The pup nestled in her arms as if content to remain there. She cuddled him close and gave him a kiss on a furry cheek. "You're a good pup, ol' champ. And we'll find ourselves a place to call home. Once I get the job set. Which reminds me, I'd better start looking. Nothing will happen with me sitting around holding you." She gave the pup another kiss and returned him to his crate.

An hour later Marissa was pounding the pavement of the downtown area. She came to a small shop selling soaps and perfumes to find an older woman hanging up a HELP WANTED sign. Marissa immediately introduced herself.

"I know your mother. Rosie Jones. She said you were coming back to town and that you'd lost your husband."

"Well, he wasn't my husband, but we were engaged."

"I'm so sorry. Anyway, do you need a job? I can offer you temporary employment for the summer season. But if business is good, it may last until Christmas."

Marissa decided it was better than nothing. At least she was establishing a foothold in the realm of working society. And she would smell good after a day in a fragrant shop. She thanked the woman, Mrs. Holden, for the opportunity, filled out the necessary paperwork, and received a brief tour of the shop's inventory that included soaps, lotions, poofy sponges, baskets, and running the cash register.

Marissa then continued along the street until she came to the edge of the college campus. She found the large theater built on the college grounds that hosted the festival each summer, modeled after the Shakespearean Globe Theater with its English-style architecture. Expectation welled up within her at the planned evening with Wayne. She would take it all in stride and without any preconceived notions. Enjoy a quiet dinner and attend the performance. *Nothing to fret over and everything to look forward to*, she told herself. If only she could believe it.

❧

Marissa was determined to enjoy the evening, even if her mind was in a whirlwind with Mom, Sammy, Anson, and everything in between. It began well enough with dinner in a nice restaurant. Wayne talked about his family and how their mothers loved the craft club. He chatted about his college days, his first job trying to use his psychologist skills that nearly ended in disaster. For a guy, he did like to talk about himself, a quality Marissa didn't recall from their time in high school. Maybe because he spent all day listening to clients spout their troubles. He had no one to hear his life's stories. And for her part, she listened as best she could, smiling at the appropriate times while slowly eating a Caesar salad sprinkled with fresh croutons.

When dinner ended, Wayne announced they would need to head for the theater. When they arrived, the preshow was in full swing out front, with the actors and actresses singing, playing lutes and harps, and even a woman in Shakespearean garb selling fruit tarts from a tray. Marissa was instantly caught up in it all. She enjoyed being transported to another world for the time being, away from the things that had burdened her these many weeks and months.

But as the play got underway, she realized perhaps *Romeo and Juliet* wasn't the most endearing tale to encourage her heart at this time. She said nothing to Wayne about it during the intermission when they took a walk in the courtyard, stretching their legs and enjoying the pleasant evening. Instead she talked about the professional acting and the costumes. "After what I did in the theater in Omaha, I can only imagine how difficult it must be to put on a major production like this."

"Many of these actors and actresses go on to star on Broadway or other big-name shows," Wayne added. "They are multitalented. As for me, I could never act on a stage."

"It can get a little nerve-racking," she admitted. "But it's also fun. You develop friendships with those who are in the show. You become a family, wanting to see the show go on, to do a performance the audience will never forget."

The time outside rejuvenated her for the remainder of the play. Marissa settled in her seat, determined to enjoy the rest of the evening. At the play's conclusion, when Romeo and Juliet each took their lives by succumbing to poison and a knife, a strange feeling swept over her. It was difficult to take in—the idea of death in love. Even upsetting, as she squirmed inside.

She looked over at Wayne, who seemed mesmerized by it all. When the play concluded, he was all smiles. "What an excellent production. Though I knew it would be. It's never been less than stellar."

Marissa managed a small smile as they wandered through the throng before finding a quiet place on the darkened street.

"Anything wrong?"

"Oh, it was a great night, Wayne. Thank you so much for asking me to go."

"I must admit *Romeo and Juliet* can be an emotional experience. But it's interesting to see that when one makes up their mind for the challenge of love, they will do whatever is needed to see it happen. And I find it admirable as well that their hearts' desire was to reunite their stricken families. And though they did die, the goal was fulfilled in the end."

Marissa didn't know what to say. Maybe she was tired of death. She wanted life. Something to hold on to. She couldn't wait then to see her dog, Sammy. And Anson even. Maybe he would be walking Goldie tomorrow morning. Then she remembered that he was in Zion National Park.

Just then she felt warmth come calling. Wayne had picked up her hand as they walked along and now held it firmly in his. She allowed the contact for the time being. It had been a nice evening after all, and they'd had a good time together.

On the drive home they said little. Just shy of Mom's house, Wayne brought the car to a stop. He turned to face her. "I hope we can get together again soon. And I'd love to have you work for me, so please consider it. I can think of no one better I'd like by my side. We'd make a great team."

"Oh Wayne, I didn't tell you. I found a job today, at a gift shop. I appreciate all you've done for me, though." She turned aside, even as his gaze lingered. She felt the wisp of a light touch as his hand slowly turned her face to meet his.

"Marissa?" He stared, perusing her every feature. His head tipped to one side, his face leaning closer, his eyelids closing. His arms drew her toward him.

She struggled out of his embrace and grabbed the door handle. "I'd better go. Good night, Wayne." She left the car and headed swiftly for the house, imagining his startled reaction, perhaps even anger that he'd been denied a kiss. Of course after a romantic Shakespearean tale, even if it did end in tragedy, he would expect a kiss to cap off the night. He probably thought he deserved it. But she could not deliver. And it was just as well. She wasn't certain about walking any romantic path right now. She wanted to take it a step at a time, not at a swift jog.

Mom had already gone to bed. Marissa opened the door to hear a high-pitched whine. She saw Sammy standing on his little legs, wagging his stumpy tail furiously. She picked him up and carried him into the backyard to do his business. A million stars greeted her from a backdrop of pure ebony. She wondered if Anson was enjoying a starlit evening over Zion with its massive sandstone walls. Or even at Bryce Canyon with a full moon veiling the famous formations in pure white.

A chill fell over her. Maybe that's why she couldn't kiss Wayne tonight. She had too much of Anson on her mind. *Lord, help me settle my heart as I'm settling here in Cedar City. Most of all, help me find my way.*

Chapter 7

Glad it worked out so you could be a part of our ministry here at the Jamboree, Anson."

Anson looked over at the smiling face of Pastor Ray, who went back to retrieve another case of water. The crowds slowly began to gather to celebrate the festivities. Along the streets were various booths—from home-made crafts and food to games and carnival rides. In front of the booths, lining the street, were automobiles of all makes and models from years' past. The event drew thousands of people to Cedar City's Main Street. And each year the church manned a booth where they gave out tracts and bottled water to thirsty Jamboree attendees.

"I am, too. Did I tell you my work schedule just changed? That means I can hang around weekends more. And show up for church more often."

"Good news. We've missed you. And I've been thinking of you, actually. There are a few events coming up that you might want to consider lending a hand with. Like the annual teen retreat late next month. I want to take the kids to Bryce. And since you know the park so well, I thought you might even want to head it up."

"Sounds good." He opened his mouth, ready to tackle the main subject on his heart—Marissa—when Pastor Ray walked off to retrieve another case of bottled water. Anson turned to peruse the sign-up sheet for manning the booth and stopped short when he saw a familiar name. *Marissa Jones. 2 p.m.* "Marissa is working the booth?" he wondered, unaware that he'd spoken out loud until he heard Pastor Ray.

"Marissa came to town a few weeks ago. She visited our church last Sunday for the first time and wanted to help. It's good for her to become involved. You know her fiancé died tragically, which is why she came back here to Cedar City. Her mother lives here."

"I heard about that." Anson then noticed the blank space on the sign-up sheet beside Marissa's name. When Pastor Ray wasn't looking, Anson added his name in the time slot. He then hurried off to bring out more water. He wondered what she would think when she saw him in the booth. Well, what did it matter? They were doing it for the town and for God. Sharing the Gospel and handing out water. And it might give him an opportunity to learn more about her and her about him.

"So is work going well?" Ray inquired.

"As well as can be expected. The usual visitor issues."

"You look like something's on your mind."

He cast the man a glance, wondering how he deduced that.

"Look, Anson, I'll be honest. Carl and I have been meeting on occasion, and he did say you might be having some relationship issues. If I can be of any help. . . I know a little about this kind of thing." He offered a grin. "And I have a fairly good track record, too, when it comes to men finding their chosen spouses in the Lord. Not that I'm some spiritual matchmaker. But God has a way of using a multitude of counselors to help us come to important decisions. I can certainly pray for you. And I'm here if you want to talk about things."

Anson appreciated the offer and told him so. It was all new waters to him, not only in relationships but also the added burden of one who had been through a tragic loss. And the loss of a fiancé, no less. The memories were still fresh, as he noted on their initial encounter on the canyon walk. He wondered how another man could fit into the picture of Marissa's life. If her heart was open to receive. If his heart was ready to accept.

"Hello! Anyone manning this booth?"

He turned to see Lucy standing there with her two sons. He grinned. "Hey, Luce. Hey, Tommy and Chris." He opened the cooler and took out water for them. "I'd hand you a pamphlet, but I think you're already on the right side of godly things, huh?"

She smiled and took the bottled water. "How's work?"

Anson wondered if that was the proverbial question of the day to loosen things up. "They had me checking on a safety issue with one of the trails in Zion. Of course I had a group of tourists from Germany asking why the trail was closed when they'd flown across the ocean to hike it. I gave them my all-American smile."

"You're so full of yourself." Lucy shook her head with a grin as she twisted off the cap and drank some water. "So are you working the booth right now?"

"Actually I'm not scheduled until two. And we're basically set up here. So if you want me to take a pair of rambunctious nephews around, I'd be happy to."

"Thanks. I was hoping you'd say that. I'm sure they don't care to go cruising craft booths, looking at pot holders and handmade wreaths."

When she told the boys Anson would take them around the Jamboree, they each tugged on his hands. "Let's go look at the cars, Anson!" they chimed together.

He smiled and led them to the cars on display—from an old-fashioned

Packard to a modern-day Porsche and Bugatti. He bought them hot dogs and popcorn. They stopped at a booth where Jamboree-goers could throw darts at balloons for prizes.

"Can we, Anson?" asked Chris.

"Sure, why not?" He wouldn't mind hurling a dart himself to build up some confidence. He plunked down the money. One after the other they threw the darts until Chris successfully popped the very last balloon. He got a small picture of a rodeo rider for his trouble. Anson then paid for his own round of darts and took care of all the balloons in rapid succession, earning a huge wooly sheep for his skill.

"You're so cool, Anson. Wait till Mom sees what you won."

Anson had to admit he was surprised and a bit sheepish himself lugging the stuffed prize around. "Speaking of your mom, we'd better find out where she is, as I've got the church booth to man in about twenty minutes." He searched the crowds milling about until he found her, petite and brunette, examining a handmade trinket.

Lucy walked out of the booth and stopped short. She burst out laughing. "Anson, what in the world? Why do you have that huge stuffed sheep?"

"Anson busted five balloons in a row!" the boys chorused in unison.

"Wow. I didn't know you had it in you."

"And look what I won, Mom!" Chris announced, holding up his revered picture.

Lucy smiled at them and then, as if on cue, led Anson over to one side while the boys hovered at a nearby booth, examining marshmallow shooters made of plastic pipes. "So I guess it went well."

"Very well. They are also fine manipulators in ordering food and prizes." He looked over at her to see her studying him intently. And again he sensed a similar distance as in their last face-to-face encounter. One he couldn't understand, as if she dearly wanted to break down a door existing between them but held back. What was it about the look on a woman's face that could send a multitude of different messages? He'd seen it in many places. With the rangers at Cedar Canyon. With Marissa on the canyon walk. Even his good friend, Diane, the cleaning lady at the Bryce Canyon Lodge. And now Lucy. Like they had some hidden agenda one must discover.

"So you aren't reading any more obituaries, are you?" she asked, staring at the sheep he held under one arm.

"No. Nothing I want to make a habit of. I was just curious to learn more about Marissa's background."

"Not sure what you can learn from that."

He wanted to say how much Marissa obviously loved Eric and how that might be a cause for concern for anyone new trying to enter the scene. He hoped in time that would not be an issue.

She then asked, "Have you ever seen a picture of this woman's fiancé?"

Anson hesitated. "No, can't say that I have. There was no photo in the listing. Wouldn't it be interesting to see one, though, after she said we looked alike."

"Huh. I'll never forget my piano teacher saying I once looked like her long-lost cousin—a famous violinist at age thirteen." Lucy laughed until she broke out into hiccups. She then ordered Tommy to return the marshmallow shooter to the barrel where he got it, even as he showed it first to her and then to Anson.

"Please, can I have it? Please, Anson?"

Anson grinned. "If I gave in and bought that, Tommy, your mother would not be happy." He took out his wallet. "Guess I'll have to get her a pot holder to ease the pain."

The boys yelped in glee as they took the money to buy the shooters. Lucy only shook her head.

"I'm trying to earn my title of uncle-of-the-year," he said with a wink.

"Well, they won't have much ammunition because I don't intend to get the marshmallows to use with them. And"—she paused and wagged her finger at him—"don't you dare think of getting them a bag of marshmallows either, little brother."

They both shared laughter until Anson realized it was time to head back to the church booth. "Stop by and meet Marissa when you can," he invited.

"Maybe I will."

Anson returned to the booth in time to relieve the two people manning it. He began piling the pamphlets into neat stacks. When he turned around, Marissa was in the back of the booth, stashing her purse behind some boxes. "What's this huge stuffed sheep doing here?" When she stood, they bumped into each other. "Oh, excuse me. . . ," she began. "Anson! What are you doing here?"

He thought he saw her visibly tremble, or maybe it was his imagination. He pointed to the sign-up sheet. "We're both manning the booth at two p.m."

"Oh." She pushed back strands of loose hair that had fallen out of the ponytail. "I didn't know anyone else had signed up. But I'm glad you did. I didn't want to do this alone."

"Jesus sent His disciples two by two. Or rather two plus three. The sheep in the back is mine. I won it tossing darts with my nephews."

She looked back at the sheep and couldn't help but grin. "I didn't know you went to this church. I thought you were like most everyone else in town, involved in the other religion, of which there seems to be a church on every corner."

He shook his head. Was that a sigh of relief he heard? "What about Wayne? What does he believe?"

"How do you know Wayne?"

Oops. "I. . .uh. . ." He realized she hadn't seen him watching them at the coffee shop a while back. "Oh, you start to know everyone in this town. Even the new people who come along. And I'll admit, I saw you drinking coffee a few weeks back—the day I showed you the ad for the puppies."

She nodded. "I've met so many new people. Especially at church. I want to be a part of the young adult group there. I was supposed to get in contact with these two girls I knew from high school, but it hasn't worked out. One of them is pregnant and pretty sick. So friends have been few until recently."

He hoped that meant she was considering him on the friendship angle. Which could be the start of something special, in time.

A couple came up then, and Marissa handed them bottles of water along with a smile. They shook their heads at the literature offered and said they were satisfied with their religion. "It isn't easy being a Christian here in town, I see," she remarked.

"Well, like most things, you stick to what you know and be salt and light wherever God places you."

A young college-aged student came up, and from the look in his eye, Anson figured he had something important to get out of his system. The guy began spouting out observations on the deity of Jesus and how their religions differed. Anson responded gently but firmly about the way Jesus had changed his life. How Jesus had been sent to bridge the gap between sinful men and God. When the young man walked off, clearly troubled, Marissa was staring at him.

"Wow. You're so good at this, Anson. Have you ever thought about becoming a pastor? Or going on missions?"

"Actually, Pastor Ray wants me to help lead the teen group when they go to Bryce Canyon later this summer."

"What? The church youth group is going to Bryce Canyon? When? I want to help. In fact, I must!"

Anson saw a fire ignite her dark and lovely eyes. More hair had fallen out of her ponytail. She undid the band, her hair cascading about her shoulders, before she caught it up once more behind her head. He stood there staring at it all. If only they hadn't gotten off on the wrong foot that first day on the canyon walk. If only the day could be repeated for the better, and they could start fresh. Like today.

She wiped her hand across her face, turned aside, and shook her head. "Oh wow. God, help me please."

Anson stepped back, startled. "I. . .I'm sorry. I didn't mean to stare. You have nice hair is all."

"It's not your fault. It's just at that moment you looked so much like. . ." She paused. "You reminded me of Eric, the way he used to look at me." She began thumbing through the stack of brochures. "But that isn't fair. I really need to get a handle on this once and for all."

"It's okay." He forced away any frustration at the continued comparisons. Eventually the man would fade from her thoughts, if he was patient. He smiled instead as more people stopped by for water on this hot afternoon. Pastor Ray dropped by also to make sure they had enough of everything. Anson and Marissa said little else for the next fifteen minutes. He wished the time hadn't deteriorated into another "Eric" moment for her. It had been going so well. He thought great strides were being made. But the past remained an ever-present shadow that left a dark imprint.

"So how's it going, Marissa?"

Anson looked up to see a tall guy with dark hair lean over the table in a casual stance. *Great.* To add another fateful twist to the day, Wayne Newberry had decided to make a sudden appearance. The broad grin on his face betrayed his distinct interest in Marissa. "I was hoping you'd be able to go around the Jamboree with me." He said nothing to Anson.

"I still have another forty minutes to work, Wayne. It's a two-hour shift."

"I can handle it if you want to go," Anson offered, but then wondered why he'd said it. Did he really want this guy latching on to her? Why didn't he push her to stay and work the entire shift?

"You've been reprieved." Wayne nodded his thanks to Anson.

"I'll go in about twenty minutes, okay? I want to at least start to finish what I began."

He opened his mouth as if to counter her, then clamped his lips shut and walked off.

"It's okay if you want to go," Anson said.

"Yes, but I signed up to do this. It's not right that he can peel me away from a commitment that I've made. Though it's nice of you to volunteer."

"Sure, no problem." He wished then Wayne wasn't in the equation of her life. He'd really like to ask her out for a bite to eat. Or another walk in the canyon. He'd even drive her to her beloved Bryce Canyon and take her to every overlook. He had some Bryce mementos at home, given to him by the concessionaire at the end of the season last year. Maybe he could give her something, like a key chain or some coasters. "So why do you like Bryce Canyon so much?"

"I accepted Christ into my heart at the canyon rim."

"Really."

"I was on a youth retreat, kind of what the pastor is planning for the teens at church. It was amazing. I'd just heard this great testimony from another youth minister on how he'd accepted Christ on an outdoor trip. We were looking at the scenery at sunset. You know that Bryce looks best at sunrise and sunset."

"Yes." *And you would, too. I can see it in my mind, with the fading sunlight reflecting in your hair. Wow.* He silenced his drifting thoughts.

"I was at one of the overlooks, and He became real in His creation. He wasn't a book or a church. God wanted me to know Him personally. It's hard to put into words."

"Yes," he said again, thinking how much he would like to run his fingers through her luxurious hair. *Knock it off.*

"Now with everything that's happened, I'd like to go back there and see what God has new for my life. And to answer any leftover questions."

"Like why your fiancé died?"

She turned. Her eyes widened slightly, revealing the appealing mocha color of them. "That could be. Maybe. I do wonder why he was called to heaven so early in life. And after we had made so many plans."

"God may tell you why. And He may not. Are you ready for either answer?"

She didn't reply. After another five minutes, Wayne reappeared, holding a melting ice cream cone, which he gave to her, accompanied by a charming smile. Anson had to hand it to Wayne for cleverly buying ice cream in an effort to lure her out of the booth. And it worked. Marissa gave Anson one final look before drifting off into the crowds. He watched her disappear while thinking on her words.

Suddenly Lucy and the nephews were standing before the booth. "Who was that, Anson?" Lucy asked. "Marissa?"

"Yes."

"She's a lovely girl."

He thought so, too. But now her lovely form clung to another man's arm.

"If God wants it to happen, it will. If not, you have to trust Him."

He looked over at her. "What was that?"

"You and Marissa. I saw her going off with that other guy. You remember the guy I was dating when Frank came on the scene. But there was nothing like Frank. Just as I believe, if this is God, there will be no stopping things between you two. No matter who or what comes on the scene."

Lucy, you've read my heart. But only God can make it happen, like you say. "Just for that, you get to take my sheep home."

She grinned. "Wow. Thanks a bunch."

Chapter 8

So are you a Christian, Wayne?" Marissa couldn't believe how quickly the question came leaping out. But since the meeting with Anson, she had to know where things stood. They'd had a pleasant enough time at the Jamboree, even though she spent most of her time thinking about Anson. Now they were back at The Grind once more, perusing life. She'd already been through so much these many months; she didn't want to start out on a wrong foot and in a relationship that was not of the Lord. Here in Cedar City, like in most Utah towns, beliefs in God took on different meanings and led one on different roads. She wanted a man who believed like she did, in the deity of Christ and eternal life through His ultimate sacrifice for sinful man.

"What led you to ask me this? Talk about sudden."

She squirmed, wondering if he considered it a personal affront. Or if he would psychoanalyze her intentions. But to her, it was important. "I don't know. My relationship with Christ means a great deal to me. You probably know that by now, especially with the work at the church booth during the Jamboree."

"Yes, I can see that, which is fine. Religion is very comforting to many people. And I go to church, if that's what you wanted to know." He mentioned the one he sometimes attended. She asked a few more questions about his true beliefs, only to watch his fingers tighten around the mug of coffee and his face grow rigid.

Marissa began to play with the strap to her purse as the meaning behind it all began to peal loud and clear.

"So what's the real reason for this?" he asked. "I'm curious."

"Well, I was talking to Anson. . ."

"The guy in the booth." He paused. "You know him?"

"I've seen him a few times. He's a park ranger or something like that. He. . ." She hesitated, wondering if she should divulge any more about her encounters with Anson. She noticed Wayne's eyes narrow and his face redden. He was sensing competition. And Marissa was sensing confusion on her part. "We walk our dogs together. I met him a few times on the canyon walk. He has a dog, Goldie."

"This isn't the same guy you thought looked like your fiancé?"

181

She sat back, realizing Wayne was indeed good at putting pieces of situations together. In fact, it downright irked her. "I. . .well. . ."

"Look, Marissa, you can't do this to yourself. It's not healthy, linking up with a guy you think is your fiancé come back to life. I'm sure it makes him uncomfortable, too."

"Maybe at first, but he doesn't seem to mind. He actually understands."

Wayne frowned as if unhappy to hear this latest development. "Marissa, I know it takes time to grieve. You need to give yourself that time. The grieving process becomes unhealthy when you start imagining situations and people, like you did with this perfect stranger. If you want, I know the name of a good psychiatrist who can—"

Marissa jumped to her feet. "I don't need a psychiatrist!" She threw the strap of her purse over her shoulder. "I'm trying to work things out, thanks very much. But one thing's for sure—I don't need someone psychoanalyzing everything I say or do. I want the freedom to explain things without thinking I'm a perpetual patient."

His features softened. "You're right. I'm sorry if I've come across like that. I just don't want you hurting any more than you already are. I care about you, Marissa. More than you know."

She slowly sat back down but could not look him in the eye. His steady, piercing gaze could drag a person in and hold them.

"I have hopes that things might be starting up again for us. We had a satisfying and healthy relationship going at one time, if you remember."

Satisfying? Healthy? She tried to consider the few times they went out for pizza in high school. She recalled the one kiss they shared. Or maybe twice, if she counted the night of the prom.

"You were an awesome prom date, too. We got an award, if you remember, for the best-looking couple. I know you've been through a lot since then, but there's no reason to think the sparks aren't still there. I believe they are. And I think it's interesting that we both decided to move back to Cedar City at the same time."

But for Marissa, sparks left over from high school weren't enough to start anything, let alone the blaze of a relationship. She feigned the need to leave, thanked him for the coffee, and headed out into the hot sun. Despite what Wayne thought, she'd really been thinking about Anson, and more than just occasionally. Daily might be a better way to frame it. She could not get out of her mind the passion in Anson's voice at the Jamboree when he shared the Gospel message with visitors at the booth. He was definitely an intriguing man. But the way he stared at her that one moment in the booth when she was fixing her hair. . .that threw her for a loop. And made her wonder if Wayne could be right about one thing—that she was setting herself up for more heartache if she didn't first release the past. Not that she would forget Eric, but she would remember that his love was in another time and place. That it was time for new wine in new wineskins, as the Bible said.

Marissa arrived at the soap shop to be met with flowery scents that nearly sent her into a sneezing fit. Mrs. Holden welcomed her with a smile. Though she tried to concentrate on her work, Marissa could only think about the conversation with Wayne. Clearly he was vexed by her decision to suggest Christianity in their relationship. Not that Eric was the most outspoken in his beliefs. They attended a nice evangelical church in Omaha. They didn't talk that much about God. Sometimes they prayed together. But she knew he was a Christian and that God had brought them together. And just as quickly had torn them apart.

She rang up a few purchases that day, even as Mrs. Holden complained about the slow business. "I'm afraid if things don't start picking up, Marissa, I'm going to have to let you go. I already warned your mother about it. But I hear you can get a fine job working for Betty's son. Like a secretary or something. Maybe you should consider it."

Marissa sighed, wondering if along with making their crafts, the women in the craft club jabbered about their lonely children in need of relationships. "I. . .well, I don't know. I hope I can continue working here. I like this job very much."

"Well, don't you worry. Betty Newberry's son is quite well off. He's a doctor. But you already know that. Betty says you two have been on a few dates already." The older woman patted her arm.

"He's been very nice," she said politely before blowing out a sigh, wishing well-meaning people would stop pushing Wayne Newberry her way. Yes, he was a nice guy. Yes, he seemed interested in her welfare. Yes, he was buying a house and that meant money. But there were also negatives as well. Things she could not ignore.

When the day ended, Marissa walked slowly toward Mom's house, distracted by her thoughts. Until she realized Sammy would need to go for a walk soon, and she hurried to relieve him of the confining crate. "Let's go on the canyon walk today, Sammy," she informed the dog. It was nice to be so close to the picturesque walk that meandered along a river and into a rocky canyon carved by wind and water. She arrived to find others walking dogs, jogging, or just enjoying the summer evening. All at once she saw a familiar golden retriever mosey on past her. "I'd know that dog anywhere," she murmured.

She heard a laugh and turned to see Anson walking toward her. "Hi. This is the last day you'll see us. I'm off again to the parks in the morning." He spoke as if it was the most natural occurrence running into her again. And maybe it was, in God's great timing.

"I thought you might be gone already, being a Monday afternoon."

"I'm on a different schedule. Except I won't be in church next Sunday. They have me working a split weekend. I thought I was over that, too. They said this is the last one, and I'll be glad. I miss church."

Marissa enjoyed hearing Anson talk about his work in the parks and also his interest in church. He then paused to look at the river. Marissa stopped and stood beside him. She enjoyed his presence, his strength, the way he and the creation surrounding him seemed to fit so well together. The two dogs decided to lie down at that moment. Sammy nestled close to Goldie's tummy. The sight brought comfort and maybe a precursor of the future.

"Look at that," Anson noted with a chuckle. "Dogs know. They're already friends." His voice drifted off. Marissa wondered if Anson could use a friend. She certainly could. She had Wayne bugging her but no other real friends to speak of since coming here. She'd been too wrapped up in her new puppy and the poofy job at the soap store, among other things. "It's good to have friends to talk to."

"I'm glad for Carl. He's a great guy. I hope you're making a few friends at church. There's a women's group that meets weekly."

"Yeah. Haven't been there yet, though the pastor's wife, Alicia, invited me." Sammy then lay on his side, all fours spread out, looking to catch a few winks. Goldie did the same.

"You should go. One thing I've found out, it's important to have people to talk to. Especially coming from the situation you did." He paused. "I. . . well, the past is good to get out."

"I'd rather leave it alone and move on. Everyone seems to think I need to talk about it. But Eric's gone. It's over and done with. Even though I have to admit, every time I see you. . ."

"You still see your fiancé sometimes?" he wondered.

Her cheeks grew hot. "Sorry. It has to stop eventually. Either that or Sammy and Goldie will have to find new buddies."

"Marissa, it's okay. I really do understand. It takes time. I'd hate to let that come between our walks."

She stared down at her feet, wishing then she'd not spooked him that first day. "It was such a dumb thing to do to you, asking if you were Eric of all things. I wish I could have a do-over where that's concerned."

"Okay. Then let's." He faced her and extended his hand. "Hi, I'm Anson McGruder. Welcome to Cedar City."

She looked first at his large hand, tanned by the sun and wind, and then at his face. She shook it, chuckling softly.

He continued. "You may not realize this, but I'd like to get to know you a little better since we're neighbors and dog lovers and, yes, Christians who need to stick together when the going gets rough."

He then turned and looked back at the river. He was being a gentleman through and through. And what did he say—something about wanting to get to know her? The mere thought made her feel even warmer under the collar of her shirt, adding to the temperature of the late summer afternoon.

"Would you like to go out for dinner sometime?"

The invitation caught her completely off guard. She whirled.

"Thought I'd land that one on you. I know you're probably going out with other guys and everything. Just thought I'd ask. Give you something to think about while I'm at work this week." He took out his wallet and withdrew a business card. "Here's my phone number and e-mail address. If you prefer texting or e-mailing, I'll understand. Let me know if it will work out for you sometime."

"Okay." She looked at the picture of him smartly dressed in a park uniform, appearing quite official. While he did resemble Eric in some ways, in the picture he was handsome and with his own extraordinary life. Anson McGruder, as he had said. She then heard him heave a sigh.

"I wish. . ." His voice drifted off.

Marissa wondered what he was about to say.

He turned to look at her, his mouth parted slightly, his hand extended. "Marissa, if you could only know how much. . ."

"Hey there!"

They turned to find a man striding up to them. Both dogs jumped up and barked greetings.

"Carl, what are you doing here?" Anson asked in astonishment. "I don't know you to walk much of anywhere, let alone here."

The man called Carl paused and looked between them both. "Ha. I figured I'd find you walking Goldie. But not taking a stroll with a fine lady." He held out his hand to Marissa. "Carl Bruce."

"Marissa Jones. Anson's mentioned you. He said you were good friends."

"I'm more like his conscience. Anyway, I'm here to tell you, Anson, that I can't keep Goldie this week. I was called out of town unexpectedly. Seems my company is doing a special trade show up in Salt Lake, and I have to leave early. I was going to call your cell but figured the walk would do me good."

Marissa saw Anson's face fall. "You can't keep Goldie this week. . . ," he repeated.

"Yeah, sorry about that."

Anson looked down at the dog sitting at his feet. "I can't put her in a kennel."

Marissa stared at both dogs sitting companionably with each other. Could she really do it? Would Mom have a coronary if she offered? "I might be able to keep her," she suddenly remarked.

Both men turned to face her. "You're going to save my reputation and my friendship if you could," Carl said with a grin.

Anson stared wide-eyed. "Wow, Marissa. This means a lot. I mean Goldie's no trouble. I can fill you in on everything. She's real easy to care for."

Carl waved at them, claiming he needed to get ready for his unexpected business trip. Anson continued to stare with more than relief on his face, but rather a look teeming with affection. He began describing Goldie's daily routine. "Do you think you can walk both dogs?"

"If not, I'll do one, then the other." She exhaled a sigh. "I just have to convince Mom it's a good idea."

"I'll pay you, of course. Eighty dollars for the week."

"You don't need to pay me."

"Actually, make it an even hundred."

"Anson, you don't need to. I'm more than happy to do it."

He stepped forward, looking as if he might supplement his gratefulness with something else. Dare she think he might kiss her by the way he'd settled his gaze on her lips? She stepped back, and he likewise retreated. "Okay, how about this? Will you go out to dinner with me when I get back as payment for watching Goldie?"

"All right." She smiled before taking the leash out of his hand. "C'mon, Goldie. Sammy. Let's see if this is going to work."

The two dogs leaped to their feet. Sammy, with his youthful exuberance, wanted to dash ahead, but Goldie kept him at an even walk.

Anson's laughter chased them down the path. "You're going to do just fine!" he called out.

The two dogs nuzzled each other's faces before stopping when she did, looking up as if to inquire if this arrangement might be permanent. "I think they will be all right."

Anson walked up and took Goldie's leash from her hand. Their fingers brushed. She lifted her gaze to see the deep blue of his eyes, matching the color of the sky above.

"I'll drop her off at seven," he said. "I hope that's not too early."

"I hope she'll be okay while I'm at work."

"No problem. She's as good as gold, hence the name Goldie."

Marissa chuckled. His fingers curled around hers and gave a small squeeze, sending tingles through her.

"Thank you so much. You're a godsend. Maybe in more ways than one."

They continued down the walk toward their respective homes. When Marissa came to her street, she offered a farewell.

"I'd be glad to come over to the house and introduce Goldie to your mom," Anson suggested.

"That's all right. It's only for a few days."

They stood looking at each other. A certain tension filled the air—of two hearts steadily developing an attraction for each other. Finally he said good-bye and turned toward his street. She watched him trot off at a fast pace with Goldie right beside him. She looked down at Sammy, who wagged his short, thin tail. "Well, we've got some fast talking to do. Pray that God gives me the words to help calm Mom when she hears that another dog is going to be in the house." But that thought didn't concern her now. What filled her mind was Anson—the intimacy of the moment with his hand holding hers. Soon she would be ready to grab hold of the future and never let go.

Chapter 9

very time I see you. . ., she began.

You still see your fiancé sometimes, he finished.

Anson thought about the conversation as he went about his business, this time at the popular Bryce Canyon National Park, where visitors littered the walkways and hovered at the overlooks, taking in the scenery of the mysterious canyon. He was considering Marissa more each day and wanted to take their budding friendship to the next level. The morning he dropped off Goldie, Marissa met him with a smile, claiming she'd convinced her mother to accept another dog if she helped paint the living room once everything was said and done. "A little finagling never hurt," she added, tossing back her thick, luxurious hair. He hoped he hadn't come on too strongly yesterday, insisting on dinner when he returned. Marissa didn't seem taken aback by it. She'd agreed to everything, after all. Even at the moment when he'd surrendered Goldie's leash to her perfectly manicured fingers complete with plum nail polish. Her steady smile followed him out the door. He only wished his interest in Marissa wasn't marred by obstacles still left to overcome. Another guy and the memory of a deceased fiancé among them.

"You haven't moved a muscle," a voice called out to him. Anson looked up to see his good friend Diane, who cleaned in the lodge. "You've been staring at the same scrap of paper for thirty minutes."

Anson finally noticed the papers strewn across the desk he'd appropriated in a room at the main lodge. He hadn't even looked at the forms outlining new park safety regulations in the past half hour. The words were a blur to his befuddled mind. He cracked a smile. "Checking up on me again, huh, Diane?"

"Someone has to." Diane sat down opposite him, a knowing smile on her face. He knew her well from his time working in Bryce. She'd come here some twenty years ago to clean at the lodge and had been in the same position ever since. When he was new to the park scene, she'd befriended him, bringing him a tin of oatmeal cookies as a welcome gift. On occasion Anson bought her a cup of coffee when the dining room wasn't filled with customers, and they'd chat about life. She told him about her family and her three sons. He'd tell her mundane things about his boring life, along with updates on Goldie.

But now his life had an unexpected twist in it and none of it boring.

"I happen to know you pretty well, Anson. What's up? I can see it in your face."

"I'm not sure where to begin."

"Whenever my sons had that look, there was usually a girl involved."

Anson looked away. "I, well. . ." Again a woman's perception amazed him, as if she could read his life in his eyes. He recalled a similar scenario at Cedar Breaks with the two inquisitive rangers. What was it about the female persuasion that sensed the unspoken?

"I raised three sons, you know. I've seen them go through every kind of situation with a girl there is. From moving in with one, to breakups, to marrying one of them. I know all the signs. So you asked her out, and she said no or something? She doesn't like you?"

"Actually I think she may like me. I'm not sure. There's another guy on the scene, too, and. . ."

Diane looked at him expectantly, waiting for the rest.

"I know we're not supposed to compare, but. . ."

The chair scraped. "Yes, that's right. You're a wonderful man, Anson, with many fine qualities."

"Yeah. Sometimes I wish I were her fiancé's double. Then I know she would take to me in an instant."

Diane stared. "What do you mean by that?"

"On the first day we met, she was fairly insistent that I was her fiancé come back to life. She'd lost him in an accident seven months ago, just before they were set to marry."

"Dear me. Maybe it's a blessing then that it's not working out, Anson. She sounds like someone you should be avoiding right now until things are better. She's obviously not over her fiancé. Maybe she needs some counseling."

"I don't think it's anything serious like that. And it's not what's causing me to pull back."

"It's the other man," she said with a nod. "Well, you'll have to do your best to win her heart, Anson. Like you won mine with a cup of coffee, making friends with a lady that could be your mother." She winked. "You have a good heart."

"I need someone to keep me on the straight and narrow."

"You already are. You just have to see yourself the way God does. That He has big plans for us. I'm not sure if yours includes this woman or not. But at least you're asking. And seeking. As the Bible says, seek and you will find when the door is open to you. It may not be that time right now. You hear what I'm saying?"

"Yes, I hear." It was heeding to faith and patience that was tough to follow.

Diane stood to her feet. "I just know you're going to find your way and that special lady to share your life with, Anson. Even if some other man might be standing in the way. God has a way of moving mountains. If God could make this beautiful place of Bryce Canyon out of rock so others can cherish it, God can certainly make something beautiful out of your hard places. If you're patient, that is."

The words rang true, even if Anson fought to accept the entire meaning of it. He gathered the papers into a folder and tucked them into a soft-sided case beside his laptop. Wandering out into the open area of the lodge, he saw several couples walking around with smiles on their faces, holding hands or with arms around each other. He'd never considered other couples until this moment. Now he wanted a hand to hold. A face to grasp close. Lips to kiss. Someone to share the splendor of the evening sunset casting a reddish glow over Bryce Canyon.

He sighed. It made no sense to think about that now. He had two more days of work to get through. And then a wondrous dinner date when he returned to Cedar City. He waited in expectation and a hope that the door to Marissa's heart would soon open wide.

꧁꧂

Anson arrived on the doorstep of the Jones residence at six p.m. to hear barking inside. He then heard a woman's voice telling one of the pups to settle down, and she'd give the dog a treat. It didn't sound like Marissa's voice, but then again he wasn't sure what her voice sounded like behind closed doors. When he knocked, he heard footsteps, and the door swung wide before him. An older woman stood there with her hair a tangled mess, a grim look on her face. "Yes?"

"I'm Anson McGruder. We've met before, at the grocery store."

"Oh, yes. I think I've seen you around town." She looked in a hurry.

"I'm here to pick up Goldie." He paused. "My dog?"

"Oh, thank goodness. It's about time. Those animals are driving me crazy. I don't know that much about dogs. I mean, I did take care of Marissa's sick dog when she ran off to be with that other man. But these two, they were something else. Marissa had to work overtime tonight, or she would be here."

Anson stepped inside to survey the humble, one-level ranch home. Goldie bounded up to him and put her front paws on his legs in a greeting. "Hey it's okay, I'm back." He then moseyed on out to the kitchen to see the woman taking food out of the fridge. "Do you have her leash and food bowls, Mrs. Jones?"

"I don't know where any of those things are. Marissa was supposed to take care of it all. Just look around. I'm sure you'll find them somewhere."

Anson stepped back into the living room, scanning the place, when his gaze fell on a picture of a couple atop a bookcase. He peered closer. The woman was Marissa. And then he saw himself standing beside her, her head resting against his shoulder. He jumped back, and when he did, he fell over Goldie and onto the floor.

"For heaven's sake!" Mrs. Jones cried, running out. "What happened? Did you hurt yourself?"

"I. . ." He rose gingerly to his feet, feeling a twinge in his tailbone. "Sorry. I—I was looking at the picture there on the bookcase and didn't see Goldie behind me."

"It's Marissa's engagement photo that she put in the paper. That's her with Eric, the one she was going to marry. I feel badly about what happened to him, but I'm glad she was able to move back here. She was too far away, living in Omaha."

He hesitated, then said, "I've never been to Omaha."

"Neither have I. But that's where Eric's family lives, so I guess he wanted to be there. Though usually the bride picks her own family to live nearby. I always thought so, anyway." She paused, staring first at him, then at Eric. "My goodness."

He sensed it. Tension. A certain strangeness. Perhaps even a sense of foreboding. "Mrs. Jones?"

"Why, you look just like him!"

Anson's face heated up quicker than an iron. He wanted to grab Goldie's leash and run, but his feet remained frozen. "Guess it's just one of those things," he managed to say.

"I guess so. Wow, it's uncanny. I can't get over it. How about that?"

He began looking around once more for Goldie's leash, wishing Rosie Jones wouldn't stare at him that way.

Suddenly the door opened, and Marissa burst in. She stopped short. "Anson! I forgot you were picking up Goldie today."

"Yes, and those two dogs nearly drove me to the insane asylum," Mrs. Jones grumbled. "But it's even more crazy. Just look at this, Marissa!" To Anson's horror, she thrust the engagement photo before Marissa's nose. "Look at this! Now look at him. Can you believe it? The eyes. And the nose and jaw. I'm telling you, they could pass as twins. If you change the hairstyle and dress them the same. I knew twins when I went to school. Dressed alike, you couldn't tell them apart."

The air left him. He had to make his escape and soon, before this escalated into something he'd rather not face. He thanked them quickly for Goldie's care and hustled out, only to hear Marissa call for him.

"Anson."

He turned and looked at her.

"I'm sorry about what Mom said. I don't know why she did that. Maybe she's afraid I'll take off again or something, if you look like Eric."

For once he was speechless. And unnerved. "You don't think I'm your fiancé come back to life, do you?"

She stood staring, her mouth dropping open. "Of course not. I was dumb to do that to you when we first met. I really hope we can forget about it."

But was it truly dumb? Especially after what just happened with her mother? Maybe they all wished this Eric were alive. That he was resurrected in Anson. And that to Anson was as creepy as any tale from the deep. Of course he did believe in the resurrection on the last day, as the Bible describes. But he wasn't that guy. Or anyone else. He was Anson McGruder. At least he prayed he still was.

"I don't know what else to say, but I'm willing to let it go," she said softly. "Okay, so you look like him in certain ways. But that's not why I like you. I like you for who you are. Nothing more, nothing less."

That alone should have sent his spirits soaring. If only he did not glance back at the window to see a shadow standing there, staring. Her mother. Maybe still holding the picture and shaking her head. *God, what am I going to do?* He knew what he had to do. Leave Marissa to Wayne and anyone else who could help. And not look back. His feet obeyed, but his heart did not. He turned once more to look back at the house. Marissa had disappeared. But her presence was even more alive and real to him. And so, too, were her expressive eyes. And her voice that told him none of this mattered, that her heart was ready to accept him. Then why did he have this stigma attached to him? How would it help propel a relationship anywhere except to no-man's-land?

God, what am I supposed to do? He sat down on the curb. Goldie promptly sat down beside him. He took out his cell. Call Pastor Ray? Or Carl? Carl would hoot and holler and tell him he should have left well enough alone. Maybe Lucy could impart a woman's perspective on this. He pressed her number but was met with a busy signal. Probably better. No sense heaping his troubles on everyone else. He tugged on the leash, bringing Goldie to her feet. He had no choice but to wait for now.

Chapter 10

Marissa hustled to the soap store. She was glad for the job to take her mind off the encounter with Anson, which rattled her more than she cared to admit. A good many tourists were out and about this hot day, which bode well for business in the store. Mrs. Holden was sure to be happy, as tourists meant money coming into the small boutique. And money meant Marissa could hold on to this job until something better opened up. Or maybe she should continue with her education and become a teacher—a career she once dreamed about when she was little.

She hurried inside and stowed away her purse, then saw the owner arranging a new set of lavender "Sleep So Nice" bath products on a shelf.

"What's the matter, dear?" asked Mrs. Holden. "You look preoccupied."

"I'm fine, thanks." She could never speak about what was happening, especially to Mrs. Holden, a fellow member of Mom's craft club. Not that Mrs. Holden wouldn't know eventually, as word spread like a wildfire in the craft club. She could see it now—Mom bringing the engagement photo to the next club meeting as if it were show-and-tell, exclaiming how Anson was a mirror image of Eric. And that meant Marissa should have nothing to do with him or any man that happened to pop into her life. Unless it was appropriate for the marriage radar screen, like Wayne Newberry. And Mrs. Newberry would be there, nodding her head in agreement and telling Mom to do whatever she could to put a snag in the relationship and get things going with Wayne. Marissa bit her lip, wishing she wouldn't entertain these thoughts. But it irritated her the way others wanted to run her life. As if she couldn't allow God to help her navigate her way through the road of a relationship, even if that road proved rather rocky.

The morning was busy, allowing her to keep her thoughts on explaining bath products to customers rather than on other things. Then the door to the shop opened, and, to her surprise, Anson walked in. Marissa smoothed the loose strands of hair behind her ears, wishing she had time to spruce up her lipstick. She pushed aside any thought of their last encounter and willed herself to greet him. "Well, stranger. What brings you to a place like this?"

Anson looked around in interest and inhaled deeply. "Ahh. I'm trying to find out what it is I'm smelling. I can't decide if it's strawberry or roses. . . ."

"Probably a mixture, I'm sure. We have strawberries and roses, among the dozens of other scents. And Mrs. Holden just got done putting a display together of lavender products. Supposedly that's good for relaxation."

"Really. I wouldn't mind seeing some. I'm getting a gift for Lucy."

Who was Lucy? She racked her brain as she led him over to the display, trying to remember if he'd mentioned a Lucy. Was she like Wayne was to her—an acquaintance from the past?

"Did you hear what I said?" He stared at her in puzzlement.

"What? Sorry, I've got a lot of things on my mind today."

"I was wondering if you thought a basket of these lavender products might make a good birthday gift."

"Oh, of course. She can spray some of the fragrance on her pillow at night to help her relax. And of course, the shower gel and lotion are relaxing as an evening bath."

"Wonder what Frank will think of the pillow thing," he said aloud, then backpedaled with a sheepish apology.

Marissa was still trying to understand who these people were.

"Frank's her husband," he added as if to answer her unspoken question. "And if he's anything like me, he doesn't know much about fragrances. I mean I take showers and brush my teeth, but I've never been one to slap on the fancy cologne. Or perfume my pillow." He chuckled, then turned serious. "I can see you're distant today."

"Sorry, I don't mean to be." For Marissa, she was on the idea that the woman was a relation, and she needn't allow the ugly green monster to emerge. Was she really jealous of another woman in Anson's life? What did that say about where Anson stood in her heart? *A lot*, she answered herself.

"And I'm sorry we ended up missing out on that dinner I promised you. Things kind of got out of hand the other evening. Any chance you're free for lunch? It will soon be that time. If I buy this nice big basket for my sister, do you think your boss will let you have an hour with me?"

Marissa stole a glance at Mrs. Holden, who was observing them with interest from the cash register. "I'm sure this purchase will make a big impression, on both Mrs. Holden and Lucy."

He smiled, picked up the basket, and headed over to the register. In a few minutes, he returned and offered her his elbow. "You're all set. She needs you back here by one."

"I never heard of making an exorbitant purchase just to take someone out to lunch. This is going to cost you more than you know."

"Lucy deserves it. She's a terrific sis. Maybe the basket will say it all when the words don't."

"I think it's a very loving gesture that she will surely appreciate. And I'm sure she's loved having you as a brother, even with the sibling differences. My sister Phyllis and I get along pretty well, even though she's five years older than me."

"Hmm. Same with us. Lucy is five years older than me. We did have our moments. And sibling squabbles. But I guess so does everyone. Except she did like to boss me around sometimes."

"Yes! I know exactly what you mean." Marissa stepped closer.

"And made me play school where she was the teacher and could give me an *F* for poor penmanship."

"Oh, Phyllis was merciless. And then I found out I'd rather be the teacher. In fact, I'd love to go back to school and become one."

"You should." He looked around the soap shop. "This place smells nice, but it isn't one of those long-term professions one can count on in life. Did you teach in Omaha?"

She shook her head. "No, I worked in a store there, too. I don't have my master's yet, and they prefer that for teaching. I guess I was too interested in the marriage degree. Too much too soon." She lapsed into silence.

After putting the basket in his car, he looked up and down the street. "Is a sandwich shop okay?"

"That would be fine."

She followed him to a shop and the counter where they ordered wraps and iced green tea. When their orders came, Anson led the way to a corner table. He said a prayer then began eating. They made small talk while he finished his sandwich in record time. "Guess I was hungry. I didn't eat breakfast."

"So what do you do on your days off?"

"Plenty to do around my house, fixing up things. I have an older place, so there's always something that needs repaired. I hang out with Carl, and sometimes we play racquetball at the college gym. Maybe I can begin hanging out with you more often." He winked. She couldn't tell if he was kidding or being serious. "Actually, I'm going to have more things to do in the coming week. Like getting ready for this big trip."

"Are you going somewhere?"

"The church teen group is going on a retreat, and Pastor Ray asked me to help. Since I know Bryce Canyon so well, he wants me to help lead it. I've been making plans for meals, devotions, things we will do while we're there. . . ."

"Bryce Canyon! That's right, I remember you saying something about that at the Jamboree." She could barely contain her excitement, even as her reaction sparked wide eyes and a grin on Anson's face. "I think I did tell you how much that park means to me."

"I do recall a hint to that effect." His smile broadened. And then his eyes turned misty, displaying a certain tenderness as if he liked what he saw.

"So do you need any help? I didn't do too much with the youth in the church I attended in Nebraska, but I do love Bryce and would like to help."

"Do you know anything about camping? Making pancakes over a propane stove? Things like that?"

"Uh. . ." How could Marissa tell him she wasn't a camper by any stretch of the imagination. Camping to her was slow room service at the Marriott. "You're camping?"

"Yes. We'll bring tents and sleeping bags. We'll cook over a propane stove."

"Wow, you really are roughing it." She hesitated. "I think we did the same thing when I was part of the youth outreach long ago. It was like one overnight. Mostly I remember the message that led me to Christ."

Anson's features softened. His head tipped to one side. "Then you should consider coming and sharing a devotion or two. It would be good to have a woman along anyway. Right now it's just Pastor Ray and me, and we do have several girls going. We need a female chaperone."

"I'm not sure how I will handle sleeping on the ground."

"I'll get you a cot if you want. And your own tent. It'll be just fine."

Marissa tried to dismiss the idea of camping to embrace what the park had to offer the teens, especially those who didn't know the Lord. And she could stay a few extra days at the lodge for a time of personal reflection. It all sounded so appealing, she could barely contain herself.

"So what do you think?" he asked, rising to his feet.

"Are we leaving?" She looked around.

"I'm just going to get us some cheesecake. Got to have dessert."

"Sounds yummy." Marissa looked down to see her half-eaten sandwich wrap. "Or maybe we can split a slice?"

Again came a grin lighting his face. Was the suggestion too intimate, asking if they could share a slice of cheesecake? Did that mean they were ready for the next step? He soon returned with a nice portion covered in strawberries, along with two forks. She continued to eat her sandwich while he took a few bites, then passed the rest her way.

He suggested a possible menu for the retreat and asked Marissa her opinion. She said spaghetti would work, thinking she might even be able to cook that kind of meal over a stove she'd never operated in her life. "Okay, count me in. So long as I can have a cot to sleep on. I don't want bugs crawling all over me." She flinched at the image of a spider dangling in her face.

"I won't allow one hairy appendage near you. But bugs are unfortunately a part of the camper's life."

She tried to eat a portion of the delicious cheesecake but found her appetite stymied by the thought of bugs. And then she thought she sensed one crawling on her arm. She shuddered and pushed the plate toward him. "It's yours. All I can think about is bugs."

He grinned and polished off the rest. "You'll do fine. I guarantee it."

Marissa liked his confidence. But she also liked the idea of basking in the beauty of Bryce Canyon. That meant more to her than anything. It would be a true start again on life. And who better to do it with than Anson?

✿❦

Marissa was now in a dilemma. She looked through her wardrobe, wondering what she was supposed to wear on a camping trip. She'd only been on one such adventure as a lowly teen many years ago. Back then it was shorts and T-shirts for the day and sweats for the evening. The majority of her clothing these days consisted of nice pants, tops, and capris. She had knock-around shorts that might suffice. She owned no hiking boots and hoped sneakers would do the trick. She looked over the things spread out on the bed, including the bottle of insect repellent on top of the pile. With the trip extended into an extra two-day stay at the lodge after the church retreat, she would need plenty more clothing than just for camping.

She dragged out the suitcase and put everything in it—shorts, pants and tops, underwear, a dress, a hoodie, a pair of sneakers, and several pairs of socks. For a moment she wanted to call Anson and get his take on a wardrobe, though guys usually didn't have much opinion on the topic. Except Anson did know everything about the great outdoors, having a job within the national parks. She picked up her cell on a whim. When he gave her a few ideas, she thanked him and turned her attention to surviving the camping part of this trip.

Mom peeked in then and gasped. "Heavens, Marissa. You're only going for five days. It looks like you're moving out." She caught herself. "You're not moving away, are you?"

"No, no. I mean, one day I will when I have the money to pay the rent. Oh, and you don't have to worry about Sammy while I'm gone. A friend is taking care of him."

Marissa was glad they'd convinced Anson's friend Carl to babysit their respective pooches while they were away. Carl took it on reluctantly but smiled a bit more when Anson promised him a huge steak dinner as payback. Anson must think the gift of food paid everyone's bill, remembering how he promised her dinner for taking care of Goldie. They had a nice lunch instead, but she wouldn't mind a fancy candlelight dinner one evening, along with a walk in the sunset.

Mom interrupted her thoughts. "I just hope you're careful out there. Who else is going besides the kids?"

"The pastor of the church, Pastor Ray. And Anson—the guy who came over here to pick up Goldie." She hesitated, thinking of the engagement photo on the bookcase and her mother's reaction. She winced.

"You mean the one who looks like Eric?" Her mother shook her head. "Really, Marissa. I don't know what to think."

"Our friendship has nothing to do with the fact that he has the same hair color as Eric. It's no big deal."

Mom paused and then asked why no other women were going as chaperones.

"I'm not sure. I hadn't thought about that."

"Well, you really need another woman going. You alone with two men and all those kids. I just don't know."

Marissa hesitated. "Okay. I'll find out." When her mom left, she was on the phone with Anson once again.

"So do you have the wardrobe figured out?" he joked.

"I think so." She rattled off her selections.

"You remind me of Lucy and how she would agonize over what to wear each day to school. It was kind of funny. And the bed would be loaded with clothes."

Marissa decided not to mention the multitude of clothing strewn across her bed. "Actually, Mom reminded me of something. Am I going with just you guys?"

"What do you mean 'just us guys'?"

"You and the pastor. I mean, it would be good to have another woman along, and I kind of agree."

"Actually, I think you're it as the female chaperone."

She sighed and sank down onto the bed. "Then I probably shouldn't go, Anson."

"What? Marissa, please don't say that."

She heard an audible groan, as if this was the worst news she could have possibly given. A part of her glowed at the thought that he cared so much and wanted her along, even if she didn't have any camping credentials to her name.

"I'll call you back," he said.

"Anson?" The call terminated.

She looked at her cell phone, pondering it. Maybe she was just being paranoid over the single woman issue. Or maybe just being careful to guard her heart as she knew the Lord would want, especially with impressionable teens whose hearts and minds were open to anything and everything.

Her cell phone suddenly vibrated in her hand, making her jump.

"I left out an important detail." His voice escalated with excitement. "Pastor Ray's wife is coming along to help out. So you can still make it, right? I mean, don't worry about what you're wearing and everything else. You'll do fine and—"

"It's okay, I'm still coming. And I've met the pastor's wife, Alicia. She's very nice."

He blew out a sigh. "Whew. Okay, great. You had me worried. See you in about an hour."

She smiled, both at his relief and at how God was orchestrating everything so far. But most of all, her heart warmed at the thought of Anson's eagerness to have her along. *God, I give this all to You. Let it be a time of knowing Your will as You once showed me long ago when I was young. Help us reach out to the teens and show them the beauty of Your creation. And. . .if there is something happening between Anson and me, make Your will known in our lives. Amen.*

Chapter 11

Anson greeted her with a huge smile and his large blue eyes when he drove up. The rear of the car was loaded with three teens, whom he introduced as Karen, Pat, and Jay. Karen and Pat issued hearty hellos while Jay only nodded his head and then looked at the small gaming device he held. Marissa managed a smile and slipped into the passenger seat while Anson struggled to place her large suitcase in the trunk.

"Looks like you brought everything," he commented when he returned, supplemented with a smile. "But I don't care. So long as you're here."

"I brought what was practical. And I'm glad to be here, too, thanks." She settled in her seat and looked back at the teens. "Did you have trouble packing, Karen? I think I had every piece of clothing I owned on my bed today."

"Oh, no. I love camping. I got everything into a small duffel bag."

Her confidence suddenly made Marissa feel a bit lower than the road beneath the car. "I hope I can figure this out," Marissa mumbled to Anson.

"You'll do fine," his soothing voice responded. "Not everyone's been camping."

"What about the pastor's wife?"

"Oh, Alicia hikes and everything," said Karen from the backseat. "They're really into the outdoors. She's even done some of the trails out in Oregon."

Super, Marissa thought, sinking even farther down into her seat. *Next to her, I'll feel like a Barbie doll.* Anson didn't have a tried-and-true chaperone to help him but just another kid in need of instruction. For now she tried to dismiss it and concentrate on what this would mean to the teens rather than thinking about herself.

At the visitor center, they stopped to wait for the van carrying the rest of the team. When they arrived, outfitted in rugged hiking apparel, Marissa glanced down at her starched cotton pants and top. She tucked her hair behind one ear and greeted Ray's wife, Alicia.

"We're going to have a great time," Alicia said. "I'm sure you've been here, right, Marissa? Most have that I know of."

"Well, a long time ago as a teen. I've been looking forward to visiting again."

She nodded, then waved the kids over to their respective vehicles. Marissa wished confidence ruled the day. Maybe she'd made a mistake volunteering to come along and be a part of this. She should have made her reservations to stay at the lodge and then hung out at the campsite and overlooks. But the lodge was expensive. The two nights she had reserved after the campout were plenty on her meager budget.

The caravan stopped at several scenic overlooks to take in the splendor of Bryce Canyon. Marissa marveled at the fascinating formations that were the canyon's trademark, along with its variegated colors, from gold and red to pure white. "Beautiful," she murmured. As a presence drew close, followed by a warm touch on her arm, goose bumps rose in response.

"I've seen the canyon so much, but I never tire of it." Anson gazed at the view from over her shoulder. She looked behind her to see his darkened face, shadowed by the sun. She couldn't tell what else he might be thinking. Or if he stared at her in a certain way. But now there was the retreat to consider and not other feelings that might be emerging.

Everyone piled into the vehicles and proceeded to the campground. Anson instructed the kids on how to set up the tents. Alicia grabbed a small nylon bag and strode over to a corner of the campsite. "This is our tent, Marissa," she said and began setting up a very tiny pup tent.

"I. . .uh. . . ," she began. "Wow, it's kind of small, isn't it?" And for sure it would never hold the cot Anson promised to bring.

"It fits two people just fine." She then took out a rolled blue foam pad.

"Anson was supposed to bring me a cot," Marissa said doubtfully.

Alicia chuckled. "A cot! You won't be able to get a cot into this tent."

"I guess not. . . ." Her confidence was leaking out quicker than faith could cap it off.

Alicia then brought out another foam pad. "I have an extra pad. You can use this if you want."

"I had Alicia bring one for you," Anson now said, venturing up to them. "I know I told you there'd be a cot, Marissa, but I thought the pad would be fine for two nights."

At that moment, she pondered the comfortable mattress and white sheets in a fine room at the Bryce Canyon Lodge. She said to Anson in a low voice, "Maybe I should rebook the rooms at the lodge for this weekend instead of Sunday and Monday nights."

"Why?"

"I can't sleep on the ground like this."

"Sure you can. And you're not directly on the ground. You're in a tent and on a pad. Alicia is great; she'll make you feel right at home. Take it easy." His gaze then drifted to the flock of teens. He lowered his voice. "You're going to need to go with the flow, Marissa. We have curious teens here who are watching everything. You'll do fine."

Marissa bit back any further comments and put on a fake smile for the group's benefit. She dragged out the huge flannel sleeping bag that Mom found in the attic and squatted down, wedging it beside Alicia's strangely shaped bag that could barely fit anyone. When she crawled out of the tent, Anson was giving directions for dinner preparations on a small stove connected to a green fuel bottle. Marissa shivered and went to dig out a fleece hoodie, thinking more and more of her inadequacy in this venture. Even at dinner when she sat with the other adults, she sensed a distance between her and the rest of them. They sat companionably together, planning the rest of the retreat, while she remained quiet.

After dinner she went to look for sticks to feed the evening campfire. Anson soon joined her. "You've been quiet. Is everything all right?"

She shrugged. "I don't know. I feel like I don't belong here."

"Of course you belong. I know you can do this, Marissa. You have many qualities the teens need." He touched her arm. Oh, how she wanted to feel his arms cradling her, imparting reassurance. She nearly threw herself into his embrace but held back.

Instead her gaze drifted to the teen group that gathered around the fire and then to the young guy named Jay, sitting by himself, staring off into space. She nudged Anson's elbow. "What's up with him? Why isn't he participating?"

"Not sure. I might have a talk with him later. God does different things in these kids, and they respond differently, too. Maybe he's a bit homesick. Or just feels out of place."

"I totally understand. I'm already homesick for my warm bed." She ignored his look and joined the circle of teens, eager for the fire's warmth.

Flames of light danced on the faces of the teens as they poked sticks of marshmallows near the glimmering embers. While they ate the gooey remains, Pastor Ray asked the group what they hoped to gain by coming on this trip. Marissa was eager to hear their responses as she settled down at a nearby picnic table to listen. She heard things like taking a walk among the hoodoos, seeing God answer a prayer, and finding out what to do with one's life. And then Jay's response: "To ask why I'm alive."

"That's important to consider, Jay," said Pastor Ray. "What is our purpose for being put here on this earth? Anyone have an answer?"

Jay's response made Marissa think of Anson. Why, she didn't know. She looked over to see him prying a melted marshmallow off a stick. Why were any of them alive at this moment in time? Why did God choose some, like

Eric, to join Him early in His heavenly realm and yet leave others here?

The teens were quiet until Karen spoke up. "Pastor Ray, that's easy. God put us here to love and worship Him. It's what we're going to do in heaven, so we might as well get a head start."

Marissa couldn't help but smile. A great response, worthy of pondering in her own walk with the Lord. They all must work out their faith with fear and trembling while here in this world, to walk with God and not against Him, seeking His will in all things. And suddenly she was on her feet, spilling out these truths to the group along with her testimony. "And God has great things in store for each of you. Just keep your minds and hearts open to Him, especially while you're here."

All of them were staring at her. She sat down sheepishly and stared at the flames of the fire.

"Marissa has made some great points," Pastor Ray said. "Good things to think about as we spend time here. Now, is anyone interested in playing some games?"

The teens quickly became engaged in a few board games, while Marissa continued to babysit the fire, throwing on a stick to feed the hungry flames. Again there came that familiar personal warmth drawing close.

"You weren't kidding when you said this place did things for you," Anson remarked, sitting down next to her.

"I just want the kids to know that God loves them, and He has a plan for their lives."

"I was able to talk to Jay, Marissa. He just found out he was adopted, so he's taking it kind of hard. He really wants someone to listen. Kids need that. Not so much pat answers to everything, but someone who will stop what they're doing and show that they care."

On the heels of this revelation, Marissa saw Jay wave at Anson, asking if he would like to play a card game.

"See what I mean?"

"That's great, Anson."

As she watched them together, engaged in the game, she realized miracles were already happening. And now she looked around the campsite to see who God might knit her with. And suddenly her feet were propelling her toward Karen. God had a way of surprising with the unexpected. And she didn't want to miss out on being a part of His big plan here at Bryce. This wasn't just about her, after all. It was also about others.

⁂

The weekend went by so fast; Marissa could hardly believe it was Sunday afternoon. She stretched her cramped muscles, reaffirming after two nights that she was not the ground sleeper Alicia and Anson hoped she'd be. But that was okay. She'd helped cook a nice meal last night with Karen, and now she and Karen were getting along well. Anson, too, had developed a friendship with Jay and promised to get together with him again.

Marissa was pleased for having survived the trip but, most of all, pleased that everything went well, as she and Anson worked together to minister to the teens. But now came the time of separation. Pastor Ray and Alicia would drive the teens back to Cedar City in their two vehicles. Anson would go his merry way with his job in the Park Service. And Marissa would spend a few days at the lodge on a personal retreat. Anson would then return Tuesday evening to pick her up.

Marissa helped the teens stuff their sleeping bags into tiny nylon bags and put the gear into a cartop carrier. Karen ventured up to give her a hug farewell.

"I'll have to visit you at the soap shop sometime," she said. "I love that place."

"Come around noon, and I'll take you out to lunch," Marissa promised.

The young teen's eyes lit up. Marissa smiled as Karen entered the van, crammed in with the other teens. When Marissa turned, Anson was standing apart from her but staring with his eyes slightly widened and lips parted in a faint smile as if he enjoyed the scene before him.

"Guess I'd better get you down to the lodge," he said, picking up her suitcase. "So you survived. I knew you would. And without a cot."

"I did, believe it or not. In a tent fit for tots. And on the hard ground." She rubbed her back. "A nice bed will do me good tonight. I'm pretty sore after it all. Too much pampering in my life, I guess."

"Sorry about the cot and everything, but I'm glad you hung in there."

"It was fun. In a painful sort of way." She entered his car, and suddenly the words weren't there. Why, she wasn't sure. Maybe because the friendly people surrounding her all weekend had acted as a buffer between her and Anson. Not that she disliked being with him. On the contrary. But now alone, without the pastor or the teens, she was left with her feelings concerning him. Anson said little as well as they drove down the park drive to the lodge, almost as if he, too, were timid and thoughtful.

"So where are you this week, park-wise?" she finally asked, hoping to talk about something rather than enduring the stillness in the car.

"They have me back checking out some visitor issues at Zion. I need to be there early tomorrow, so I plan to head over there tonight." He paused. "I wish I could spend more time with you, but. . ."

"Of course you have your job. This is my time to be with God anyway."

"We all need that. I'm alone days with the long drives to the parks, so I have plenty of time to think and pray."

How she wanted to know what filled Anson's mind and his heart during all that driving. Was it thoughts of the past and plans for the future? Could she possibly be in some future equation? After spending the weekend with him, watching him interact with the teens, and especially Jay, Marissa liked Anson's characteristics more and more. He had both the compassionate and adventuresome sides that made an attractive picture. As well as displaying a merciful heart.

He drove up in front of the lodge. "All set?"

"Yes. Thanks for the ride."

"See you Tuesday night."

She nodded and rolled her suitcase up to the doors before turning to watch him drive off. She was alone. Of course there was plenty to see and do. The beauty of the park was at her beck and call. But without him, there was something strangely absent, like a part of her was missing. *Lord, I pray You do a work in my heart during my time here.*

After settling into her room, Marissa took a walk to a nearby overlook. Already early evening, the crowds had greatly diminished. At Sunset Point, she observed the Bryce Canyon amphitheater in all its glory, including the famous Thor's Hammer formation. Marissa marveled at it all and took time to search out every unique aspect of the canyon.

The teens had come here on Saturday, and Anson gave them a talk about the canyon and how scientists claimed it was formed. He supplemented it with a discussion about God's hand in creation. Marissa thought he would make a good science professor. Standing there at the overlook, she could still picture him—his large hand acknowledging the expanse of a red-and-gold-colored canyon, his voice heightened with excitement. The vision continued to stir her heart in a way she didn't think would happen so soon. But for now, she must settle these loud thoughts of Anson and, instead, concentrate on what God might be saying.

The next day, Marissa spent the morning at an overlook with her Bible in hand, studying scripture and writing thoughts in a journal. She once kept a journal back in college when the pressures of life caused her to seek God's guidance. She thought back to the important entries made during college, like the first time she laid eyes on Eric in her chemistry class. The dates. The ski trips they took.

Suddenly she was transported back to a snowy day on the slopes when she'd lost her way. Eric had skied up to help her. When he offered her a hand, they both found themselves in the snow instead, laughing. She might have thought love was born right there. Eric had also been intellectual and more of a homebody. Except for his fascination with skiing, he stuck to home, his computer, and his work. He liked being in Omaha, surrounded by family and friends, when not lured by the call of the slopes that he loved with a passion.

And then she thought of Anson and the activities they had done together in just a short amount of time. Walking their dogs in Cedar Canyon. Handing out bottles of water at the July Jamboree. Helping minister to the teens. Marissa bent over the journal and began to write. Thoughts of Anson filled her. The pleasant conversation. His smile. The touch of his hand on her shoulder. His face illuminated by the campfire the other night as he laughed with the teens. She had moved on with life. But now she wondered, as she drew a heart in childlike fashion in the margin of the paper, if she was also ready to move on with love? And did Anson feel the same way? Or was it too soon to even consider such a thing?

She closed the journal and took in the view before her. It appeared like a painting with hoodoos like miniature stone statues aligned in rows. They could have been an army of soldiers ready for duty or tree trunks without their limbs. Even an old city from biblical times, with caves for dwellings. But this was a land God had created. And the same place where He once breathed into her heart a desire to know Him. Not in book form or in church form but in the reality of what He'd created her to be. His child.

Marissa stood to her feet, her heart at peace. Now a longing rose up within. She felt in her pocket for her cell phone, wondering if it was too presumptuous to call Anson and ask how his day was going. She'd had his information keyed into her phone log ever since he'd given her his business card. She hesitated before pressing the key.

"Hello?"

"Anson? Hi, this is Marissa."

She heard static and then one or two words. She walked down the trail, hoping for a better signal. Again came some mismatched words about Tuesday. Suddenly the signal was lost. Reluctantly she pocketed the phone then walked around for a time before heading back to the lodge.

When she arrived, a matronly woman, dressed in the uniform of a maid, was sticking a note on her door. "Excuse me? Can I help you?"

The woman jumped. "Oh my goodness, you startled me!"

"I'm sorry. Did you need something?"

"Oh honey, I was just putting this note here. It's from Anson." She paused to stare at her. "You wouldn't happen to be that young lady he was telling me about? The one who'd lost her fiancé?"

Marissa blinked, wondering how in the world a strange woman would know that.

As if to answer her unspoken question, the woman hurried on. "I'm Diane. Anson and I are good friends. He told me about your situation. I was so sorry to hear about your loss."

"Thank you. It's been hard, but I've had help along the way. Family and friends."

"That's good. Anson is a wonderful young man. But I was sad to see him troubled when we talked last. I wish I knew the words to say to him."

Marissa wondered what she meant. How was he troubled? By her? Was she doing something wrong by being so involved in his life?

"He's a dear, sweet man. And I know how important it is to take things one step at a time. Not to rush, especially when there's another man involved. And you need to find out, too, what you're supposed to do and who you're supposed to be with. You know what I mean? I used to say that to my boys. They didn't seem to want to listen. One got a divorce a year after his marriage. Another lives with his girlfriend."

Marissa's hands began to sweat. "I want to do what's right."

"Of course you do. Just be sure, if he's not the one you believe you should marry, that you let him go and not lead him on. Anson's a wonderful man. I guess I don't want to see him hurt but happy. You know what I mean? You're a bright, pretty girl. I know things will be just perfect, if they are meant to be." She smiled, said good-bye, and moved off down the hall.

Marissa was unsure what to think. She took the note off the door and wadded it up. All the feelings she'd experienced by the overlook—the scriptures, the memories, thinking God might be leading her heart, all the thoughts of Anson—were now replaced with questions. Was she doing the right thing? Was Anson the right man for her? Was she leading him on? Maybe she should pull back for a time, just to make certain of her heart and his. *God, I need Your timetable and Your wisdom. Not mine.*

Chapter 12

The following day Marissa decided on a long walk—a journey of the heart into God's creation. The trail she chose took her below the canyon rim for a hike among towers of sandstone, drenched in the colors of red and orange. Some appeared like castles. Others made her feel insignificant, standing alongside these tall stones of strength and purpose. She would have enjoyed it more were it not for the conversation at the lodge yesterday. It must have been providential that Diane was there, right when Marissa arrived, to share her thoughts. After all, wasn't Marissa here to listen? Perhaps the words had come from God through the woman's lips to her ears. Gazing up at the rocky pinnacles, she asked once more to hear God's voice. Only the sound of the wind whistling through the canyon and rustling the sparse vegetation answered her.

A few hikers passed by, heading in the opposite direction. Marissa continued on until she came to a trail junction. She sat down to consider which direction to take. If only she'd thought to bring the brochure that described the hike. Her tongue ran across her dry lips, and she suddenly realized something else she lacked. She had no water. "Some hiker I am," she grumbled. *I can't seem to plan anything. Not my life, not even a simple walk.*

"Looking for a guide, miss?"

Marissa glanced up, the sun's rays shining in her face, to see a dark figure towering over her. When she stood, she recognized Anson in his park uniform. "Anson! What are you doing here? I thought you weren't coming until tonight."

"I went to your room and found out you were gone. So I decided to take a wander while waiting for you. Did you get my message? I left one at the front desk yesterday after our call broke up. I asked them to deliver it and to let you know I'd be in the park early."

The note. The one she'd wadded up after the conversation with Diane. "I didn't read it, sorry."

Anson shook his head, smirking. "I've heard of people being absent-minded." He hesitated. "Is something wrong?"

"I. . .well, no." She knew it wasn't the truth, but at this point it made no sense to go into it. Instead she followed him up the steep trail as he described his time at Zion.

She paused to catch her breath while he seemed unaffected by the trail's challenge. "You're in good shape. You're not even winded."

"I hike a lot of trails. Goes with the territory." Again he paused to look at her. "I'm not sure, Marissa, but you don't seem yourself. Did something happen?"

He was beginning to read her emotions like a book. Better even than Wayne. "I'm fine."

He said no more but continued the trip through the cavernous rock. When they arrived back on top of the rim, Marissa was heaving. Her mouth was as dry as sandpaper. She watched Anson take out his water bottle and drink thirstily. "You don't have water with you?" he asked.

She shook her head. "No, and I'm dying of thirst, I'll have to admit."

"C'mon, follow me." He headed for the general store and to the back entrance where he hailed a worker. In a matter of moments, he presented her with two bottles of cold water.

"Thanks. I guess being an employee of the park does have its advantages."

"One time on a scorching day, I went down the trail with a daypack full of water bottles. I gave them all out. I wondered how many of those visitors would have suffered heat exhaustion that day."

"You're like the cavalry, Anson. It's what you're good at." His head tipped slightly to one side, perusing her. She quickly shifted topics. "So what did your note say anyway?"

"That I had Tuesday afternoon off and wanted to know if you might be free for dinner at the lodge? I still owe you a dinner, you know, for taking care of Goldie."

"We had lunch."

"Hardly the same thing. So are you free, or is your calendar full?"

He grinned as if knowing full well she had nothing else planned. But things still cluttered her mind. "I'm not sure, Anson."

His smile evaporated. "Okay, there is something wrong." He moved to a picnic table under some pine trees and sat down. "You have to tell me, Marissa. Was it something on the retreat?"

"Oh, no. I had a great time. I learned a lot. It's. . ." She looked off into the distance. "Well, I met an older lady at the lodge who knows you."

"You met Diane?"

"Yes. She was the one who delivered the note to my room. She. . .well, she cares a lot about you. And doesn't want things to go wrong, I guess."

His face reddened. "Oops. I did tell her about you. She's like a mother to me. I don't have one now, you know. I guess she wanted to help."

"Maybe it would be better if we both. . .kind of slowed down."

"Slowed down? What do you mean by that? Like not having dinner tonight?"

"No. I. . .I. . ." She hesitated. How could she tell him that she wanted assurance in these matters of the heart? Proof that if she fostered a new relationship, it wouldn't be ruined, too. Like Eric's.

"Marissa, please don't let one person's opinion drive everything. Diane can be a bit nosy, but she means well. We'll take this one step at a time and see where God is leading. I'm fine with that."

She considered it before allowing her gaze to encompass his face. She was no longer seeing anyone but Anson—for who he was and all that God meant for him to be. "Okay."

"So do you want to go out to dinner with me? Or would you rather wait?"

"Dinner would be fine, thanks."

His hand found hers and squeezed it slightly. No further words were needed until they sat down opposite each other in the dining room. Anson talked about his work in the parks and the visitors he'd helped. A few times he called out to several people he knew—a waitress here, a fellow employee there. Marissa observed this with interest as she slowly ate her meal.

Afterward he suggested a stroll by the overlooks to see the final rays of the setting sun pour forth their glory into Bryce Canyon. They stood there, watching the fading sunlight turn the canyon into different colors. "This is the best time of day to come here," he said softly in her ear.

The warmth of his hand slowly embraced the small of her back. She didn't pull away but fought to remain still, hoping she wouldn't tremble. His arms drew her closer. The kiss began gently, like a testing of waters, then slowly strengthened. When she opened her eyes, he was still looking at her, though he'd stepped back with his hands now tucked into the pockets of his trousers. They said nothing for several long moments.

"Guess we'd better get going," he finally said. "I'm sure you need to be back for work Wednesday."

"Yes. My bank account can't take another night here."

"I kind of wondered how you were able to afford two nights. The rates are pretty steep." They walked the path back to the lodge.

"Oh, Eric had given me money back in Omaha and. . ." She stopped. "Never mind."

"Marissa, it's okay to talk about him. He was a big part of your life for a time. I read the obituary."

"What?"

His face reddened. "Just that I know you loved him a lot."

"Yeah, I did. Once."

He said nothing more.

Anson wasn't certain why he was doing it, but once more he had Eric's obituary displayed on his computer screen. The words that played over in his mind. *And his beloved fiancée, Marissa Jones, who will miss him dearly.*

This doesn't mean he is her forever love, he reasoned. *Or that she will never consider marriage again. Only that she misses the man.* He shouldn't let it affect him. There was nothing in it to concern him but for an active imagination. But then Marissa doubted whether they should be together. As if it were a bad omen.

The cell phone rang, disturbing his thoughts. Lucy. "Oh Anson, I just wanted to tell you, the gift basket of bath products was wonderful. I loved what you picked out. Or you and whatever lady picked it out, that is."

"Hi, Luce," he said absently, his fingers running over the keyboard. He drew away from the screen to concentrate on the call. "Glad you liked it. And I did get some good advice from Marissa, actually. She works at the bath store."

"Oh, the one you were telling me about at the Jamboree." She paused. "Sounds like you're on the computer, huh? I heard keys clicking."

"Yeah, just glancing at that obituary again. Wondering if I should go check out Omaha sometime." He chuckled.

"Hey, Anson. . . ," she began.

"There's nothing new here, of course. I'm just trying to figure out where Marissa and I stand with each other. One moment I think things are going great. Then there's another curveball thrown that I have to handle."

"I'm looking at the obituary right now, too," she said.

"I shouldn't be reading things into it. Like there's competition or something. I mean, the guy is gone. Though there is one other guy I should ask about. That psychologist friend of hers. But she hasn't mentioned him much lately."

"Actually there may be something to all this. Things you don't know." There came a lengthy pause.

Oh no. "Like what?" He tried not to tense up, but he did. The tightness ran down his arms and crept up into his neck. And then there came twinges of a headache at his temples. *Great. She knows something about Marissa and Wayne. That's why Marissa had all those doubts at Bryce Canyon.*

"I thought maybe there could be something. Especially when your friend Marissa said how much you looked like her fiancé. I thought, no way. Then I saw the name and city in the obituary."

Huh? "Luce, you're not making any sense."

"Anson, I made a promise to Mom long ago. She asked me never to tell you, but you really need to know. It's your right. Especially with all that's happened."

Anson's palms began to sweat. "Luce. . ."

"Look, I'll just come right out and say it. You. . .you were adopted by Dad and Mom. I was five when Mom and Dad brought you home from the hospital at Park City. I remember it well, though. You were so tiny and frail. You looked like one of my baby dolls."

He could barely draw a breath, as if the wind had been knocked out of him. "What? No way."

"It's true."

"How can that be? Mom told me how they had to keep me in the hospital and all for several weeks. I had some health issues and everything. . . ." Anson paused, feeling like the carpet had been ripped out from underneath him. "She—she had all the baby stuff. The baby picture, the little blue cap they put on the boy babies. . .the whole nine yards. It was all kept in that trunk in the master bedroom."

"Yes, that's true. But you were still adopted. Mom and Dad found out about you through someone at their church. They drove up to Park City, took one look at you, and immediately wanted you."

His gaze traveled to the screen. "So what does that have to do with the obituary?"

"It was a teen pregnancy. The mother had twins. She kept one twin and left the other at the hospital in Park City, which was you. The mother's name was Henrietta Clay."

The words on the screen glared at him. Henrietta Clay. Park City. "No way." He stood to his feet and nearly dropped the phone.

"Anson, we don't know for certain if this is your birth mother in the obituary. It may be just a freak coincidence. But even if it is true, it doesn't matter. Dad and Mom loved you very much. And I do, too, even if you were an ornery little brother who always seemed to get his way." She tried to laugh, but it came out sounding like hiccups.

"But if it does turn out to be true. . ."

"Then that man in the obituary could be your twin brother." The words came out in a near whisper.

Twin brother? And that meant. . .Marissa was engaged to. . .my brother? He stood to his feet and began to pace. "Look, I need to go."

"Anson, wait. I know this is a major shock. But we love you. Mom and Dad loved you. I'm sorry they aren't here to tell you this. But you must believe it."

Lucy's words were like some far-off melody. He told her a quick good-bye and stumbled blindly around the house with Goldie by his side whimpering.

And then he thought of the first meeting with Marissa at the canyon walk. Marissa. . .who nearly fainted when she thought she was seeing Eric. And in all likelihood she was, if it were true. . .that she was the girlfriend and even the fiancée to some past link he never knew existed. Another identity, even if he could not make himself believe it. He returned once more to the computer and printed out the obituary. He looked at the mother's name, alive and well in Omaha. A mother who had helped plan Marissa's wedding, of all things. His fingers crinkled the paper.

Anson glanced over at a family portrait sitting on the bureau, taken a few short years ago. He examined it carefully for the first time—of Dad, Mom, Lucy, and him. He realized at that moment he had nothing in common with them, save the last name. The family characteristics of dark hair and brown eyes. The dimple on the chin. The short stature. He didn't look a thing like them—with his sandy-colored hair, blue eyes, squared-off jaw, and six-foot frame. He had no connection to them. Not one drop of family blood ran in his veins. He returned to the computer and did a search until he found a yearbook picture of Eric. He didn't look that much like him, in Anson's opinion. Maybe this was all a mistake.

Now what was he supposed to do? He did the only thing he could do at the moment. Pray hard. And get his best friend Carl over to his place as soon as possible.

⅋

"You're not making this up, are you?" Carl searched Anson's face. "No, I can see you're not. Sounds like something you hear on the news. I mean, Lucy was only five when it supposedly happened. How would she know all the facts?"

"Evidently Mom told her everything before she died. There's probably documentation somewhere. Lucy will find it, no doubt. Wow, I wish she had been kidding. But it would have been a sick joke, for sure."

"Anson, I don't know what to say. Wow. The mere idea that your love interest may have been set to marry your twin before he died. . .I mean, talk about coincidences. In fact, it's surreal."

"It makes me think of a picture I once saw on the Internet, of a tin can half open and worms slithering out. Talk about opening up a can of worms... and more."

"So if you find out it's true, which it may be, what do you plan to do?"

"Do? I have no idea. I just found out about this an hour ago. A few minutes can turn your life upside down."

"Okay, yeah. So say you're adopted. Many kids are. I mean you had great parents. A great sister. All that is good. And it may be you love the woman who might have been in love with your brother." His face colored. "I see what you mean. It is a tough situation."

"The idea that Marissa knows my birth mother. Had active interactions with her. Can you believe this?"

"So I'm guessing you haven't yet told Marissa."

"How am I going to do that? As it is, we were already on fragile turf. Have been from the beginning. Now I know why." He began to pace once more. "You realize, if the truth comes out, I'll only be a resurrected Eric in her eyes. Back to life, just as the Bible says."

Carl sighed. "Eventually this is gonna come out. You can't keep it a secret. The pieces will fall into place. Once the facts are established, the sooner you tell her, the better."

"You mean the quicker everything explodes. And I don't. . .I don't want that to happen."

Carl managed a smile. "You love her a lot, huh?"

"Yeah, big-time."

He blew out a sigh. "I don't know, Anson. The ball is in your court. You've been given a shocker for sure. I'd first confirm this all with Lucy via documentation or whatever. Make certain of the facts. Maybe talk to Pastor Ray about it. See what the next step should be. But if it ends up being true, you're gonna have to level with Marissa. And then see what happens. You can't undo the past, but you can live for the future. So walk this out and see what happens."

Walk it out? How? He was now stumbling about blindly, ready to fall flat on his face.

Chapter 13

Marissa reminisced about the kiss shared at Sunset Point above Bryce Canyon. While the canyon had once served to bring her closer to God, now it was bringing her close to a man she still knew so little about but thought she'd known forever. And that was hard to understand. Maybe it was because of his similarities to Eric. But Anson was his own man through and through. His was one of determination. Of allowing nothing to come between them, especially the way he held her firmly in his arms. And she did not shrink back either but welcomed it. She'd come to Cedar City looking for a new start in everything, including love. And she had found it in ways she never thought possible.

She sat on the floor, staring at the cell phone, contemplating calling Anson. Already Wayne had called, trying to snag her for another round of coffee at The Grind. She'd politely refused. Suddenly the phone jingled. She swiped it up and answered breathlessly, hoping it was Anson. Instead it was a voice she hadn't expected to hear.

"Marissa, how are you?"

She nearly lost her grip on Sammy, whom she held in the other arm. She gently put him on the floor and stood to her feet. "Why, Mrs. Donaldson!"

"Please, you know you can call me Retta. How are you? We haven't talked in so long."

Marissa smiled at the warm voice of Eric's mother. She told her about her first weeks in Cedar City, the job, and her new canine companion. Then she wondered how to broach the subject of Anson. Would the woman think it too soon to be in a relationship after Eric's death? That it trampled the memory of Eric she had nursed for the last few years? "Also, I met someone. A really great guy here in Cedar City."

"Oh, how nice. I know Eric would want you to be happy. What's his name?"

Marissa breathed easier at her acceptance. "His name's Anson. He works in the national parks like Bryce Canyon. He's a really nice guy. We walk our dogs together." She added a few more details, nothing much, but enough to let her know that life was moving forward.

"I was looking over some pictures, which is why I decided to call you. First to find out how you are. And I've been thinking." She hesitated. "Reminiscing, I suppose. It was a long time ago. But I wonder. . .with Eric gone, if it might be good to find out. . ."

Confused, Marissa wondered what she was trying to say.

"I'm sorry. I know I'm not making much sense. I guess it doesn't matter now. You see, Eric was a twin. He—he didn't know. No one knew but his father and me. We never told Mark either."

Eric's younger brother, newly married and living in a suburb of Omaha.

"This happened before I met my husband, Gene. I was a troubled teenager. I became pregnant with twins. My mother could help me with one of them. But we decided to give the other twin away. We left him at the hospital in Park City."

A chill swept through her. She opened her mouth to speak, but nothing came out.

"Eric never knew he had a brother. Or Mark a half brother. Maybe now is the time Mark knew. And maybe we could somehow find that brother. My twin son."

"Eric has a twin somewhere," she repeated, thinking aloud. Suddenly words came back to haunt her. And visions. The meeting with Anson at the park when she thought she saw Eric. Her mother throwing the photo of Eric in her face, claiming they could be twins if they dressed alike. Marissa took to her feet and ran for her room, dragging out the photo album.

"Are you still there, Marissa?"

"Yes, I am. Sorry. I'm looking at pictures, too."

"I guess I caught you at a bad time."

"No. I just. . .I don't know what to say."

"I'm sorry. I shouldn't have said anything."

"No, I'm glad you did." But her thoughts were in motion. *It can't possibly be him.* She began to chuckle. *Right, Marissa. He was born in St. George, you know.*

"All I can say is, if by some miracle I do find him, I hope we can meet. And I hope he can somehow understand why I did what I did so long ago."

"I guess you can only take this one step at a time," she said slowly. Retta offered a few more comments, asked that Marissa stay in touch, then said good-bye. Marissa sat on the floor as Sammy waddled up and began to paw at the cell phone. How does one find out if there is any truth to a wild-goose chase? She pushed the pup off her lap and headed for her laptop. She searched here and there, and on a whim, looked for the McGruders in St. George. She found a listing. George and Patricia McGruder. Deceased, as Anson had said. Two children. Anson McGruder and Lucinda McGruder Green.

"There has to be adoption papers on file." She slumped over the laptop. It made little sense to do this. He couldn't possibly be the one. There was nothing to substantiate it but a few physical similarities. She gazed once more at the pictures of Eric. She then compared them to a few she'd taken of Anson on her cell phone during the teen outing at Bryce Canyon. The similarities were few and far between now. It had all been her imagination from the beginning. "So much for that."

Sammy had stretched out on the carpet at her feet, ready for an afternoon doze. "Guess I should take the hint and let sleeping dogs lie. Thanks for the reminder, Sammy." Until she glanced once more at the names on the laptop. Did some more searching on Lucinda "Lucy" Green. And came up with a phone number in St. George.

≈❀

Anson could barely concentrate on his work. He tried in vain to center his thoughts, his visions, his plans solely on Marissa. If only there weren't fresh barricades set against this relationship. The barricades of twins, adoption, a mother who may have once been the future mother-in-law to the woman he loved. Couple this with the special encounter at Bryce. He would take Marissa there again if he could hold her hand, gaze into her eyes, and share another kiss. He touched his lips briefly in memory.

A chill swept over him. Now everything had changed in a moment's notice. So much for Marissa being at the point of accepting him. With all this coming to a head, he had no idea what the future held. *I have to leave that up to God. He knows better than me.* He tried to dismiss it as he began checking over a comparison of visitor stats for a study to be presented at a business meeting the following morning. But the God equation still lurked in the back of his mind. One plus one equals two. *God, what are Your plusses and minuses for me? Is Marissa the big plus I've been waiting for? And what about the minus that seems to be hanging over us? What is going to happen with that? Does it all add up to zero?*

All at once his cell rang. He answered quickly, not bothering to check the ID. A soft, feminine voice greeted him. He straightened, his hand tightening around the phone. "Marissa! Hi."

"I'm sorry to call you like this when you're working."

"You can call me anytime."

"Thanks. I really need to talk to you. I thought maybe you might be at Bryce today."

"No. Not today. But I would gladly make it today. Every day, in fact." *Except. . .wow, do you realize you may have been engaged to my long-lost brother?* He couldn't believe he was actually thinking this. It sounded so foreign to him,

217

so inexplicable, like some tale told by a Hollywood flick. He should keep such thoughts bottled up. Especially when they had no basis in fact yet.

Her soft chuckle flooded him with warmth and made him yearn for another moment like the one they had shared at Sunset Point. Or maybe she would like to come here. Cedar Breaks was a lot like Bryce, though smaller. Mira and Sandy, the two rangers at the visitor center, would love to meet her. He and Marissa could talk, walk around the park, and maybe even share another kiss. And forget all about adoptions and twins and the whole show.

"Did you hear what I said, Anson?"

"Sorry, Marissa. Yes, I heard. I was thinking that maybe you'd like to come up here with me sometime and see Cedar Breaks."

"I've been there. Well, a long time ago. Anyway, when are you coming back to town? I have something I need to talk about."

"I can be there tonight if you want. I'm only an hour away." He didn't tell her the rest of the story, that he had a big meeting the next day at the national monument headquarters over at Grand Staircase-Escalante. That could wait. Besides he was curious to know what she wanted to talk about. And then he realized he needed to talk to her, too. Though he had no idea how he would ever broach the subject of adoption and twins. He would leave it alone for now. "Are you okay?"

"Yes. I—I just need to talk."

"I'll be there around six p.m." When he hung up, a sudden wave of doubt assailed him. He didn't like the sound of her voice. There was no way she could know about his past, could she? Or was it something else? A new set of worries plagued him when he should be concentrating on the reports for the upcoming meeting. He tried his best to focus on his work, even as he kept one eye trained on the clock.

When the time finally came, he drove straight to Marissa's. She sat outside on the porch with Sammy in her lap, as if waiting expectantly. She hooked the leash to the porch railing and walked over to his car. "C'mon up to the porch and have a seat. I made some lemonade. Are you hungry? Did you have dinner yet? I can make up some sandwiches, too, besides what I have here."

He followed, barely able to contain himself. "I'm fine. Don't worry about it. So what's up? You sounded serious on the phone."

She said nothing but poured him a glass of lemonade. He shook his head when she offered fruit and cheese on a glass plate. It was a nice little spread, hardly illustrative of some difficult discussion to follow. She then took a seat and popped a grape in her mouth. "How was work?"

"Okay. I've got a huge meeting tomorrow though, at Escalante. Which means I have to finish my report and then leave at the crack of dawn to make it there in time."

Her face instantly fell. "I'm sorry, Anson. I should have asked if this was a good time or not."

Uh-oh. That did not come out right. "It's always a good time when I'm with you."

His comment made her blush, and he was glad to have rescued the conversation. "I—I talked to Eric's mother this afternoon. She called."

His hand froze around the lemonade glass. "Oh?" He barely choked out the word before he began coughing. She came up behind him and gently rapped him on the back. "I–I'm okay."

She stood behind him, waiting. After a few moments, she stepped back and returned to her seat. "She. . .she was pretty emotional. Told me a few things about Eric I never knew. He didn't either."

Anson said nothing, only waited for what seemed like an eternity.

"She said Eric was a twin. It was a teen pregnancy. She kept him, but she gave the other away."

Anson quickly put down the glass before he dropped it. Things were slowly starting to add up. "Marissa, I just found out I was adopted. In Park City."

"I know. Lucy told me about it. I—I called her. I had to find out. She plans to locate the paperwork to confirm it. But she seems pretty confident. So if it turns out to be true. . ."

Then I'd say you have similar taste in men. He let the comment rest in his brain and, instead, stared across the street at nothing in particular. He then looked over to see Marissa's probing gaze, one that left him uncomfortable. "Then we know, I guess."

"Eric's mom so much wants to meet the child she had to give away. It means a living link to the child she lost. She's such a nice lady. She's. . ."

He stood to his feet. "Yep. She made a choice, didn't she? Keep the good one and dump off the damaged goods." He recalled then the health problems he'd had at birth, or so he'd been told. Ill and frail. It had come down to survival of the fittest among twins. And suddenly he was angry.

Marissa was, too. "Anson, that's an awful thing to say. She's heartbroken over what happened. And it's not like you had an awful childhood. You lived just fine. Your adopted parents loved you. Cared for you. It must have been a heartrending decision for her. She was so young. A troubled teen."

"Look, I need to get ready for tomorrow's meeting. I–I'll call you."

He dared not dwell on the distraught look on her face or her eyes staring at him. He stepped off the stairs and walked to his car. *Now what, Anson?* He couldn't answer his own question. Instead he entered his car and heard his cell phone beeping from where he'd plugged it into the car charger. He swiped it up to check the number. Pastor Ray had called. He listened to the voice mail.

"Sorry to bother you like this, Anson, but the young guy from the retreat, Jay, wants to talk to you. He just found out something about his birth mother. He thought you would understand. He trusts you. Thanks." Anson found a pen and scrap of paper and jotted down the phone number. *It never rains, but it pours,* he thought. Just as he'd begun to find out about his past, here comes a young guy with a similar problem. Could he handle it?

He punched in the number. The mother said Jay had gone to the diner to hang out with friends. Anson quickly headed downtown to the diner where the young people often gathered. He could easily make out Jay, hunkered down in a booth with his handheld game as if trying to shut out the world while his buddies talked around him. For an instant Anson realized he was like that young man. After hearing the news today, he'd tried to shut out those who cared, like Marissa. But now he could do something about it rather than wallow in self-pity.

He slid into a seat opposite Jay. "Hey, there."

Immediately the teen put down his gaming device. "What are you doing here, Anson?"

"Pastor Ray called. Said you heard some news."

Jay bent his head and said nothing.

Anson studied him—the red flush of his cheeks, the way his fingers moved across the buttons on his handheld game when clearly his mind was elsewhere. "I got some news today, too," Anson went on. "You won't believe it."

Jay's head popped up, and his eyebrows narrowed. "What kind of news?"

"I heard from my sister that I'm adopted, just like you. The mother was a teenager when she had me."

"My real mother lives in Park City. And now she wants to see me. I don't know if I should meet her."

Park City. The city name struck him full force. "Wow. Well. . .uh. . . I know it's tough, Jay. You need to search your heart. It was a hard thing for our mothers to do, you know. Give us away when they knew they couldn't care for us." He inhaled a sharp breath. "They—they had to make some tough decisions. And we can be glad that God kept us alive when our birth mothers could have done the terrible thing, like get an abortion. We had loving parents who adopted us and gave us everything we needed." He shut his eyes briefly, thankful for that. He was alive. And loved. More than he realized.

"But what will I say if I see her?"

"What does the Bible say to do?" *Yes, what does it say, Anson? Consider it.*

The words came to him, words that even now ministered to his own searching heart. "Show God's love. Maybe thank her for giving you life. And for making the decision to have you. We're all adopted sons and daughters, you know. Not just here on earth. God mentions in His Word that we have received the Spirit of adoption in which we cry out 'Abba, Father.' We want to know our fathers here and our Father in heaven. God understands our situation much better than anyone. And He can make it all work out if you give it to Him and trust Him with it." Anson sighed in relief, thankful for those words, even if he'd spoken them. He needed to hear them just as much as Jay.

Jay nodded. "She's gonna call my mother tonight. They're gonna set up a place and time to meet."

"I think it's a good idea. It will settle all those questions you've had in your heart."

"So are you going to see your birth mother?"

Anson hesitated. "I don't know yet. I'm still trying to put the pieces of the puzzle together. Find out if the facts are true. But if God wants us to meet, then it will happen the way it's supposed to happen."

Jay nodded, and the tense lines running across his youthful face began to relax. "Thanks for talking to me, Anson."

"Anytime, Jay. I mean it. Take care. I'll pray for you." He headed out but not with the normal lift to his step. Instead he was weighed down by the very words he had spoken. What would he do if he found out he and Eric were related as he suspected? Could he go to Omaha and face the woman who had kept Eric and not him? Could he show the love that he'd just preached about to Jay?

Chapter 14

I've been so worried about you. You haven't answered your phone in several days."

Anson was surprised to see Marissa standing outside his home with Sammy on the leash. Goldie made a flying leap off his front porch, and the two dogs barked as if greeting each other like long lost pals. "They remember each other." He looked on until he could no longer ignore Marissa's probing gaze. "Sorry I haven't called. I was waiting for the right time to see you."

"The right time. . . ," she began blankly.

"Yeah. You know there's a right time for everything under the sun. It's biblical."

He watched Marissa shift back and forth in agitation. "Anson, don't you dare leave me in the dark. . ."

"Lucy found the paperwork. In a safe locked away. It confirms it. The birth mother was Henrietta Clay of Park City. Now Mrs. Henrietta Donaldson of Omaha, Nebraska. In fact, Lucy even went ahead and called this woman. They talked quite a bit. I guess the call you placed to Lucy gave her the courage to go ahead and find out."

The only sound for a moment was the cool wind whistling around the house. A change in the season was definitely in the air, in more ways than one. He saw her shiver. "Do you want to come in? You look cold."

Marissa shook her head. He left to fetch his jacket. When he returned she was still in the same spot as if frozen in place. She did accept the jacket with shaky thanks. "Well, we kind of figured that would be the answer." She studied him for a few moments. "So were you identical twins? I'm not sure if you are. I mean, you do look the same, but. . ."

"I don't know about that part. But I was born later. Seems Eric came before midnight on February twenty-eighth. And I followed after midnight March first. So he's technically the older brother."

"Are you. . .are you going to talk to Mrs. Donaldson?"

"I don't know. It will be hard asking why she thought Eric good enough to keep and not me." He couldn't believe he still said it. There it was—a continued deep-seated anger. Why he had it, he didn't know. In fact, it was foolish. But it was there nonetheless.

222

Marissa sensed it, too, for she took a step backward and looked down at the sidewalk. Then to his surprise, she tugged on Sammy's leash and headed up the stairs of the porch to plunk down in a chair. He assumed she would have walked away. Each day he was realizing what a special woman she was. And Eric must have known it, too. Marissa was turning out to be one in a million. A woman of godly virtue and beauty. He ought to feel blessed if he were not struggling at the moment.

"I know this has to be tough, Anson. But it's also a miracle in many ways. I mean, if we hadn't met, if I hadn't had such a freak-out the day I saw you in that canyon, all these other things. . .none of this would have come out. And you would not know who you are. And Eric's mom would not have known what became of her other child."

Anson said nothing for a long moment. He realized he'd been spared in many ways. God had preserved him, maybe even for this moment in time.

"Anson, talk to me."

"Sorry about what I said earlier." He scratched Goldie around her ears. "I'm still trying to work this all out. I probably should go see her. I mean, she lost someone close. She had to go through tough decisions as a teen. It would be good for her to know that one of us survives."

"Anson, just remember. This was a teen pregnancy. She was a child herself. Scared. Lonely. You can't condemn her for what she did. At least she gave you life. And you had a good life. Still do. We live in this world for God, even if we are temporary residents. To make the most of what He has in store for us, and to do it all for His glory."

"Wow, look at the preacher lady." He cracked a grin.

She blushed and stared at the porch floor. At that moment, she was the most beautiful woman in the world to him. Were it not for the seriousness of their discussion, he would take her in his arms and kiss her appealing lips. *And you were once engaged to my brother. My brother loved you. My brother was going to marry you.* The thoughts cut him to the quick. *Can you possibly love me for who I am?*

"I never was much of a preacher," she admitted. "I kept my Christianity mostly to myself. But you've brought it out, Anson. You have a gift, reaching out to young people and others. I like what you do."

"And how about the man? Do you like him also?"

Now her flushed face and dark eyes centered on him. "Yes, I like the man very much. And his name is Anson. He's strong. Determined. Loves dogs. Walks a lot. Camps. Wears a snazzy uniform. Preaches up a storm. Should maybe do missions or lead a church someday. Reaches out to hurting teens. And anyone who works in Bryce Canyon is a bonus feature in my book."

Anson took her hand in his, marveling at its softness. She smelled sweet, of some bath product at the shop where she worked. "Okay. Then let me walk this out."

Her hand slipped out of his. "Just promise me you won't do it alone. If you can, ask Pastor Ray or Carl to help. We're supposed to bear one another's burdens."

He nodded and watched her carry Sammy down the steps and place him on the sidewalk. He'd been blessed by the love and concern of family and friends. He knew that. And Marissa had his best interests at heart. But he must seek peace and pursue it. Peace in the realm of closure so he and Marissa could enjoy learning all there was to know about each other.

❧

The next day Marissa was surprised to find Pastor Ray's wife, Alicia, at the front door. She hadn't seen her since the teen retreat. Upon hearing who the visitor was, Mom immediately invited Alicia in for coffee and a slice of chocolate cake. Alicia smiled politely and found a place on the sofa, but her gaze never left Marissa. She sipped the coffee and ate the cake while asking how Marissa's time had been so far in Cedar City. And if she had recuperated from the retreat.

Marissa looked to Mom, who began edging her way to the door. "I'll let you two talk," Mom said. "I've got a few errands to run."

Marissa sighed in relief, thankful Mom understood. Last night Marissa had decided to clue Mom in on the latest developments. After revealing that Anson was indeed Eric's twin, Mom gaped in shock. "I knew it. They look so alike." She marveled at the information. When she had recovered from the shock, she was all business.

"And now what, Marissa? What do you plan to do?"

"I'm going to leave that in God's hands, Mom. But I will tell you that I like Anson very much. And not because of what we found out the other day. He's very special in his own way. And God has brought us together."

"I thought all this time you and Wayne were getting along. Betty said. . ."

"Wayne isn't for me. I don't know why, but he makes me uncomfortable. Anson doesn't." She must have had some dreamy look at the mention of Anson, as Mom's lips had contorted into a frown.

"Well, at least this Anson lives in Cedar City. And he did seem like a polite young man when he came here looking for his dog. I like a man who respects others."

Marissa was grateful for small things. But now she turned her attention to Alicia. "The retreat was special. I wonder what the future holds, though. Especially with Anson."

224

Alicia laid the fork on the plate and put the dish on the coffee table. "Anson told Ray what happened. And right now they're on their way to Omaha. They took an early flight."

Marissa jumped to her feet. "What?"

"Anson didn't want you to know about it until after they'd left. It was something he needed to do. Ray and he talked it over, prayed about it, and we all felt it was the right thing after Ray talked to the birth mother."

That may be, but all Marissa felt was disappointment. She'd been left out of the most important event in his life. Anson was going to see Eric's mother. If that were not difficult enough, he'd decided to go without telling her. After everything they had gone through these past few months. . .Anson had chosen not to involve her. "I think Anson has this strange impression that I'm only attracted to him because of Eric. I just wish I could convince him. . .everyone, that's not the case. God has done something new here. Anson is his own person. A fascinating and interesting man." She sank back down into the sofa.

"I can see you care about him very much." Alicia supplemented her words with a knowing smile. "Not that you couldn't tell from the retreat, the way you both talked and stared at each other."

Marissa gripped the sofa pillow resting beside her, wondering if it had been that obvious to everyone. "I do love him, Alicia. I know that. I just wish. . ." She hesitated. "Maybe the trip to Omaha will get us through this." *Even if I'm not a part of it*, she added silently. Anson had warned her ahead of time he wanted to walk this out in his own way. And likely he didn't want to burden her any more than she already was. Even if deep down she wanted to share that burden with him.

"We want to see a good conclusion for everyone involved. So why don't we pray for them and for the journey?"

Marissa nodded, closed her eyes, and listened as Alicia offered a prayer of help and protection for the two men journeying to Omaha. "May Your will be done here, God. And we pray for forgiveness, reconciliation, and healing to come forth. In Jesus' name. Amen." When Alicia left that evening, Marissa sat back, relaxed, at ease about the situation for the first time.

❧

The next day Marissa tried to busy herself with her job at the soap shop, all the while wondering when she would hear from Anson. She chose not to call him just yet, not wishing to interrupt whatever might be happening in Omaha. She could only pray for a good outcome, as Alicia said. A satisfying ending, one a reader often wished for in a romance novel, where the man and woman overcome obstacles to embrace love.

She wanted that conclusion in her life. At one time, she may have thought she was robbed of it, but all things were working together for good, as scripture promised. Eric was in a better place. And Marissa was on the path God had placed her, on the road with the man she believed was the one for her. Even if Anson was going back to where she and Eric once lived and dreamed and had nearly gotten married. To see the woman who was Anson's real mother. She shook her head, wondering at it all.

The bells to the shop door tinkled, and Marissa looked up to see a tall figure walk in. He looked around until his gaze fell on her. She froze with her hand on a bath product on an upper shelf. She finally let go of the box and turned, tucking strands of hair behind one ear. "Hi, Wayne."

"So this is where you work."

"Yes, for now. And it looks like I might be kept on at least through the New Year, which is good news."

His lips were drawn into a frown, his gaze never leaving her. "Can we talk?"

Marissa looked around for her boss and saw her near the cash register. She gestured him to the back room. "Yes?"

"I really think you're headed for trouble, Marissa. I feel as a psychologist and a friend that I need to warn you."

"What are you talking about?" Suddenly she thought of Anson and wondered if Wayne had heard some dreadful news concerning Anson and the trip.

"Your mother told my mother what happened. How Anson and Eric are related. Marissa, I can tell you from a psychologist point of view that what you're doing isn't healthy at all. You're losing your identity to someone who is only a figment of your imagination. You've chosen an unhealthy path here, resurrecting someone in your mind who is dead. You've never really accepted the fact that your fiancé is gone."

The words buzzed in her brain like a hive of angry bees. "That's not true. . . ," she began, though the doubts were clearly besieging her, robbing her of much-needed faith. "I'm choosing to trust God and. . ."

"I didn't study all this for nothing. It's obvious you have unresolved grief. You need some serious counseling to overcome it, Marissa. It's the only avenue available to deal with this issue. In fact, I'm going to set up an appointment for you with a psychiatrist."

Marissa ground her teeth. "Let's get real about things. Maybe it's you who isn't being honest, Wayne. Like you've never gotten over what we had or didn't have back in high school. You're the one living in some fantasy world. Thinking we're still old prom dates who need to move on with a relationship that's really dead in the water."

226

His face hardened like clay in a hot oven. His whole body became rigid. "Now you're getting defensive."

"And you're not? Stop playing doctor for a minute, Wayne, and see what's going on here. I'm moving on with life. Yes, Anson and Eric were brothers. Yes, I lost Eric going on nine months now. But Anson is not Eric. He is his own man as Eric was his own man. And Anson is everything I could ever want and need in my life." She set her gaze to the floor, but she stood her ground. "Look, I know you were there for me when I first got here, and for that I'm grateful. But that doesn't mean I want anything more than a friendship. Obviously you won't allow that to happen. You want it all."

"Marissa, I value your friendship. Which is why I'm here to warn you—"

"Of what? What is there to warn me of? You have nothing to base this so-called diagnosis on except for some mothers in a craft club who thought they could plan out their children's lives. But I'm trusting God to work things out. He knows my heart better than you or anyone."

"Even if it might be causing irreparable damage?" He stepped forward. "Marissa, be reasonable."

"I'm the most reasonable person there is. And I'm willing to live with my decision. I only ask that you let me."

Wayne shoved his hands into his pockets. There came a look of longing in his eyes, as if he wished things were different. Finally he turned and walked out into the main showroom. Before he left the shop, he looked back. "I'll be here for you, Marissa, if you change your mind."

"If you want to stay friends, that would be fine. But any more than that, I can't give you."

The door to the shop closed with the tinkling of bells. She breathed a sigh of relief for her decision and the strength of her faith despite the sudden doubt that had tried to weaken it. And with it, her love for Anson had grown, even if he wasn't here to see it.

≈

Anson stood at the front door, which was decorated with a cheerful wreath of dried flowers. His palms were wet. He shifted back and forth, sighing repeatedly. He looked to Ray for help, and the man gave him an encouraging smile. He stood there, wondering what he would say. He knew already the woman was looking forward to seeing him. She had eagerly accepted the invitation for them to stop by, even if her voice was filled with emotion.

He knocked. The door flew open to reveal a modest-looking woman. Young in the face. Bleached blond hair and blue eyes.

"Please come in," she invited. He immediately noticed the fragrant aroma of freshly baked cookies. She had laid out a platter of large chocolate chip cookies on the coffee table along with other finger foods.

"This is my husband, Gene," she said. Her hands were shaking.

Anson politely shook the man's hand and took a seat on the sofa. They all sat quietly while Pastor Ray made small talk. Then he saw the photo, a huge portrait of a smiling Eric. And suddenly goose bumps broke out. He stood to his feet and went over to examine the photo. "So that's him?"

"Yes," said the trembling voice of the mother. She walked over and stood beside him. "That's Eric."

"Were we identical?" The question burst out of him.

"I'm not sure. But you were twins. Oh, if you could only know." She paused. "I tried. I wanted you so much. But I couldn't. It wasn't possible and—"

"It doesn't matter. None of that matters now."

She opened her mouth as if to counter it, then looked to her husband. "Come and tell me about yourself." She led the way back to the chairs.

Anson did so, though he found it difficult making eye contact as he spoke. He needed to, but something held him back. He wasn't sure what. Maybe he should have let her finish what she'd begun earlier. . .telling him about the past and why she'd done what she did. He needed this to go well. To be a friendly meeting. But maybe other things needed to come out of this, also.

"I know you said it doesn't matter. . . ," she began again, straightening in her chair. She looked him in the eye, and he met her gaze. "I was only seventeen and pregnant with twins. I was told, you see, that I couldn't carry both of you. I was told that one would have to be taken so the other could survive. My mother would not hear of anything like that, and I'm glad. But I knew, too, after you were born that we couldn't take care of you both. And you were sickly also as a newborn. You needed special care at the hospital. It made sense at the time."

"I understand why you did what you did." He could picture her back then, scared and alone with two boys, and one struggling for life. She could do nothing else but leave him at the hospital and pray for the right parents. And God had been faithful.

"I thought a lot about you these many years. I wondered what nice family had adopted you. What you looked liked. What you enjoyed. How school went. If you had friends."

Anson fished out his wallet then and showed her pictures of his parents, now gone.

"Aren't they wonderful people." She wiped a tear from her eye. "I'm so glad. If they were alive, I would thank them over and over for all they have done." She looked at him again. "And now. . .I can hardly believe, but you and

Marissa are seeing each other. And it was totally by accident."

"Pretty amazing, I'll have to admit." He sighed, then added, "She's a terrific woman."

"Yes, she is. And I'm glad my son. . .well, both my sons, love her. She's sweet, kind, and devoted. I am so glad she moved to Cedar City. You can't know how glad I am." She closed her eyes. "Thank you, Lord. It was Your perfect plan."

When she opened them, Anson was looking directly at her. And though he did not know her as a son should, he wanted to learn more of her. And to bring that part into whatever his future held. With that, he promised to remain in contact.

Anson finished the pilgrimage at the cemetery with Pastor Ray accompanying him. Looking at the marbled stone with Eric's name chiseled on it, he wondered what it might have been like to have a brother. To play football with, to hike, even to ski, though he'd heard from their mother of Eric's excellent abilities in that area. He saw a pot of flowers there. He wondered if Marissa still had a bond with this man, even in death. If it was something that could be overcome in the days ahead. Or if he would have to let her go.

⁊❦

"Well, this has been a quite a trip," Pastor Ray commented as they began the flight home. "How are you taking it, Anson?"

"I'm doing okay, Ray," he said with confidence. Sunlight streamed through the window of the plane. A new day had come, and with it, a new outlook on life. "It went better than I thought. I knew it would be tough, but I needed to do it."

"You can move on," Ray added. "Though you do plan to stay in contact, which is good."

Anson nodded. He wanted to move on, to change course, hoping it would lead him to Marissa. Marissa, whom he wanted to carry off into another spectacular sunset like the one they had witnessed over Bryce Canyon. She'd giggle in his ear, her hands around his neck, pressing her face into his, her hair scented with something from the soap shop where she worked. At their feet would be Sammy and Goldie. He only prayed that Eric's memory did not exist in the middle of it all.

"You all right?"

"Yeah." He paused, deciding he might as well get these thoughts out in the open, too, as he had with everything else. "I've been thinking of asking Marissa to marry me. I really love her very much. But now I wonder if it's a good idea, especially after all this." He glanced over at Ray, who stared back, his face deadpan.

229

"Well, I thought that's why we were doing this."

"Huh?"

"Why we were making the trip. Eric is in a better place. God is interested in us finding healing. And that also means moving on in His grace and in faith. Of course, Alicia and I would like it, too, if you could set up a few premarital counseling sessions with us. We recommend it for new couples looking to marry."

"I don't know if Marissa's going to agree anyway. With all this now out in the open, it might send her running in the opposite direction."

"To where? Anson, she has no other place to go but forward. Wait and see. I think you'll be pleasantly surprised."

When they landed in Salt Lake, Marissa felt so close even though they still had a several-hour road trip back to Cedar City. He could hear her voice and see her fabulous hair swept up by the wind and her dark eyes staring into his. It was a vision that remained with him and, he prayed, a vision that would last.

Chapter 15

Life was a journey of unpredictability, as Anson had discovered. Twists and turns. Canyons and mountains. But with God, it could only lead to happiness. Anson was ready to open the door and receive whatever awaited him. He knocked, anticipating the wide-eyed look of surprise on Marissa's face before glee escaped her lips, her hair cascading over her shoulders. And then the feel of her arms around him as they embraced.

Instead, Mrs. Jones met him at the door with Sammy barking faintly in the background. "Marissa's at work. Something about doing inventory for the upcoming Christmas season. I wouldn't bother her at the store right now."

"Oh. Okay." He backpedaled until her voice stopped him short.

"You really do like her, don't you?"

Anson stared. His hands fumbled for the pockets of his cargo pants. "I . . . she's a wonderful person, Mrs. Jones. A caring and gentle woman. She wants to make others feel good about themselves. She loves God and wants to do His will. She seeks Him in everything and in every situation. And I know she loves you."

Rosie Jones stood there quietly. He wondered if that was a tear hovering in the corner of her eye. "I hope she does. I think she believes I'm just a mean old lady. But all I have is my daughters. I want what's best for them."

"As do all mothers, Mrs. Jones. I'm sure Marissa knows that."

"I'm not sure she does. I know I can be hard. Maybe I have some unforgiveness for her leaving like she did. Which wasn't her fault. She was following what she thought she should do. I shouldn't blame her for my unhappiness."

Anson stayed quiet, uncertain how to respond.

"But you seem like a nice man. I must admit, I was so amazed to learn you were Eric's brother. Marissa told me, you see. Maybe it would have been better for me to have gotten to know him. I mean, it's too late now. But at least I can get to know you."

"That would be great, Mrs. Jones. I'd be glad to be a personal escort, too, whenever you want to visit one of the parks around here."

She smiled. "And that dog of yours—well, I'm not a big dog lover, but that dog Goldie was very sweet. She followed me everywhere. I think once Marissa leaves, I might look into getting a golden retriever for myself."

Anson smiled. "I'd be happy to help train the new dog you end up getting, Mrs. Jones."

"Thank you. That's sweet of you." She hesitated. "Would you like a lemon bar? They're Marissa's favorite." She went back inside and soon returned with a paper plate of bars in a Ziploc bag.

"Thanks. It was nice talking to you."

"And you. Good-bye." For the first time, he saw her smile. And with that, a smile formed in his heart, and a confirmation, too, of what his heart had been speaking. He only hoped Marissa felt the same way.

≈❧

Marissa's cell phone rang early that afternoon. It was him at last. Marissa could barely handle her phone, her hand was shaking so. "Anson? Oh Anson, I've been waiting to hear from you! Why haven't you called me?"

"I'm sorry. I—I wanted to wait for the right time and place. Did Alicia tell you?"

"Yes, she did." Marissa waited, switching the phone from one ear to the other, her curiosity beyond her control to keep still. "Anson?"

"I'll tell you more when I see you. But I can say that it went well. Very well, in fact. And I was glad Pastor Ray was with me."

"Oh Anson, I'm so glad!" Tears sprang into her eyes. Tears for everything and especially for him. She could hear him breathing over the phone and wished his arms were holding her right now, his face pressed close to hers, feeling his warm breath fanning her cheek. Even on the phone he felt so close, she could nearly touch him. "When. . .when can I see you? After I get off work?"

"I'll pick you up."

"I'm off at four. Don't be a minute late." She could hear the grin in his voice as he promised to be right on time. When she clicked off the phone, four p.m. could not come soon enough.

≈❧

Marissa could barely get through the rest of the day, her mind buzzed so. She paced continuously around the shop, looking for things to do, no matter how mundane. After the count was complete, she picked up a feather duster and began swiping away specks of dirt. Even her hands trembled along with the rapid beating of her heart.

"I can tell you can't wait to see Anson," Mrs. Holden observed.

Marissa whirled. "You know he's back?"

"I talked to Rosie at noon. Anson stopped by your house this morning."

The feather duster swiped a glass canister of bath salts, sending it crashing to the floor. The glass shattered. "Oh, no! I'm so sorry, Mrs. Holden."

The woman only laughed as a strong scent of lavender filled the shop. Marissa quickly fetched the broom. "You can take it out of my pay."

"Don't worry about it."

"I wonder why he didn't come by then to see me. I mean he did call, but. . ." She thought it odd he would see Mom but not her. Had something occurred in Omaha that made him reluctant to stop by? Or had Mom said something that might have put a barb in their relationship? She swept up the salts into a dustpan and dumped it in the trash.

"You'll see him soon," Mrs. Holden said matter-of-factly.

"I guess." She dearly wanted to ask Mrs. Holden if she could leave early. It was all she could do to contain herself. Yet when the time came, instead of expectation, Marissa was tired. Weary of everything. Of life's issues, especially. She dragged herself out the door, trying hard not to cry when she spotted a familiar SUV parked outside.

"Going my way?" a voice called out the window.

How she wished she could be cheerful when she saw Anson's smiling face. Instead she only felt irritation on many fronts. "Why did you wait to see me? You went to see Mom and not me? Is something wrong?"

The smile disappeared from his face. "Sorry. I thought I'd let you do your work. Your mom said you were pretty busy."

"I would have made time for you day or night, Anson." Marissa wished herself to stay calm, knowing none of this was his fault. She finally slipped into the passenger seat and fastened the seat belt. "So where are we going?"

"Surprise. And don't worry, your mom is taking care of Sammy. This is our time to be together."

For a time she didn't know what to say. And neither did he. The situation had left them both speechless, on the hunt for the right words and emotions after what they had endured. At last Anson opened up. About the meeting in Omaha. Seeing Mrs. Donaldson. The promise to remain in contact with her. "She really cares a lot about you," he said. "Like the daughter she doesn't have."

Marissa smiled. "She is a nice woman. I'm glad, even if this was difficult for you, Anson. Even with her loss, she's gained a son. Not that you are Eric," she added quickly.

He stared at the road ahead. "And what about you? What have you gained?"

"A man who cares about me. And thinks of me more than just a friend from the school yard."

"I think I know what you mean. I've wanted that, too. Someone who cares, and someone I can care about. And one who doesn't think of me as, well. . .someone else."

If Marissa were behind the wheel, she would have brought the car to a stop. As it was, she pointed to the side of the road and asked him to pull over.

"What's wrong?"

"Plenty." Marissa leaned over, took his face in her hands, and kissed him soundly on the lips. "There. That's just to remind you who I care about, Anson McGruder. Okay, you may be the younger brother by two hours of the man I was once engaged to. But you're more than I could ever hope for."

Anson said nothing for a moment, as if paralyzed by the sudden encounter. "Uh. . .do you. . .do you mind if we keep going? We can make it in time if we do."

"Where are we going anyway?" She glanced around. "Actually, I think I have a clue." She settled back to enjoy the remainder of the drive and the man taking her to the place she loved most. Only she was curious to know what deadline he was trying to make. As they drove into Bryce Canyon National Park, she thought perhaps he had an evening meeting to attend. Or maybe another fateful encounter with Diane, the cleaning lady and his second mother, though Marissa couldn't imagine why. Instead he pulled into the parking lot near the lodge, just as the sun was beginning its descent toward the horizon. Bryce Canyon would soon reveal its inner beauty under the fading rays.

"Ah, I see what you mean by wanting to make it on time," she said, laughing as he opened her car door. They strolled the paths as they had once before, in another time, and watched the sun set.

"Is it any different now?" he suddenly asked her.

"If you mean, is it different from the last time I was here, yes. I was full of questions. I thought they might have been answered, but there were some doubts thrown in for good measure."

"You don't have doubts now? Even after everything's been revealed?"

"It's actually what makes the doubts nonexistent now, Anson. The questions are answered. Though I know it will take time for the both of us to get used to the idea of who you are." She allowed his arms to encircle her as they took in the sunset over the famous canyon.

"Then would you mind if perhaps we call on Pastor Ray and Alicia?"

She looked into his eyes.

"They offered some counseling sessions. For those who one day want to. . ." He hesitated. "I know we still need time to digest it all. Who I am. Who you are and were."

Her heart began to flutter. "Like in premarital counseling?" She saw his cheeks flush. Then a quick nod of his head. "I think that's a good idea, Anson. One step at a time."

"It's all we'll ever do. I promise. Whether it be the canyon walk, the Navaho loop walk in Bryce, or life's walk."

She welcomed the determination and commitment in his kiss. "Good. I can't wait to start!"

WASATCH LOVE

Dedication

To Mary Kessler. And to Marge, Juli, and the other secretaries and service reps of Great American. My husband, Steve, thanks you for all you do, and so do I.

Chapter 1

I'm going to get into this thing one way or another."

Brenda Stewart struggled, wondering how in the world she could zip a dress with her arms twisted at odd angles behind her back. After a few more tugs, she managed to zip it to the nape of her neck. She then tugged down the fabric and looked in the mirror. The dress appeared stretched beyond measure over her large bosom, rounded stomach, and thick waist. So much for the aerobics class she'd started attending a few weeks ago. None of it seemed to have affected her figure. And just when Dad decided that his "punkin" needed to get her life in order. To him that meant taking a flying leap and finding an intended.

She wished Dad would dispense with the *punkin* part. Right now she felt like a punkin—or *pumpkin*, rather. Size 14 wasn't a flattering number to her, no matter how hard she tried to alter her image with a different dress. The clerks at the boutiques took one look at her and shook their heads before rummaging in racks tucked in the far corners of their stores, hunting down the right size. Like this black dress with spaghetti straps that, according to the tag, was a size 14 but fit more like a 12. She didn't remember it being so tight in the bodice. Maybe she had starved herself the day she tried it on.

But she couldn't worry about it now. The cocktail party would begin soon. Stanley, the chauffeur, would be heralding his arrival via the intercom. And she had yet to make up her face.

Brenda couldn't figure out how she'd gotten so far behind. Too much on her mind, she supposed. Although Dad always complained she was no keeper of time, that she inherited the trait from her mother.

She'd just begun to apply the foundation when Stanley called up.

"Great," Brenda mumbled and ran to answer the buzz. "Give me five minutes, Stanley," she said into the intercom. She then peeked out the front window.

He stepped away from the building, looked up at her window, and pointed to his watch. She blew out a sigh and returned to the mirror. Now the makeup routine turned into an act of desperation. She plastered on the foundation, blush, and eye makeup in rapid fashion rather than methodically, with care, as she normally did, as if it were art in the making.

Stanley again hailed her. She knew the reason for his impatience. The man would face a reprimand from dear old Dad if he delivered her to the function late. Dad always did stick up for her and her needs. But she didn't like seeing other people suffer for it. At the ripe age of thirty, she'd learned that she needed to take responsibility for her actions. When the timing was right, that is.

Brenda grabbed her evening bag and lace shawl, shoved her pudgy feet into narrow black high heels, and rushed out the door. When she arrived at the car, an agitated Stanley opened the passenger door and again looked at his watch. "Don't worry," Brenda told him. "I'll tell Dad it's my fault."

He said nothing but shut the door and made for the driver's seat. Brenda snapped open a lighted compact to check her eyes. Considering the quick paint job, they didn't look half bad in the dim light. She'd just begun putting on lipstick when the car stopped at a light, nearly causing her to color her cheek instead. She sighed and waited, looking out the window at the passing city streets of Salt Lake and people roaming the lit sidewalks. A wave of sadness flowed through her then. Sad she didn't feel in control of her own destiny. Sad that someone else was always at the helm. And then a sense of desperation hit her—an urgency to do something different before it was too late.

Stanley brought the limo to a smooth stop in front of the ritzy hotel where the party would take place. Brenda quickly finished putting on the lipstick, closed up her purse, and readied herself for whatever the evening brought. Time to put on the plastic-coated smile of perfect teeth—a smile that had cost Dad a bundle—along with the charm that befit the daughter of the CEO of Stewart Enterprises.

An *I-am-the-top-dog's-daughter* grin occupied her face as one by one people came up to greet her. As if on cue, everyone smiled back. A stately couple walked up. Mr. Grafton, the company treasurer, and his wife, sporting a 'do of mixed red and blond tones as if the hairdresser couldn't make up her mind which color to use.

"Brenda, darling, you look wonderful," Mrs. Grafton purred, flicking her eyelashes coated in a thick layer of mascara. "Is that a new dress? It looks fabulous on you."

I'm sure you don't mean a word, Brenda thought but smiled anyway. Most of the people in attendance had dollar signs in their eyes and hopes for advancement on their countenances. They savored a piece of the Stewart homemade pie, sweet and tantalizing to the financial taste buds. "Yes, it is a new dress, thank you," she said politely.

"And you are *not* going to the party unescorted, Miss Stewart," came a familiar voice from behind the roving people.

Don't mind if I do, thank you, Mr. James Ensley. Again she flicked her famous smile corrected with a stint of braces and a retainer, followed by whitening gel. Dad probably wished now he could spruce up her figure.

Jim Ensley's large hand easily slipped around her elbow. Like everyone else, Jim looked for a way to climb up the corporate ladder. One giant step for man. The VP promotion step, that is. And on the heels of an engagement ring if he and Dad had their way. Jim was one of the few guys on Dad's short list of prospective grooms, though she was certain he was a few years younger than her. But she didn't want to marry him. Nor anyone else for that matter.

"I can find my own way, thank you."

"I'm sure you can, but I won't allow it. And what a fabulous dress. I love a woman in black."

Is that what you say to all your ladies? She dearly wanted to blurt it out loud but instead came back with a demure, "You're just too kind, Mr. Ensley."

His dark eyebrows rose in response. She had to admit Jim sported superb looks. Thick, dark eyebrows framed a pair of luminous eyes reminiscent of the finest chocolate truffle. And he had dark, wavy hair that matched his eyes. Not an ounce of fat anywhere on his lean body. He must have a girlfriend or two or three tucked away somewhere in his life. She'd seen him texting at odd times during board meetings or talking away on his cell. And he always had his iPad open. Whenever she tried to sneak a look, the page was on a company field. She had to admit he was a hard worker and just the right kind of guy to have at Dad's side. If only she didn't have doubts about his real intentions.

"C'mon, you have no more interest in me than in a wildebeest."

Jim turned, his face but inches away and a bit too close for comfort. "What did you say?"

"Never mind. So what are you going to tell—let me see—Christine when you see her? That you're escorting another woman to a party?" She knew about Christine. A cute thing but shy. Brenda could hardly call herself shy.

He said nothing, and for once Brenda thought she might have hit a nerve. But it soon disappeared when they arrived in the large banquet hall where a live band played a robust set. Dad never went cheap when it came to company affairs, and tonight was no exception.

Jim propelled her over to where the company execs and numerous guests were ordering cocktails from the open bar. Sometimes Brenda indulged in a mixed drink, but tonight she didn't feel like it. She wanted to keep her senses at full strength, senses that already were depressed by everything around her. People gazing at her from the right and the left. Men wanting to edge in on her company, even if it meant associating with a wildebeest tucked in a black silk dress.

Dad came forward then and gave her a hug. He smiled for all the women who elbowed their husbands or dates and cooed at the sight of father and daughter. "Glad you finally made it, punkin. Stanley brought you late again, I see."

"It was totally my fault, Dad. My makeup wouldn't go on right. Let it go, please."

Dad nodded and said no more. Brenda sighed, thankful she did have some pull around here, even if she felt as if she were being dragged in too many directions. But Dad needed her. And she needed him. All they had was each other, along with the megacorporation that was Stewart Enterprises, a company that sold medical equipment. And she, Brenda, was the chief promotional guru of it all. She thought about that as a tray of hors d'oeuvres passed by her nose.

Brenda snatched a cracker decorated with cheese and pimento. Looking at it, she envisioned the delicate zipper holding her dress suddenly popping. She promptly threw the cracker in the trash and turned to seek out a glass of sparkling Perrier and nearly collided with Jim holding two champagne glasses. He offered her one.

"No thanks."

Again Jim's nearly black eyebrows rose. Everyone, except her, clasped an alcoholic drink. Did she now present some new symbol, posing as a humble, teetotaling wildebeest?

And why pick a wildebeest—those hulking creatures she'd seen on Animal Planet? They were large and ugly and probably smelly.

Yes, Brenda could call herself robust, but she kept herself well groomed. She looked at her nails, which were perfectly shaped and polished as only a good manicurist could do. She was no wildebeest. Or anything else, it seemed. Just another promotional tool of the company tonight, outfitted in tight black.

A couple of women younger than Brenda wandered by, but not before telling her how fabulous her dress looked. *Fabulous* must be the code word of the evening. She'd heard it said at least a dozen times. Maybe if she felt fabulous in the dress, the word might ring true.

"I see Jim wasted no time snagging you tonight." Brenda's good friend Rita came to stand beside her. She ate crackers one after another, washed down with champagne that would no doubt make her giggly. Brenda tried not to concentrate on her friend's hourglass figure, which never changed no matter what food passed between her lips. If only she possessed a high metabolism rate like Rita.

Brenda shrugged, looking instead at the food on Rita's plate and wishing she could devour it all.

Rita's eyebrows rose—yet another sign tonight along with the word *fabulous*. Everyone's eyebrows formed perfect arches as if they couldn't believe what they were seeing and hearing. That might be more truthful.

"At least he's up and coming in the company," Rita continued. "He has plenty of things going for him, even if he is full of himself. And don't forget, he gave you Snowy."

"Yes, I love Snowy. But I also have the rich father who is his boss. Makes me look good, even if my figure doesn't."

Rita sighed. "Hey girl, you're very attractive. And I know there's a guy out there somewhere who will love you for who you are."

"I would take him in an instant. How about the company janitor?"

"Charlie Creasy? You're awful, girl."

Brenda knew Charlie, fresh out of community college where he'd flunked out. Besides she was eight years his senior. The two women broke out in loud laughter. Dad glanced in her direction and smiled, looking pleased that his darling punkin was enjoying herself. Brenda couldn't tell him that what she really wanted to do was slip away from this scene and take a walk. She felt closed in here, nearly unable to breathe.

In fact, she liked the idea so much, she soon made her escape from Rita and ducked out into the lobby when no one was watching.

No one but Jim, that is, who had radar built into the sides and back of his head. He met her outside the double-wide oak doors.

"Much better out here, huh?"

"Look, I kind of want to be alone. Where is Christine anyway? Why didn't you invite her?"

"We broke up. Brenda, I need to tell you something. About me, your dad, and. . ."

Brenda smirked. "Oh I know. You broke up with Christine because Dad sat you down in the office and gave you an offer you couldn't refuse. Right?"

Jim stared at her, his face flushed.

Brenda continued. "He said, 'Jim, if you keep your head on straight and your eyes off other women, you'll get the vice presidency served up on a silver platter and my punkin to boot. A VP and CEO's daughter make a good match.' Am I right?"

He coughed. "Brenda, c'mon."

"Maybe I should ask him." Brenda moved off toward the doors leading to the ballroom.

"Wait a minute." His choking words made her pause. "Okay, we did have

243

a meeting. But I didn't break up with Christine because of some ultimatum. I did it because she wanted out. It was the right thing to do. We were drifting apart anyway." He paused, loosening the collar of his shirt, breathing deeply as if the air failed to reach his lungs. "He did say the vice presidency is a possibility. He likes me. Is that so wrong? And he talks about you all the time. He knows you're lonely. He said you were getting—"

"Older and fatter but not much wiser."

"He didn't say that. Your father loves you very much. He wants what's best for you."

"Good. Because what's best for me right now is to be left alone."

Jim said nothing for a moment. He then walked over and emptied his drink into the garbage. The move surprised Brenda, as if he, too, wanted to be clearheaded like her. "I know you may not believe me, but there are people who want you happy. Me, for one."

"Why?"

"Why?" he repeated. His ears turned red to match his face.

"You don't really know the real me. You know me as part of the company only. And no one can forget these chubby cheeks." She pinched them to emphasize the point. "Other than that, why would you want me happy?"

"Because it's the right thing to want for someone else."

For once Brenda was uncertain how to respond. Instead, she nodded and walked off down the ornate hallway of the hotel, praying he wouldn't follow her like some shadow. At the end of the hall, she turned to look. He was nowhere in sight. She breathed a sigh of relief.

≈⟡

Jim could feel the heat in his face, and the words still lodged in his throat as if they were a perpetual plug. He went to get himself a long drink out of the water fountain. When he turned around, she'd vanished.

Yes, he admitted there were other motives. Other needs. Things she didn't know about, but it was not for her or anyone else to get involved with right now. He would make the money required, and that meant securing the VP position. And if her father meant for him also to marry the stubborn and highly opinionated daughter to make things right, he would do that as well. Too much lay at stake not to.

Jim sighed and headed back into the party.

"Where's Brenda, Jim?" Mr. Stewart asked, looking around as if hoping to spot his daughter in her silky black dress.

"She said she was getting too warm and went out for some air, I think."

He nodded. "You spoke to her?"

"Yes sir. She does have her own way of doing things, as you know. And she's quite smart in the ways of—"

"Yes, she is indeed smart," Mr. Stewart interrupted. "Gets that from me." He chuckled and slapped Jim on the shoulder blade. "Go get yourself another drink. And make sure she's having fun, okay?"

But Jim had had enough drinking for one night. He wished he didn't feel so desperate in his situation. He owed more than he could pay. And he had no choice but to call on others to help him. Even if it meant obtaining help from the unpredictable Brenda, her father, and the company.

Jim straightened his bow tie and returned once more to the foyer to see her pacing before the glass doors. Every so often the doors opened, emitting a bit of refreshing air that swept the black dress around her legs. Those legs didn't look chubby to him, even though Brenda complained about her figure. In fact, they looked rather shapely and appealing. As did the rest of her.

He wondered how he could reach into her mind—a sharp mind that seemed to have things figured out. What could he do to enter her world? A world that seemed in another galaxy from his. He sucked in his breath, realizing he'd have to tread carefully.

"I'm back," he said as he walked up to her, smiling.

"Dad sent you out here to check on me."

He ignored her intuitiveness. "I was getting concerned. I thought you might have left."

Brenda laughed and swept back a bit of her auburn-tinted hair. "Oh come on, you weren't worried."

"You don't seem yourself tonight. And I can tell you'd rather be somewhere else than here. So let's find a quiet place. I have some new classical CDs I like quite a bit."

She looked directly at him, still and thoughtful. "You don't like modern music?"

Jim smiled inwardly, glad he had drawn her interest. "Classical is one of my favorites. Helps me relax when it gets too stressful. You need to do something else to get your mind off work and life."

"I go to aerobics class. When I remember, that is. And as you can see, I have a hard time remembering."

"I'm not sure what you mean."

"No, probably not. Guys don't care about stuff like looks, flabby arms, that kind of thing." She rubbed her arms as if suddenly chilled. He slipped off his jacket and offered it to her. She stepped back as if surprised before taking it and shrugging into it.

"So what do you say?" Jim pressed. "Would you like to come over to my place and listen to some classical music? Maybe have a cup of coffee?"

"Okay, but no funny stuff. I've got the red phone line."

"I'm not a fool." *Nor are you, Miss Stewart.* Mrs. Ensley would sound nice. . .if only he loved her the way he should.

Chapter 2

Brenda went right home from Jim's, but nothing could erase the discomfort left over from the evening. She looked in the mirror to see smears of mascara encircling her eyes. She looked like a raccoon. But raccoons lived a simple existence in the woods. The only thing they were concerned about was clean food—she'd heard something about them washing their food. If only life could be that simple. But not her life. And what had transpired tonight had made it even more complicated.

So what had she done? Allowed classical music and tender words to sweep her into some kind of romantic mood. She liked Jim's kisses. He told her how beautiful she was. That she was no wildebeest. She had so much going for her. She loved hearing the words, especially after trying so hard to fit into that black dress. The words fed a hungry soul searching for acceptance.

Now Brenda felt as if life had become one big trap. She needed to break free from it, but how? She tried to relax and lie down after taking a shower, but distress filled her. At least she hadn't spent the whole night there, but she might as well have. She had given away everything else the evening had to offer.

Sleep refused to come as Brenda tossed and turned. Her senses were still riveted on the night. The hum of classical music filling his apartment. The aroma of freshly brewed coffee in the air. Then came the kissing. He was a good kisser. The lights dimming one by one.

When everything was done, she found herself saying she was sorry. To whom, she didn't know. Maybe to herself.

"You shouldn't go home this time of night, Brenda," Jim had said softly, standing there in a pair of navy blue sleep pants and black shirt half unbuttoned and hanging loose. She shuddered at the picture. What did it prove in the end? The music and caresses and kisses and everything else that followed were now painful memories wrapped in guilt.

Brenda peered at the clock. One in the morning.

She really needed to talk. Rita would be up.

She wasted no time and called. Confessed to what had happened.

Rita yawned as if it meant little. Said everything would look different in the morning. "Don't get hung up about it. And remember that Jim has lots of potential, and he did give you Snowy. That shows he cares."

At that moment Snowy the cat jumped up on her bed and nuzzled her. Snowy, short for Snow White. Supposedly Prince Charming had done his deed. And this night, Jim seemed like a prince. But she did not feel anything like a princess. Far from it. She didn't know who she was anymore.

"I need a vacation, Rita. Some place to go, even for a few hours."

Rita yawned again and told her to get some sleep. Brenda hung up and thought about the plan.

Where could she go for a short getaway? Salt Lake City was flanked by a dead and odiferous lake on one side and huge pointy mountains on the other. She'd gone up to those mountains a couple of times for a company picnic. The Wasatch range. She remembered swatting the bothersome mosquitoes. But maybe she should go back there for a day. Escape in general and reexamine priorities. Straighten out the curves in her life. And inform Jim Ensley he'd have to go it alone, even if Dad wanted another outcome for the both of them. She no longer fit into the equation of his life. Or anyone else's, it seemed.

Brenda stood to her feet and dried her eyes before looking at her Smartphone to conduct a search. She would take a drive and think things through. Even get lost somewhere. Lose herself in another place rather than the places of corporate heads and parties and tight black dresses and encounters at midnight. Anywhere but here.

Brenda began to make plans. It wasn't the first time she'd tried to make a daylong escape. There had been other times. Even that weeklong trip to Monterey. It would be good for her sanity. As long as she didn't get in over her head with this. But what did it matter? She was already sinking fast.

❧

I've got to call her. I have to apologize. This could be the end. Jim paced then looked at the clock. Two in the morning. He couldn't call her now, even though he was certain she wasn't asleep. He'd never planned to go all the way. All he wanted was to listen to some classical music and drink coffee. Get to know each other more than simple business associates on company turf. Engage in some affection and niceties to make her feel better.

But Brenda Stewart proved more alluring than he expected. She'd been like a drug the way she clung to him, her black dress flowing. Intoxicating like a drink, which he consumed little of at the party. He wanted to fulfill her needs as well as his. But now he sensed the confusion. And he worried over what the recklessness might have cost him.

He pushed back his hair and paced once more. He'd have to take a chance and call. He must stop what could rapidly turn into a mortal bleed, draining him of his future, but most of all, hurting the one he cared for.

The ringing of her cell resting on the nightstand made Brenda leap. Normally she turned it off at night; she must have left it on accidentally. Now she peeked at it to see Jim's number. *No way. I can't.* She waited. Then she picked up the phone with a shaky hand to listen to the voice mail.

"Brenda, I'm really sorry about what happened," came his deep but gentle masculine voice. She could picture him sitting on the edge of the bed, still clad in his black shirt—it did look nice. The prince all the way. They were similar at least in one respect—the princess of the company in her black dress and the prince in his black shirt. His hair slicked back. His dark eyes wide and probing. "I know we went over the top, and I know you are bothered by it. I hope we can forget this and just let it go. Please. Call me."

"Sure," she hissed. "Thanks a lot." But Jim wasn't the only one to blame. She could have walked out of there when things began heating up. And should have. But she didn't. She wanted it all, too. The so-called affection, the love. Only it wasn't love at all. The idea that what they'd done was called making love was a total misnomer. And she ought to know that by now, having slipped up before with a previous boyfriend years ago. The act temporarily satisfied some selfish need, releasing some pent-up, uncontrolled passion that should be kept under lock and key until the right time and place—in marriage.

Brenda looked over at her nightstand and took up the small Bible sitting beside the alarm clock, the Bible her grandmother had given to a much younger Brenda. She kept it there more as a good luck charm than anything. But now she had a deep desire to read it. To find something good out of what happened. Like forgiveness for herself. And maybe for Jim as well.

Jim paced, again on edge. The phone rang, but she didn't answer. He couldn't believe she lay there in peaceful slumber after all this. Maybe she wasn't as upset as he first thought, though she did bolt from his place as if she were. Refusing even a ride home or the help of Stanley, the chauffeur. He had called a taxi for her instead. He then asked if she wanted to spend the night. He didn't think it would matter. They would only sleep. And that's when she stormed out without looking back.

Now Jim feared the consequences to follow, especially if she was upset by the rendezvous. If word got out to her father, Jim might very well see a pink slip on his desk come Monday morning. *What a dumb thing to do.* And not just for the possibility of receiving a pink slip, but because that pink slip could spell the end of his plans. He couldn't afford to let that happen.

Again Jim tried to call. Again the phone went to Brenda's voice mail. He could do nothing more but try to get some sleep. At least it was now Sunday.

He could sleep in and then think of a way out of this.

When Jim awoke, he still sat in the chair in the living room. The sunlight of a new day seeped through the window. He looked around then and saw that Brenda had left her lacy black shawl draped across the sofa. He stood and picked it up. The fabric was soft to the touch with the scent of her perfume still lingering on it.

They did talk last night, even in the midst of everything. She claimed she was lonely but didn't know why. She said she wanted more out of life, to fulfill dreams, though she claimed she didn't know what those dreams were.

Brenda Stewart, daughter of the CEO of Stewart Enterprises. She had her own condo and her own chauffeur, and she barely had to work except to promote her dad's company at various company functions and boardroom gatherings. It seemed the perfect life, at least outwardly.

He squeezed the shawl. And yet, even with the passion and discovery last night, even with all she had, the dissatisfaction remained.

Now it caused him to rethink his life. His advancements. What he wanted— and needed. And whether he was doing the right thing in this company.

Jim looked out the window of his apartment. The streets of Salt Lake were fairly quiet this Sunday except for those going to their respective churches. He'd visited a few churches of various doctrines and slants in his life. He went to one that sang hymns. He attended another where the guitars, drums, and clapping made him feel jittery. None of them seemed right.

He now headed for the kitchen and found the makings of a sandwich still sitting on the counter from last night. He was hungry for something else in life. But what? Sex and food were not sufficient.

His cell rang. He hurried to answer it, not even bothering to check who it was. He only hoped and prayed—and did murmur a prayer—that the caller was Brenda.

"I can't find my daughter, Jim. She won't answer her phone. Do you know where she is?"

"Mr. Stewart! I. . .uh, I don't know where she is."

"The maître d' saw you leave the party last night together. And Stanley said he didn't drive her home."

"Sir? We, uh, we did come here to listen to some classical music. I called a taxi for her. She left after midnight."

"I wonder why she won't answer her phone."

"Maybe she went to church."

He paused, and Jim heard coughing. "Church? I never considered that. I wasn't aware she's going to church."

Jim then heard voices in the background. One sounded like Geoff Bruce giving Mr. Stewart his opinion on what to do.

"Are you certain she isn't there?" Brenda's father asked again. "Sometimes she likes to play these little games. If you're hiding anything from me, Jim. . ."

Jim felt the perspiration break out on his forehead and thought about last night. "Sir, I swear to you she isn't here."

Again he heard Geoff's voice. The fact irritated him. Geoff Bruce stood next in line to grab the coveted VP spot if he failed. And he dare not fail. A life depended on it.

"I believe you. I apologize for coming across so harshly." Mr. Stewart sighed. "I have some important people arriving. She's supposed to be here at the brunch we're having later, to give a big presentation on the benefits of the company. She has that PowerPoint presentation, a new one I approved only last week." He sighed once more. "I'll try back later. Call me if you hear anything."

"All right, sir."

"Of course I expect you here, too. Ten o'clock sharp. I want to introduce you."

"Oh yes, sir. Thank you, sir." At least Mr. Stewart didn't make a big deal that Brenda had been at his place last night. If she made an issue out of it, though, it could land him in plenty of hot water. He had time to think it all through before arriving for the brunch. Come up with some reassurance to save both their reputations and likely the job as well.

But now Jim's thoughts turned to Brenda's whereabouts. She never mentioned going to church on Sundays. No one he knew in Stewart Enterprises attended church. But perhaps they ought to consider a little spiritual guidance. Couldn't hurt. After all, nothing else was working in the peace department. He sure didn't feel any peace over this current set of circumstances. And neither did Brenda for that matter, according to what she divulged last night.

Jim went over to the coffeemaker, dumped out the old grounds, and made a fresh pot. He again caught the scent of Brenda's heady perfume. It permeated his place. He recalled how they had come into the kitchen last night when he offered to make coffee. She stood there, her head tipped to one side, the silky dress draped around her legs, a smile on her face when she said she'd love some. The aroma of brewing coffee filled the air. And then she kissed him, playfully. Kind of a peck. Arms encircling his neck. His arms curled around her. And they indulged in a little more kissing. It went from there.

Jim shook his head and concentrated on the morning's activities. He showered and fixed himself some scrambled eggs to tide him over until the brunch. He decided to be the company advocate instead of Brenda. Act confident even if he didn't feel it. Do all he could to help Mr. Stewart and the company succeed in obtaining more contracts. But above all, he hoped Brenda would call her father soon or things would not go well.

His cell rang again.

"Has she called you yet?"

"No, Mr. Stewart. I still haven't heard from her."

"Blast it, where did she go? She knows it's important to be here today. She knows what to say. I need her."

Jim cringed when he heard the words *I need her*. Everyone needed Brenda. And she knew it. She was needed for pleasure, for a prop, for anything to see that money and power and this world called Stewart Enterprises could go on. Used by him, too. Suddenly he was saddened by the fact.

"Jim, are you listening?"

"Yes, sir."

"I'm counting on you to pull this thing off for me since she isn't here. So hurry up and get down to the office boardroom."

"Of course, sir."

Jim heard a sigh and perhaps a fist hitting the table. And then silence. But now he rushed around, gathering his briefcase and netbook, hoping his suit looked good. Everything else faded. He returned to work mode, determined to mend a breach Mr. Stewart didn't even know existed. He would do his best with the situation. And change some things that needed changing. Like where he stood with Brenda.

❧

Brenda had no idea where she was going until she saw the signs for a ski resort. She recalled coming to the resort long ago to ski. After falling at least a dozen times, she finally ended up inside the lodge sipping on hot chocolate and massaging her frozen toes.

Now it was early summer with only a smattering of snow hidden in cold niches within the mountains. She drove into the resort area to see many cars parked there. Adults and children, dressed in their Sunday best, headed into the lodge. It looked as if a church group had rented the place for a fancy brunch.

Then she remembered something Dad had told her recently. About some executives and a classy Sunday brunch today and how he really needed her there to help him sell the company and what they had to offer in medical supplies. She'd even come up with a new presentation, too, with music and sound effects. Dad loved it.

"Oh no!" Brenda looked at her cell, checking the time to find it well past the start of the brunch. Dad sometimes got long-winded. She could still go and make a grand entrance and a brief presentation. She was good at impromptu presentations. Or she used to be, if she hadn't lost that skill along with everything else.

Brenda drove until she found cell coverage. "Dad, I'm so sorry about the brunch. I totally forgot."

"I'm glad you're all right, Brenda. But if you could come right now and at least meet these hospital administrators, it would be helpful."

"I'm still an hour away."

"An hour away?" He hurled a curse then swiftly apologized. "Just come as soon as you can." And then added, "Please."

Brenda said she would. She felt bad she had let him down. She and Dad only had each other since the day Mother ditched them both, nearly crushing Dad's spirit as well as his health. He even experienced episodes of chest pain the doctor called angina. Brenda stood determined to help Dad whenever she could, especially on the business side of things. Anything to alleviate the stress and avoid problems with his heart. Though in the back of her mind lingered her need for space to call her own, whether it be a drive back into the Wasatch for some time away or a major trip.

Brenda left the pristine mountain scenery to enter the city and a maze of stone buildings, roads, sidewalks, and other monuments to man. Arriving at the headquarters of Stewart Enterprises, she took stock of her appearance. At least she'd thought to wear a pair of nice black slacks and top. It should be a suit, but she would have to let that go. Brenda touched up her makeup, sprayed on some perfume, and hurried inside.

In the boardroom, a few people still lingered around the massive table, chatting. Empty coffee cups and plates half filled with sweet rolls remained. And there sat Jim Ensley on her father's right. Their gazes met briefly before Jim dropped his gaze to stare at his iPad.

"Ah, and here's my angel, everyone," Dad announced, standing to his feet. "I'd like you to meet my daughter, Brenda."

At least he didn't call her "punkin." Brenda performed her radiant smile and shook each hand while making pleasant comments. She hoped whatever came out of her mouth would portray Dad and Stewart Enterprises as a company these medical professionals could trust for their every need. Each of them offered a return smile and nod. She then took a seat at the far end of the table, away from Jim, who refused to look her way after their initial glance.

A server inquired if she would like breakfast. "Just bring me something like an iced caramel macchiato, the kind Starbucks makes, if you know what I mean."

"Well, I think we've about wrapped up this meeting unless anyone has any questions," Dad announced. Murmurs circulated as professionals stuffed handouts into folders and put away laptops and computer tablets. "Thank you all for coming."

The executives stood, shaking hands, thanking Dad for the invitation. Jim was by his side, fixed in place, until the invited guests left the boardroom.

"I'll see you for dinner tonight, punkin?" Dad asked. "We can catch up."

Brenda nodded, and her father left. With Jim still there, she decided to stand her ground also, even if she did lose her footing last night. Not to mention that the specialty coffee had arrived. She sipped it while watching Jim look around for the padded computer case. "All business today," she observed. "The pleasure part we got out of the way."

"Look, I'm sorry about last night," he said quickly, still refusing to meet her gaze. "I left you a message."

"Well, I'm not sorry."

Jim straightened. His intense brown eyes focused on her in surprise. She had to admit she did like the look of them, like Hershey Kisses. "You're not? I thought you were. You went marching out like. . ."

"Last night opened my eyes to a lot of things. And I'm doing some soul-searching right now, too. Reading the Bible and stuff like that."

"Oh. Okay. Sure."

She laughed. "The man who agrees with everything. So I take it Dad doesn't know?"

"Of course not. Why should he? We're adults. What we do in private stays in private."

"Unless God wants it shouted from the roof. I think I read that somewhere." A flush began to fill his face, and she thought she saw him flinch. "Does that scare you?"

"Our private lives should remain that way—private."

"Unless a person doesn't want it to be. What would dear old Dad think to find his nearly second-in-command taking advantage of his daughter one dark and dreary night after a party?"

"You know that's not what happened, Brenda." He grimaced, yet his gaze looked like a deer caught in the headlights. "If you want to see me fired, you can certainly do it. You have the power. But I can tell you, it won't change a thing. Or make you feel any better."

Brenda stood and folded her arms. "See you fired? I have no plans like that. You mean too much to Dad. You're like a son to him. He needs you right now in the company. And you're a good worker. But I would prefer if from now on we stay away from each other."

Jim blew out a sigh. She saw his hesitation, as if he didn't want to agree to that kind of ultimatum. And she thought she knew the reason why. Because of Dad. Dad's desire for her marriage, especially if Jim ended up the VP of the company. It would fit a CEO's daughter well. They would make a fine executive portrait, no matter how miserably it ended up.

Brenda bit her lip, angry over what happened last night. Oh, how she disliked him right then. But really, she disliked herself. And wished she could relive yesterday with a clean slate and a new heart.

Chapter 3

I really need to get out of here. Spiritually and emotionally.

Brenda couldn't do it physically for any length of time. She had her function at Dad's company, her condo, and her cat, though Rita would take care of Snowy. Something quick perhaps, like a day outing. She considered returning to the ski resort in the mountains where the people dressed for church gathered for a Sunday brunch. Anywhere but here in the city.

Her cell beeped with an incoming text message from Jim. He'd been contacting her nonstop since their unfortunate encounter a week ago. Asking how she was. If she needed anything. And telling her he was sorry at least a dozen times. Something was definitely eating him. Maybe like her, he felt unsettled, too. After reading the Bible, Brenda found some solace in asking God to forgive her for their night of indiscretion. Like the one scripture that talked about God removing one's transgressions as far as the east is from the west. Maybe she should clue Jim in on the scripture she found, though she didn't think he was the religious type.

She checked the text message. Jim asked if she wanted to go to lunch. She texted him back, saying she had her aerobics class. Nothing more popped up.

Brenda put down the phone to look at her aerobics things—the gym shorts, the sports bra, the sports shoes. Instead, she went and found a different pair of shorts and a T-shirt. She located a lavender-colored hoodie and a pair of velour lounging pants. And then her purple water bottle. *What am I doing, really?* Her mind was blank. Finally she grabbed the small Bible she'd read the last few nights. Time to discover some nutrition for the soul. Things Grandma once shared when Brenda didn't care to listen. Until now, when they really seemed to matter.

She jammed everything into an old daypack from high school—one decorated with jeweled stickers and other teen memorabilia—blowing off the dust bunnies accumulated from the closet. "What are you doing, girl?" she asked herself, using Rita's lingo.

Brenda looked out the window. No sign of Stanley yet. He normally came about this time to take her to the aerobics class. Not that she couldn't drive herself places, but Dad liked her to be carted around in a horse and carriage of steel. He paid the chauffeur good money, he said. But today Stanley could have the day off.

She took up the car keys. In an afterthought, she wrote out a note and stuck it to the door, just in case Stanley decided to check on her personally. She nodded in satisfaction.

Now she was ready to leave. *I'm on my own. Good-bye, world. Hello, whatever is waiting for me out there.*

Brenda then drove back to the place she'd visited on Sunday—the ski resort in the Wasatch Mountains. When she arrived, the lodge stood still and silent, the parking lot empty. The ski lifts were frozen in place. Green slopes met her gaze. No college-aged people were walking around in their big clunky ski boots or toting snowboards while calling out to each other. With the advent of summer, the resort looked almost eerie.

Brenda returned to her car and drove down the winding road. All at once she saw a parking lot with a small view overlooking a green valley. How different it appeared from the bland buildings and sea of humanity that was Salt Lake City. Or the drab gray of the Great Salt Lake itself. The tranquil scene appealed to her wandering soul. She threw on her daypack and began walking down the trail leading into the green meadow and forest beyond. She had no idea where it led, but as long as it led away from life for the time being, that was a good thing.

Cool, clear air filled her lungs. The brisk breeze made goose bumps break out on her arms. She stopped and donned the hoodie and lounging pants, glad she had thought to bring them. A nice walk beat the idea of standing in an overheated gym, staring at women who looked ten times fitter than she. Or looking at her rounded reflection in the mirrored walls as they performed their routines. The mirrors teased the participant into working out so the new you would emerge. Except Brenda had yet to see any fruit from all the sweat.

Here there were no mirrors, no huffing and puffing of women trying to exercise in beat to whatever music blared over the sound system. Here the chirping birds provided the music, accompanied by the wind rustling the leaves. Brenda compared the sounds of nature in no-man's-land to the ranting of friends and family—nature was oh-so pleasant to the ears and for the psyche. Still, she could hardly believe what she was doing, following a lone trail to nowhere. But at least for the first time, she felt peace.

❦

"Why isn't she answering her cell?" Mr. Stewart paced before wheeling to face his secretary, Gracie, who quaked in the doorway. "Get Stanley on the line right now."

Jim watched the man warily. "Brenda did text me to say she was going to her aerobics class, sir."

"But I just called there. She never arrived. No one has seen or heard from her. Blast it, why does she do this to me? She's just like her mother."

"Stanley is on line two, sir," the secretary interrupted.

Mr. Stewart snatched up the phone and barked long and loud while Jim stood there, feeling as if he were slowly sinking into the thick carpet. Once more the daughter had gone missing, and once more the boss was highly agitated.

"What do you mean she left a note? Well, read it to me." He waited then slammed down the phone. "I can't believe this. If I die of a heart attack. . ." He turned to Jim. "The note only said she was giving Stanley the day off. That she would drive herself. Nothing else."

"I'm sure she's fine." Jim stepped back when his boss glared at him.

"Platitudes don't work, Mr. Ensley. I want facts. I want to know where she went. The note added she would drive to her aerobics class. But she obviously never arrived."

"Sir, we know she isn't fond of the class. She could be anywhere—from some boutique to the nearest Starbucks."

Mr. Stewart began to pace. "Try her cell again."

Jim obliged, knowing what would happen. The call immediately transferred to voice mail. He then added a text message, though the last time they communicated, she'd given him the brush-off about lunch. Said she was going to the aerobics class. Maybe her father was right and something bad had happened.

A chill swept over Jim as he pocketed the phone. This wasn't about him anymore. Or his plans. This was about a young woman who had failed to show up at her intended destination. He now paced with Brenda's father before blurting out, "Sir, we should call the police and let them know."

Mr. Stewart's face turned ashen. "The police?"

"Sir, you're an important man. And you have money. This is your only daughter we're talking about. She never arrived at her intended destination. . . ." Jim saw the man's face whiten even more as he stumbled over to a large chair and sank into it. The man ran his hand over his face.

"Do you think she could have been. . . Oh no! Call at once!"

Jim wasted no time dialing 911. And was promptly told by the authorities to wait at least twenty-four to even forty-eight hours on a missing person. That might as well be a lifetime to a father. And to him.

He looked out the window above the busy city streets of Salt Lake City. Once again guilt rose up in him—a wish that he could redo the last few days, weeks, even months. Then maybe there would be a different outcome. Brenda hinted at unhappiness on her part. He'd been deaf to it, thinking only of his cause, even if it was one of necessity. *I wish she knew the truth of why I need the VP spot. Why us being together would help. I'm not a selfish monster. There are reasons for these actions. . .good reasons. . . .*

And he needed to divulge those reasons soon, even if he believed them too personal to involve others.

&⁊

No one ever said Brenda was graceful, despite the multitude of ballet lessons she'd taken at a young age. In the aerobics classes, she often tripped over her own feet. Today proved it again. Despite the fact that she enjoyed the walk on this early summer day, she never saw the protruding root until it was too late. And suddenly she found herself on the ground with a sickening pain in her right ankle.

Now she sat where she'd fallen as the ankle bruised and swelled. She'd walked roughly two hours and had no idea how far she'd come or where she was. The fact that she'd taken a few detours off the main drag while deep in thought didn't help. But now the pain in her ankle concerned her the most. In time, so did the cool wind blowing, sending shivers racing through her.

Looking at her cell phone, she saw no reception. It would be only a few hours before the sun set and cold seeped across the Wasatch. The tension of her predicament radiated to her ankle, making it hurt even worse.

This whole idea had been dumb from the get-go, and the accident proved it. "Super-de-duper, Brenda," she grumbled. "Another fine mess you've gotten yourself into." After a bit she grabbed hold of a nearby sapling and struggled to her feet. A tree branch on the ground became a walking stick of sorts. She tried hobbling down the trail but only succeeded in going about a hundred feet before pain halted her progression. Tears of frustration clouded her vision. *Here I am, Miss Glamorous, the CEO's daughter, muddy, hungry, tired, and with a bad ankle to top it.* She could just imagine how she looked, her hair sticking out in every direction and her eye makeup smeared. She didn't smell terrific either. Right now all she wanted was her cozy condo, a shower, and her bed. And an ice pack to soothe the throbbing in her ankle.

Again tears teased her eyes. She thought she had done the right thing by seeking God in this pretty place. Instead, she was rewarded with a sprained ankle. God made everything, didn't He? Why did He put that root there to trip her up? What was the lesson to be gained in this?

Brenda banged the ground in frustration and wondered how long it would take Dad to summon a search party to track her down. She could picture it already: an Amber Alert put out for his punkin—even though she was an adult. He would be convinced she'd been whisked away by some stranger. But it was the woods that held her captive, as did her battered ankle. Maybe her own disappointment, too.

Just then Brenda heard branches breaking. Fear gnawed at her with icy teeth, sending tremors shooting through her. She struggled to her feet once more and headed into the woods, sliding down behind some brush. She didn't want to be seen right now, alone and injured. Unless it was some law officer Dad sent. She wouldn't put it past him to send them out in force.

Instead, it was a guy with a beard, wearing a big red flannel shirt and heavy work boots. He stopped too close to her hiding place for comfort. Brenda's anxiety rose to a new pitch. She prayed furiously that she would become invisible. She hoped he could not hear her rapid breathing or her heart pounding in her chest.

"Are you okay?" the guy asked. He had the eyes of a hawk, seeing right through the brush.

"No. I hurt my ankle."

"I don't live too far from here. I can give you a hand and let the authorities know where you're at."

Brenda hesitated. *Go to some stranger's house? That didn't sound wise at all.*

"I know you don't know me. I'm Rick Malone. I've lived here for about fifteen years in the cabin my dad built. That is, before they began putting in all the fancy homes up here."

It all sounded believable, but again the warning bells were going off. She wanted to tell him she was fine, except for the fact that she was getting colder by the minute.

As if on cue, he opened a daypack and took out a fleece pullover. "Here, put this on. Hypothermia can be a real problem up here, especially in the changes of season when people aren't prepared."

She accepted it but tried to avoid direct eye contact. It smelled of manly soap, which seemed strange out here in the woods.

"I do need to head back, though," said Rick. "I left my niece alone with her younger brother. Though she's almost fourteen, she can get a little scatterbrained."

A niece and nephew lived at his house? That sounded like a better situation. So long as he wasn't telling her a tall tale. *Oh God, please don't let it be so.*

Rick fished out a picture then as if sensing her apprehension. "See? This is them a few years ago. Tina was twelve then and still didn't mind posing for the camera, if you know teen girls. And Cody's nine, though he's seven in the picture."

Brenda found her voice. "They. . .they're cute."

"Quite the pair. Tina can be a challenge. She likes to stay up all hours of the night. But they like being here for a visit. And I like having them while I'm on vacation."

"Where are their parents?"

"Right at this moment, enjoying a cruise."

Rick did seem to have all the right answers, using smooth, quick speech and giving a lot of details. If he was taking care of his niece and nephew like a good uncle, he must be all right. Besides that, her ankle was hurting worse, and her teeth chattered despite her clenched jaw. She couldn't stay on the cold ground anymore.

She made up her mind. "I can hardly walk, you know."

"I'll help you." He came forward and offered her a hand up. His mannerisms were gentle, even if his rugged features made her feel anxious. She wasn't certain she liked his hand on her arm, supporting her as they took it slow along the trail. Daylight was rapidly fading. She hoped they would find safety soon.

Rick took out a headlamp from his daypack and switched it on. Brenda chuckled at the contraption strapped to his forehead, flashing a beam of light this way and that along the trail. He looked like a cyclops with the glowing beacon. "Not the conventional flashlight," she murmured.

"No, but it does the trick. Puts a whole new thought on the idea of God as a light on my path. That's what I think about when I wear it. His Word is a lamp to my feet and a light on my path. It helps me see things more clearly."

Brenda silently wished the light had shone brightly before she tripped over the root. Now in the distance she made out flickers of golden light.

"My cabin," Rick pointed out. "Beyond that is a housing development. When Dad first built the place, we were alone out here. But no more. Now there's quite a few fancy homes. You can see them better in the daylight."

Brenda gulped. She hadn't planned to spend the night here. Was he offering?

"It's about time you got back!" shouted a young voice.

Brenda heaved a sigh of relief when a teen girl emerged from the cabin, aiming a large flashlight to illuminate the rest of the path. So far everything Rick had told her was true. The anxiety melted away as Brenda smiled at the girl.

"I found an injured hiker," he said. "Get me some ice in a bag, will you, Tina?"

Tina moved off to fetch the ice as Brenda and Rick entered the house. Brenda promptly lay down on the sofa while Rick found a few pillows to prop up her injured limb. When the ice bag was in place, Brenda looked at the teen standing before her.

Tina had ratty red hair that hung in strings. She looked unkempt in jeans and a T-shirt. More like a tomboy. Brenda would love to take her under her wing and properly groom her. Tina would feel better, and Brenda would feel as if she'd finally done something meaningful for someone else.

Then another young person entered the living room, a boy carrying a new Lego creation. He looked about nine as Rick had said. "Who's that, Uncle Rick?"

"A lady who fell while walking and hurt herself, Cody."

"I'm Brenda," she added. "Brenda Stewart."

The boy nodded and trudged out of the room. Brenda realized then that she knew so little about kids. Maybe it was high time she did and vowed to at least get to know Tina and Cody. "Sorry to be such a bother," she said to Rick.

"I'm just glad I found you when I did. Wouldn't have been good spending a night in the Wasatch with the temperatures dropping. You might not have made it. God was watching over you."

The mere mention of her ordeal sent another chill racing through Brenda. She adjusted the ice bag on her throbbing ankle. "I actually was in the woods to spend time with God."

"Really? That's good to hear. I like having my quiet time in the woods. Nothing like a walk to take oneself away from the cares of the world and concentrate on what God might be saying. So when did you get saved?"

Brenda stared at Rick. Saved? Saved from what? He couldn't mean the woods. He knew perfectly well he'd saved her from finding herself a human ice cube come morning. "Uh. . .it's hard to say exactly when," she faltered.

"Yeah, some have an instant conversion. For others it can come over the course of many years."

His words proved all the more confusing. Conversion? She did come to the mountains for something new in her life. Was this what he was hinting at?

"For me it came instantly. The day it happened, I knew something had changed. I was glad I happened to walk into that InterVarsity meeting. I thought I was going to some other meeting at my college campus, you see. They had switched rooms. And when the guest speaker started talking about God and how one needs a Savior to bring them into fellowship with God, I knew it was exactly what I needed to hear." He smiled when Tina appeared with a sandwich and a glass of milk. "Thanks, Tina. That was nice of you. I'm sure Brenda's hungry."

Brenda managed to tug her attention away from Rick's strange words to the ham sandwich and milk that appeared to be whole, not skim. But right now she cared less about counting calories. Hunger ruled the day. She took it with thanks and began eating.

Tina plunked down in a nearby chair, pushing stringy strands of red hair from her face. "So where do you come from?"

"Salt Lake. My father owns Stewart Enterprises, a medical warehousing facility. It's one of the top companies there. We have the best. . ." She stopped, realizing she certainly didn't need to sell this family on the company. She nearly laughed at how much Dad and the company were ingrained in her being. She hoped soon to discover the real Brenda among all the trappings. Maybe if she had been like Rick and walked into a wrong meeting somewhere. . .

Tina shrugged. "I'm not from around here." She sat back in the chair. "I'm only here because my parents think I'm still too young to stay by myself while they go on a cruise. Fourteen is old enough, in my opinion. Probably thought we'd get busted for something. Cody would get into trouble, and I wouldn't be able to handle it."

"That can happen," Rick added. "It takes a lot to care for someone younger. Look at the time I'm having with you two, and I'm way older."

Brenda had to snicker at this, even as Tina declared, "I'll be fourteen at the end of the week, you know." The girl gave Rick a steely-eyed look. Brenda was starting to like her. The girl was a younger version of Brenda when she was a teen, standing up to authority and wanting her independence. Except the girl needed some serious grooming, with her scraggly red hair and washed-out complexion.

"Well, happy birthday early," Brenda added. The comment brought a smile to the teen's face.

"Thanks."

Rick then turned to face Brenda and declared, "Think we ought to get your ankle checked out at a hospital?"

Brenda straightened, and the ice pack fell off her ankle. She could see it now, the mere thought of having to tell everyone at home what had happened. Her father doting over her. Jim's chocolate-colored eyes. "Really, I think some ice and rest would help most."

Rick gave her a surprised look. "Anyone we should contact who may be worried about you?"

"I'll take care of it. I have my cell phone with me. But I don't think it's a good idea to move my ankle for a while. It does hurt." She hoped he would let her spend the night. She didn't care to add that the thought of returning to city life, surrounded by people who no more cared for her than an inanimate object, fueled the urgency to stay put.

Well, maybe they did care. At least Dad cared, even if he could be over-protective. Did Jim care? Fat chance, unless the VP position came with it.

"Let her stay, Uncle Rick. She's comfortable here and it's late," declared Tina.

RED ROCK WEDDINGS

"I could sleep on the sofa," Brenda added. "I won't be any trouble."

"No, you can have the guest room, and Tina can sleep out here. She's used to roughing it at times, even on a sofa."

Brenda smiled, glad Tina helped convince Rick to let her spend the night. It would make the circumstances easier maybe. Right now she needed to preserve her spiritual and emotional sanity, as it still stood on fragile ground.

"You should let someone know where you are," Rick insisted.

In resignation, Brenda took out her cell and speed-dialed Rita's number. She needed her friend to look after Snowy anyway.

"Brenda, where in the world are you?"

Brenda gave her the abbreviated version of her whereabouts with one eye trained on the family sitting nearby.

"What? You're in some guy's cabin in the mountains?" Rita sounded aghast. "What kind of a vacation is that? I thought you'd fly to Venice like we once talked about. You and mountains just don't go together."

Brenda nearly laughed. "No, I'm not in Venice on a gondola ride. I'm in a safe place. I twisted my ankle, and some nice people are taking care of me. I really don't want to move it tonight. So that's why I'm here."

"Brenda, you're hurt?"

"No big deal. I'll be home tomorrow. I'm with a nice religious family."

"Want me to let your dad know? I mean, you probably should."

Brenda thought on that one. Of course she should. But she was thirty, after all. This was her life. Her opportunity to live a little on her own. She didn't want her father calling and interfering. "No, that's okay. I. . .I'll let him know soon. Just keep quiet about this. I'll be home tomorrow."

"Girl, I don't know if. . ."

"It will be fine. I can be gone for a day or two without everyone getting upset. Just let me do this, Rita. Please. I need it."

"Well, okay. I'll feed Snowy."

"Thanks. I owe you."

"Yeah, more than you know. Just be sure you call your dad. If you don't tell him, he's liable to send out the dog team to rescue you. And what about Jim? What should I say to him if I see him?"

Brenda tensed. "It's none of his business, actually."

"I'm sure he'll be worried."

Brenda's gaze traveled to Rick. "I don't really care what he thinks. He's not my bodyguard." For some reason Brenda saw a vision of Jim's face then. The concern radiating in his dark eyes. His hand reaching out to grasp hers and hold it close to his cheek. His lips ready to kiss. She flinched and shook her head to ward off the image.

"Okay, it's in your hands, Brenda."

The phone clicked, even as Brenda considered it. She should have asked Rita to call her father. But she didn't need the hassle of it right now. Brenda wanted to be her own woman. To control her destiny for at least a day. She would contact Dad in the morning.

Brenda then caught sight of the uncle, niece, and nephew staring at her. She managed a small smile. "Okay. All set."

"Are you sure?" Rick asked in a dubious voice.

"Oh, Rita gets a little overprotective. Everything's fine." Brenda turned away, hoping her face didn't reveal her thoughts—that she would hear it from Dad and everyone else when she arrived back in civilization. Dad would tell her how this affected his heart, furthering his angina attacks. That they had promised long ago—after Mother left—to be there for each other. She bit her lip and looked at her phone.

Cody then came out with a game of checkers, inviting her to play. And she promptly forgot all about Dad and everything else.

☙

Later that evening, Brenda decided to hobble to the guest room and relax. Rick shooed the kids off to bed over Tina's protest, claiming she was quite old enough to stay up. Brenda could just imagine trying to keep a girl like Tina under control. Now Brenda understood a bit of what Dad and Mother went through in trying to raise their headstrong daughter who thought she knew everything. Just then she saw Rick peek into the room. He did not come in but stood in the hallway to one side and asked if she needed anything. Brenda shook her head.

"Okay, well I'm going to read. If you need anything, just let me know." He moved off to another room, leaving Brenda to consider her life and everything in between. Choices. Future. Her dad freaking out over her wandering soul. Jim rushing to her side, probably ready to offer a red velvet pillow to rest her foot on, accompanied by a marriage license.

Brenda lifted her leg to examine her ankle. The ice had helped cut down on the swelling. Rick offered a few pain pills earlier. He seemed to know a lot about injuries suffered in the woods. He was quite a caring individual. It made her feel warm inside to think of him. Someone who cared, without preconceived notions driving him to do so.

Brenda took out her cell phone and looked at the text messages. Several popped up from Jim, asking where she was and about her physical condition. There were also several frantic voice mails from him. "Brenda, we're real worried here. You weren't at the aerobics class. Please, if you decided to take a minivacation, I can understand that. But let me know you're okay."

Brenda wondered at the genuine concern in his voice. But she refused to call him. Instead, she gazed around the interior of the room and the walls made of sturdy logs. A log cabin in the woods with all the charm and quaintness of Laura Ingalls Wilder's *Little House in the Big Woods*. It gave comfort. A place of temporary belonging. A refuge from what lurked in the valley below. She would love to stay here forever.

If only she could.

Chapter 4

"Jim!"

He barely heard his boss's voice above the melee unfolding in the office. When Brenda had still failed to show or call by early the next morning, a few police officers arrived at the boss's insistence. Marge, the head secretary, carried a tray filled with cups of coffee and doughnuts and offered them to the eager officials.

"Sir, what can I do?" Jim asked. Lines of tension creased the older man's pasty white face. He prayed the man wouldn't have a heart attack.

"Go out and look for her, Jim. Please. Find her, will you? And call her friends."

The voice bordered on desperation, as if the man was willing to place everything squarely on Jim's shoulders. The piercing blue of the man's eyes, so like Brenda's, bore into his. Jim needed to be here for this man and for Brenda. He needed to find her and reach out to her. To make things work out, even if they were preconceived plans in his mind. "Yes, sir, of course I will. I'll scout out all her usual places, ask her friends, see if anyone has been in contact with her. I'll keep the authorities abreast of any developments also."

The man nodded wearily before accepting a cup of coffee from Marge. Jim stole away into his office to pack up a few items. There were only a few places he knew of to look. A few friends. *Where did you go, fine lady? Was it on my account?* But he could no more read Brenda's mind than anyone else's. He could only go on hunches. And right now things were not adding up. And they could be leading to things he didn't even want to ponder.

❧

"We don't know where she is at this point, Rita. She won't answer her cell. She didn't show up for aerobics class like she said she would."

"She's fine. Rest assured." Rita chuckled.

Jim watched the tall brunette—Brenda's best friend, with perfect legs and a perfect figure to match—stride over to the couch in the lobby of the company building. She sat down with all the flair of a model and crossed her shapely legs in a sweeping motion. He shook his head and focused his gaze on a potted fern in the far corner of the room. "How can you say that? She's not where she's supposed to be."

"You got that right. And she knows it, too. I think you and her pops are both blind as newborn kittens. The girl's totally unhappy. And she knows you're after her on account of her money and position. That's the reason you want the wedding bells to peal, isn't it?"

Jim redirected his gaze on Rita. "That's not why. . . ," he began, uncertain what to say.

"Of course it is. We had it all figured out. Though I told Brenda you were better than nothing. There's a bunch of losers out there. At least you were headed in the right direction, with proper advancement and all in her dad's company. And her dad likes you. Plus you got her Snowy, whom she adores. But you get sidetracked too easily."

"Rita, if you only knew the whole story. . . ."

Rita ignored him. "You guys think you have it all planned out. But we women have the edge, you see. Female intuition that is one step ahead of anything you can come up with. Brenda always knew what things were about. She decided enough with the games, and it's time to get on with her life."

"So she left town?"

"Yeah. Right now I need to go feed Snowy."

Jim flew to his feet, wondering if Brenda had skipped town on his account. He swept back his dark hair with quick strokes of his hand. "Where did she go? I mean, did she talk about places she wanted to visit?"

"Let's see. There's a list. Las Vegas. Monterey—she loves that place. I even heard her talk about Venice. Now that would be the premier vacation destination for an executive's daughter but best for a honeymoon experience."

"You think she flew overseas?" How would he ever tell the boss that one? His daughter had taken the first flight to Europe to ride in a gondola and feast on Italian cuisine. If he did tell him, then it would all come to a head. The boss would find out what unfolded the other night. Jim would be blamed for feeding Brenda's unhappiness and precipitating her subsequent flight. And he would find himself with no job, no future, and no way to fulfill what must be done.

"Look, she just went off for a few days to be by herself." Rita paused, her eyes narrowing as if to study him. "You look all worried, Jim. You've got those lines running horizontally across your forehead. And are those crow's feet on a guy as young as you?"

He ignored the comment. "Yes, I'm worried." More than he realized. Something was happening here. He *really* was concerned about Brenda.

"Well, it's your own fault. You can't fake a relationship. Though I have stuck up for you in front of Brenda. I did want to give you a chance. I mean, you're a great-looking guy with a promising future. But women can see right through the fakery. We know all the tactics. The putting-on-the-charm, sweep-the-lady-off-her-feet routine. And yeah, Brenda told me about you two. How you got it on last week after the party."

Oh man. Terrific. So Brenda went and told her friends what happened. This was going from bad to worse. Now the whole world knew, and in time, so would the head honcho. "I told her I was sorry. I got carried away." *And she did, too,* he added in defense. *She kissed me first.* As lame as that excuse sounded at the moment, he didn't dare speak it aloud.

"Look, this isn't about me anymore," Jim continued. "I just want to make sure Brenda's okay."

"She's fine."

"Rita, if you know where she is and aren't telling me, you need to say so now. Her father is already talking about a heart attack or something if this goes on, and he isn't a young man. In fact, he looked real pale and weak when I left him."

Rita's features softened. "Look, I don't know where she is, exactly. She did call me, and she said she was fine."

"What? She called?"

"Yes. She said she'd be home today. That she would take care of things." Rita looked at her watch and stood to her feet. "Sorry, but I need to go over to her place and check on Snowy. Good thing the manager knows me."

Snowy, i.e., Snow White. The cat he'd given her. The cat she adored. Though he could hardly call himself Prince Charming in this whole thing, even if he had given her the pet. She probably likened him to some dastardly villain out to use and abuse.

"Look, may I go with you to Brenda's? To see if she left a note or something, giving us a clue as to where she might be."

Rita cast him a look over her shoulder. "Okay, fine. But no rummaging around and making a mess."

Jim sighed. Too late for the mess. Way too late.

❧

Jim hadn't been in Brenda's condo for close to a year, and now curiosity got the better of him. While Rita searched the place, meowing and performing other cat impersonations to coax Snow White out of hiding, Jim looked around the condo decorated in contemporary flair. He checked the calendar on the fridge but saw nothing unusual, save that yesterday was the aerobics class. He opened the fridge to see unopened bottles of Perrier, a cheese cube and veggie tray left from some party, a box of éclairs, and a sandwich in a Panera Bread wrapper.

"Don't tell me you're raiding the fridge!" Rita exclaimed.

Startled, Jim quickly closed the door.

"Honestly, that's a guy for you. Always thinking about his next meal."

"I didn't mean anything by it." He felt as if he were making one mistake after another. "I wish she'd told you where she went."

"Well, I can tell from the looks of the bedroom that she had no intention of going to her aerobics class. All her stuff for the class is still there. A couple dresser drawers were left open. The hall closet's also open, and I know she keeps some bags and stuff in there. So she did some packing."

"To head out of town," Jim concluded. "But why wouldn't she at least tell her father? I mean, they are pretty close."

"Dear Jim, wake up and smell the coffee. If you wanted to get away and be alone, would you tell everyone where you were going? Especially an over-protective father who would then try to track you down and plead with you to come home before his heart goes wild?"

"I wouldn't want to worry my family." Speaking of which, he glanced at his watch. He was still safe on the time. He would need to call and check in soon.

"Nice, but most don't think like that. In fact, I'm kind of surprised to hear you say it."

Just then Jim heard an earnest meow and saw the pure white cat patter down the hallway and into the kitchen.

"C'mere, girl, let me get you some kitty food," Rita crooned.

Jim watched Rita open up a can of cat food and dump it into a dish. "I'm a real nice guy once you get to know me, Rita. I'll admit I've made some mistakes. But who hasn't."

Rita glanced over at him.

"And yeah, last week was a big mistake. We both got carried away. Besides, Brenda is a nice-looking woman."

Rita's eyebrows rose as if questioning his sincerity.

"She is. She has a lot going for her." Jim was being truthful. Brenda did have plenty going for her. Wit, charm, determination, but tempered by an uncertainty about her future.

"Get real, Jim. You know you don't love her. We all know the endgame in all this. Bed then wed. And pick up the bonus check on the way out."

He stepped backward and stared. The words were like fists pummeling his stomach and ringing loudly in his ears. Is this what he'd been doing? He answered his own question with a resounding, *Yeah*.

"Like I said before, this is a means to an end. It's how it is in the corporate world. Good thing Brenda left it for a short time away. And maybe it would be better if she left you completely behind." She gestured him to the door, locked it, then strode off, leaving Jim in the hallway outside Brenda's condo.

The words Brenda had spoken came to the surface of his memory. About taking up the Bible and reading some scripture. He wondered why he remembered that particular statement. Jim didn't even remember if he owned a Bible.

The cell phone played a tune. "Yes, Mr. Stewart?"

"The police believe they've found Brenda's car, Jim. Abandoned on Trappers Loop Road, not far from Ogden. In the national forest."

"Huh? You mean in the Wasatch? Why would she be up there?" He couldn't picture the stoic Brenda on any woodland trail. She barely walked the neighborhood, except to the nearest Starbucks.

"There's talk it could have been an abduction and she was driven there, especially when I told them she hates the woods. It's the only thing that makes sense. There's no reason on earth she would be in a place like that."

Jim's fingers tightened around the phone.

"So can you get on up there right now, Jim? Where are you?"

"I, uh. . ." He looked once more at Brenda's door. "Brenda's friend, Rita, and I were over at her place. Rita was feeding the cat, and I—I was looking for clues."

"All right. But I need you to go. I'll be there just as soon as I can. They are going to arrange for a search party in the area, just in case she took off into the nearby woods and got lost. I can't even imagine Brenda taking a hike of all things. It's not in her nature. Someone must have taken her there against her will. And I told the police that fact. She was supposed to be at her aerobics class." His voice cracked. "I hope she's okay. She's all I have."

"We'll find her, sir."

There was silence. Jim checked the connection, but it was lost. Lost, just like Brenda. And now he grew even more worried for the young woman with auburn hair. More than anything else in this tightening world of his. Now he was connected to Brenda emotionally. He knew it deep down. He had to do whatever he could to find her and set things right. And leave the future to future's sake.

He only wished Rita had told him more. Like where Brenda was exactly.

He tried Brenda's cell again. He heard a click. Someone answered, but all he heard was a strange noise. *Oh no.* "Brenda? Brenda, is that you? Please answer. Please. Hello? Hello, are you there? Can you hear me? Are you in trouble? Please tell me."

"Yes, I'm in trouble. I'm hurt and—"

Jim heard nothing more. He tried again, but it went to voice mail.

She's hurt? Panic assailed him. His mind was a mass of jumbled thoughts. He must do something. His face felt damp, his palms even more so.

He paced, the anxiety full blown. He would have no peace, either, until she was safely back home. Forget what Rita said—claiming she was okay. The game had changed. Brenda was injured and helpless.

He needed to tell Mr. Stewart this new development. And pray the man would not collapse. He would let the boss come up with the next course of action. Jim frowned. If only the police hadn't been so flippant about all this. Waiting crucial hours for a young woman who failed to appear. Hours that might have avoided injury or worse.

Jim heaved a sigh and placed the call. He told Mr. Stewart about Rita and then what Brenda managed to say under obvious duress. The man hurled a curse, angry that Brenda had confided in Rita and not her own father. But his anger rapidly turned to worry about Brenda's cryptic message and the helplessness he felt.

Jim tried to calm his boss's anxiety as best he could. "Maybe her phone went dead. She can't recharge it. But she was able to tell us a few things. I wish I knew more."

"I'm calling the authorities back right now. Blast them! I won't wait a minute longer. I want her found. Who knows what might have happened? And get Rita down here to my office. She has some explaining to do if she wants to keep her job."

Jim's face colored at the accusations. He thought of Rita facing unemployment. "Sir, Rita helped as best she could. It seems Brenda was vague with everyone. I don't know why your daughter did this, but. . ."

The man sighed. "I'm so tired, Jim. I—I don't feel well."

"You just rest. I'll place the call, sir. I'm here. Anything you need."

"Thank you. I don't know what I'd do without you."

Normally this news would have excited Jim. The vice presidency was almost certain. But at that moment, Jim didn't care. None of it mattered. The only thing concerning him now was Brenda.

Brenda, you need to know once and for all that people do care. Though I know I've failed to show it. I need to change, somehow. But I need my circumstances to change with it.

And there, he had no idea what to do.

Chapter 5

Brenda looked at the phone on the dresser. That wasn't a very nice thing to do to Jim, she knew. But deep inside, anger lurked. She was mad at everyone and everything, including herself and this dumb ankle, now bruised and swollen. All she wanted to do was take a simple walk and ask God about some stuff in her life.

Tears stung her eyes. She sniffed as they came fast and furious. She needed a tissue badly. The towel where the ice pack rested would have to do. She plucked it up and used the corner to blow her nose. "Okay, so now what do I do?"

At least a new day had dawned. The sun was shining. The birds were singing, the sky was blue, and her ankle didn't hurt like it did last night. This place was doing wonders for her. She had to stay just a little longer to see what else might happen.

The next sensation she experienced was the aroma of freshly brewed coffee tickling her nose. Slowly rising to her feet, she limped down the hall. She heard movement in the kitchen. Rick looked at her from the doorway. "Do you take milk and sugar in your coffee?"

She sat down in a chair at the kitchen table. "Milk and artificial sweetener, if you have it. If not, regular sugar will do."

"So how did you sleep?" he asked from behind the open refrigerator door. Soon he was handing her a mug of fresh brew.

"Not bad. Tina and I talked in the middle of the night. She came to my room. She's a night owl, like you said."

His eyebrow lifted. "You had a talk with Tina?"

"Yeah, girl stuff. Makeup. Clothes. Nothing a guy would be interested in."

He chuckled. "Oh, I see. Makes sense. Probably good for her, too. All she's had for a week is male influence."

Brenda sipped the coffee and found it better than Starbucks. What was it about the mountains that brought out the best in the people and the coffee? She'd consider building her own home here someday if it wasn't so far removed from modern conveniences like a good boutique. She blinked, thinking on it, when she saw a gray tabby skirt across the door on the back deck. "You have a cat!"

"That's Charley. He likes to spend his time outdoors. He's a good mouser."

"I have a cat. Snowy. Short for Snow White. She's great company. I had a dog growing up, which I guess my parents thought would make a good substitute for a sibling. But after the dog bit me, I didn't have that anymore either." She paused then and thought of Jim. Why, she didn't know.

"Animals make great companions."

"Yes, they do." Brenda was really enjoying this moment. The warmth of the mug cradled in her hands. The sunlight streaming across her face. And the strength of Rick, a fellow cat owner and a man who was proving more intriguing the longer she sat listening to him. Obviously he wasn't married. He wore no wedding band. This could get interesting. "Anyway, during our talk last night, I told Tina I'd take her to my beautician and give her a royal makeover for a special birthday gift. My treat. She seemed to like the idea." Brenda stretched out her legs and glanced down, wishing she wasn't wearing dirty clothes from yesterday. She looked up, but Rick kept his gaze fixed on his coffee mug.

"Well, if you can do it sometime in the next few days, but I'm not sure how with your injury. Pretty soon their parents will be returning from the cruise and coming here to pick them up."

Brenda wondered how she would get around with her injured ankle. At least Stanley could drive. Wouldn't Tina love that idea—being chauffeured in a limo to the beautician?

"You have a funny smirk on your face," Rick said with a grin. At last he was looking at her. "Like someone deep into planning."

"Oh, I'm thinking about some great ways to impress your niece. She's gonna have a blast. If you can bring me my daypack, I've got my wallet in there. I can give you my business card with my cell number and all so we can stay in contact about the plans."

Rick obliged. "Which reminds me. We should get ahold of your family or friends and let them know how you are."

Brenda's fingers fumbled for the buckles to the daypack. "Don't you remember? I already talked to my friend Rita. And I. . .I, uh, also placed a call to my dad's business associate. So. . .I can leave whenever I'm ready." She didn't go into details of Jim's frantic plea on the phone and how she'd hung up on him before they'd exchanged any words.

"Okay, great. I feel better if people know where you are and that you're safe."

Brenda didn't feel as great as she had when she woke up, knowing she'd contrived some mixed-up story to keep her here. But things were already at work in her heart, more so than anything she endured in the lowlands amid the bustle of life in traffic, buildings, and people hurrying about. Or the sight of Dad pacing back and forth. Or Jim staring with his huge brown eyes, pleading with her to be reasonable. She glanced up then to check out Rick's eye color and decided they were green. What a perfect color to match the area where he lived.

Brenda took out a business card with the Stewart Enterprises logo and her contact information. "Here's my card. When I get out of here, call me in a day or two after I get settled. Stanley can take Tina to all the great spots around Salt Lake. And have her done up in style before she goes home."

"I know she will like that very much. Thanks for your generous offer."

Her heart stirred as she watched Rick's large fingers curl around the card and tuck it into the pocket of his flannel shirt. He then asked if she liked bacon and eggs. They would have a late brunch.

Brenda decided she could certainly forgo her typical breakfast of a glass of juice or nothing at all. She smiled and said that would be fine.

He went back to the fridge while she remained at the table, watching his every move and relishing the time. It felt like a vacation in a way, though no one in their right mind would consider nursing a sprained ankle anything like a vacation. But if people were made privy to her rather unfulfilling lifestyle, this was definitely time well spent.

While Rick cooked, they talked about the Wasatch and her trip to Monterey. Soon the delectable aroma of bacon filled the cabin. The scent made her think of the great outdoors. The brunches she endured at company functions were of the continental type—mainly fruit-filled danish and melon. Dad refused to eat the typical eggs and meat because of his high cholesterol. But it seemed natural, here in this rustic setting, to have a down-to-earth, country-style brunch of eggs sunny-side up, accompanied by crisp bacon and biscuits.

The aroma soon stirred to life the other members of the family. Tina and Cody ventured into the kitchen dressed in sweatshirts and jeans, eager for something to eat. Cody promptly sat down beside Brenda. "So how long are you gonna be here?"

"Just today. I have to get back to Salt Lake. My dad is probably worried about me."

"My dad isn't worried about me."

Brenda wondered about that comment as the boy fiddled with the Lego model he'd built last night. "What's that?"

"A spaceship. Can't you tell? See, here's the radar unit. And these are the engines that make it go into space. You gotta have good engines to make it go that far away."

"I know. I wonder how powerful the engines must be that once carried the space shuttle into space. Like those big orange solid boosters they use on liftoff."

Cody's eyes widened, and he straightened in interest. "Yeah. I asked Dad to take me there. He said maybe someday. It's a long ways from here to Florida and the Kennedy Space Center."

Brenda's vacation dreams of late consisted of a gondola ride in Venice or shopping in Monterey. But traveling to see the launch sites in Florida—what a unique concept. "It must be a neat place to visit."

"Okay, it's ready!" came Rick's cheery voice.

Brenda gazed at the small wooden table set with four plates, a bowl of scrambled eggs, a platter of biscuits, and fragrant slices of bacon all neatly arranged on a plate. A true family-style meal. She blinked back the sudden tears, wondering when she had ever been treated to such a gathering. She couldn't recall.

"You okay?" Rick asked her in concern. "Is it your ankle? Maybe we should bring your breakfast to the sofa and let you rest."

"No way. I would never pass up sitting around a table with family for anything." She sat down opposite Rick with the kids on either side. Rick bowed his head and spoke a powerful blessing that could have made the food change color if God so desired. Rick talked as if he truly believed God would hear every word of his prayer. If only Brenda had that kind of faith. Despite her desire to know God more, something was missing in the God angle, but she couldn't quite put her finger on it.

"Did Brenda tell you she's gonna take me to a real beautician, Uncle Rick?" Tina announced. "I'll be totally glam!"

"I think it's a great idea."

Brenda smiled at seeing the joy radiating on the girl's face. Then a thought came to mind. "Hey, we could start the process right now. I have my cosmetic bag in my daypack. We can wash your hair, put it up in curlers, and I can do your face."

Tina looked over at her while Cody scrunched up his face. "Curlers," he said with a laugh. "Where are you gonna find curlers?"

"Shut up, dork," Tina said to her brother. "I have my curling iron with me."

"That will work fine. I'm better with that than curlers anyway." Brenda enjoyed the rest of the meal. It tasted so good that she had seconds. Washed down with orange juice, nothing else in the world satisfied at that moment.

"Can we get started right now?" Tina wondered. "Cody and I can do the dishes up real quick."

"I'd help, but. . . ," Brenda began.

Rick shook his head. "Don't worry about it. Take it easy. Maybe go rest your ankle on the sofa if you want." He then came over and whispered, "I'm just glad you're giving Tina all this attention. This will be the highlight of her time here, for sure."

Brenda sighed, smiling deep within. Little did Rick know, but these last twenty-four hours had also been the highlight of her life.

In no time she was instructing Tina how to pat dry freshly washed hair in a fluffy towel instead of rubbing it. She then set to work using Tina's blow-dryer, followed by the curling iron. "You're gonna just love this when I'm through. We'll try some makeup, too."

Brenda rummaged in the pack for her cosmetic bag. She took out lipstick, foundation, shadow, and mascara. "I've got to get some of this," Tina cooed, picking up each product to examine it. "But Mom would go postal if she knew you were doing this, especially the makeup stuff."

"We can buy some when you come see me. If your mom won't mind."

Tina's grin stretched from one side of her face to the other. When Rick returned from performing his outdoor errands, he stopped short in the door-way. "Wow. There's a young woman in my home."

"She's going to look even better as soon as we finish curling her hair and putting on some makeup." Brenda picked up a small mirror to gaze at her-self. It both amazed and disgusted her to see the dark circles under her eyes. Yesterday's makeup had long since vanished. "And wow, right now I look hideous." She began tracing a bit of under-eye makeup to cover the dark circles.

"You do not!" the family said in a chorus.

Brenda laughed. "I've never known myself to go without makeup. I must be changing. Here comes the new me." Though the mere idea did unnerve her, especially since she was dressed in day-old clothes and her hair looked like an animal's nesting material. If she weren't leaving soon to go home, she'd ask for a shower and some of Rick's clothes to wear. Maybe she would anyway, once she finished with Tina's hair.

Suddenly she caught sight of Rick gazing at her in the mirror's reflection. She felt her face warm. *Ooh, nice, Brenda. Way to make him look!* She put the makeup away, thinking of the man staring at her, hoping this might be the beginning of something good between them.

And suddenly she had a vision of Jim—his face hovering over hers in the dim lighting of his apartment. The warmth of Rick's attention rapidly turned to anxiety for the future. Soon this would all come to an end. She would return to Salt Lake and her responsibilities, as well as serve an overbearing and overly concerned father in the company. And have to deal with Jim as Dad's sidekick.

Not a pleasant prospect in the least.

"Let me put some makeup on," Tina pleaded.

Brenda surrendered a sponge and a bottle of makeup to Tina. Meanwhile she checked her cell phone for messages. Three popped up, all from Jim, pleading with her to call him if she could. Instead, she thought about life in the fast lane of the corporate world compared to life here in the Wasatch. Stress versus peace. Parties versus family breakfasts and washing a young teen's hair. A gondola in Venice versus a trip to the Kennedy Space Center.

"Brenda, how's this look?" Tina asked. Brenda added some finishing touches, followed by the eye makeup. She then took a small comb and carefully fluffed the teen's hair. "You're gonna love this. Go look in a mirror and see the new Tina."

Tina trudged off, and Brenda heard a shriek. She tensed, wondering what could be wrong. "What a 'do!" Tina cried. "Uncle Rick, you gotta come see this!"

Brenda couldn't help but limp behind Rick to the bathroom, eager to see his reaction. Tina's hazel eyes were wide as she gazed at her reflection in the mirror.

"Tina, you're a beautiful young woman," Rick said with a smile. "Though I thought that before the makeup and hairstyle."

"Oh Brenda, how can I ever thank you? I'll look so good to Al."

"Al?" Brenda and Rick said in unison before looking at each other.

Tina's face reddened. "He's just a homeboy," she mumbled.

A boyfriend no doubt. Fourteen was the age for first love to bloom. Brenda remembered it well from her high school days, one of many boyfriends to come. And who was on the list this time? If she could count Rick as one, she wouldn't hesitate, even though they'd known each other less than twenty-four hours. And despite the fact she would love to get Rick into a Ralph Lauren polo instead of the frumpy flannel shirt. Some nice Nike tennis shoes instead of work boots. Cut the beard down to a goatee. She stood there imagining it all.

"What?" Rick asked.

"I was thinking about your makeover. Like changing the beard to a goatee. And your hair gelled. A nice blue tailored shirt."

"Flannel is warm up here in the mountains."

"You have to admit, though, flannel is not the most appealing item in the closet." She laughed then until she saw his gaze drift elsewhere. A slight flush tinted his rugged face as if the comment flustered him. Could there be an attraction building? It made her tingle just to think about it. She prayed it would remain and even grow.

A thunderous pounding sounded on the door.

Brenda limped after Rick to the living room. He answered the door, only to have it burst open before him. Men in uniforms charged inside. Red and blue strobe lights of several police cars flashed before the open door.

Tina screamed. Cody stared wide-eyed, clutching his Lego spaceship so hard, several of the plastic bricks popped off.

"Officer, what's the matter. . . ," Rick began.

"Not a word, pal."

An officer whirled to face Brenda. "Are you Miss Stewart?"

"Yes, but. . ."

"The rescue squad is here. Please lie down on the stretcher and let the EMTs check you over."

Men rolled a stretcher into the house while the officer motioned to his comrades. "Round up those two kids. They need to come with us."

"I don't understand! What is this?" Brenda lay down on the stretcher, but not before looking at Rick who was held at bay by two police officers.

She tried to blink, but everything was a blur, including the image of her father looking down on her, flanked by Jim Ensley, as the EMTs pushed the stretcher outdoors.

"Oh punkin, I was so worried!" Dad's lower lip trembled. His eyes were bloodshot. He looked awful. Brenda would have worried more for his health if not for the scene before her, coupled with the thought of Rick being taken in by the police.

"Dad, what is this? What in the world are you doing? Why are the police—"

"Did that man do anything to you? So help me if he put one finger on you."

"What? Are you all crazy?" She struggled to sit up. "Rick didn't kidnap me or anything like that. He found me in the woods and—"

Dad patted her shoulder. "It's going to be all right. Jim, follow the ambulance to the hospital, please. She's badly hurt. Not to mention emotionally distraught."

"It's just my ankle." Brenda tried to sit up and see what was happening to Rick's family. "Where are they taking Rick? What's going to happen to the kids?"

"Don't worry about them," Dad said in a low growl. "It's you I'm worried about."

"Dad, Rick didn't do anything wrong. He—"

"You've been through enough of an ordeal." He nodded to the ambulance attendants. "She needs to go to the hospital right now."

"It's just my ankle." No one seemed to listen or even care. Brenda then caught sight of Jim and the concerned look on his face. He of all people might be her last link to sanity. "Jim, please, why won't anyone listen to me?"

"It's going to be okay, Brenda." He took hold of her hand. "I'm here. We were able to trace your whereabouts using your cell phone. I figured you were using it to try and signal us. Especially when you told me you were in trouble."

Oh no! "That's not true. I. . ." Again she strained to see Rick hustled out of the house, followed by the kids, who pled with the authorities that their uncle was not a criminal. *This is a nightmare!*

The doors to the ambulance shut before her, sealing the family from her view. Anguished thoughts raced through her mind. *What is going on? This is all my fault. God, help us, please! Help Rick and the kids!*

Chapter 6

Jim tried not to pace inside the waiting area of the emergency room, but neither would he sit down. Mr. Stewart left to grab a cup of coffee with explicit instructions for Jim to inform him the moment he heard any news of Brenda's condition. Jim knew hospitals well. They seemed a mainstay of his life these days. He forced away that thought to concentrate on what was happening right now and the feelings he battled inside. It didn't help that news reporters called and texted his cell constantly, asking for updates and clarification of the situation up in the Wasatch. Not only did he have a battle of the heart to contend with, but an outward battle, too.

Jim gave the reporters a brief rundown of what had transpired. But when Mr. Stewart got word the press was hounding them, the man's face reddened. "You aren't to say anything, Jim. That's why I have Delores, the company spokesperson." *In other words, Jim, clam up.*

Now Jim's cell rang again, showing a local number. *More battles*, he thought, and ignored it. He walked over to a large window in the waiting area, hoping for a glimpse of nature to remove his mind from this place and everything else that had transpired. Instead, he saw a mobile television unit with its telltale satellite antenna pull into the emergency room parking lot, as if they planned a live broadcast. *Great.* He wanted to hide, but there was nowhere to go.

He took out his phone to call Delores to come handle this, but before he could punch in her number, a man and a woman outfitted in suits entered the room. They looked around, spied him, and immediately hurried over.

"Mr. Ensley, can you give us an update on Miss Stewart?" the woman asked, notepad and pen ready.

"Please direct your questions to the company spokesperson, Delores Williams, who will arrive shortly."

"Surely you must have some statement about this event. I mean, you did try to contact Miss Stewart, and because she left her cell phone on, you were able to trace her whereabouts."

Jim opened his mouth to respond then closed it, refusing to be baited. *How did they learn all that?* he wondered.

The reporter picked up on the nonverbal signal like a coyote on a scent.

281

"We heard the man involved is being questioned by the authorities. Have you ever seen him before? Like around the company?"

"Never," he said shortly. "That's all I'm going to say."

The reporter cracked a small grin as if pleased she'd broken down some invisible barricade. "They say he had two children with him. Was there any reason to think the kids were in danger?"

"I know nothing about that. You'll need to check with Child and Family Services."

"Tell us how you're feeling at the moment, Mr. Ensley."

"Relieved. And very glad Brenda is alive and unharmed."

The woman nodded and turned to leave when her eyes widened. Immediately she hurried to the elevator where Mr. Stewart was exiting with a cup of coffee in hand. "Sir, a statement if you will about these events concerning your daughter. Mr. Ensley just provided us with his."

"Jim, I told you not to talk to the reporters!" the man barked.

Jim balked at the sharp tone and nearly slid down the wall. "Sir, I barely said anything. Only that I was relieved Brenda's okay."

"We have no idea if she's okay," he retorted. "It's obvious she's been through an ordeal. She might have been brainwashed by a monster in his hideaway and who knows what else."

Jim saw the reporter madly scribbling down his boss's words. "Look, he doesn't mean any of that," he informed the reporter. "It's unsubstantiated."

"It's his statement."

Jim wanted to rip the notepad out of her hand. Just then a nurse and doctor exited from the main treatment area. Jim ignored the reporters flocking after them and went with Mr. Stewart into the examination room. When the double-wide doors clanged shut, barricading the wolves on the hunt, he breathed a sigh of relief.

"How is she?" Mr. Stewart asked the doctor as he mopped his forehead with a handkerchief.

"Oh she's fine. Has a sprained ankle. We x-rayed it, and nothing is broken. She will need physical therapy for it. Should be as good as new in about four to six weeks. I have it in an Aircast."

"A cast!"

"It's just a temporary splint so she doesn't reinjure it. She will need ice, and I have written a prescription for pain medicine."

"I will hire a private-duty nurse to help her the next few days. Jim, see to it. Ask Marge to look up the best agency in the city."

The doctor balked. "Sir, I don't think that's necessary, but—"

"If it were your daughter, you would. How is she mentally?"

"Very angry, I must say. And confused by all the police presence."

"You see?" Mr. Stewart whirled to face Jim. "She's now confused and agitated. Can you imagine what might have happened up there?"

The young physician stared at him. "Sir, according to the young lady, the man in question only provided her a place to stay after she injured her ankle. I heard her tell the police and—"

"Fine for you to say. I happen to be her father. I am the CEO of a major medical firm. And I know my own daughter. She's never run off like this without telling someone. Brenda contacted my assistant here and told him she was in trouble. That's all she was able to say before that man cut off communication. She had to be sneaky and leave her phone on. I would like to say she gets her sneaky ways from me, but that's more like her mother."

The young doctor swiped back locks of his dark hair before looking at his clipboard. "Well, she can go home."

Mr. Stewart nodded and sighed. "Good, good." His phone beeped. "Jim, go help Brenda, please. I need to answer this and then call Stanley to come get us."

Jim nodded and approached the curtain that concealed Brenda. She lay on the narrow bed, her face tense in what looked like agonizing pain. Her ankle lay encased in the clear plastic of the Aircast, which was fastened with Velcro. He'd seen such contraptions, as the company dealt in medical supplies. He just never thought he'd see Brenda wearing one. "Are you all right?" he asked gently. "You look like you're in pain. Should I call the nurse?"

"No, I'm not okay. And I'm not in pain. I'm absolutely furious at you two for what you did. How could you bring in the brute squad like that? How could you do that to Rick and the kids? Are you crazy? Where are they anyway?"

Jim stepped back under the onslaught of her words. "Brenda, it was up to the authorities to decide on the course of action. You told me you were in trouble. When you wouldn't answer your phone, we did what we thought was best." He lowered his voice. "Look, the reporters are everywhere. Your father is convinced something happened to you. You're gonna have to be careful when you leave here and not say anything right now."

Brenda's eyes glinted sharp like daggers looking to slice through him. "Well, the truth is gonna come out. I gave my statement to the police. Rick helped me when I hurt my ankle. He gave me a place to stay. We had a wonderful brunch. I plan to tell those reporters how an innocent man and his niece and nephew were hauled away for no good reason and—"

"Brenda, you can't do that. Think of your father. The company. I really had no say in what was done, only that—"

"And why didn't you? Why didn't you help, Jim? Huh?" She paused, her face redder, as Jim thought on that. "Please leave. I need to get dressed. This hospital gown is an embarrassment."

Jim did so, though his ears still rang with Brenda's accusations. But what was he to do? He had her father's concern on one side and Brenda's on the other. And he stood in the middle, feeling as though he were being squashed between them. But despite that, he believed something was wrong. Like the strange call saying she was hurt. The way her car stood abandoned in a place she had never been to before, off some road in the wilderness. Mr. Stewart had given them all cause for concern. It seemed the right thing to do, sending out the authorities.

Jim wished he could convince Brenda he wasn't the bad guy. He cared about her. In fact, seeing her injured and lying in a hospital bed was tough, more than she or anyone could know.

All this—the hospital, her injury, everything—reminded him of painful things. Things he couldn't control but wished he could. The only thing he tried to control was the money flow. But that felt so shallow and uncaring at this moment. And even that might be in jeopardy with this latest round of unfortunate events.

An orderly soon arrived with a wheelchair to take Brenda out to the car. Jim stood by to help, but Brenda ignored him. She left the vase of roses he'd brought sitting on the table. He picked it up. "You forgot your roses."

"I meant to forget them, thank you," she hissed.

Jim walked beside the wheelchair anyway, carrying the roses.

Mr. Stewart stood in the lobby, finishing a phone call. A smile spread across the man's withered face. "I am so glad to see you, punkin. How are you?"

Brenda looked at the flock of reporters standing ready, armed to the teeth with various electronic devices—recorders and a few cameras—all corralled in one area by hospital security. They readied the cameras and microphones for her statement. She waved cheerily. "I'm doing better." She smiled for the cameras and held up her injured foot, displaying the splint. "I'm going to live, guys. Thank you for your concern and for the concern of Stewart Enterprises, the number one place for medical equipment."

The barrage of questioning began.

"Can you tell us what happened, Miss Stewart?"

"Is there any truth to a rumor that you were held hostage in the perpetrator's cabin?"

"Can you tell us what it was like?"

"Are you glad to be going home?"

Jim watched as Brenda struggled to form answers. Finally she said, "Yes,

I'm glad to be going home. My ankle is doing well. And I'm sure every rumor of what went on will be laid to rest. That's all I have to say about the matter." She smiled and waved.

Jim admired her fortitude. What she didn't say spoke volumes to him. It showed her obvious love and respect for her father. And just then he noticed her look at him before her gaze darted away.

Stanley helped Brenda into the limo and shut the door, the tinted windows sealing her from view. Which was probably for the best. After all this, it was doubtful she'd ever speak to him again. A lost cause for the time being. He needed to figure out another way, but that might depend on Mr. Stewart opening the closed door between them.

Jim's cell rang, and he tensed at the number. He swiftly answered. "Pam? Pam, are you okay?"

"I had to call you, Jim. I feel so awful today."

"It's going to be okay."

"I wish you were here. I saw on the news something about Stewart Enterprises and the daughter lost or something in the mountains. Was she found?"

"Yes, Brenda's been found, and she's doing okay. We're just leaving the hospital now. Things got a little out of hand, though." *More than a little.*

"I hate hospitals. Doctors. The whole show. And this chemo makes me sick."

"I know, Pam. I know it's tough. Hang in there."

"I miss you. You're the only one who cares. Well, I know that isn't true. But you know what I mean."

"It will be okay."

"Thank you for what you're doing. It means so much; I can't even say."

"Look, I gotta run. I'll see you soon." Jim hung up, determination welling up within him. He strode forward and entered the driver's seat of his car. He would remain by the Stewart family's side, in every situation, no matter what. He would obtain the vice presidency of the company. He had no choice when he thought of the voice of desperation that tugged at the very core of his being.

And now prayer rose up within him. *God, if You're really there somewhere, please make these things work out. Not for me. I don't deserve any of it. For my sister, Pam. She's all I've got. She deserves it all. Everything I can give her and more.*

❧

"You really must keep the ice pack on, Miss Stewart."

Brenda was about ready to hurl a sofa pillow at the private-duty nurse Dad had hired. She was some dame from the fifties it seemed, with a beehive hairdo and a smell like mothballs. She wore a standard nurse's uniform—a dress that came above the knees and a white cap. She wondered where in the world Dad had dug her up from. "No thanks, I don't need ice on my ankle right now. I'm feeling a whole lot better. So you can leave."

The nurse looked at her with a pair of steel blue eyes and lashes coated in too much mascara. "But I was hired to—"

"I know, but since I'm the patient and doing just fine, there's no reason for you to stay. Thanks for all your help." Brenda didn't explain the real reason for the early dismissal. Ever since she got home, she had been itching to find out what happened to Rick and the kids. And she didn't want a nosy nurse around while she went about investigating.

The nurse reluctantly picked up her handbag, which looked more like a piece of carry-on luggage, and admonished Brenda to use the ice pack and keep her foot elevated on the pillows. Brenda responded with a sweet smile and replaced the ice pack. When the door to the condo closed, Brenda tossed it aside and came to her feet, wincing in pain. Right now nothing else mattered but finding out if Rick had been released yet. After the hospital interview, he should have been let go. She placed a call directly to the police.

"Sorry, I can't provide that kind of information," came the obnoxious response from whomever they had screening the calls.

"But I'm the supposed victim. I gave the police needed information in the case." Brenda didn't watch all those crime dramas for nothing.

After a bit a man came on the line with a voice so deep he could have been a radio personality. "This is Officer Hendricks."

"Yes sir. I'm Brenda Stewart, the one you all rescued this morning. I talked to one of your men at the hospital and. . ."

"We're still sorting out the facts. And Mr. Malone has been cooperating."

"I would like to know when he's going to be released."

"I don't have that information yet. Likely soon."

First query down. "And what about the kids who were with him? I'm so worried about them."

"You'll have to contact Child and Family Services directly, ma'am."

Brenda could just picture Tina in the care of some foster family, giving them a run for their money. If Tina didn't run away first, which was entirely possible. And poor Cody was probably scared to pieces. The mere thought of his distraught face, his fingers holding tight to his Lego spaceship, sent tears welling up in Brenda. If only there was some way she could take care of them. They liked her well enough. It was the least she could do for Rick until they were all reunited. "Well, thank you for your help. You've greatly relieved my mind."

She pushed the END button on her phone and considered it all. Maybe if she went down there and pressed the issue, the police would immediately release him. Then they could go get the kids together. She'd buy them ice cream and apologize a dozen times if needed.

Brenda placed a call to Stanley. When she had the chauffeur on the line, she gave him strict orders to come get her, no questions asked.

"But Miss Stewart, I'm not supposed to," he protested. "I'm under orders not to drive you anywhere right now. You just got home and—"

"Oh yes you can, Stanley, or I can make life quite miserable."

"But Miss Stewart. . ." He paused then finally said he would be there in ten minutes, but she would need to clear it first with Dad.

Brenda nodded, satisfied with how the plan was shaping up. But then she felt a renewed pain in her injured ankle and hobbled over to take a couple pain pills. Just the thought of Rick still holed up in some nondescript interview room, like the kind she'd seen on *Law and Order*, after he had fed her bacon and eggs a few hours before, made her want to burst into tears. It didn't matter what her ankle felt like. He must be feeling much worse. And probably steaming mad. She wasn't sure what more she could do to quicken Rick's release, but she would try everything. And then beg Rick to forgive her and her father.

She hobbled over to a mirror to reapply her makeup then dressed in a pair of slacks and a tight-fitting top, with clunky earrings and a necklace to match. Only the best for today's rescue mission. She planned to do this right and see Rick set free.

Her cell rang. "Forget it," she told the phone when she saw Jim's number on the screen. But refusal might prompt the man to knock down her door, thinking she'd collapsed or something.

"Hello?" she said as she struggled to reach her purse on the floor.

"You sound like you're in the middle of something. Shouldn't you be resting?"

"I am resting." Oh no, another lie. "I—I just dropped something. I need Nancy Nurse to get it for me."

Jim was silent on the other end. He then said quietly, "You sent her away, right?"

Brenda gripped the phone. How in the world did he know that? "I didn't need her anymore. It's a waste of hard-earned money."

"Okay, where are you going, Brenda? Stanley just called me and said you asked him to come get you but wouldn't say why or where."

"Oh for heaven's sake. I want to. . .to, uh. . .get my hair done. Have you ever been out in the woods and had your hair end up looking like you'd just taken a dive in a tub of grease? I guess not. Guys don't care about things like that."

Brenda knew she'd have to pay Stanley dearly to inform Jim he'd taken her to the hairdresser and not her intended destination. But what choice did she have? The way Jim and her dad had acted by having Rick hauled away for questioning, anything could happen.

"Okay. I can understand that." Jim sighed. "I'm just afraid you're risking more damage to that ankle of yours if you keep getting up and around. You're supposed to rest it for a week according to the discharge instructions from the emergency room."

He sounded like a man who cared, but she wondered why. She had a hard time believing him. If only Jim responded to her needs like Rick. Rick with the smile, the gentle approach, the wonderful brunch with his family. Just the thought of Rick standing there in his flannel shirt, even if he could use a good change of attire and a decent haircut and shave, sent a strange warmth surging through her.

"I'd like to come over tonight and bring you some dinner," Jim continued. "If that's okay."

"I'm sure Nancy Nurse will cook up something good."

"The nurse is only supposed to be there until five from what Marge told me. So I will bring over dinner. I know several good take-out places. I can help out, too, if you need anything done. I'll go home before bedtime."

"Sorry, I prefer not to go down that road again, thanks. Been there and regretted it ever since."

He paused. "Okay, I'm sorry it came out that way. I only meant to say that I want to help. I won't stay or try anything or—"

"Yeah, but there are too many traps to walk into." Brenda knew she couldn't pin the blame on him for their night of indiscretion. It takes two to make situations happen. And her lapses of judgment left much to be desired. Her fingers tightened around the small rectangular phone as the silence ensued. She looked to see if they were still connected. They were.

Finally Jim said one or two additional things, though she hardly heard them when the doorbell rang. She muttered a quick good-bye and hung up. Grabbing the purse that still lay on the floor, she hobbled over to see Stanley, clutching his cap and looking quite nervous. "How could you tattle to Jim about me wanting to leave?" she seethed. "This is between you and me."

"I'm sorry, Miss Stewart, but you're not supposed to leave, not with your injury," Stanley said in a tremulous voice. "You're going to get me into a lot of trouble. I—I need this job."

"Don't worry about your job. I'm in charge. And I already informed Jim that I'm going to the hairdresser. But first I need you to drive me directly to police headquarters downtown."

"Miss Stewart!"

"Just do it. Please."

The man shook his head but said no more, to Brenda's relief. This emotional roller-coaster ride was wearing her down. What she wouldn't give to do something relaxing for a change, like take a long dip in a Jacuzzi, complete with foaming bubbles. A trip to the police station, followed by Jim bringing dinner, did nothing to perpetuate a peaceful feeling. Her life was turned upside down. She was seeing and doing things all the wrong way. And she had no idea how to turn things right-side up.

Chapter 7

Jim could hardly contain himself as he sat behind the wheel of his car. He'd intercepted Stanley in front of the condo as the man was about ready to whisk Brenda away on her beauty errand, informing Stanley he would take care of it. At first she raised a fuss, then she quieted down when he'd agreed to drive her to her intended destination—police headquarters—though it was against his better judgment.

Now Brenda winced as she tried to move her foot into a better position before opting to elevate it on the dashboard. So much had changed in the last week, it nearly made his head spin—from his interest in being with Brenda at her father's big shindig, to the night of indiscretion, to the frantic worrying over her whereabouts, and now to everything that had transpired with this hermit living in the woods. He hoped things might soon change between them. Despite the irritation plastered on Brenda's face whenever they were together, he was thinking more and more about her. And in a different way. Not for what he wanted or for what his sister, Pam, needed. But in ways he couldn't quite put his finger on.

"You haven't said anything," Jim finally observed. "Still mad I took over Stanley's rightful job?"

"No. Actually, I'm curious to know why you're doing this. And not putting up a major fuss that my plan is not the hairdresser but somewhere else."

"Because I care about you." He said it, but he doubted she believed it. The raised eyebrows above her stark blue eyes verified it.

"Now, c'mon, Jim. What you really care about is your pending status in the company hierarchy. A VP and CEO daughter kind of go hand in hand, don't you think?"

"Look, I won't deny that I'm interested in the VP spot. I mean, who wouldn't want advancement in their career?"

How he wanted to go on and tell her the reason he needed the advancement. That he wasn't some selfish, egotistical brute. He had legitimate reasons for making as much money as possible—and quickly. How could he tell her that his sister needed a life-saving measure—and soon?

He opened his mouth to explain it all. Then he saw her foot and her gaze drifting to the window and realized she had other things on her mind.

Important things to a woman like Brenda. Now was not the time to delve into his troubles.

Thinking on it all, he nearly missed the turn for police headquarters until Brenda shouted in his ear. When they arrived, Brenda immediately opened the door and eased herself out, wincing in pain. "Just wait here," she ordered. Despite the pain in her face, she still proved the sergeant in command. "This will only take a few minutes, I hope and pray."

"I think you need a little help getting there. You aren't walking very well." He got out of the car and went around to the passenger door where he offered her his arm.

Brenda shook her head and limped into the building under her own strength.

Jim reluctantly remained in the car, rapping on the steering wheel, wondering what she was doing in there. He checked his e-mail via his phone and made some calls. Finally after twenty minutes, Brenda opened the door to the station and motioned to him.

"They need a statement from you," she said when he arrived.

"What?"

"Look," she said in a low voice. "You need to vouch for me. Tell them this was a mistake. Rick has to get out of here. He's got to get the kids."

Jim felt the heat building under his shirt, knowing what her father would say. The boss was convinced his daughter had been carried off by some strange guy who may have qualified for the Unabomber tucked away in his mountain-top cabin. "Brenda, maybe your father should be making the statement. He brought the charge and—"

"He won't do it. I don't know why. . . . Well, I think I know why. Anyway, can you please help me get Rick released immediately?"

"Okay. All right." Jim walked in and did what she asked, all the while praying Mr. Stewart wouldn't castigate him. With the necessary paperwork filled out, Jim turned to see a brawny man with a beard, dressed in a red flannel shirt, lumber out. The man didn't look Jim's way but stood before the desk as the final papers were readied. The man tried to remain calm, but Jim could clearly see the pinched look on his face with flaming cheeks that matched his shirt. Symbols of a silent rage?

"Do you have any idea where they've taken my niece and nephew?" the man asked the receptionist. When she said Child and Family Services, he gave a look that could have melted wax then ambled out. Still he ignored Jim. Well, the guy didn't know him anyway.

But as Jim followed, he could see that Brenda sure knew the guy. She called the man Rick and nearly threw her arms around the man. She told him through tearful gasps how sorry she was for everything and how she would help him get Tina and Cody back even if it took her life savings. Watching her gush over the man, Jim suddenly felt something he hadn't anticipated.

Jealousy.

After watching the interaction for another minute or two, Jim finally strode over. "Brenda, you really need to be getting back home and resting that ankle."

"Yes, that's a good idea," Rick agreed. "Who are you?"

"Jim Ensley. I work for Brenda's father." They politely shook hands.

"I am so, so sorry for all this, Rick," Brenda went on, her lower lip trembling. "You helped me so much when I hurt my ankle. This is just awful. Can I at least help you get the kids back?"

"No, I'll handle it. You need to take care of yourself. Promise me you will."

"Yes, yes, I will." Brenda's eyes were large and luminous, like two huge marbles glinting in the sunlight as her gaze focused on Rick. Jim felt his agitation grow. She looked like she would do anything for the man. And what did she know of him? Practically nothing. She then opened her purse and took out her business card. "Please, Rick, please call me when you all are safely back home. I really want to see Tina. I promised her a new hairstyle and makeup session for her birthday, and I intend to keep it. I won't go back on my word."

He did take the card, to Jim's surprise. Said something about how glad he was that Brenda wanted to help Tina. Then offered a stiff good-bye.

Brenda stood perfectly still as if frozen, watching him walk away. Then she began limping after him. "Rick, please wait! Let us at least go with you to Child and Family Services."

But he shook his head and said he'd rather do this alone. Brenda sighed in dismay and slowly limped back to Jim's car. "He despises me. I can tell."

"I didn't know he was supposed to like you."

Brenda gritted her teeth while giving Jim her rendition of the evil eye. "We got along very well. He cooked a wonderful brunch this morning."

"I make really good blueberry waffles."

"And his niece and nephew are so needy. Especially Tina. She's a teenager, and we both know what a tough age that is. I want to help her. I plan to take her to a beautician to get a makeover for her birthday."

"So you plan to help her by turning her into a beauty queen?"

Brenda exhaled loudly as if blowing out flames like a dragon. "Yes, Mr. Ensley. I want to strengthen a young girl's self-esteem and show her that she's beautiful. And give her something important to think about. If everything's not ruined now."

Jim opened his mouth, ready to cast the blame for that on her father, but clammed up at the last minute. She glanced his way as if surprised he did not respond.

They returned in silence to the condo where Jim ordered Chinese take-out. Brenda got herself an ice pack and headed for the sofa. "This is not going to be another one of those moments, Jim."

"I have no intention of staying to eat or anything else, Brenda. The food will be delivered right to your door. I'll leave you the cash to pay for it."

She blinked in surprise. "You aren't eating?"

"No. I can tell you'd rather eat with Genghis Khan than me. Though I do want you to know that I care about you. I know I've made some really big mistakes in the past. I'm trying to overcome them. I want to be able to care for you like this Rick did, if you'll only give me the chance. Even make you the best blueberry waffles you've ever eaten." His voice drifted off as he took a bill out of his wallet and plunked it on her coffee table. Then he strode for the door.

"Hey Jim? Thanks for everything."

Jim whirled. He wanted to say something but only nodded and left. He wondered as he pressed the button for the elevator if he'd made any inroads into Brenda's life. But after the scene at the police headquarters, Brenda only had eyes for one person. Some strange guy who lived in the wilds of the Wasatch.

≈≋

Brenda could hardly eat her egg roll as she watched the evening news. Somehow reporters had managed to track Rick down as he went to Child and Family Services in search of Tina and Cody. He stood before the cameras, still clad in the same red flannel shirt, while reporters accosted him. It seemed hard to believe this was the same man who had helped her out in the woods and then cared for her in his home. She blinked back a tear, watching his sagging shoulders and his tired face.

"The only thing I will tell you is that I was cleared of any wrongdoing," Rick said flatly. "Now I just want to go home."

Someone asked if he was going to sue for false arrest. Brenda held her breath, wondering what he would say.

"I only want to get my niece and nephew back and forget about this."

"Oh dear Rick," she said to the screen. "I'm so sorry for getting you into this mess. For having an overprotective father." How she wanted to call Dad up right now and yell at him. But what good would it do? Besides, he didn't need her stress, and she didn't need to stir up more problems, like further trumped-up charges. She thought at times she had the upper hand with Dad. But most of the time he held the reins of command. And it made her mad to think he did and how that attitude led her to escape into the Wasatch.

Brenda now shifted her ankle, and the ice pack fell off. How she wished this whole mess had never happened. Life was one disaster after another. There must be a way to clean it up.

Her cell rang. Dad. At least it wasn't another reporter. She'd received a number of calls tonight with unrecognizable local numbers, even text messages asking for her statement on the news broadcast. Still, she drew in a breath, knowing the fury to come. "Hi, Dad."

"Punkin, I'm so worried about you. As soon as I saw the news tonight, I immediately called and asked them why that man was released. They said there was nothing to hold him for."

Brenda could imagine him, pacing back and forth, his tie undone, his face red. She wished he would settle down. She didn't want him to have a heart attack.

"Dad, look. Rick didn't do anything wrong. I hurt my ankle, and he helped me. He's got two kids. Or rather a niece and nephew. You can relax. He's okay. Believe me."

He acted as though he'd gone deaf. "I called Jim, and he told me he took you down there to see that man. Why, Brenda?"

"Jim did it for me. I asked him to." She took a deep breath. "Dad, both these guys have helped me. Don't blame them. They're innocent."

"I don't understand why you're acting like this," he wailed. "Did that man brainwash you? You know what happened to Elizabeth Smart. She was brainwashed and actually wanted to live with her captors. She couldn't even leave them. That couple forced her to dress up, parading around town and everything."

"Oh for heaven's sake, Dad. I wasn't brainwashed. I'm not a little girl either. Look, I went out for a walk in the woods, and I sprained my ankle. Rick came along and found me and took me to his cabin so I could put ice on it. I met his niece and nephew. They are really sweet kids. Are you listening to anything I'm saying?"

There was silence, then he offered a subdued good-bye.

Brenda looked at the cell in bewilderment, wondering why her father was reacting this way. None of it made sense. If only something or someone could calm him, give him peace, reassure him, and tell him things were okay.

Forget any rest tonight. This was turning into another full-blown nightmare. And she only had herself to blame. For taking off like she did and not telling anyone. For using her phone to play a trick on Jim. For every ill in her life. And for others reaping what she had sown.

She wiped a tear that crept down her cheek and finally called Rita. "I'm in trouble, Rita."

"Oh no! Not again. Girl, you need to get yourself a bodyguard."

"No, not that kind of trouble. With Dad, that is. He's got it in his head that because I didn't want the guy who helped me, Rick, put in jail, he must have brainwashed me. The man helped me, for crying out loud. He rescued me. I could have been dead on a trail with my ankle busted. This is crazy. How do I make Dad see reason?"

"I saw on the news how the man was released. That was quick."

"Jim helped me. We went down there and filled in some details. Jim sided with me on Rick's innocence."

"Huh? How in the world did you get Jim to do that?"

Brenda wondered, too. At first Jim wanted anything and everything to do with making it big in Dad's company. But to go against the boss and seek Rick's release went against his plans. Maybe there was more here than met the eye. Like a smidgen of truth behind the words Jim had spoken—that he did care about her. Not for all the wrong reasons but maybe for a few right ones.

"Brenda, are you still there?"

"Yeah. I don't know why Jim did what he did."

"He must have known it would land him in hot water with your dad. I think, girlfriend, the man really likes you. And not for status, promotion, or other things. It's gone beyond that. I've seen changes in the man these last few days. He was worried sick while you were gone."

"Well, fine and dandy," Brenda said in irritation. She wasn't interested in hearing about Jim's changing moods right now. She would rather think about Rick. And how she wanted to see him again—even if he did live in the woods and wear unfashionable clothes. To see his smile and eat another of his wonderful breakfasts around the kitchen table. To live a life of freedom and peace. "I'm not interested in Jim. If it weren't for this stupid ankle of mine, I'd drive myself back up there and see Rick. I'm pretty sure I could get him to ask me out."

"Are you crazy? You can't go back and see that man."

"Why not? Honestly, no one cares to know the truth. I wish I had taped everything as proof. I got along great with the kids. I even promised Rick's niece I'd take her to a stylist for her birthday." Brenda straightened. "And that's coming up. Her birthday. I have to do it. A promise is a promise."

"Brenda, honey, you're better off in the city and not in the wilderness. It's doing strange things to you."

But her thoughts were on Tina. She said a hasty good-bye to Rita, cutting her off midsentence, and began to think. She couldn't go back on her promise to Tina. And if she did see Tina, she would see Rick.

❧

After a few days passed, Brenda again considered her plan to take Tina for a makeover. Time was running out. She looked at her right ankle and grimaced. She practiced pressing her foot downward to the floor like the motion of pressing on the accelerator in a car and felt a throbbing pain. *I'll never be able to drive myself up there. And even if I could, I don't really know where Rick lives.*

Brenda considered who could help. Stanley was out of the question. What about Jim? Every day since the ordeal, Jim had called, asking her condition. And every day the delivery guy came with food. Jim knew where Rick lived. He'd driven up to the Wasatch. He came with the entire brute squad and her father. He probably still had the location programmed into his GPS.

She tapped on the armrest with her fingernails. How could she convince him to take her up there? That might be stretching his good intentions too far. But she must try. It hadn't taken much at the police station to change Jim's mind. Rita said that there were things changing in the heart of Jim Ensley. And he ought to be willing to assist her in this latest endeavor—helping a teen feel better about herself while making Brenda feel better in the process.

Brenda left him a message. "Hi, Jim. I wanted to tell you how much I appreciate everything you've done. It means a great deal to me. Give me a call when you get this, okay?" She sighed, deciding her voice sounded appropriately sultry and convincing.

Until she recalled her Bible, still tucked inside her daypack from the adventure in the Wasatch. She took it out and sifted through the tissue-thin pages. What did God think of these issues in her life? She honestly didn't know. It must be in the book somewhere for her to consider. She was trying to bless someone in need, like Tina for her birthday, as well as make amends with Rick. That had to score points with God. As well as help in the peace and contentment department. Right?

Chapter 8

Jim stared long and hard at the quiet features as his sister's hand grasped his. The hand felt bony, as if her flesh was melting away. He resisted the urge to grip the hand harder under the force of his helplessness. That's what cancer did—acted like some vile monster, feeding off the poor and innocent, the kindhearted and gentle, taking over like an enemy or demon. He'd never been very religious like most in this city, but right now he sensed some kind of evil presence infecting her. And he planned to defeat the enemy of cancer, somehow, someway.

Pam stirred then and began to moan. Jim immediately hit the CALL button. Whenever she groaned, he rang for help. And then the perturbed nurse would arrive as though she were wholly tired of the routine and him.

"It's not time for her medicine," the nurse said matter-of-factly, flicking off the call light.

"Then get me the doctor. I want the dosage increased."

"If we increase it any more, Mr. Ensley, your sister's respirations will slow. And that could set her up for pneumonia. You see, she's resting now."

Jim looked at Pam to find she had quieted. Now he retreated once more into his shell of helplessness and distress. Inwardly his heart and soul moaned, wanting to arrest this thing taking over her blood, this aggressive form of leukemia. After a year of remission, it had come back with a vengeance. Her only hope now was a bone marrow transplant. Donors were available. But they needed money.

His cell vibrated in his pocket. He released Pam's hand long enough to look at the ID. He stood quickly and moved away from the bed. "Hello? Brenda?"

"Hi, Jim. Bet you're surprised to hear from me. Did you get my message?"

He looked over at his sister who stirred again. "No, I haven't checked my messages. How's your ankle doing?"

"I plan to live a good, long life. Hey, I need a huge favor."

Jim straightened. "Sure. Anything." Silence came over the phone. He checked to see if they were still connected. "Hello?"

"Yeah, I'm still here. I just don't know what you're going to say to this. But I made a promise, and I have to fulfill it. And only you can help me. No one else in the whole world can do it."

How could Jim tell her that promises were a two-way street—that her father's company also had something he needed, as he looked once more at Pam. Like a VP spot and the money for the transplant. Maybe Brenda would vouch for him. Tell her father he would make an excellent VP. He pushed the thought out of his mind. "What do you need?"

"Okay, look, you know how to get to his place. You drove up there with my dad. I need to see them again. I made a promise."

None of this was making much sense until she managed to blurt out about the young girl named Tina, her birthday, and some kind of special trip to mark the occasion. "Does this have anything to do with that flannel guy?" he asked.

"He has a name. It's Rick. And yes, I need you to drive me up there today so I can give Tina her birthday gift. It's very important. I'd drive myself, but my foot won't allow me. Besides, I don't know how to get there. And neither does Stanley."

Jim hesitated, wondering what Mr. Stewart would say when he found out he'd taken the man's daughter to the enemy's lair. He glanced back at Pam and grimaced. This web was getting tighter.

"Jim, are you still there? Where are you anyway?"

"I. . ." Pam stirred and opened her eyes. "It's personal business. Look, I don't know about this, Brenda. Your father is likely to get real upset if he finds out."

"He doesn't have to know. He won't if you don't tell him. Please?"

Pam turned slowly and looked over at Jim. A small smile creased her dry lips.

"I'll be there in half an hour," Jim said quickly. He hung up and came to her bedside. "Are you in pain?"

She moved about in the bed. "No, I think I'm all right. Who was that?"

"Brenda."

She shook her head. "Oh Jim, I wish you didn't have to put yourself into a corner like this. I know what you're trying to do. I only wish. . ." He saw her eyes glimmer with tears.

"Pam, you need this transplant. It's your only option left."

"But it's so expensive. And without insurance. . ."

"Don't worry. I'm taking care of it. I told you that. The only thing you need to concentrate on is fighting this thing and getting well." He stooped to kiss her on the forehead. "I'll be back as soon as I can. Brenda needs a lift, and I'm her willing chauffeur for the day."

Jim turned to leave, but he felt the light wisp of a touch. Pam's hand fumbled for his. "I love you, Jim. I want you happy. You know. . .it's okay to love someone else. And care for them."

Jim managed a smile, but the words struck him in a strange way. He walked out the door, turning at once into his business mode, even as he considered her words. Did he have trouble expressing love for someone because of what was happening with Pam? Could a gravely ill sister paralyze a person's emotions and make them refuse to love another?

He shook his head. He wouldn't psychoanalyze himself. He would do what needed to be done. Drive Brenda on her own errand of mercy, even if it was to Flannel Guy's house of all places. And try to maintain his status in the company, as any day now Mr. Stewart was set to announce his VP selection. He only prayed these little maneuvers with Brenda wouldn't do him in as far as the position was concerned.

Jim arrived at Brenda's condo to see her standing by the door, looking very chic in slim-fitting pants, a jeweled top, and plenty of makeup. How he wished she'd get that dolled up for him. But then again, why would she?

Brenda entered his car, a shiny gray BMW with leather seats and all the amenities. A car he might have to sell soon for some quick cash. Especially if Mr. Stewart delayed his VP selection.

She wriggled her nose. "You smell weird, Jim. Like antiseptic."

"I was at the hospital visiting a relative." It came out so quickly, he didn't realize he'd said it until he did.

"Really? I'm sorry. I didn't know anyone in your family was sick. I hope it isn't serious. You know, you never say much about yourself. Are you being secretive or something?"

"No more secretive than you. But at least I don't go running off to the mountains."

Brenda flinched. Her face then contorted into a look of dismay. "There were perfectly good reasons for that. And you know the primary reason was—"

"I know. I could say I'm sorry a dozen times, but it doesn't seem to do any good." Glancing out of the corner of his eye, he suddenly saw her face relax, her eyes grow large, her lips become red and full. The contrast proved startling. And rather beautiful, too. "Are you ever going to forgive and forget?"

She said nothing but only looked out the window.

They drove for a while. He made small talk. After about half an hour, he stopped at an intersection. "I'm not sure where to turn next."

"Oh no. You've got to remember, Jim. This is very important. Don't you have it programmed in your GPS?"

He shook his head. "Don't you have his phone number so you can ask for directions?"

"Yeah I do, but he won't answer his phone. It only goes to voice mail, and it says his box is full. Probably with inquiries from nosy reporters. The family's been through so much. Rick likely turned his cell phone off. I'd do that if I were him."

"Well, right now we could use a little navigational help, as I'm not sure at all where to go. And my GPS is useless without at least a partial address."

"Something must look familiar. Go ahead and take a left. I remember going this way to take my walk in the woods."

After a time she pointed out a small parking area. "See? That's where I parked my car for the walk. Dad had one of his employees come up and drive my car home."

Jim drove on, wondering what was to become of all this. He didn't like the idea of taking her to see a guy she obviously had feelings for. Maybe he was thinking too much and not showing her how he cared. How he had plenty more to offer than anyone living in the woods of the Wasatch.

Just then he jerked the wheel, sending Brenda falling against him. She righted herself quickly, but at once he saw the red flood her cheeks. She smelled nice, of some perfume that made him a bit heady.

The road turned to gravel, and all at once they were in front of the modest log home.

"Oh wow, Jim, you did it!" Brenda turned and threw her arms around him. "Thank you so much."

How he wanted to curl his arms around her but refrained. She disengaged herself from the embrace and made her way out of the car. He waited, just like another Stanley, all the while wondering what good would come of this in the end.

And then his cell rang. Brenda's father. *Super. Just what I need right now.*

"Jim, I need you at the office as soon as possible. We may be losing a valuable account, and only you can talk them into staying on board with us."

Jim panicked, looking at Rick's log cabin and then the time, realizing he was a good hour away from work. "I. . .uh. . .I've been visiting a sick relative, sir. And taking care of other responsibilities." *Like your daughter.*

"Oh. Well, how soon can you get here? I don't want to rush you, but this account is very important."

"As soon as I can, sir."

"Very good. And have you seen Brenda? I only get her voice mail. I hate it when her phone is off. Makes me think she's run away again."

"Yes, she's fine. And watching out for her ankle as only she can do." Which meant not at all.

"Good, good."

The boss sounded happy, and Jim realized his boss would be even happier if Jim could get the client back on board with the company. And maybe the VP position would be wrapped up in one nice package, and his troubles would melt away.

Guess Brenda will have to cut short her visit with Flannel Guy. Jim looked at the quiet house. No voices, no movement, no nothing. In fact, it was strangely quiet. Too quiet. For an instant, panic seized him. He'd better find out what was going on. And then hightail it back to Salt Lake.

☙❧

"You don't know how sorry I am for what happened." Brenda sat at the table, nursing the cup of coffee Rick had made her. She could clearly see the changes that had come over the family. Cody refused to speak to her. Tina at least ventured out to say hi, but suspicion clouded her face. Brenda saw the makeshift Happy Birthday sign for Tina in the kitchen and a lopsided chocolate cake on the counter surrounded by a few birthday cards. She couldn't help the lump in her throat at how everything was turned upside down for the girl. Brenda must make things right.

"It's not your fault," Rick assured Brenda. "Is it, Tina?"

The girl shrugged and returned to scratching the table with her fingernail.

"Well, the reason I'm here is to announce that I have a surprise for Tina."

At this the young teen looked up, curiosity lighting a fire to her hazel eyes. "What surprise?"

"If I told you, it wouldn't be a surprise. Any chance you can come with me for a few hours?"

Rick shook his head. "Sorry, Brenda, but I don't want Tina leaving the house. I barely got these kids back."

Now Tina turned to Rick and pouted. "Oh Uncle Rick, don't do this to me. It's my birthday. Brenda has a surprise for me." Her face cracked into a smile. "And I think I know what it is. Please?"

Just then the door slowly creaked open, and a male voice offered a sheepish hello. Rick went to see who it was.

"Hello. I'm Jim Ensley." Jim offered his hand.

"I remember seeing you at the police station. Thank you for resolving that issue so fast." Rick offered a quick handshake then turned toward Brenda. "So is this your driver?" His voice held a warning tone.

"I'm sorry, Rick, but with my ankle hurt I can't drive. Jim agreed to bring me up here. I'll return Tina by this evening. I promise on a. . ." She paused. "On the Bible. My word."

Rick thought for a moment or two, clearly not happy. But the look on the girl's face made him relent. "Okay. You have your cell phone, right, Tina? And you will stay in contact with me." The girl nodded, accompanied by all sorts of gratitude. But Brenda could clearly see the road map of tension outlined on Rick's face. How she wished she could calm his anxiety.

Jim mumbled something about needing to see to some errands. Tina picked up her purse and said good-bye to her uncle. Brenda watched the exchange, wondering what it would be like to feel Rick's arms around her. Rick caught her gazing at him, and for an instant, she felt something pass between them. He then looked away as if embarrassed by the fact.

Brenda smiled to herself, glad for this short but sweet encounter. Maybe it would lead to other things. Like a date with the guy. And a way to get him out of flannel forever and into something more appealing. She had never been one to suggest a date, but maybe Rick needed some coaxing. Time to force the hermit in the Wasatch to experience life and love. Maybe after a nice day with Tina, he might be more open to it. Especially if she brought Tina back glowing like a model.

Brenda smiled, liking the plan more and more, until she saw Jim cast a glance at her as if he could read her mind. She straightened and put on a serious countenance. But inside, her heart raced with anticipation.

❧

"We're going to have the perfect day, Tina," Brenda announced, glancing back at the girl who had said little since entering Jim's car. The girl's fingers stroked the fine, soft leather of the seats.

Suddenly a loud noise made Brenda jump. Tina had plugged her iPod into some speaker system in the back. "Oops, my B," she said quickly. "I just wanted to see how this speaker system works. This is so sick!" she added to Jim. "You must be loaded."

"Wish I was," he murmured. "A good car is necessary in the corporate world. Goes with all the flash."

"I wish my dad had this kind of car. It's awesome. We only end up with old ones. Maybe that's why Mom and Dad never got along. She was always saying we didn't have enough money for stuff."

Brenda looked back to see Tina playing with a cup holder. "I thought they did have money. That's why they're on the cruise. Your uncle told me."

"They're on it to get back together. Before they get a divorce or something, I guess."

Brenda sighed. Cleary she could see how hurt Tina was. And in this situation Brenda saw herself. Her mother had taken off when Dad got too caught up in his work. They weren't divorced, but Mother lived her own life in a New York City apartment on the stipend Dad gave her each month. Brenda hadn't seen her in five years.

"A cruise is a wonderful way to reconnect," Brenda said. "I've been on one. They're nice. Lots of couples roaming the decks arm in arm." She and Tina continued to chat about cruises and other vacation spots. Only then did she notice Jim's absence in the conversation. He looked preoccupied by something. Rigid lines had formed on his face, and his gaze focused straight ahead. And then his phone rang.

"Please don't say anything about this trip," Brenda pleaded.

Jim made small talk, said he'd be there soon, and clicked the phone off. "I can't play chauffeur anymore, Brenda. I'll drop you off at your place, but you'll have to get Stanley to take you around. I have to get to work pronto."

"Who's Stanley?" Tina piped up. "My uncle doesn't want me riding around with strange guys."

"Stanley is only my chauffeur," Brenda explained. "Ever been in a limo?"

Tina inhaled a sharp breath and fell back against the seat, her hand over her heart as if to still it. "Oh, tell me this is a dream. I get to ride in a limo?"

"Uh-huh."

"Oh, this is going to be the best birthday ever! I'm so glad you got lost, Brenda, and Uncle Rick found you. I mean I'm not glad you got hurt. But, well, you know what I mean."

Brenda laughed. She loved hearing the teen's exclamations of joy. How she wished she had done something like this earlier in her life. Taken her eyes off herself and focused them on someone else for a change. Looking over at Jim, she had him to thank, of all people in the world. He'd gone over and beyond the call of duty. Helping get Rick out of hot water with the law. Fetching Tina. Providing a nice Chinese feast among the many take-out meals. Trying to make amends on many fronts, it seemed.

But personal things did lurk in his life. She wondered about that until Jim pulled up to the condo complex. And just as quickly the thought faded under the expectation of another adventure.

Chapter 9

J im wished he could tell someone what was going on in his life. The secrets were getting to him—not only secrets having to do with family issues but also his personal feelings. New things were at work, like his growing attraction for Brenda. No longer did he think of her as simply the boss's daughter. She was a real woman with feelings and with her own dreams. And yes, an ability to attract others, like this guy from the Wasatch. Not that he thought Flannel Guy was falling head over heels for her. But obviously Brenda had decided Rick was her new specialty coffee, so to speak. What could he do about it, if anything at all?

Jim had to put it aside for the time being. Mr. Stewart was again calling him on his cell, asking his arrival time. And then there came a voice mail from a frail Pam, claiming she needed to see him and hoping he would be there in the evening. He blew out a sigh. Everyone needed him, and it was wearing him down. First Brenda, for her list of errands. Pam, for comfort. Mr. Stewart, to keep operations running smoothly.

When was he going to call on some real help to deal with these situations? Like that great Someone way up there on yonder throne. Likely God looked down at Jim this very moment and wondered what the man was doing with his life. Jim wished he knew. If only it could be spelled out, like a direct memo from heaven. Maybe there was something to Brenda's turning to the Bible in her time of need. She talked about it after their ill-fated rendezvous that one night and how she wanted to seek God. Jim ought to consider it. A godly path might actually lead him somewhere other than a dead-end street.

Tires screeching, Jim arrived at the parking lot of Stewart Enterprises. He hurried inside, greeted by Gracie, the boss's stern-looking secretary. "Better get in there, Jim. Mr. Stewart is not happy."

Just what he needed. Another confrontation. And then his cell rang. He looked at the open door leading to the boardroom and then looked at his phone. Ducking into the hallway, he answered it and heard an unrecognizable voice.

"Mr. Ensley, this is the head nurse. I wanted to let you know that your sister is having a rough time. She asked me to call you."

Panic seized him. "A rough time? What do you mean?"

"It's nothing life threatening. Just pain and anxiety, we think. We gave her medicine, but I know how much she finds comfort in you."

Jim looked over his shoulder to see Gracie shaking her head and pointing to her watch. His feet began propelling him toward the boardroom. "I'll be there when I can."

He headed inside, trying not to appear stressed, but he already knew he was too late for that. And Jim was about to become even more frazzled once Mr. Stewart leveled his guns in Jim's direction.

The meeting proved to be subdued in tone. Mr. Stewart did not bark or ask why Jim was late. Instead, he took Jim aside to thank him for watching over his punkin. To tell him he was sorry about the sick relative. But now they must get to work and salvage important accounts. Nothing else mattered.

Jim's fingers touched the phone in his pocket. Work and Pam. A fine balancing act, to say the least. He nodded like the dutiful employee he was, agreeing to the list of demands to follow up on clients, to ready the reports that were due, and everything else.

God, I need to do all these things. They are all important. My work. Pam. Brenda. I need help. He straightened, realizing prayer had taken hold of his thoughts. It felt like the right thing to do. He ought to tell Brenda about his prayerful mood. If only she wasn't so hooked on Flannel Guy. This prayerful path in life might lead to something new and better.

❧

Brenda had watched Tina's beautification with a sense of satisfaction. Never before had she felt this way. For the first time in her life, she had made it possible for someone else to be pampered. She savored the joy in seeing the beautician massage Tina's scalp with perfumed shampoo and then give her a new 'do using scissors and a blow-dryer. Now they were at the makeup counter of a fancy department store where Tina was getting her first makeover. The young teen looked as if she was having the time of her life.

"See, you apply the base like this to the eyelid," the girl explained. "The powdered shadow goes over the top."

"This is so sick!" Tina exclaimed. When the girl finished, Tina stared in the mirror. "Brenda, you've got to see me!"

"I am seeing you. You look wonderful."

"Sure hope my parents don't go postal. Mom always said I was supposed to wait until I was sixteen for makeup."

Brenda wondered if she might get in trouble for having taken the girl to get the makeover. But Rick agreed to it. It was on his head not hers. And what a fine head he possessed, too, even if he was the outdoor type. There were strength and purpose in his rugged nature. A freedom that steered clear of societal norms and lifestyles. The chance to be whoever God wanted him to be.

"Let's celebrate by having lunch," Brenda suggested. "I know a good place."

"Great. I'm starving." Tina hopped off the stool but not before gazing at her appearance from different angles. The clerk gave Tina a nylon bag filled with cosmetics. She looked over at Brenda with large eyes.

"Don't worry, it's a gift," Brenda assured her with a laugh. "Happy birthday."

"Oh, you are so awesome." Tina launched into her friends' reaction when she returned home sporting her new look. Then she added, "Al won't believe it's me. Do you have a boyfriend, Brenda?"

A vision of Jim flashed through Brenda's mind at that instant. He had been caring in many ways, but he could never be that kind of man to her. Even if he wanted to. Or more likely, was desperate to. But her own desperation turned instead to the girl's uncle and the memory of Rick's cheery voice, his excellent cooking, and his kind words. How she would love to have him as a boyfriend.

"You aren't saying anything."

"Right now I don't happen to have one. Guys come and go. Makes me wonder why we go through the whole boyfriend routine and the breakups that follow. I'm thinking now that I'll only get my next boyfriend if I know I'm going to marry him in the end."

Tina looked over, tipping her head in such a way as if to question such a strange proclamation. "Why?"

"Too much heartache not to. Life is tough enough. Shopping around for a guy like he's clothing on a rack does not make for interesting times. It can leave you feeling used." Brenda realized then how much she wanted to be loved for who she was as a person, not because of her father or the family bank account. Love based on personal worth, like Rita once said back at the office party.

"Yeah, I can see that. I see breakups all the time. Even some of my friends have gone through it. One of my friends broke up with three different guys."

Just then Stanley drove the company limo up to a classy restaurant where patrons stared at their arrival. Tina soaked up the attention like water to a sponge. She shook back her hair, laughing, pretending as if she were some Hollywood star arriving on the red carpet. None of the attention moved Brenda. Maybe she had been at this game far too long. Brenda only followed the starstruck girl into the restaurant where a waiter showed them to over-stuffed chairs.

"Oh, I am so loving this life," Tina purred as a waiter promptly filled their goblets with water and presented menus in leather portfolios. "Can I order a cheeseburger?"

"It's your birthday. Order whatever you want."

Tina did just that, ordering the typical teen fare of cheeseburger, fries, and a chocolate milkshake. Brenda stuck to a grilled chicken salad. She asked Tina what kinds of activities she liked and listened as the girl related her social networking online, participation in school plays, and playing the flute in the school band. "I never learned to play an instrument," Brenda mused, stirring the ice around in the goblet of tea brought by the waiter.

"I only do it because my parents made me. They say learning an instrument is important to entering college. I don't know why. It doesn't make sense. But honestly, they don't make sense a lot of times anyway."

"Sometimes it seems that way. I used to think that, but really, parents know more than you realize. And many times they are right. They have your best interests at heart." Brenda vowed to try and remember her own words, even with Dad sending the commandos to raid Rick's cabin the other day. He did it because he cared, as crazy as it seemed.

"I think I'd rather live somewhere else. Like with you, maybe."

Brenda nearly laughed out loud. Looking into Tina's large eyes, Brenda could see the girl was serious. "I don't think your parents will go for that right now."

Tina began slurping down her milkshake. "Who cares? We'll have fun. How about it? Can I move in?"

"Uh. . ." Brenda hesitated. The waiter arrived with their orders. "Let's go ahead and eat." The matter temporarily forgotten, they ate while Tina exclaimed over the best-tasting burger in the world. To Brenda a salad was a salad, but to this girl sitting before her, even the food was extraordinary. It made Brenda realize how good she'd had it. And how she no longer enjoyed things like Tina did but rather took them for granted.

In midbite, Tina again popped the question about moving in. "I want to live your life. It's so much more exciting than mine."

"I'll tell you, Tina, I have a cat, and she doesn't like strangers. And I guess when one lives alone long enough, you get used to things. Besides, you've got school to finish. Great friends back home. Even if your parents aren't the best in the world—and whose are?—they'd really miss you if you left."

"Maybe." She said little else as they finished up the meal.

Exiting the restaurant a short time later, Tina's exuberance melted away to thoughtful silence. With the birthday extravaganza wrapping up, Brenda's thoughts turned from the moody teen to Rick, wondering what she should say when they saw each other.

Tina directed Stanley where to go as they headed into the Wasatch. Brenda chatted about a few mundane things as the city of Salt Lake became replaced by trees and grassy green meadows, flanked by the sharp, rocky peaks of the mountains. Soon they were pulling into the long, narrow gravel road leading to Rick's mountain hideaway. Brenda tried to imagine herself driving down this road as his wife. The image proved unsettling.

She pushed her musings aside when the man walked out, his face all smiles, his arms open wide in a greeting. How Brenda would love to run into those arms that he actually extended to Tina. Cody ran out then, looking to investigate the limo and pepper Stanley with questions.

"Wow, and who is the new woman arriving on my doorstep?" Rick exclaimed. He then remarked to Brenda, "I didn't even recognize her."

Brenda smiled. "She had a good time, I think."

Rick chuckled. "After all this, I hope you can stay for a visit and dinner, Brenda. I'm doing up my famous fried chicken." He paused. "And your chauffeur is more than welcome to eat as well."

"I'll send Stanley on his way and call him back when I need him to return. Or maybe you can drive me home if you have time?" She hesitated, hoping he would. To her delight, Rick agreed. Inwardly she smiled. A dinner invite and a ride home. So far, so good.

Once inside, Tina spent an hour telling stories of the hair salon, the makeover, the fine lunch, and the limo ride. "I told Brenda I want to live with her, but she said I still have a few more years left in high school."

"Uh. . .yeah," Rick agreed, his eyebrows raising. "Just a few years. Fourteen is pretty young to be thinking of getting out on your own. You need to finish high school. And then there's college."

Tina relaxed against the sofa. "Oh, but she has the most wonderful life, Uncle Rick. I could get used to it real quick."

"But this is a great life right here," Brenda pointed out. "Your uncle lives a nice, simple existence. No sense of the hurry-up lifestyle or modern things taking up time and space. It's peaceful, too."

"It's too quiet," Tina complained. "There's no one to talk to here. And he doesn't have a computer. I can't even get on Facebook."

Brenda laughed, joined by Rick. "So we see where the teen interest really lies," Brenda mused. She looked to Rick, but he wasn't staring at her, much to her dismay. She wished he would. She thought she looked pretty good, after all. While the makeup people were doing their work on Tina, Brenda had spruced hers up and made sure her hair was in place. Maybe Rick wished she sported the outdoor look. She should have shown up in flannel garb from L.L.Bean, along with a windswept hairdo.

She looked down at her tailored pants and short jacket over a glittering sleeveless blouse, gleaming purse, and even high heels. Not the rugged woman for a rugged man. More like someone for a professional.

After a time Rick excused himself to make dinner. Brenda followed, asking if she could help, knowing her cooking skills amounted to sliding a Lean Cuisine meal into the microwave or calling for take-out. He said he could handle it, but she remained in the kitchen, hoping beyond hope that something might build between them.

Rick made small talk of his early days cooking and the work he was doing on an old car. He talked of his job as an auto mechanic.

Brenda tried to digest this, thinking of him arriving home every night covered in grease. She quickly changed the subject. "What do you do for fun?" she now asked, taking up the plates he had put on the counter to place around the table.

"You have to ask?" At that moment their eyes met, the first hopeful sign she'd seen. "This is the Wasatch. I like hiking. And skiing in winter. Sometimes I go into Ogden or Salt Lake to visit friends. I also like to head up to Idaho. Ever been rafting?"

Brenda shook her head.

"I did it once, in Hell's Canyon. Never go into Hell's Canyon on your first time out rafting. That place was unbelievable."

The more he talked, the more Brenda was feeling like some porcelain doll that might break if he squeezed too much. How she wanted to be a part of his life. But right now she felt as if she were standing to one side, peering in, watching silvery flakes fall on a woodland cabin in some snow globe, far removed from the scene. "I would love to go on a drive sometime," she said brightly. "Like to Idaho. Or anywhere you want." She winced, realizing how desperate that sounded.

Rick melted away into his cooking, facing the stove, his back to her. He said little after that.

At dinner Cody talked of going home soon to see his friends. Tina cooed about the lifestyle of the rich and famous. The fried chicken proved tasty, as did the potatoes and fresh green beans. Brenda pondered what to do concerning Rick. She refused to abandon the idea of a date. Maybe if they stepped out onto the porch and looked into the star-covered skies, he would suggest it. Start small, like a simple walk down the road, and work their way up. Brenda believed she and Rick had been brought together for some reason. Even if that reason still proved unclear.

Chapter 10

A week of working all day and staying the night at the hospital wore Jim close to the breaking point. He yawned, asking the head secretary, Marge, if she would make another fresh pot of coffee. He'd arrived late to the office, having worn the same clothes from yesterday, not even stopping at home to shower and change. He'd spent the night sitting at Pam's bedside or trying to catch a few winks in the visitor lounge before she would call for him. At least now Pam rested comfortably, though he was dead on his feet.

Jim loosened his tie and tried to focus on the spreadsheets in his computer, but all he saw was blurred images. The data made even less sense. If he didn't get these forms right, Mr. Stewart would find something else to get after him about. Or more likely, someone else to fill his seat.

"Tough night?"

Jim peered up to see Geoff Bruce looking in from the hallway. He'd forgotten about the Swedish wonder, ready to snatch up the vice presidency position without hesitation. "I have a sick relative," he blurted out.

"Oh, sorry to hear that. Is it serious?"

"Kind of. But I plan to get the reports done, don't worry."

"I'm not worried; only Mr. Stewart is. If you're having family issues, maybe you should take a leave of absence. There is such a thing as family leave."

Sure, and when I get back, you'll be sitting tall in the office right next to Mr. Stewart's. And I'll be demoted to the janitorial staff. That wouldn't help Pam's situation or his. Jim had to think fast on his feet, even with the few brain cells functioning and legs wobbly from fatigue. "I'm okay. I've got a handle on it."

Geoff left just as Marge came in with some fresh brew. She was a motherly type with graying hair. She'd been with the company for years. Perhaps even when Brenda was in diapers. Jim nearly felt the compulsion to spill the beans of his life into her lap. He often wondered why he hadn't yet. Maybe he didn't want to drag Pam's situation through a labyrinth of people outside the family and have to listen to their varying opinions. Besides, he could handle it. He was in control. He planned to beat this thing, just as he planned to win in the company. But at times the urge to tell someone that

310

his sister must have a bone marrow transplant soon if she was going to beat the leukemia was like a wall of water asking to be set free over the spillway. The pressure was mounting to the breaking point.

"You all right, Jim?" Marge now asked, setting the mug beside him.

"Sure. Just didn't get much sleep."

"Well, you're going to have to try and get the reports done. Mr. Stewart was asking about them yesterday. They were due in."

They were due yesterday? In a panic, he looked through his calendar and saw that they were actually past due by a few days. Where was his mind? Lost in a puddle of confusion. Or at Pam's bedside. "I'll get them done today."

She nodded and left him to his work, but nothing happened. The fog over his mind increased.

By 3:00 p.m. he still hadn't finished when Marge called over the intercom that the boss wanted to see him. Jim felt the pressure rising like that of a pressure cooker. Now the praying came easily. *God, I'm in kind of a jam here. Please help me out of this somehow.*

Mr. Stewart was shuffling papers when Jim arrived. The man was never still, always either rearranging things or pacing. "So what's going on, Jim? It's not like you to fall behind in your work. Geoff tells me you have family problems."

Great. "I'm sorry for the delay on the reports, sir. I'll get them done."

"I'm not sure you can, and it's got me mighty concerned. You realize I'm about to make some changes here in the company hierarchy. I've got to have top people by my side that I can rely on to make things work. There's competition out there for this business. Other clients and hospitals will go elsewhere for their equipment if we don't keep them in line." The man's eyes now leveled at him. His nose twitched. "I really do like you, Jim. You're like a son to me in many ways. But I see things going on in you that aren't right. You haven't had a disagreement with my daughter, have you?"

Your daughter, my dear sir, has flown the coop to hang out with Flannel Guy of the Wasatch. He said nothing, though, and shook his head.

"Actually I'm growing more and more concerned about Brenda. I'm hoping you know what's going on. I've heard rumors, for instance, that she seems infatuated with the man who kidnapped her."

"She has gone to see him and the family," Jim admitted.

Her father's lips contorted into a frown of displeasure. "That is totally unacceptable. I thought you two were getting along well. Don't tell me you're letting me down in that area, too, Jim."

Wow, two strikes. If he came up with a third. . .out. "Brenda is pretty strong-willed," Jim managed to say.

"I'll agree with you on that one. Which is why I need you to do me a huge favor. And it's going to require a firm hand and determination."

"Sir?"

"I need to put a stop to this wandering heart of hers. She may be strong-willed, but I know you two have also been close in the past. I need you to intervene. To put a stop to her visits with that kidnapper. Whatever it takes. Stanley told me, too, how he's taken her up there. I reprimanded him, of course. But I'll pay you to take her somewhere to get her mind off things, like this man. Maybe a vacation. Like the Caribbean. She's even talked of going to Venice. I don't want my daughter falling for the bad guy."

Jim hardly thought of Rick as some criminal. He actually appeared like a nice, ordinary individual who unfortunately got caught up in Brenda's flight or fight response. But from the look on Mr. Stewart's face, he was dead serious. "I'm not sure what I can do, sir. As I said, Brenda is her own person. We've already seen what happens when we try to intervene. She takes off full speed ahead."

"Then you're going to have to take her somewhere. Anywhere. As long as it's away from Salt Lake. And while you're at it, find out more about this man and his intentions. See how far this has gone."

To Jim's amazement, Mr. Stewart began pulling large bills out of a locked drawer, including a $1,000 bill with a president's face Jim didn't recognize. "Sir?"

"Here's some money for the trip. And a little bonus to keep Brenda away from the man. If you need Marge to make the trip arrangements, let her know."

Jim stared at the money, wondering what it added up to and how much more was locked away in the drawer. Surely enough to put a small down payment on Pam's treatment. Or enough to get the ball rolling. But the longer he looked at it, the stranger he felt. At one time, money was all that mattered. Now the idea made him feel guilty. There had to be other ways. Turning to nobler acts to win the heart of a disillusioned woman. And surrendering Pam to some Higher Power who could provide for her needs.

Jim gently pushed the stack of bills aside. "Don't worry about the money right now, sir. I'll do what I can about seeing this man. If I need it for a trip, I'll let you know."

Mr. Stewart's face broke into a wide grin. "Interesting. You've just scored a big bonus with me, young man. I like how you think." He returned the money to the locked drawer and then stood to his feet. Jim did the same. "Let me know what happens. The cash is here if you need it."

Jim shook the man's hand, but instead of relief, he felt the fog around his life growing thicker by the minute. Take care of Brenda. Meet Rick. Get the reports done. Be with Pam. If life was a jungle, he stood in the thick of it. And armed with only a machete of determination to cut his way through.

೧ೱ

Now that Jim had an ultimatum from the boss and more than enough stress to fill the inside of a battle cruiser, he wished he had a membership in a fitness club. He thought of Brenda and her aerobics class. It would do him good to pump iron on a machine. With every weight lifted, he'd imagine the weights of his dying sister, work, Brenda, everything falling from his shoulders.

With the reports finally done the next morning and the clock nearing noon, Jim readjusted the mirror in his car as he sat in the parking lot of Stewart Enterprises, wondering what to do first. He decided to put out feelers and see what happened. First he called Brenda's cell, hoping she would agree to have lunch with him. It only skipped to voice mail. He left no message. She might be screening her calls anyway. And if he wasn't the man of her dreams, she would likely ignore him.

Jim then considered Rick, wondering what harm there could be in moseying on up to the Wasatch and doing a little investigative work. Finding out for himself as well as for the boss where things stood between Rick and Brenda. He'd know better then how to deal with Brenda and if drastic measures were required. Like Mr. Stewart's idea of a whirlwind vacation.

But if Rick and Brenda had already signed a mental pact to some future commitment, no amount of money or a trip to Venice would work. He would then have to report to the boss that Brenda had made up her mind. And Mr. Stewart could locate another fairy godmother to turn his "punkin" into a gilded carriage, and good luck with it. Jim would wash his hands of it. But if a door was open, that is, if Rick and Brenda were only friends or casual acquaintances, then Jim had an opportunity to wedge his size 12 shoe in there.

Jim stopped at a market to pick up a basket of cheese and sausage for the visit, along with a tin of cookies for the kids if they were still around. Brenda really liked the girl, Tina. It must have made her feel motherly, taking the young girl under her wing. And suddenly he was thinking of his own kids. And hers. Teaching them. Nurturing them. Praying for them, especially in the vulnerable teen years. He thought on that last activity. The idea of prayer was coming even easier these days. Especially with his fully loaded plate.

The drive into the Wasatch went faster than he had anticipated, thanks to his GPS. Jim stopped halfway down the gravel road, nursing a pang of apprehension. What in the world would he say when he arrived? "Hi, how are you? Leave the boss's daughter alone. Hey Rick, can you please let me try and gain Brenda's attention? Can you let us see where we are going in our relationship?

Or really, can you just lay low for now?"

Jim drove on in determination to meet Rick man-to-man.

A young boy sat on the porch steps, holding what looked like something made of Legos. Jim put down the window and smiled at the boy. "Hey there. Got your Legos, I see. I used to play with them when I was your age."

The boy stood, startled, and rushed into the house yelling for Rick as Jim exited the car. All at once the man appeared, outfitted in his usual flannel apparel, even though the day was quite warm. "Hi. Can I help you?"

"I'm not sure if you remember me, but I drove Brenda here to pick up Tina for her birthday outing."

"Oh yeah. Of course." Rick's hands slid into the pockets of his jeans.

"I just wanted to drop by and bring you something. An apology, really, for everything we put you through, with the police and all." Jim handed him the basket of goodies.

"You didn't need to do that. But thanks."

"Well, we were really concerned about Brenda, but I think we took it too seriously. Brenda's like family to all of us at the company. I've gotten to know her fairly well."

Rick nodded and pointed to two wicker chairs. "Have a seat."

Jim then took up the can of cookies and held it out to Cody, who stood a distance away, peering at him cautiously. "You like cookies?"

The boy's face brightened. He hurried forward and took the can. "I sure do. Thanks! But Tina won't eat any. She says she's too fat."

Rick snickered. "Teens. Ever since Brenda took Tina on that makeover trip, she's been in the bathroom for hours."

"Actually, I haven't seen much of Brenda these days. Is she okay?"

Rick straightened in his seat. "I don't know. I mean, she was here to drop off Tina last week. I did take her back to town. But we don't stay in contact, which is probably for the better. She's been very nice to Tina, but I think she's hoping for something to happen between us. And I can't allow that to happen."

At this, Jim nearly jumped out of his seat. He fought to maintain his composure and simply nodded. But inwardly he was grinning from ear to ear.

Rick traced his finger across the armrest of the chair before his gaze drifted off to the far woods. "You see. . .I'm married."

Jim's mouth fell open before he realized it and quickly shut it. "Oh," he managed to sputter.

"My wife, Marta, left about two months ago to live with her parents in Idaho. We've had some disagreements. She wasn't too crazy about life here. And I think she was upset that we hadn't had any kids yet. I love her very much. I wanted to give her some space to think things through, but I think I gave her too much. I don't want her to slip away. When Brenda was here, I realized how easy it is to trip up. I'm glad Brenda took Tina under her wing. But I don't want this to lead to something between Brenda and me, if you know what I mean." He looked down at the basket Jim had brought.

"Sorry we sent your life into a tailspin like this."

"Actually, Brenda may have been a blessing in disguise. It made me realize that I need to get my marriage back on track again. Tina and Cody go home next week. I need to call Marta and set things right. We've been apart too long. The Bible talks about being apart for prayer. But then you're to come together quickly to avoid temptation. And I'm seeing firsthand the truth behind that."

Jim sat, staring with Rick at the basket he'd brought. He wondered what, if anything, he could add to this serious conversation. *Nothing, actually.* Anything Bible related was foreign territory to him.

"Sorry to dump all this on you. But I wanted you to know that I'm not in any way pursuing Brenda. All I did was help her out with her ankle. And allowed her to help my niece."

"You need to let Brenda know," Jim said to him. "She can easily develop her own ideas about things." And then he realized what this news would do to her. Make her want to run again. Maybe to no-man's-land where no one could find her. Jim must keep that from happening. He needed to be sympathetic. Provide a shoulder for her to cry on, so to speak. And not because of any money thrown at him by her father. The mere idea made him cringe. Jim would provide his strong, steady shoulder because he cared. No strings attached whatsoever.

"I will do that, thanks. I'm glad I have God to give me guidance in this. I'm not sure what I'd do without it." Rick stood to his feet, and Jim did as well. He offered his hand. "Thanks for stopping by."

Jim thought on Rick's words. God's guidance? How does God guide someone in these matters of life? Wasn't He just a church building? A hymn? Platitudes? Jim coughed. "Okay, sure. Good seeing you." He ambled off, his mind a whirlwind, both in gratefulness and confusion.

While driving down the mountain, Jim's cell beeped a voice mail. "I saw you called," said a familiar voice. "Tell Dad I'll call him tonight."

Jim punched in the key to her number. It rang and she answered.

"Jim?"

"Brenda, hey, you'll never guess where—"

"I left a message. So Dad has you tracking me down again, I see. You're better than any bloodhound. You should get a new profession." She chuckled scornfully.

"Want to get some coffee?"

"Can't. I'm heading out to a new jewelry store Rita said I need to check out."

"Brenda, I—I want to let you know. . .I'm on my way back from seeing Rick."

There was silence for a split second. And then a thunderous "What? What on earth were you doing up there?" Before he could answer, the words rushed out. "No, don't tell me. It's my life. Don't you guys get it? I can see who I want, when I want. I can date who I want, too. So just lay off."

"Brenda, he's married." He heard a clatter. Had she just fainted? "Brenda? Are you okay?"

And then there came a feeble "Stop it. You're making it up."

"No, I swear to you. We sat on the porch, and Rick told me. He's been estranged from his wife for the past two months. He plans to go see her to reconcile once the kids leave. He wanted you to know."

"No, no." He heard gasping.

"Brenda, please don't hang up. Brenda, there's something I want to say. I really care about you and—"

"You only care about Dad's company."

His hand gripped the phone. "Brenda, look, I don't want anything between us. Not money, not the company, not your dad, not past mistakes. . . I have to say this. I have a sister…a sister who is really ill. She has leukemia and. . ." He heard nothing and checked the connection. She'd terminated the call before she heard the reasons.

"Blast it," he muttered, borrowing her father's favorite saying. *Why do I bother? Brenda doesn't care about me or anything else but her own world. Now she'll leave again, most likely. Fly to some foreign land. What's the use?* He paused and thought on Rick's words shared that afternoon. Of a God interested in guiding the things of life.

Hey God. I know I don't know You. But I'm really trying to turn over new leaves in my life. Don't let Brenda run again. Let her know somehow that I do care.

Chapter 11

Girl, get ahold of yourself. You've used up all the tissues in my purse."
Brenda blew her nose, but the tears kept coming fast and furiously, as they had all last night. She cried most of the time with Snowy in her arms. Now a few managed to find their way to the croutons atop her chef salad, turning them slightly soggy. Lunch and misery didn't go hand in hand. "What am I going to do, Rita?"

"You're going to move on and be glad you didn't get involved with a married man. That's what you're going to do."

I nearly got involved with a married man. What kind of woman am I? First the one-night stand with Jim. Now this. Her life had turned into a genuine soap opera.

"Brenda, don't go blaming yourself. It's not your fault. You found the man attractive. There's nothing wrong with that. And you didn't know he was married."

She began to hiccup. "What's the matter with me? Talk about looking for love in all the wrong places. Another oldies tune come to life. That's me all over."

Rita shook her head and ate a forkful of her chef salad. "I just find it odd that Jim was up there and found out about it."

In an instant her tears vanished. "Do you. . .do you think he made it up?"

Rita shrugged. "I'm sure he didn't. But it wouldn't hurt to find out the truth for yourself. I know Jim wants his hooks in you. He has from day one. He's got some plans he wants fulfilled, and you're a big part of them."

"He said once he needed money. What in the world does he need money for, I wonder? He already makes decent pay. Unless he wants a villa on the Mediterranean or something."

"Did you ever ask him?"

"Why should I? I'm not interested in his personal life. But now I do want to find out why he's interfering with mine. And resorting to lies."

"You don't know if he's lying. I only said it might be good to find out the truth instead of hearsay. And take it from there."

Brenda nodded and tried to pick up her fork to eat. When would Jim ever stay out of her life? But then she thought about Jim's call and what he'd said. His words struck her in a strange way and made her wonder if what he said was true. That things had changed. That he cared. There were times Jim seemed different. Could she believe it? Or was that a lie, too?

Rita looked at her phone and began texting. "Wow, I'm gonna have to run, girlfriend. Got to head back to the company. Geoff needs me to do some research for him. You okay?"

"Oh sure. No problem." She managed a smile, but inwardly she felt dried up and barren like that massive salty desert that lurked past the Great Salt Lake. Rita plopped down some bills to cover the check, waved, and left in a flourish. Brenda thought of her friend with her stylish figure and confidence in life. And she didn't even have a boyfriend that Brenda knew of. Or if Rita did, she never let it get to her like these scenarios had for Brenda.

Brenda took out her cell phone and paged down to Rick's number. What could she possibly say to him so she didn't sound like a fool? How should she broach the topic? Especially if Jim had lied—though inwardly she knew he hadn't. What reason would he have to do such a thing? *Unless he really wants me and will stop at nothing.*

The waiter came over to clear the dishes. Brenda ordered a hot fudge sundae. Her nerves must be working overtime for her to spoil the diet. But she felt she deserved it, even if her body didn't. Hot fudge might ease the pain inside. The pain of wondering, searching, stumbling about blindly, finding innumerable traps with no way out. And the common denominator in all these things was Jim Ensley. He'd become a genuine wrecking ball to her life.

The sundae arrived, but it tasted like sugar topped with dark food coloring and sprayed with fat. Brenda ate two bites, paid the check, and left. Misery clouded her every step. She needed to call Rick right now to straighten this out. When she did get ahold of him, he agreed to meet her at 3:00 at the coffee shop. But Brenda still wasn't sure how to go about this. She wished Rita had given her talking points before she went her way. Like how to uncover the truth. Where things stood between them. And if some estranged wife was caught in the middle of it all.

After a half hour of window shopping in which she saw nothing but black and gray, Brenda headed for her car, glad her ankle was better so she could drive without Stanley's assistance. Another advance for independence, in a strange sort of way. She drove until she came to her favorite coffee shop. She could use an iced caramel macchiato right now. And someone to share it with—someone she yearned to know, and someone who really cared about her. Someone truly unattached and unafraid.

A half hour later she was on her second coffee drink when Rick stepped through the door. Her heart leaped. He looked perfect, dressed in a polo shirt and slacks. She barely recognized him out of his flannel element. Their eyes met, and he came over, sliding his hands casually into his pockets. "Hi."

"Hi. Thanks so much for meeting me. Can I get you a coffee?"

Rick shook his head and looked around the establishment. His mind was elsewhere. Or was it nerves? She couldn't tell. Then again, she really knew nothing about him. Even if she did yearn to know everything.

"You're probably wondering why I asked you here."

"I think I can guess."

She straightened. "You can?"

"Well, maybe not." He went to buy a cup of coffee. Brenda shifted in her seat. Maybe it would have been better to do this all over the phone. But she needed a face-to-face encounter for something this serious. To get the truth out in the open. Yet a part of her didn't want the truth. She wanted her fantasy world instead. A date with Rick. A moonlit walk, even if it was on some backwoods trail in the Wasatch. Enjoying another country breakfast with family in the warmth of a house, cozier than the white paint and modern deco of her condo. To have what he possessed. Contentment.

Only now Rick didn't look content. He appeared fidgety, fumbling with his cup, turning it slowly before taking a drink. A question might thaw the ice rapidly solidifying this meeting. "How's Tina doing?"

"Well, you changed something in her, that's for sure. She occupies the bathroom 24/7. It's not that bad, but she likes staring at herself in the mirror more and more. I do think she has more self-confidence. I really appreciate your taking her under your wing like that and making her feel special."

"I had fun."

"They go back to their parents in a few days. And they aren't too happy about it." Rick took a healthy swallow of coffee.

Brenda waited, hoping beyond hope that all of Jim's reporting was false, that when the kids left, she and Rick could pursue a relationship. Finally she blurted out, "Jim told me you two talked."

"Yes, he came to see me yesterday. He brought us a huge basket of goodies and cookies for the kids."

Brenda sat back, slightly startled. "That was nice of him."

"He felt pretty bad about what happened with the police and all. I had no idea you were such an important lady."

"Dad tends to overreact when it comes to his daughter. And the reaction means little when one doesn't understand where the daughter stands in life and the direction she wants to take." Brenda could not believe the feelings came streaming out. But then she caught a glimpse of Rick's face, and she breathed in sharply. He wore a look of compassion.

"Sometimes it's hard to know which direction to take. I had a feeling when I found you on the trail that you weren't sure where you were going. Not just literally, but in life, too. It isn't easy to map it out. Sometimes you just have to walk the path and see where it leads. There's a favorite scripture of mine I like to think about during times like this. 'Man plans the way, but the Lord directs the path.' I think you just need the Lord directing your life, Brenda. You've been trying to do it your way. Why not try His way?"

"I have been reading the Bible and all. It's kind of comforting." She saw Rick take out his wallet, and she drew in a breath of expectation. But he only gave her a card for the church he attended—an evangelical church in the city.

"Come visit some Sunday. The pastor would be more than happy to answer any questions you might have." He paused. "And Brenda, there's something else you need to know."

Brenda's fingers curled around the card. "I think I know," she said softly. "Jim told me. He said you're married."

"Yes, I am. I plan to get back together with my wife. It was wrong of me not to come out and tell you. I realize I need to walk the path of my marriage and not run from it. To stay the course even if it's bumpy and leads to tough places. But it's the path I must walk. I married 'till death do us part.'"

Brenda nodded, though she forced back the tears trying to make their appearance. "Well, I should have known it was too good to be true. That a nice guy like you would already be hitched."

Brenda, it doesn't mean a dead end in your life. You just have to see where God wants you to go. Once you give Him control, you're going to see things work out in ways you never imagined." Rick finished his coffee. "I hope you don't mind, but I need to head back. The place is a mess, and the kids are in charge of cleaning it up. Which means not much is going to happen while I'm away."

"Okay." She barely choked out the word.

Rick stood and looked down at her with eyes that looked oh so tender. "Brenda. . .I. . ."

Just tell me you have feelings for me, Rick. Tell me I'm pretty. Kind. And that you're in love with me, and the wife thing is gone for good. Please!

"Brenda, I'm sorry to have led you on like this. Truly I am. Forgive me." He heaved another sigh, turned, and left without another glance. She saw him through the window walking briskly down the sidewalk, his steps long, his head held high.

But all Brenda saw before her was a dark and lonely road. The light had gone out. Anger rose up within her. Maybe Rick might not have gone back to his wife if Jim hadn't interfered. They might have been set to divorce, and

Rick would be free. And she would have been happy. . . .

✑❧

A few days later, everything came to a head. Dad sat there, his face turning from red to redder as if it were flame kissed over the fire. "I'm not sure what to think."

"I know I've never asked you who to hire and fire. But this is my professional opinion, and there are others who will back me up on it in the company. I've heard the complaints. He comes to work unkempt. He's been late. The reports. . .well, look at them." Brenda offered the stack of reports after she had Geoff Bruce go over them and splatter them with his red ink.

The man wiped his perspiring face and nodded grimly.

"Maybe he drinks. He acts like it. Who knows what he does? But we can't keep him on here." Brenda felt her cheeks flaming. One lie piled on top of the other and set ablaze, with her on top of the burning pyre. She felt the heat.

"He drinks on the job? Blast it, I knew there were things up with him. His work output's been way down. He's been sloppy." Dad dragged his fingers across his head of thinning gray hair. "I had such high hopes for him. I thought he would be a good match for you, too. You need someone in your life, punkin."

"Not him, I can tell you that. In fact, not anyone." She said it with such anger that her father rolled his chair backward. He then stood to his feet, his arms open wide. Brenda submitted reluctantly. "Don't worry about this. It's out of your hands. Let it go and try to be happy."

Try to be happy. Impossible now. She hurt too much, and she had to cast that hurt on someone else. Someone needed to pay for the disappointment. And the lot fell to Jim Ensley, supposedly the last man standing in all this. Only he wouldn't be standing much longer.

When Brenda left the office, it seemed like everyone was staring at her, though it was likely her imagination. Whispers abounded in office corners. She hurried out of the building and found a bench to sit on. She thought back to the times she and Jim spent together. *I wanted to feel loved. Or some kind of feeling. Anything other than what's inside of me. And now what do I feel after all is said and done?*

Brenda thought it would be vindication, getting the man canned. Instead, there was only misery. And now a terrible guilt to top it off.

321

Chapter 12

Jim knew something was wrong the moment he opened the door to the building. It began with the floor attendant who gave him a strange look. Stepping into the elevator, Jim saw a co-worker, Melissa, and greeted her. She looked away and took out her cell to place some impromptu call.

What's going on? Probably nothing. After all, he didn't seem to have many friends these days. More and more he was feeling like an outsider. The only time he believed he did anything right was at Pam's bedside. And the floor staff of the hospital agreed, telling him how much better Pam did when he came to visit. Energetic. Happy. And in less pain.

But something was definitely wrong here at Stewart Enterprises. When he entered the office, Marge stood like some security guard, her arms folded and her face rigid.

"Jim, you need to report to Mr. Stewart's office immediately."

Jim froze. "I can't even drop off my bag?"

She shook her head and turned on her heel to head back to her desk.

"Marge, whatever this is about, I didn't do anything wrong. The reports are logged in as I promised."

She looked back at him, and for an instant he saw the look of a mother. His mother, now gone. He choked up for a moment. Mom always knew what to say and do. She would have understood any mistakes. She would have provided comfort. If only she hadn't succumbed to the same cancer that Pam battled right now. Sometimes he even wished Dad were here, though the man had remarried and now lived with his new family in California. Jim talked to him a few times about Pam's condition. But Dad had a new life, and now it was just Pam and him. Alone.

"Jim, I really can't talk about this," Marge continued. "You need to go see Mr. Stewart. He's waiting for you."

Jim forced back the emotion, heaved a sigh, and walked toward the ominous office. He peeked in the open door to see the man with his shoulders hunched, pacing back and forth before peering out the large plate-glass window to the streets of Salt Lake below. When he heard Jim's footsteps, he whirled.

"This is it. It's done. After this meeting, you'll have fifteen minutes to pack up your things."

Jim almost dropped his coffee cup. "W–what? Sir—I—"

"I've heard the complaints all around. And from my own daughter. Rumors you're even drinking on the job."

"What? Sir, that's not true at all."

"Your work output proves otherwise. Lack of concentration. Sloppiness."

Jim couldn't control the tremors. "Sir. . .please let me explain about my sister and—"

"There is nothing more to say. I'm sorry, but the company no longer needs you." He flicked the intercom switch. "Marge, send in Geoff Bruce, my new vice president."

The man paused. His face blanched, his voice choking. "I—I had such high hopes for you here in the company, Jim. You used to be very good at what you do. You once gave this company 110 percent. I thought you would make a good son-in-law, too. I trusted you to do what's right. And you let me down. I'm sorry, but this is good-bye."

Jim backpedaled, nearly running into Geoff who materialized behind him. He expected the Swedish wonder to be wearing a look of triumph on his face. Instead, the man's features were masked in seriousness.

Jim walked slowly to his office, numb from head to foot, his thoughts spinning. Where in the world had this rumor of drinking come from? He didn't drink. Half the company drank. What in the world?

Then he considered it all. Brenda must have marched in there spouting off. *She's angry.* Angry over the man she can't and shouldn't have. Angry about everything. He was doomed by false accusations and misunderstanding.

I've been fired when I need that job the most.

Jim looked up then and saw Marge standing in the doorway. His face felt as if it were on fire. He could say nothing to her or anyone else. Shame filled him. The quicker he got out of here, the better.

When Jim gathered what stuff he wanted, which wasn't much, he walked out into the main office area. Everyone ignored him but Marge. Could that be the crook of a smile he saw on her face?

He stopped before her. "I just wanted to thank you for everything you've done for me here, Marge. You were like a mom to me." He didn't wait for a response but moved off toward the bank of elevators. Until he heard the patter of footsteps behind him, and he turned.

It was Marge. "Jim, I know there are always two sides to a story. I know you've had it tough here at work. And there are rumors floating around. But I believe the truth will come out in the end. And I believe God is watching out for you."

Yeah, some great God up there. My sister is dying. My job is gone. He said nothing to Marge though. The elevator doors slid open. And in an instant, they closed on Marge's compassionate face and this place. Forever.

A tear glazed his eye. Not for himself really. But for the one who depended on him. Pam. Now he would fail her, too.

Once outside the building, Jim snatched out his cell. He refused to let this go down without at least confronting Brenda. He punched the number, and to his surprise she answered.

"Brenda, why? Why did you do this to me?"

He heard nothing. Maybe some paper rattling. A sigh.

He went on. "I thought we'd settled things. I thought things were settled with Rick, too. What does any of this prove?" Again he heard nothing and looked at the phone. They were still connected, probably by a thread. He inhaled a breath. "Talk to me," he said, trying to keep his voice calm. "We need to talk about this."

Jim looked again, and the call had terminated. He nearly threw the phone in frustration. *Why is this happening? What does this serve in the end? If this is supposed to make things better, I'd sure like to know how.*

Jim walked the sidewalks. He didn't know where to go or what to do. He felt empty. Without purpose. He finally went back to his car and drove to the hospital. At least he could sit by Pam's bedside and watch the disease cripple her bloodstream and her body. At that moment he wished he were in her place. *God, if you can't make this right, then let Pam live and let me die. I deserve it.*

❦

Jim's words reverberated in Brenda's heart and mind, even as she tried to go through the tasks of the day, like following up on some clients of Dad's and doing other mundane tasks. But she couldn't forget his distraught voice over the phone or the guilt she felt for having done what she did. All of this consumed her, so much that she felt paralyzed.

Her cell phone rang. She prayed it wasn't Jim with another emotional plea tugging on her heartstrings.

"I heard the news!" cried Rita. "Girl, it's all over the company. I can't believe you got Jim fired."

"I. . ." For once she didn't know what to say.

"Why did you do it?" She didn't wait for a response. "You know what I think? You're mad at Jim because he got in the way of your relationship with Rick. I mean, it looks pretty suspicious. Look at the timing of it all."

Brenda bit her lip, realizing her friend could read her like a book. It scared and humbled her. "Well, Jim only wanted to use me for money and for a prominent position in Dad's company. You know that."

"Your dad really liked him. Like a son. He wanted Jim by his side. But I think the times Jim had with you turned him upside down. Made his work go haywire and everything else. You had him running back and forth on your little errands. You had him jumping through hoops. It was getting ridiculous. And for what? To be with a married man?"

"I didn't know Rick was married. I—"

"You need to stop using others to cover up what's going on inside of you. Honestly, Brenda, you need to grow up."

The call terminated. Brenda stood there stunned. Never in her life had her best friend hung up on her. Brenda knew Rita spoke the truth, but she was unsure how to deal with it. She looked at her cell and the picture of ocean waves on the screensaver. How pretty it appeared. Peaceful. Pleasant. Soothing. But waves like a tsunami could also wipe out everything and everyone. And she'd stirred up one big tsunami that took out those she cared about. Yes, including Jim. Jim, the guy who stayed by her side. Jim, who would do things for her even if it upset Dad. Jim, who cared and cared a lot.

And now one thing he said in the past stuck out in her mind. He'd said, "I don't want anything else between us. Not money, not the company, not your dad," before she had hung up the phone that day. And then she remembered the words that resounded with nearly every meeting: *I care about you.*

Now Jim was unemployed. He was reduced to nothing because of her.

Brenda placed a call to Marge the secretary, knowing the motherly woman would let her in on what was happening in the company circle. "So Dad let Jim go."

"Yes. Jim packed up his office and everything. I never saw a sadder man. Whatever happened between you two, you need to do what is right, Brenda."

She inhaled a sharp breath and confessed to Marge the whole scenario with Rick.

Marge sighed. "Oh Brenda."

"Jim's wanted a relationship with me from the get-go. I thought maybe it was because of the VP spot. That he didn't care about me personally. But things changed after the incident in the Wasatch. I just. . .I just let this whole Rick thing come between us."

"You need to tell your father the truth, don't you think?"

Brenda didn't say anything, but the words were clear—from Rita and now from Marge. She had to fix the mess she'd created. Tell dear old Dad she was not his innocent punkin. She had issues. She needed fixing. "I should probably talk to Jim, too. And try to get his job back pronto."

"I think that's a good idea. Even if you both made mistakes, God forgives. Then you can forgive yourselves."

"Do you go to church?"

"Why, yes. But knowing God is much more than just going to church. It's seeing Him for who He really is—a personal Savior who wants to come into your life and fellowship with you."

"Rick thought like that. The other guy I liked, the one who's married. He talked about God like that."

"God wants to be real to you and talk to you, just like you and I are talking over the phone. The Bible says if we knock on the door, He will answer and come in and dine with us. I think you really need to knock and knock hard. And I know He's waiting to answer and come into your heart."

Brenda licked her lips at the mere thought. Fellowship with Jesus. Even dine with Jesus. It seemed so strange to her. How often she pictured God as some obtrusive figure way up yonder. But not the way Marge painted Him. Marge made God sound powerful yet personal, too. To be worshipped, revered, and loved. She realized if she did want that fellowship, she would need to restore what was lost. She must make tracks now to repair the damage.

Brenda grabbed her car keys. The last time she'd been there turned into a fateful night of disappointment. Now it could lead to redemption.

≈❧

Brenda knocked on Jim's apartment door, but no one answered. Jim was gone, likely off to find out what to do with his life now that she had destroyed it. Maybe he'd escaped like she had, though likely not to the Wasatch. In Utah there weren't many other places to flee lest one headed out of state. West took a person to the snow-white wasteland of the Great Salt Desert, while south took a person to a barren wilderness of red rocks and sagebrush. North was Idaho. She wondered then where he might be found and took out her cell. Calls were impersonal. She needed to look him in the eye. Tell him about the talk with Marge. Ask if they might seek God together and turn this around somehow.

Brenda headed to the elevator and nearly bumped into a flashy woman in high heels who was exiting. She hoped the woman lived on Jim's floor. "Excuse me. Do you happen to know Jim Ensley who lives in apartment C?"

The woman spun about. "Sure, I know Jim. He's never there though." She held out her hand. "I'm Juli. Without the *e*."

"I'm a—a friend of his. Brenda. I'm trying to track him down."

"I'm sure Jim's still at the hospital. He spends most of his time there these days."

Brenda grew rigid. "The hospital?" She recalled the one time he said he was visiting someone in the hospital. "Is someone sick? Was there an accident?"

"His sister is very sick. She has leukemia. From what he told me the last time we talked, if she doesn't get that bone marrow transplant soon, it will be too late."

Brenda felt her mouth drop open and quickly shut it. "Uh, okay, thanks." Numbness drifted over her. All this time, from the company halls to the Wasatch to everything in between, Jim had a sick sister. *Brenda Lorraine Stewart, how could you?*

Brenda didn't even wait for the elevator. She ran to the nearest stairs and charged down all five flights. She didn't care that she was out of breath when she reached the ground level. *Jim, how could I have done this to you? All this time. Everything you were going through. Okay, yeah, that one night we were wrong. But from that moment on, you tried to reach out to me. To make amends. To be there, even though you also had a sister battling leukemia. And who did I care about? Me. Poor, little ol' me.*

Brenda stepped on the gas and raced to the hospital. Breathless, she asked if there was a Pam Ensley listed as a patient. When she discovered the room number and obtained a visitor pass, she hurried for the elevator. Until she saw the bright windows of the gift shop. She looked through the many items and settled on a bear dressed as a ballerina, thinking of all those lessons she took as a little girl. The sight of it made her want to cry. *I'm such a fool, God. Only thinking of myself. That's all I've ever done. One selfish brat. God, help me make this right. Help me know what to do.*

With the bear in hand, she pressed the elevator button with a shaky finger. *I can do this,* she told herself. *I have to do this. Oh God, help me.*

Brenda headed down the hall, went past the nurses' station, and stopped before the door. She peeked inside. Jim was there, slumped in a chair, unmoving, like a permanent fixture of the room. The woman in the bed was asleep but peaceful. A machine ticked by her bedside. They both had the same dark hair color and nose. Brenda realized something else as she looked at Jim. He was a steadfast man who refused to abandon the lowly or, in this case, the sick. He would stay by one's side no matter what happened. He would've stayed by her side, too, if she hadn't pushed him away.

Brenda tiptoed in and stood still for a moment, then she lightly touched his arm. Instantly Jim jolted awake. When he saw her, he jumped up. "Brenda!"

"Jim, I'm so sorry. For everything." And without thinking she dashed into his arms. And his arms curled about her. She heaved a sigh.

"How did you find out?"

"The woman, Juli, in your apartment complex. She told me how you were spending all your time here. I—I can't believe this. If I had known. . .I never would have—"

"Don't worry about it."

"I'm such a fool. A selfish, spoiled brat. A liar. A. . ." She couldn't go on.

He disengaged from the embrace. "No. I'm the selfish one."

"What? Are you kidding? How can you say that? You don't have a selfish bone in you."

"Yeah, I do. I wanted to fight this battle my own way. To be the victor in it. It might have appeared noble, trying to advance up the corporate ladder and maybe getting you along with it, but it was still selfish ambition and everything else."

Just then his sister stirred and opened her eyes. "Jim?"

"Pam, I want you to meet someone. This is Brenda."

Brenda expected revulsion. Instead, the woman's lips parted into a faint smile. "It's nice to finally meet you. Jim's told me so much about you."

"I—I brought you something." Brenda presented the bear.

"Oh Jim, look! Remember how I took ballet lessons as a girl? I wanted so much to be a professional dancer."

Tears teased Brenda's eyes.

"You're going to get your wish, Pam," Jim told her softly. "I just know it. You deserve to have a dream come true."

"And I know it, too," Brenda added with equal conviction. She saw Jim gaze at her face and his lips quiver in a small smile. "It's going to okay."

Chapter 13

I don't know how you can even look at me," Brenda said slowly, stirring her coffee laced with cream and sugar. No iced caramel macchiato today. Just simple coffee, cream, and sugar. It felt right.

But Jim did look her squarely in the eye, even as he sipped his coffee. "I know you're sorry for what happened. The problem is, I doubt it can be fixed. Opinions are formed. There's a stigma attached. No one looks at you the same. Even if you do smooth things over with your father, I could never go back to work at Stewart Enterprises."

Brenda straightened. "But you have to. What about Pam?"

"I'll get work elsewhere. I have a pretty good résumé. I could probably land an advertising job. Or even in a medical outlet, since I have sales experience. I just wish. . ." His voice died away.

Brenda wished, too, that things were different, that none of this had ever happened. Maybe if they had met in another time and place, they might have pursued a pure relationship. Time well spent at a nice dinner. Walks in the moonlight. Holding hands. Conversation. Enjoying the innocence of love without delving into the ways of the world, kindled by selfish desires. They would have fallen in love the way it was meant to be. But it hadn't happened that way. They were saddled with their present circumstances and the consequences of their actions.

"Well, I'm glad you can probably land a job. I feel a little better. Not much, but a little. I guess I can see why it's probably not good to go back to Dad's company."

"I need to look forward and not backward. And I need to pursue Pam's care now. She needs the transplant. They have a donor. But without the money. . ."

"Leave that to me."

"Look, Brenda, this isn't your cause. I was wrong to make it other people's cause."

"We're supposed to help each other. I discovered that with Tina. That's why we're here. All my troubles seem so petty when I see someone like your sister struggling with life and death, and you along with her. We're here to help each other, not to be personal monuments to selfishness. Besides, I would

329

love Pam to become a dancer. So if Pam can fulfill her dream, it would be good. Do what needs to be done. There will be money for it."

Jim grew quiet, and Brenda did, too, wondering what might be circulating in his mind. For the first time, she examined his characteristics—his deep-set, coffee-colored eyes. His wavy brown hair. A tiny mole on his upper right cheek. She never really looked closely at him until now. He'd only been one dimensional to her. But the moment she saw him at Pam's bedside and the care he displayed, the way he'd given up everything to see his sister made whole, that one dimension became many. Her admiration soared. And maybe other things as well.

Just then she saw a small smile form on his face as if he noticed her perusing him. He flushed. She smiled in return.

Jim stood then and went over to the cafeteria line to purchase something. He returned with a piece of layered chocolate cake on a plate for her. "Chocolate is the right thing to eat at certain times in life."

"I love chocolate, and I haven't eaten anything all day." The cake tasted good for a hospital cafeteria cake, with fudgy frosting inside and out. Heavenly, just like him and those fudgy brown eyes of his. After a few bites, she asked if he wanted some. He shook his head and only sat there watching her eat. "Now that there are no longer any presumptions on either part, we can find out what makes each other tick," he suggested.

"That would be nice," she said, scraping the last bit of frosting off the plate. "In a nutshell, as the only Stewart offspring and heir to the throne, I'm it for my dad. My mother left when I was a teen to stake out a claim on the East Coast. New York City to be exact. The one dog I did have left a scar on my leg from a bite, hence the reason I will forever remain a cat owner. And I was addicted to caramel macchiatos until today."

"I'm sure that wasn't easy for you, having your parents split like that when you were young."

She shrugged. "Probably not. I'm sure some psychologist would look at it and say that's where my wires got crossed. But Dad has always been there for me. We're a team. Though I think I've seen how I need to go my own way. Find out my life apart from him and the company. And find out what I'm meant to do. But I'll admit, I miss not having a mother to talk to about things."

"Mine isn't here either. She died of leukemia. The same thing Pam has."

Brenda gaped. "Wow, I didn't know that."

"It's bad stuff. Which is why I want to see Pam live when our mom didn't."

"Jim, I wish you'd said something about this sooner."

"Well, there were times I tried. Other things kind of got in the way, and—"

"Yeah. Lots of stuff. Dumb stuff, too. Stuff that sent me in the wrong direction when people needed me most." Brenda looked at her cell phone. "I didn't realize how late it is. I need to run."

"Okay."

She noted his disappointment but realized she'd have to move fast if she were to set things spinning in the right direction. If she played it all correctly, something good might still come out of the rubbish.

She stood to her feet, as did Jim. "Thanks for the cake."

"Sure." He opened his mouth to say more but didn't. "Thanks for coming. It meant a lot."

Brenda smiled and exited swiftly, her brain a mass of jumbled thoughts. How does one put Humpty Dumpty back together after she pushed him right over the cliff and watched him break into a million pieces? What kind of superglue could repair something like that? But at least at the moment she didn't feel so burdened. A weight had lifted from her shoulders. More than likely it was the burden of guilt. If only she didn't have to contend with the aftereffects of bad decisions. But for the pale young woman lying in the hospital bed and the man with eyes as appealing as the cake she'd just eaten, Brenda would do all she could and more.

☙

As usual Dad was entertaining physicians and hospital administrators in the company boardroom when Brenda arrived at Stewart Enterprises. She paced outside the doors until she noticed Marge the secretary looking at her. When Marge finally moved to serve her a mug of coffee, Brenda smiled her thanks.

"I know it isn't any of my business. And I shouldn't be asking personal questions. But is everything all right? I know you've gone through quite a bit and—"

"Actually, I've learned in the past few hours that there are people who have legitimate sufferings compared to the measly overrated stuff I go through, Marge." Brenda sipped the simple brew. "Tastes good. You always do make the best."

The older woman backpedaled. "What kind of suffering do you mean, dear?"

"For instance, I'm sure no one in this whole place knows that Jim Ensley has been caring for his dying sister these last few weeks. I sure didn't, and I feel terrible about it."

Marge stared wide-eyed. "What?"

"That's why I'm here. To wake up everyone and tell them to come together and help someone in need. It doesn't take government or other higher-ups to help. People can step up and make things happen. So I want to get money together for her care as soon as possible. She needs a transplant and has no insurance."

Marge laughed. "I think I'm seeing a new Brenda Stewart standing before me."

"Yeah, and high time, too. I also need to tell everyone in this office that I was an idiot. What I said about Jim wasn't true. I want to make things right."

Suddenly she felt Marge's arms around her. "I'm so glad, honey. I've been praying for you and for Jim. I just knew there were more things here than met the eye. But I had no idea he had a sick sister."

"No one knew. I'm not sure why he didn't share it. But at least we can do something about it. And I need you to help me."

"Sure. Anything."

"I need you to write up a company memo for me." Marge scurried to take up her pad and pen. "Here's what I want it to say: 'To the employees of Stewart Enterprises. I regret to inform you that the manner and subsequent termination of Jim Ensley from this company was brought about under false pretenses. Any and all allegations brought against Mr. Ensley were completely and utterly false. He is an honorable and upright man and deserves our respect and support. Mr. Ensley especially needs your support now as he has a very sick family member who is currently in the hospital. Miss Stewart regrets the firing of this man and hopes you will consider a generous contribution to a fund in his sister's name so that she may receive a lifesaving bone marrow transplant. Signed, Brenda Stewart.'"

Marge looked at it and sighed. "Honey, don't you think you'd better clear this with your father first?"

"No. This is my decision. And since I have no idea how long that meeting of his is going to last, I want this sent out as soon as possible. I'm sure Dad will be calling me tonight about it. But the memo will already be out, so he won't have any way to stop it."

"I'll get an e-mail sent out." She paused. "I must say I didn't think this would happen so soon. You realize that people will now wonder even more what is going on. It could have the opposite effect."

"I don't think so. The people in this company are good people. We will come together to help in a time of need."

The older woman smiled and nodded. "You're a lovely young woman, Brenda. And you have so much going for you."

"I'm not sure about that." Tears teased her eyes when she thought of Rita. "Most everyone dislikes me. What's the use?"

Just then the woman's arm encircled her. "Honey, I don't dislike you at all. And neither does God. He did a great thing for you, you know. He sent His Son to die for you. It's the greatest gift of love anyone can give. Dying for another." She went then and took up her purse. "Here, take this little booklet with you. Read it over. Call me if you want. We'll talk about what real love is all about."

Brenda dried her eyes and nodded, taking the booklet. She drifted out of the building and into the day that had turned unexpectedly warm. But at least the sun still shone.

☙

Brenda had barely opened the door to her condo when her cell rang. She struggled with a bag of groceries, feeling better about things as she had selected nice veggies and healthy items. She commanded herself to attend her aerobics class now that her ankle was better. She wanted to look good and feel good. And she made a commitment to attend church this Sunday.

Brenda glanced at the number. Dad. *Uh-oh, am I ready?* She thought then of Pam in the bed, wasting away to nothing, and found the courage to answer. "Hey, Dad."

The words rushed out. "Brenda, what in the world were you doing sending out a company-wide memo without consulting me?"

"You were in a business meeting."

"Don't you understand what this does? It undermines my authority. I'm supposed to be heading all this. You've pulled the rug out from underneath me."

"What we both did to Jim was wrong."

"You were the one who came into my office with the accusations from everyone and—"

"I know, Dad. I was wrong. Really wrong. I only did it because I thought Jim was interfering in my life. And come to find out, he was helping me big-time from making a really huge mistake. Even you didn't want me hooked up with Rick, the guy from the Wasatch."

"You mean the man who kidnapped you? You bet I didn't. I don't know who is worse—Jim or that man."

"For heaven's sake, Dad, Rick didn't kidnap me. He helped me when I was injured. I owe him a lot, but not my love. Jim found out he's married. I had no right to try and make things happen with Rick. Or blame Jim for it by getting him fired."

"Brenda, I. . ." Silence met her ears.

She sighed. "Dad, look, I'm sorry, but I have to make things right. Jim's got a sister who's dying. That's why his work output was running behind. Why he sometimes came to work late. And the other things we talked about. He was taking care of Pam. I saw her in the hospital. She has cancer. They need money. Can we do something about this? Like get money together quickly to aid in her treatment?"

"Honestly, I can't keep up with you."

"We're in the medical business anyway, Dad. You've got all those fancy clients. We could probably get the procedure done cut rate. Or at least the supplies for it. Who knows?" When silence met her ears, she said tentatively, "Dad?"

"Brenda, you'll be the death of me one of these days. I just can't keep up with you anymore." He sighed long and loud. "I'll see what can be done. But if you're asking me to hire Jim back, I can't. I've already filled his position."

"Already? Well, he said he's planning to get something else. He doesn't want to come back."

Again Dad hesitated. "Brenda, I love you, but you've got to stop playing with life and act like an adult one of these days."

"I know. I'm sorry I've been a pain in the neck, Dad." She closed her eyes, thinking of the mental turmoil she had brewed in such a short amount of time. But she heard words of love from him anyway, even after all that had happened. Despite everything, he loved her.

When the call ended, Brenda sat thinking on those words. She opened the booklet Marge had given her. As she read it, she realized that God stood ready and willing to forgive her mistakes. The tears spilled out. And so, too, did words of prayer as she asked God to forgive her. She looked up and saw the grocery bags still sitting on the counter. She opened the cupboards and the fridge. Into the garbage went all the junk. Doughnuts. Chocolate milk. Filled cupcakes. Chip bags. Out with the old, in with the new, as the old adage said. And the new never felt so inviting.

Then she thought of Jim. Jim, who didn't shirk when it came to dangerous situations. Jim, bold and courageous. Jim, steadfast and sure, just as he looked at his sister's bedside, seeking to overcome the death wish placed on Pam's worn body. He wasn't afraid of anything. He dealt with everything head-on. Most of all, he dealt with her, Brenda. And cared for her. Even when she wrecked his life.

He really is some guy, Brenda thought. She considered his handsome features. The dark eyes that matched his hair. His charming smile. His nice frame and large, inviting hands. Right then she yearned to be with him. To talk to him. Discover his likes, dislikes, everything she could. And help see him and his sister through this minefield of cancer safely to the other side.

At that moment Snowy made an appearance. Brenda scooped the cat into her arms, nuzzling the soft white fur. *I know Prince Charming gave Snow*

White the kiss of life. I've had kisses that meant nothing. What would it be like to kiss the man she loved? She hoped to find that out real soon and licked her lips in anticipation of such an encounter. "What do you think about that, Snowy? Time to kiss a real Prince Charming?" A meow echoed in her ear, followed by a purr. "Exactly."

Chapter 14

If the roller coaster of life could give ups and downs and forward and backward motions, it had done all that and more. Jim was still reeling from it, hoping it wouldn't make him dizzy in the spirit. In one moment he'd been an outcast to everyone and everything. The next he'd been elevated to near hero status, all because of the simple devotion to family that everyone should have regardless of one's circumstances.

But he had to admit, Brenda Stewart's about-face proved the greatest miracle. He never thought she would react the way she did when she found out about Pam. During the past few weeks, he and Brenda took every opportunity to be together. Especially as she arranged the all-out fund-raising for Pam's care. Employees and even clients of Stewart Enterprises, led by Marge, came out to give of their resources and wish his sister well. Now with money flowing and Pam receiving the bone marrow transplant, Jim felt a new high he didn't think he would ever experience.

With all this came a rush of new feelings inside him. No longer did he and Brenda serve some means to a selfish end. They were becoming of one mind and heart. They were acting more like a couple, working together, helping one another in need. The plastic-coated images were gone. Now they could look at each other with new eyes and, yes, new hearts.

Jim was grateful, too, she'd pulled out all stops to see that Pam received the proper medical treatment. Brenda was not some spoiled daughter of a successful CEO. She was a woman with a loving heart to give to those in need. One who had her own bout of cancer in a way, not of the body but of the spirit and soul, robbing her of joy and peace. Not that Jim understood spiritual things. Brenda had tried to clue him in by showing him the booklet Marge had given her. He'd read it and wondered what it really meant. There must be something to this relationship with God. Rick had even shared about it at his cabin in the mountains.

Jim pulled out his cell phone and called the very guy he'd once thought was his competition for Brenda's affections. Flannel Guy, Rick Malone.

"Jim, it's good to hear from you."

The enthusiastic greeting surprised Jim—and opened the door wide for frank conversation. "I've got some questions about, well, God."

"Sure."

Uncertain how to begin, Jim managed to stumble his way through, asking about right and wrong, sacrifice, and other things. And Rick patiently told him of the saving knowledge of Christ. It all seemed foreign to Jim. Rick then invited Jim and Brenda to come to his church—a strong evangelical fellowship of believers where Jim could learn more about salvation through Christ. "Well, I'm not sure what's going to happen with that," Jim said. "I haven't yet sprung all this on Brenda. But she may come. A secretary at work gave her some small booklet about God."

"And Jim, I have something to tell you. Since our talk a few weeks back, I've been talking to my wife, Marta. We're in the communication stage of things. I plan to see her tonight. It's going to work out. I believe it."

"That's good to hear, Rick."

"Look, I also have to say this, Jim. The great things that happened here, with my niece and my marriage, are all because of Brenda's visit to the Wasatch. I know that sounds kind of strange, but God uses all things for His purposes."

"Really." He never considered that Brenda's flight paved the way for reconciliation and even love.

When Jim hung up the phone, he was on the Internet, looking to send Brenda a huge bouquet of flowers from a well-known and excellent source, better even than the shops in Salt Lake. At first he considered a simple summer bouquet. Then he decided to go all out with the ultimate bouquet—a dozen long-stemmed red roses. He'd given them once before at the hospital when she was evaluated after the incident in the Wasatch. But this time he gave them out of everything in his heart. And he wanted the best. He ordered them delivered in a cut-glass vase. And threw in a box of chocolates with them, recalling how much she liked the cake at the cafeteria. Roses and chocolates went hand in hand.

Now Jim wondered what she would think about going to Rick's church, knowing how she once felt about the man. But he must put aside any misconceptions and concentrate on the good to be found in seeking God for their lives. Jim paused. What a unique concept. He'd thought about God when this cancer came stalking his family. Wondering if God really cared that His creation suffered and even died. But everyone had to die from something. It was just a matter of when. After that, then what? Rick said Jesus was the way to heaven. That death need not be a terrifying prospect. There was more to life and death than what met the eye.

But Jim was glad Pam had a chance to live. When he received the good news that the transplant operation had gone well and she was recovering nicely, he rejoiced even more. Yeah, he needed to go to church. Forget all the other reasons. He needed to thank God.

Several days later Jim got a call. When he hung up, he nearly jumped but instead shouted, "Yeah!" A pharmaceutical company had called to set up an interview for a job in a couple of hours. Things were definitely looking up after the bout of doldrums. He made a dash for the bedroom to get his suit to take to the cleaners. And while he waited, he could get a new haircut and check on Pam's progress.

Jim dropped off the suit and headed to the barber for a quick cut. He stopped by the hospital to check with the nursing staff about Pam. And there he saw Brenda in the hospital lobby. "Brenda."

She whirled and stared. "Oh Jim. I was asking about Pam and. . . Wow, your hair looks good. What's the occasion?"

"Job interview. Cephalon is interviewing me later on this afternoon." Jim thought she would be happy for him, but instead, she lowered her face.

"I take it Dad didn't offer you another job. I thought maybe it might happen, with everyone coming out to help Pam and all. Well, at least he can give you a recommendation for this new job. I hope he does."

"Brenda, even if your father did offer me a job, I don't think I could go back there. This is a great opportunity if I get it. I hope you understand."

"Sure. It's just. . ." Brenda hesitated. "I don't like how this turned out. And it's all because of me." Tears came as Jim gestured her to some chairs in the lobby.

"You can forget blaming yourself. We both made mistakes, and we'll get through them. I think I know a good way to start." He paused. "First off, I talked to Rick again. He wanted to thank you for going to the Wasatch."

"What?" Her face took on the color of a cherry.

"He said it helped pave the way to where things are right now, reconciling with his wife. And he was thankful about his niece."

"I got an e-mail from Tina. She sent me a picture. She looks great." Brenda paused. "I just don't believe you actually talked to him."

"Well, I had a couple questions about God. Rick explained a good deal of it. He's invited us to come to his church this Sunday."

"That's nice." Brenda looked away and turned silent. Jim tried to push aside any nagging reservations. But then Brenda turned the tide of conversation and talked about Pam. "They'll be allowing visitors soon. They are monitoring her blood work."

"I appreciate your coming here to check, Brenda." He took up her hand in his and was pleased to see she didn't pull away. In fact, her fingers curled slowly around his, making his hopes rise. "Got time to grab one of your favorites? A caramel macchiato?"

She looked at her watch. "There are no meetings to attend for Dad at the moment and no aerobics class right now. I just realized what a boring life I lead."

"Your life isn't so boring," he said, leading the way out the hospital entrance and to his car.

"It is for me. Go to meetings. Smile a lot and give a great PowerPoint presentation. Go to parties. Pretend to drink when I don't care to. Go to aerobics class. Pretend to look and act graceful when it isn't in my genetic makeup."

He pulled up to the coffee shop—one of Brenda's favorite hangouts. And soon they were at a small table drinking coffee and talking. Or rather, Brenda talked while Jim listened. She opened up about life growing up as an only child. She talked about a yearning to travel to Venice, which Jim filed away for future reference. Oh, how he would love to surprise her with a trip like that as a honeymoon destination.

Honeymoon destination? Jim, where are you going with this? Do you want to spend your life with Brenda Stewart? Just don't pretend to fall in love, Brenda. Please. It has to be the real McCoy. The real deal or no deal at all.

"What is it?" she asked, probing his face with large, glossy blue eyes and the corner of her lip upturned. "You're wearing a strange expression on your face. Is it something I said?"

"I just hope we can be real with each other, like we are right now. No more pretending. No more games. I don't want us to be anything but genuine. And truthful. Open with each other. It's what a relationship is all about."

"So are we in a relationship, Jim?"

He gave her a quick glance before his gaze darted to the street. "Do you want us to be?"

"Well, after everything I've put you through, I'm surprised you're even mentioning the idea. I know I helped raise money for Pam's treatment, but I wanted to do that. As for other things, I've been downright dastardly."

"I'm grateful for what you did for Pam. As far as the two of us are concerned, let's take it one step at a time."

Brenda wriggled her nose, and at that instant, she looked cute to him. Adorable. Both. "No wonder Dad liked you. You can look at things from every angle. Plan it out. Make it work."

"Yeah, but our plans don't always work the way we think. And sometimes I'm glad they don't. Life has a way of bringing surprises instead, better than anything we try to have a hand in doing. It makes it right in the end." Jim checked the time on his phone. "I'd better go. Need to pick up my suit. The interview is in an hour."

They stood, and suddenly he felt a warm kiss on his lips. A shock wave raced through him.

"For luck. Hope the interview goes beyond what you want. And, I guess, this is to start the process of being genuine."

"Wow. Thanks." He smiled, and she did, too. When he dropped her off at her car, he hoped the roses he ordered the other day were waiting for her. He hoped it signaled to her his own idea of being genuine. Red roses indicated the next step up. If she was willing to take that step with him.

వ❀

Brenda felt like she was flying on a cloud, and certainly not because of the caramel macchiato, as delicious and potent as it was. But because of new and different things. Maybe even love. She entered the apartment building only to stop short when the manager stood in the foyer as if waiting for her. He held a huge white box. "This came for you, Miss Stewart."

Brenda thanked him. Many times clients of Dad's would send her flowers as a way of warming up to the company. But normally they came right to the office. She hurried to her condo to open the box and found long-stemmed roses carefully preserved in a cut-glass vase, accompanied by the finest dark chocolate truffles. The long-stemmed roses were slightly open, with a delicate and earthy aroma. "Wow, someone is doing it up big." She unsealed the envelope while Snowy wrapped her furry self around Brenda's legs.

I'd love to start over with us and see what happens. Are you game?
Jim

Am I? Wow! She fingered a soft, velvety petal. How often she wished for a chance to start over. Was it possible to begin again? Looking at the exquisite bouquet, she realized Jim offered a solid hint to that effect. Brenda peeled back the cellophane wrapper and popped a truffle in her mouth. It melted to a velvety smoothness on her tongue. Was this Jim's unique and romantic way of being genuine, as he had spoken about at the coffee shop?

Only time would tell. They must first walk the walk and find out which way to go. She thought then of the invitation to visit church. Could she go to Rick's church and not harbor ill will or anything else? It would be a crucial test for her and for them. To see what happened and how things had changed.

Brenda scooped Snowy into her arms. "I think I'll go to church, Snow White. It's the only way I'm going to find out where everything stands, especially with my new Prince Charming. And see if I'm still standing when all is said and done." *And maybe fall madly in love in the process.*

Jim never thought Brenda looked more radiant than on Sunday morning when he picked her up for the services. She said nothing about the roses, and he wondered if she'd received them. But from the smile on her face and the way she sighed, he had a feeling she did. For his part, he was in a good mood also, having learned he'd picked up the job with the pharmaceutical company where he'd interviewed. And after church he was going to see Pam for the first time since the transplant.

But now he needed to get through this next chapter of life. The church chapter and running into Rick. Or rather, waiting to see what happened between Rick and Brenda. And if what Rick had said on the phone was true—that the man was indeed getting back together with his wife.

"Looks like we might get a storm." Brenda pointed at the bank of dark clouds hovering over the Wasatch. Summer storms were not uncommon in Salt Lake, and Jim had been through enough personal storms to last a lifetime. He hoped it wasn't some omen of the day. But even if the sun failed to shine, he was determined to make this a good day.

"I'm sure you're just dying to find out what I think," she now commented.

"What you think? About what?"

"Wondering if I'm game or not. Isn't that how you put it?"

Jim drew a blank until she reminded him of the note that came with the roses. "That's right. I couldn't remember how I worded it. But I hope it's okay to look at things new. A good way to start, anyway."

"I agree."

Brenda smoothed out her skirt that still showed a good deal of her legs, looking lean and real good. He admonished himself to keep his eyes on the road.

At last they pulled into the parking lot of a humble building. Several people lingered outside and smiled at them as they exited the car. Already Jim felt acceptance, and they hadn't even set foot inside the building. Was this what it was like to be surrounded by the people of God? Just like the day Jim went to see Rick. Acceptance without judgment.

They took a seat in the rear of the sanctuary and listened to the opening prayer and music. Every so often Jim cast a look in Brenda's direction to see her sitting quietly, obviously engaged in the service. And Jim felt something happening to him, too. Some kind of working in his heart, though he wasn't exactly sure what. When it came time for the message, the pastor spoke of the many people Jesus had ministered to without retribution. Harlots. Tax collectors. Selfish and scheming men. Jesus desired everyone to come to Him with open hearts ready to receive Him. When the message concluded, Jim felt his heart opening wide. He saw it touched Brenda, too. She jumped to her feet, eager to share in the final song. And then a subdued feeling came over her as she sat down to open her Bible, revealing a crinkled page signed in faded blue pen.

"I have something I need to show you, Jim. See this? My grandmother gave this Bible to me. She once told me about Jesus long ago, when I was little. Of course when you're little, you think they're just fascinating stories. She tried to tell me the truth even at a young age. To trust in God and not in myself."

Jim didn't know what to say but remained silent, trying to absorb her words. Just then he heard a slight noise and looked up to find a smiling Rick standing over them.

"Hey! So glad you were able to come today."

Jim noticed a petite woman with short brown hair standing nearby. When Rick introduced her as his wife, Marta, Jim breathed a sigh of relief. Then Jim felt Brenda draw closer to his own side, even as she thanked Rick for helping her that day up in the mountains.

"This is the young lady I found on the trail in the Wasatch," Rick told his wife. "She'd sprained her ankle. And yes, I did have that mistaken run-in with the law, only because of her father's concern. But it all worked out. For the good, I might add."

"Yeah, Rick helped a lot. And he also talked about God," Brenda added. "In fact, to both me and Jim. And invited us here today."

Marta nodded, looking over at Rick. "I've often told him he should be a minister. He has a gift. Actually, many great gifts." She said the words slowly as if savoring each of them.

"Well, we all have things to learn," Jim added. "I must say your pastor does a good job at explaining things."

"He does," Rick agreed. "And if you ever want to get together, Jim, let me know. We have a men's group that meets regularly. Brenda, there's a women's group." He moved off to a table to fetch some pamphlets. Returning and handing them to Jim and Brenda, he said, "This tells you all about the groups. It's good to knit yourselves with others who can pray with you and hold you up. I can't begin to tell you how helpful it is to have a brother to pray with. Especially when I sometimes go off-trail in matters of life. I've had my own burning bushes of revelation. We all do."

"Thanks." Jim wanted to say more but realized the time had come to depart, especially where they were all concerned. God had done a work through their circumstances. Each person had been used to help the other through that time in the Wasatch. A time that brought a healing of their hearts and minds. And now love.

He spoke these things aloud to Brenda once they were inside the car.

"It really is amazing, Jim," she agreed. "And it was good to see that Rick had reconciled." She paused. Her fingers curled around his arm. "You know, I never did thank you for what you did. Going up there to Rick's place and finding out what was happening. Saving me from some major issues as well as major embarrassment. Making me see things in a new light."

Jim didn't know what to say. Instead, he took up her hand and gave a squeeze. "I don't want to lose you, Brenda. We're meant to be together. I've known it all along." He allowed the words to resonate until she nodded. He never was so sure in his life. He only prayed she was sure, too.

Chapter 15

Brenda couldn't believe she was going to another party. But this time things were much different. Jim asked her to attend his first company function for the new pharmaceutical company where he worked. She looked at the black dress hanging in the closet and decided a new one was in order—something different but still with flair. She called on Rita to help her pick one out.

"So I hear things are really heating up between you and Jim," Rita mused as they headed for the first boutique. "I never thought I'd live to see the day. Especially after everything that's happened between you two."

"Things are not heating up. That makes it sound like all we want is the physical side of things."

Rita laughed. "Who's kidding? You sure did at first."

"Yeah, and it was shallow. I'm seeing now why it's better to wait until marriage. There's an added dimension when love and commitment are in the equation. And there isn't any guilt either." She fingered a silky dress on the rack, only to see Rita retreat as if her words had hit some unknown mark. Rita's tawny-colored skin tone deepened with a blush.

"I can't believe you of all people are saying that."

"Okay, maybe I did want to experience love. But it wasn't love, Rita. And I'm starting to find out what love is really all about. And it's not the physical. That part's important, sure, when the time is right. But I'm enjoying just being with Jim. Talking, enjoying some trips. Can you believe we just went out to Antelope Island last weekend?" She blushed when recalling the trip and the sweet kiss they shared while looking back on Salt Lake City and the Wasatch in the distance.

"Ew, that place? I can't even imagine." Rita sniffed the air as if expecting to smell the strange odors that permeated the place from the Great Salt Lake surrounding the island.

"Yes, and we had a great time. He's a lot of fun. I'm learning so much more about him." She took out a deep wine-colored dress. "What do you think of this?"

Rita shrugged. "I don't know. Right now I feel like I've stepped into a church scene with all the dos and don'ts rather than having fun shopping.

This isn't what I bargained for."

"Sorry. I didn't mean it to come across that way. It's just that I'm learning a lot of things. But speaking of church, you should come with us. They have a great women's group. We even meet at Starbucks on occasion."

"Oh great. Now you're a member of the church club, too. Terrific." She began sidestepping away.

Brenda took the dress and headed toward the dressing room. "It's just a suggestion. I like the peace I found there. I've never really had that in my life, you know." She quickly slipped out of her pants and top, thinking on her words. And not only the peace but how much she was falling for Jim as each day passed. She only hoped she could do what she told Rita and not find herself tempted like before. The old had passed away, as the pastor had said in church last Sunday. The new had come. Time to put the teachings and words into action. She prayed a new vessel was being created to hold to what she'd learned and help her not to slip backward.

Brenda stepped out of the dressing room and breathed a sigh of relief that Rita had not left, even with everything she'd talked about. "What do you think?"

"Girl, I'd say you've been transformed inside and out. What size is the dress?"

"I don't know." When Brenda took it off, she checked the tag. "No way. Rita, it's a twelve!" she squealed from behind the door. "It's got to be the cut of the dress. I've only lost about five pounds."

"Sometimes that's all it takes, girlfriend."

Yeah, five pounds of mostly emotional baggage lugging me down in life. Isn't that the truth? Brenda slipped the dress back onto its padded hanger and emerged from the small room. "Well, that was painless and profitable. I've got a dress."

"And I've never seen you happier. I guess there's something to be said about what's going on. I've known you a long time, Brenda. It's good to see a smile on your face. You look like a new woman."

It's also good to finally feel alive and not like the walking dead. She nearly wanted to skip but held herself to a dignified walk all the way to the counter to have the purchase rung up.

With the dress tucked away in a plastic garment bag, they went in search of shoes and found a pair of slingbacks on sale with a purse to match. She was all set for the night of her life. But as Rita walked alongside her to the car, Brenda noticed that her friend had become quiet. Rita didn't act her usual, confident self, as if she held the world in her hands. Brenda wondered about it until they entered the car.

"Brenda, I need to tell you something. I. . ." Rita hesitated. A tense look came over her face. Her eyes darted away. "I slept with Geoff."

"You mean Geoff Bruce? Dad's new VP?"

Rita nodded. "Yeah. After what you said in the dress shop, well, I've been feeling weird about it the past week. Only I didn't want to think about it. I figured it was only one night, you know. No big deal. But I've seen how it affected you. How you changed because of it. And it got me thinking."

"Was it worth it?"

"I don't know. I mean, he doesn't care we did it. Everyone does it these days. To find out if you're compatible or something."

"How is sleeping with someone going to tell you if you should spend the rest of your life with him? Is it going to help when you get into trouble? When there are problems? When money gets tight or someone gets sick? Love isn't just about getting physical. Though the physical aspects can be nice when it's in the right atmosphere, like marriage. But it takes time to get to know each other. What one thinks. What one likes or doesn't like. And really, letting go of our own wants and needs and letting God take care of them."

"Girl, you are really into this God thing."

"Yeah. I'm finding out He's really all I'll ever need. He knows me better than anyone. He can make my dreams come true, if I let Him." She explained to Rita how she became a Christian.

Out of the corner of her eye, she saw Rita sit back with her head against the headrest, her once-pinched face relaxing. Could it be that some of this might be rubbing off on Rita? Brenda hoped so as she kept driving and suddenly pulled into the hospital parking lot.

Rita straightened and gave her a look. "What's going on? Why are we stopping here?"

"Gonna make a brief visit to check on a friend."

Rita looked at her quizzically. Brenda asked if she wanted to come along, to which Rita shrugged and exited the car. "So who's here?"

"You remember the fund-raising campaign for Pam," Brenda said. "I'll introduce you. Oh hey, you aren't sick, are you?"

"What? No, of course not. Why are you asking me that?"

"They don't want anyone sick to visit. It's hospital policy for transplant patients."

Rita shook her head and followed Brenda into the elevator to the second floor. Inside the hospital room, a petite, brown-haired woman sat in a chair surfing the television channels. "Brenda!"

"Hey, Pam. How are you doing?"

"Good news. They're going to release me tomorrow."

"Wow, that is fabulous news. I'd like you to meet a good friend of mine. This is Rita. Rita, this is Pam, Jim's sister."

At this, Rita gave Brenda a look of amazement before smiling sheepishly and adding her own greeting.

"Rita also works at Stewart Enterprises," Brenda explained.

At this, Pam's face brightened and words gushed out of her, thanking Rita and the other employees of the company who helped her and sent cards and flowers. "I wouldn't be alive if it weren't for you all. Thank you so much."

Rita appeared taken aback. "I'm just glad we could help."

Brenda suddenly saw the highfalutin and opinionated Rita changing into a woman of thoughtfulness. One could not help but be humbled at the sight of Pam Ensley and all she had been through. Brenda went on, talking to Rita about Jim who spent night and day with Pam and the courage that got her through.

"Along with some much-needed help by good friends here in the city," Pam confessed. She then said softly, "I don't know if you're aware of it, Brenda, but my brother really likes you. Rather, I know Jim's in love with you. He always has been, I think. Even when things didn't look right. Like the time when you hurt your ankle and were hanging out with that other guy. Even when I was really sick, I could see how much you meant to Jim. He was always talking about you. Kind of clues you in right there. I just told him he needed to let go. That it was okay to love someone."

Brenda smiled, the warmth flowing like a stream through her as she cast Rita a glance. "All things work together for good. We talked about that at the last women's meeting at church."

"That's one of my favorite verses," Pam added. "And it really is working together. All of it."

The small talk lasted for a bit longer before Brenda declared she needed to get ready for a party at Jim's new company.

"Yeah, he's looking forward to it," Pam said with a smile. "Thanks for coming to see me."

Brenda headed out, followed by a sheepish Rita. When they returned to the car, Rita could only utter, "Wow."

" 'Wow,' what?"

"I don't know. Just plain 'wow.' Girl, I'm glad you helped her out. And we all saw the light. The girl's alive and breathing because of it. It's pretty neat."

Brenda laughed. "I'm glad, too, Rita. You don't know how glad."

"Yeah," she agreed.

Oh yeah indeed, Brenda thought. Amazing, in fact. But she believed in her heart the best was yet to come.

She dropped Rita off then headed back to ready herself for the party. Brenda loved the way the gown draped over her figure. It was neither tight nor loose but just right. A necklace of golden baubles and large hoop earrings completed the outfit. Her heart skipped a beat. She felt like a teenager on her first date. Everything felt fresh and new.

The intercom in her condo buzzed. "Hi, beautiful," came a deep voice.

"You have no idea if I'm beautiful or not," she said with a chuckle.

"Brenda, if you came out wearing jeans and a sweatshirt and your hair standing up in every direction, you'd still be the most beautiful vision to me. But I know you would never look like that. I know you. At least I'm trying to get to know you as each day goes by. I still have plenty to learn."

"Don't we all. I'll be right down." Brenda felt as if she were floating on a cloud as she entered the elevator. And right into Jim's arms as he stood by the open doorway, anticipating her arrival. Suddenly his lips were swooping down on hers, drenching them with a reservoir of love he held deep inside. "Wow, what a greeting," she said breathlessly.

"Wow, what a dress. You and Rita picked out a nice one."

"I found it, actually." She grabbed his hand and held it tight in hers. "I'm glad Rita came along. I talked to her some. Had a good conversation, actually. She went with me to see Pam."

"You saw Pam?"

"She's being released tomorrow. She looks so good, Jim. So different from when I first saw her in the hospital."

"Yes." Jim held the door open for her. "A miracle."

"It's all been a miracle." She glanced over at him as he entered the driver's seat. "None of it is because of any one person either. It's all of us working together to do what's right."

"I know you did a lot for Pam. Raising all that money in such a short amount of time to help with her treatment. I just hope you don't think. . ." He hesitated. "I hope you don't think I'm trying to pay you back. I never can, you know."

"Can we pay God back for all that He's done for us? There is this little thing in the Bible called love, Jim. I saw someone in need, someone too ill to do anything to save herself. I saw a devoted man—who would do anything to save the one he loves. I saw that I could also offer some of that same love in return."

They drove in silence, each one in deep thought, though Jim's hand held on to hers the entire ride. When he pulled up in front of the hotel, Brenda had a swift flashback to the night many weeks ago when she was wearing the black dress at Dad's shindig. At first she wished it all hadn't happened, but now she was glad it had. It led her onto a path of true healing in many ways.

But tonight was a new night. Stepping out of the vehicle, Brenda would be escorted to another function by the man named Jim Ensley. This time she was eager to have a good time in his presence without any preconceived notions, hidden agendas, or anything else. Just the freedom and the peace to be who God meant them to be.

Jim took her elbow and escorted her into the ballroom. And suddenly she found smiling faces greeting her and Jim with enthusiasm, drawing them into separate circles of conversation. No one here called her 'punkin' or put on words or images in an effort to get on her good side. While Brenda remained a CEO's daughter, she could be another person here, one who blended in with the crowd. She could talk and laugh and make plans for get-togethers over coffee. She was just another woman at the party and with a wonderful man by her side. Brenda loved every minute of it.

☙❧

"You look like you enjoyed yourself," Jim commented after the party was over.

"You'll never believe what happened. Several of the women invited me to join their reading group. Can you imagine that? Me, reading! Guess it's high time I got a little more culture in me besides shopping and drinking caramel macchiatos. I know I still need my aerobics class, but I could use some diversity in my life. And time with others, too." She sighed and leaned back. "It was a nice gathering, Jim. They're nice people. I'm glad you're a part of them. You belong there."

"I'm glad it worked out that way, too. I like the people. I like my position. It's enough to meet my needs and be able to wine and dine the woman I love."

"Don't worry about the wine and dine part. Just be yourself. Nothing more, nothing less."

The moon shone bright, casting a veil of white over them. Jim then steered the car into a park. He turned and grasped her hands in his. "I love you, Brenda."

She smiled. "I love you, too."

"Would you like to help me become the man I believe I'm supposed to be?"

Brenda gaped, wondering what in the world he meant. Until a small velvet box appeared in his hand. She began feeling dizzy. "Jim, you can't possibly mean. . ."

"Okay, a car is a strange place to ask, but I can't wait any longer. I thought about asking at the party, but all the people. . ." He paused.

"Jim. . ." Brenda covered her mouth with her hand. His coffee-colored eyes looked directly into hers. Tremors afflicted her. The strong Brenda now felt mushy all over. It was like some far-off dream, only this dream had become a reality right before her eyes. And when she least expected it.

"Brenda Stewart, will you marry me? I want to be your husband, devoted to you and you alone."

"Yes! Yes, I will," Brenda said breathlessly. Jim leaned over, his arms encircling Brenda, and gave her the sweetest kiss that had ever touched her lips. A kiss of devotion. And pure love. Prince Charming all the way.

Beyond their car, the Wasatch Range sparkled in the moonlight with renewed life. How often she had gazed at the jagged peaks and thought nothing of them. They had always been a part of the scenery here in Salt Lake, along with the buildings and the Great Salt Lake itself. But now she gazed at the mountain range with new eyes and a new heart, thankful to God for helping transport her into the arms of the man she loved.

A Letter to Our Readers

Dear Readers:

In order that we might better contribute to your reading enjoyment, we would appreciate you taking a few minutes to respond to the following questions. When completed, please return to the following: Fiction Editor, Barbour Publishing, Inc., P.O. Box 719, Uhrichsville, OH 44683.

1. Did you enjoy reading *Red Rock Weddings* by Lauralee Bliss?
   ❑ Very much. I would like to see more books like this.
   ❑ Moderately—I would have enjoyed it more if _____
   _____
   _____

2. What influenced your decision to purchase this book?
   (Check those that apply.)
   ❑ Cover   ❑ Back cover copy   ❑ Title   ❑ Price
   ❑ Friends   ❑ Publicity   ❑ Other

3. Which story was your favorite?
   ❑ *Love's Winding Path*   ❑ *Heart of Mine*
   ❑ *Wasatch Love*

4. Please check your age range:
   ❑ Under 18   ❑ 18–24   ❑ 25–34
   ❑ 35–45   ❑ 46–55   ❑ Over 55

5. How many hours per week do you read? _____

Name _____

Occupation _____

Address _____

City_____ State _____ Zip_____

E-mail _____